The
ANGEL
OF
VIENNA

BOOKS BY KATE HEWITT

KATE HEWITT

The

ANGEL

OF

VIENNA

bookouture

Published by Bookouture in 2022

An imprint of Storyfire Ltd.
Carmelite House
50 Victoria Embankment
London EC4Y 0DZ

www.bookouture.com

ISBN: 978-1-80019-304-8
eBook ISBN: 978-1-80019-303-1

To the 789 who lost their lives at Am Spiegelgrund.

PROLOGUE

VIENNA, AUGUST 1946

A crowd has gathered outside of the courtroom under a summer's sky, the air balmy and warm, the sunshine like a benediction, but the faces of those standing there are haggard and drawn, arms folded, gazes lowered, as they wait in silence, in expectation, but not in hope. It is too late for hope.

In the back of the crowd, a woman stands, holding the hand of a young boy. Her whole body is alert, straining, an energy seeming to make her thrum or crackle, as she stares at the doors of the court as if she could make them open by sheer force of will. She has waited a long time for this moment.

Next to her, a man smelling of sauerkraut and cigarettes shifts wearily as a sigh escapes him. His face is unshaven, his eyes hollow as he stares ahead blankly. The woman wonders what has brought him here, whom he has lost.

It is the end of the first round of the Am Steinhof trials— "the child killers" as the newspapers have called them. Everyone in Vienna has acted as if they are scandalized by the news, shaking their heads and clucking their tongues as if they never knew, couldn't have even imagined. They are victims, after all, every one of them in this, the first country Hitler oppressed, or so they all say now. Never mind that, after the Anschluss, Austria accomplished in five days what took Germany five years—bundling the Jews into buses and trains, along with so many other unwanted—including the children.

The woman knows how it really was. She remembers how it was a secret they were all compelled to keep—complicit, if not willing, although plenty were, and more than willing. Eager. Yet to hear people speak now, you'd think no one had been a Nazi at all.

The door of the courtroom opens and although no one moves, it feels as if the crowd surges forward. The woman's hand tightens on the boy's; he tilts his head up to her, his hazel eyes glinting in silent question, and she gives him a reassuring smile, or tries to. It has been a long, hard road to get here, to a place where they are safe, they are well, they almost have enough food to eat. Of course, it is hard for everyone; the whole country is wrecked, everyone starving, trying to rebuild a world from the ashes, but how do you even begin?

A man emerges from the courtroom to stand on the steps outside, but it is no one official, and the crowd, almost as one, slumps, a collectively held breath released as they continue to wait.

"They're about to read the verdict," he calls out, and the woman feels the energy steal through the crowd again, as people straighten, mouths drawn tightly, eyes narrowed and flashing.

Have they all lost someone to the hospital's regime, or are they here merely for idle curiosity, to see what has happened to the dreaded Dr. Illing, the second medical director of Am Spiegelgrund, the name now notorious? Jekelius, his predecessor—the woman remembers *him*—is now in a Soviet prison camp, his fate already decided, or as good as. But as for the others—Illing, Hubsch, Türk, Katschenka—their fates will be decided today. Guilt or innocence. Justice or mockery.

The woman did not sit in on any of the trials. She could not bear to see Illing or any of the others telling their lies, their faces shining with earnest conviction as they tried to explain away their heinous, murderous deeds.

They had no quality of life whatsoever, no ability to be healed or cured, no possibility of work or enjoyment... I took my responsibilities very seriously, and when one had advocated this dying, it was an absolute blessing...

She read that much in the newspaper, and it was enough to bring a familiar rush of fury to the fore, along with that old, drowning sense of helplessness.

Even here, on a sweltering summer's day, she can feel herself back there, in the parkland of Am Steinhof, the bite of autumn in the air. She remembers the icy drenching of fear, the acid tang of it on her tongue, the way her stomach swooped and then hollowed out as hands scrambled on stone and they heard the tramp of boots, the barking of dogs, the distant shouts. *Halt! Halt!* Then the terrible crack of a gunshot, shattering the stillness of a chilly night.

The boy's hand tightens on hers and she looks up, drawing her breath in sharply, for the door of the courtroom has opened again, and now a bailiff stands there, his expression sober. Finally, the verdict will be announced. Finally, she will know if justice, at long last, has been served.

Yet, she wonders bleakly, can justice ever be served? One life, for how many? Hundreds, even thousands, over the years. She saved only a handful, and even now, all the others haunt her dreams, along with her waking, so when she closes her eyes, she still sees their thin faces, their desperate eyes, feels the weight of their unutterable despair. She knows, and unlike so many others who long only to forget the war with all its tragedies, she never will. She will never let herself, because those children must not be forgotten. No, she thinks as she stares hard at the man about to read the verdict, she will always, always remember...

CHAPTER 1

HEIM HOCHLAND, STEINHÖRING, GERMANY, OCTOBER 1940

"Push!"

Hannah Stern gave the laboring woman—a girl, really, at only sixteen—a briskly encouraging smile as she crouched between her legs. She was hardy and round-cheeked, a devout member of the *Bund Deutscher Mädel*, with a photograph of Hitler under her pillow and a child in her belly. Like far too many naïve young girls, she'd become a bit too friendly with one of the *Hitlerjugend* back home in Stuttgart, and she'd found herself here.

Well, Hannah thought, heaven knew it could be worse for the poor girl. A lot worse. Heim Hochland was a paradise compared to what most girls in her situation faced. It was thanks to her wheat-blond mane, and those china-blue eyes, not to mention her perfect pedigree of purity, that she was here at all.

"I can't…" the girl, Elsa, grunted, braced on her elbows, red-faced from trying, her blond hair clinging to her plump cheeks in damp, sticky strands. "I *can't*."

"You'll have to, I'm afraid," Hannah replied with a quick, bracing smile. "It's the only way, as I'm sure you know. What comes up must go down, and what goes in must come out, babies included."

"But the doctor... I should have a doctor!" This came out in a wail. Even in the throes of labor, Elsa sounded aggrieved, even a bit petulant. She'd been promised so much in this maternity home, with its steeply pitched roof and colorful shutters, the deep blue lake and the oversized statue of the breastfeeding mother looming in the garden, her Aryan face gazing proudly down at the infant in her arms. The best medical care was offered in an atmosphere that felt like a holiday—games and music at nights, the occasional party, even dancing, although it was meant to be forbidden. Walks in the garden, fresh cream and butter, bread and meat... life here was indeed a holiday compared to what other Germans were facing, in this, the second year of war.

"I know what you've been promised," Hannah told her placatingly, "but I'm afraid the doctor is busy in Berlin." As he so very often was, as the medical director of the entire *Lebensborn* program, started five years ago to improve the birth rate of Aryan Germans. It was left to women like Hannah, a nurse now stepping in as midwife despite current laws to the contrary, to see the babies born. It was not the first time she'd had to deliver a baby here at Heim Hochland, even though her official duty as a pediatric nurse was the care of the infants and children in the nursery, bouncing babies and pink-cheeked toddlers who looked to her to be their mother, if only for a little while. With doctors needing to trot off to bustling places to look important, rules were forgotten or simply scrapped.

Hannah didn't mind; she liked feeling useful, and the miracle of birth amazed her every time—the held breath, the sudden cry, the sweep of relief and joy. Besides, these children were fortunate, blessed, to be adopted into families who would love and care for them. She was only sorry when the children she'd come to care for despite her best intentions to remain at least a little bit aloof suddenly disappeared from the nursery and her life.

Now she gave Elsa a look of sympathy as the laboring girl groaned again, her head falling back once more on the pillow. She had not been the easiest of patients during her time at the maternity home, complaining about almost everything, but she was little more than a child, if one fervently devoted to her *Führer*, willing to give her baby up to the cause she so ardently believed in. Hannah couldn't help but feel sorry for her.

Elsa's body convulsed, and Hannah bent down, squinting to see the tuft of blond hair peeking out like a promise, a good Aryan baby, just as the girl wanted. "The baby is coming, Elsa," she told her, "whether you want it to or not. Push, and it will be easier, I promise. It's hard work being a mother, and it begins now!" She injected a teasing note into her voice, hoping to lighten the mood. "What do you think you get a *mutterkreuz* for?"

"As if I'd ever have four..." Elsa muttered, panting. The award, with three classes, had been introduced two years ago. Women who had four children received a bronze medal.

"Oh, go for gold! Have eight at least," Hannah replied cheerfully as Elsa gave another groan that seemed to come from the depths of her being and the baby's head emerged, reddened and pulsing, damp blond hair smeared with blood cradled in Hannah's capable hands.

As Elsa let out another groan, the baby added its own startled shrieks to the noise and the girl struggled up onto her elbows. "Well?" she demanded breathlessly. "Is it a boy for the *Führer*?"

Hannah gazed down at the child for a few taut seconds, its tiny, perfectly formed body able to be held in her one hand—ten fingers, ten toes, limbs strong and straight, deep blue eyes staring straight up at her, almost as if he knew.

"Yes," she said quietly. "It's a boy. A beautiful baby boy."

"Oh, thank heaven! Thank the *Führer!*"

The *Führer*, Hannah thought grimly, would have precious little to do with this poor child, although all to do with the place he'd been birthed—Heim Hochland, less than an hour east of Munich, one of the discreet and luxurious maternity homes set up for girls like Elsa, who could prove their purity to four generations and were willing to surrender their blond, blue-eyed babies into the care of the Fatherland.

"Let me see him," Elsa implored as, quickly and neatly, Hannah scooped the baby up in one arm, clipping the cord as the new mother sagged back against the sweat-dampened sheets. "I want to hold him."

The boy was intended for adoption by a worthy couple in a matter of weeks—an SS officer, his blushing bride, so far childless. Perhaps that woman would receive a *mutterkreuz* one day, but not, Hannah knew with a sorrowful twist in her gut, with this baby.

"It's time for the placenta, now," she said, ignoring Elsa's request. "Push again, not too fast, easy does it..."

With another groan, Elsa expelled the placenta in a gush of fluid and blood, falling back onto the sheets with exhaustion. "*Mein Gott*, is it done yet?" she demanded as Hannah, still holding the baby, tidied things away. "Let me hold him!"

Hannah hesitated, and then wordlessly she handed the tiny baby to Elsa.

Elsa's motherly, expectant smile morphed into a look of horror as she caught sight of the child's face. "What's wrong with him?" she cried, thrusting the baby away from her as if he was so much rubbish, and quickly Hannah scooped him up, cradled him close to her chest, one hand covering his tiny, damp head with an instinctive protectiveness as he let out a bleating cry.

"He has a cleft palate," she explained calmly. "The roof of his mouth has not joined together properly, but it can be fixed.

Quite easily, in fact, a simple surgery when he is a few months old."

"Fixed." Elsa spoke as if she did not understand the word. She did not want to. She did not, Hannah suspected, want a baby who had to be *fixed*.

"He is a completely healthy boy, otherwise," Hannah continued quietly. "Listen to his cry." The boy let out another lusty bellow, and she couldn't keep from smiling as she gazed down at his dark blue eyes, so wide and clear. Besides the lip, she thought, he really was perfect. Surely the doctors would see that, as well?

Elsa's lips trembled and she shook her head. "Take him away."

"Elsa..." Hannah protested instinctively, even though she knew there was no point. The baby would have been taken away from Elsa anyway in a few days, perhaps a week. Why not now?

And where would he go?

It was her duty as acting midwife to report the details of a birth, cleft palate included; it would be impossible for her not to do so. If she didn't, she would be disciplined or worse, and someone else would make the report, anyway. These things could not be hidden, not in a place like this.

And because of that report, Hannah knew, he would be taken away, not to the SS officer and his wife, but most likely to an orphanage—but what family would want to adopt him, with his lip like that? Physical perfection was not just the ideal these days, but the standard as well as the requirement. Babies like this one would end up languishing in an orphans' asylum somewhere; perhaps the nuns in charge would be kind to him. Hannah certainly hoped so.

Drawing the blanket over the corner of his face, she walked quickly out of the room toward the nursery.

· · ·

Later, after she'd left the baby with another nurse in charge who'd clucked her tongue at the sight of his face, Hannah went outside, in desperate need of a forbidden cigarette. She stood alone in the chill breeze of an October evening as the first stars came out above the expanse of dark blue water lapping the gardens of the home. She let her mind empty out, concentrating only on the cold, distant stars, so remote and beautiful; the smooth and empty expanse of lake, stretching out in the darkness; the smoke floating upwards in lazy, ephemeral curls before fading away into the night.

"A shame for Elsa." Gerda, a nurse from Munich with a placid face and a stolid manner, joined her out on the terrace, glancing at her cigarette once with pointed indifference even though nurses, especially nurses at Nazi maternity homes, weren't meant to smoke. Hannah didn't all that often, but tonight, with the baby's unblinking blue eyes and twisted lip fresh in her mind, she'd needed the short respite a cigarette offered.

"She seemed more angry than grieving," she remarked, her gaze still on the stars.

"And so she is. Nine months waddling around with stretch marks and swollen ankles, and all for nothing!" Gerda spoke with the complacency of a mother with three blond-haired children back in Munich, farmed out to relatives so she could work here, her husband fighting in Norway. A good mother and wife in every way, although not yet deserving of the *mutterkreuz*.

"She still has a baby at the end of it," Hannah remarked quietly. "With beautiful blue eyes."

Gerda made a dismissive noise, and Hannah sighed. Why was she bothering to argue the point? She knew it would do no good. Nurses were not meant to have opinions, and even if they did, they certainly didn't offer them to doctors or anyone else in charge. She had no power or choice here, and if she had, she could hardly change the whole system, the world they lived in now, that required perfection and demanded obedience. The baby would be cared for, at least, and who was to say he wouldn't find a better family someday, kinder than a fervent SS officer and his wife?

With another sigh, she gazed out at the darkening night as she and Gerda both listened to the whisper of the wind in the poplars. To Hannah, the sound seemed vaguely threatening, like the murmur of gossips, whispers of warning. When she'd come to Heim Hochland from Berlin back in 1936, she'd enjoyed the peace and solitude out here in the country, and also the luxury and comfort the *Lebensborn* maternity homes promised their staff, as well as their mothers—soft beds, nice linen, plentiful food, evenings around the fire or piano. *An easy life,* she'd thought, *and wouldn't that be a change.*

As time had marched on, however, as laws had been passed and war was declared, she'd begun to feel, more and more, a strange restlessness, a deepening disquietude, even in the midst of such ease and contentment. Smiling babies, complacent mothers, good food—what, really, was there not to enjoy? And yet, increasingly, she'd struggled to find pleasure in her work, in the longed-for ease of her life. In addition to the pregnant mothers who came to the home, little blond children had started to be brought in, pale-faced children who spoke no German and cried for their mothers. Hannah held them at night and stroked their hair and tried not to think about how they had come here, or why.

"You'll have to report it, you know," Gerda told her. "There will be trouble for you if you don't."

Hannah flicked the smoldering butt of her cigarette toward the water, its black expanse opaque and fathomless under the night sky. "I already have," she replied, an ache of regret in her voice, because of course she'd filled out the form as soon as he'd been born. She'd had to. She held onto the faint hope that it might mean a better life for the boy, at least one day.

Silently, she turned to head back into the home, its gracious rooms now quiet and empty.

"Nurse Stern." The voice of the home's matron was a clipped bark, authoritative and firm, whether she was addressing a recalcitrant toddler or a competent nurse. She strode toward Hannah as she came into the home, her mouth pressed into a thin, disapproving line.

"Yes, Matron?" Hannah straightened, heels together, chin lifted.

"A telegram has arrived for you from Berlin. Most unusual." Her blue eyes narrowed as she regarded Hannah with a slight air of disapproval, as if looking for some fault.

Having qualified in 1932, a year before the Nazis had reorganized the way nurses were trained and changed much of the curriculum to fit their dogmatic beliefs about racial purity and hygiene, Hannah knew she was not the matron's idea of an ideal Nazi nurse, not like one of the fanatical Brown Sisters, handpicked to train under the Nazi regime and relentlessly devoted to their *Führer*. No, she kept her own counsel and reserved her judgement, but the gaze she gave the matron was clear and firm, with only a hint of challenge.

Even after four years at Heim Hochland, she remained tight-lipped about her background; to the matron, a telegram meant she was either important or in trouble, and no doubt she'd prefer the latter, so she could replace Hannah with someone who showed a bit more nationalistic fervor.

"Thank you," she said, and held out her hand.

After a few seconds' considered pause, the matron placed the telegram in it and then folded her arms, waiting for Hannah to open it. There was no way, Hannah knew, she could walk away without letting her superior know what the mysterious missive held.

She turned slightly as she ran her thumbnail underneath

the envelope's seal, doing her best to angle the thin slip of paper from the older woman's prying eyes.

"Well?" the matron asked after Hannah had scanned the few lines. "Is it some emergency?"

"I am wanted in Berlin." Which made her sound far more important than she was, but Hannah took a perverse pleasure in the matron's suppressed gasp of shock, the way her eyes narrowed in displeasure. She did not like being taken by surprise.

"Wanted in Berlin," she repeated coldly. "What can you possibly mean?"

Was the woman imagining—Hannah thought with a wry twist of her lips—that she would have to report to the Gestapo in Prinz-Albrecht-Strasse, shaking in her shoes? She was probably hoping for such a thing. *I always thought Nurse Stern was suspect, her* Hitlergruss *a bit too slow off the mark.*

"My brother is an officer in the Abwehr," she told the matron. After a career in the army, Georg Strasser had moved to military intelligence at the start of the war. "Naturally, it is not something I often discuss. He requires my presence in Berlin immediately."

With her eyes still narrowed, the matron held out her hand and Hannah gave her the telegram. The few lines said exactly what she had—Georg asked that she visit him at his home as soon as possible. He would send a train ticket in the post. No explanation, no apologies, and why should there be? The only reason she was at Heim Hochland, or even a nurse in the first place, was because of her brother. Her half-brother, to be precise, but she had no intention of offering that information to the purse-lipped matron.

"In Berlin," she repeated, in annoyance now rather than suspicion, "and no explanation as to why? You are needed here, Nurse Stern. You have duties—"

Hannah tucked the telegram back its envelope. "If you feel I can disobey my brother..."

"His summoning you can have nothing to do with his position."

Hannah chose to remain silent. She doubted very much indeed that Georg's rather officious summons had anything to do with his position in military intelligence, but she did not wish to say so. Let the matron, with her cold eyes and severe manner, wonder.

"It is very inconvenient for us here at Heim Hochland, Nurse Stern," the matron continued. "You are needed at your duties."

Hannah bowed her head, as meek as the matron could possibly please. They both knew there was no way she could refuse a military officer's request. "I understand, Matron."

The older woman gave an exasperated hiss between her teeth. "Oh, very well. You may send your reply. I suppose you are not all that valuable."

Hannah nodded her thanks and turned to go, before she hesitated, and then resolutely turned back. "Matron... the boy who was born this evening, to Elsa Werling?"

"What of him, Nurse Stern?"

The older woman's tone was ominously repressive, but Hannah pressed on anyway, driven by a need greater than that of self-preservation. "He was completely healthy, save for his cleft lip. You know that can be operated on quite easily, when he's a few months old? Completely fixed."

The matron's gaze narrowed to two slits of scorn. "Are you a doctor, Nurse Stern? Was I not made aware of your promotion?"

Hannah kept the woman's hostile gaze. "The procedure is common knowledge. It really is easily done—"

"That child is not your concern."

"Where will he go?" Hannah dared to press further, needing to know. "An orphanage?"

The matron pressed her lips together. "Yes," she replied after a second's pause. "An orphanage. He will be well looked after, Nurse Stern, do not doubt, but you must see he can no longer be adopted by a member of the SS."

Reluctantly, Hannah nodded and then, at the matron's dismissal, walked slowly upstairs.

Her room was in the attic, high above the more comfortable nurseries and dormitories, with a single bed and a bureau, a washstand and nothing else. Still, it had sufficed, and she had enjoyed her work, yet even so, Hannah realized she was relieved to be absenting herself from Heim Hochland, from the deepening disquiet she'd felt in this place, among the narrow-eyed Brown Sisters and the sanctimonious matron, all of them always watching, waiting to catch you out.

Still, she wondered what her half-brother could possibly want with her. In the four years since Georg had arranged her position here, he had not written or communicated with her once, not that she'd expected him to. He'd made it clear from the beginning that their relationship had been a matter of duty and resentment rather than any affection. In fact, he had not laid eyes on her until ten years ago, when, at just eighteen years old, she had stood at the edge of the Invalids' Cemetery, a sodden and bedraggled figure, and watched as their father was lowered into the ground. Georg, then a man of forty, had walked toward her, the rain sluicing off the shoulders of his greatcoat.

"You're Hannah, aren't you?" he'd said, his tone matter-of-fact rather than kind. "My father's daughter." His bastard daughter, although it seemed Georg was too much of a gentleman to point out what they both obviously knew. He was the last of three brothers, two having been killed in the muddy trenches in France, and he'd looked at Hannah in quiet appraisal, his only sibling left.

She'd stared at him wordlessly, this half-brother she'd never met although she'd glimpsed him once years before, with the rest of his family, from a distance in the Tiergarten, when she'd been only ten or eleven, following their merry family outing like a beggar searching for scraps.

From that day of the funeral in 1930, Georg Strasser had decided to take something of an interest in his half-sister; he'd arranged and paid for her nurse's training at the Charité, without giving her the option of choosing a different path. Hannah had sometimes wondered what he might have said if she'd asked to train as a secretary or teacher, or even an opera singer. His nostrils would have flared, his lips thinning, as he informed her that was quite, *quite* impossible. Which, of course, it was.

Considering her own dire circumstances at the time, Hannah had not been in a position to tell Georg anything but a heartfelt thank you. He had been her savior, and she could not begrudge the fact he was a reluctant one.

And he *had* been generous, in his own way, although it was offered so grudgingly that it often felt more like stinginess, and he had never suggested a deeper relationship than what they had—a few terse meetings over the course of a decade.

She had never been invited to the Strasser home; she had never met his wife, a fluttering thing in white satin she'd once seen getting into a car, a flash of glossy hair and red lipstick, dark eyes in a pale, made-up face. She'd never been part of her half-brother's life in any way that was meaningful or affec-tionate or *real*, and yet here he was, summoning her to his stately home in leafy Grunewald—why? For what?

She would find out soon enough, Hannah supposed as, back in her bedroom, she stripped off her uniform and slipped into her nightgown. She had learned over the last three years not to seem too curious about anything. Not to ask questions, especially ones you didn't want the answers to. Never mutter under your breath, roll your eyes, make a joke, even look so much as skeptical. Anything that could make a fervent nurse or ardent officer question your loyalty.

It was a lesson she'd already had drilled into her as a child, among the tough streets and dirty tenements of Neukölln, but it had been cemented here at Heim Hochland. Mind your own business. Keep quiet, just do your job. Like her old neighbor Hilde would have said, *anything for a quiet life.*

Now, with a quick brush of her teeth, a slap of her cheeks with water from the pitcher, Hannah took down her scraped-up hair, and then hopped between the chilly bedsheets.

As she lay there staring at the patch of starlit sky visible from her small attic window and trying not to shiver, she found herself not thinking of her half-brother or his surprising request, but of a nameless baby boy with unblinking blue eyes who had looked up at her with trust and wonder, as if he could see straight into her soul.

Hannah closed her eyes against that bit of sky and willed sleep to come.

CHAPTER 2

BERLIN, OCTOBER 1940

The maid who answered Hannah's knock took in her worn coat and nurse's uniform with a deliberate sniff, and then instructed she wait in the hall while she went to see if Major Strasser was 'at home'. He certainly was at home, Hannah thought. She'd seen his car, a sleek black Mercedes, in the driveway, as she'd knocked on the door.

It was five days since she'd received her brother's telegram, four since the train ticket had arrived in the post, handed over by the matron with silent, simmering disapproval. Hannah had packed up her things at Heim Hochland—she didn't have much —and had taken the slow, trundling journey past Bavarian fields rippling under an autumn sun toward Berlin, the Fatherland's beating heart, and her half-brother's summons.

It had been three years since she'd been in the city of her birth; she'd had no real reason to return, and in any case, no money to make the journey. A nurse's wages did not run to leisure trips, and the memories of her childhood in Neukölln were not ones she particularly wished to revisit, although she thought she might call on her old neighbor Hilde while she was in the city.

Hannah heard the maid's murmuring in the study off the hall, her brother's rumbling response. She wondered if he'd offer her supper; after the six-hour train journey, where she'd eaten nothing but black bread and some hard cheese, her stomach was growling. And what about a bed? No, Georg's generosity would certainly not run to that. He would not even think of it, and she would have to beg a place on Hilde's kitchen floor before returning to Heim Hochland—or to whatever her brother bade her to do, for surely it was going to be something.

"Major Strasser will see you now, *Schwester*," the maid said, her manner prissily severe, and Hannah murmured her thanks as she followed the woman with her black dress, neat cap and white-frilled apron, into her brother's study.

The room was richly decorated and pleasantly warm, its wood-paneled walls lined with leather-spined books and heavy, ruby-colored velvet curtains drawn across the windows, a cheerful fire crackling in the grate, despite the national scarcity of coal.

The maid closed the door behind Hannah as her half-brother rose from his desk, bracing his hands on its surface, cherry wood inlaid with leather. He looked so different from her, with her light brown hair and eyes, her small, slender frame like her mother's, while Georg Strasser took after their father—the dark hair cut short and now gray at the temples, his body large and muscular, topping six feet by several inches, and, now at fifty, only just beginning to run to fat.

"Major Strasser," Hannah greeted him formally, inclining her head. "*Guten nacht.*"

"*Guten nacht*, Hannah." His lips thinned at the sight of the small, battered suitcase she was still holding. Did he think she would ask if she could stay the night? Well, she wouldn't. He gave a brisk nod and a click of his heels that revealed his Prussian heritage as well as his military background. "Thank you for coming."

"Did I have a choice?" Hannah tried to speak lightly but there was a slightly waspish edge to her voice that she regretted. Scoring such paltry points was surely beneath them both. Georg had lifted her from the gutter; the least he deserved was her courtesy.

"How have you been keeping?" he asked, his tone as formal as ever, one hand tucked into his waistcoat. "The Bavarian countryside must be more pleasant than Berlin, especially in wartime." There was a pointedness to his tone that Hannah knew was to remind her that the only reason she was enjoying the peaceful countryside was thanks to him. "When I was in touch with Dr. Ebner, he spoke highly of you."

"How kind of him," Hannah replied, although, in fact, while there were sixteen nurses at Heim Hochland, she doubted Dr. Ebner could pick her out from a well-starched line of them, never mind speak highly of her. She might have been working there for four years, but to an eminent man like Ebner, she was entirely forgettable. She always had been.

Georg gestured to one of the comfortable club chairs framing the fireplace with its glowing embers and welcoming warmth. "Please, do sit down."

Silently, Hannah eased herself into a chair, placing the suitcase at her feet and her hands in her lap.

Georg sat opposite her, his bearing as proud as ever as he gave her a look that was caught, as it always seemed to be, between haughty and welcoming.

"Well, dear brother," Hannah remarked pleasantly, "as lovely as it is to visit after all these years, I am wondering what could possibly cause you to summon me all the way from near Munich, and in wartime, no less. I hope you aren't unwell."

"I am in good health, thank you," Georg replied stiffly.

He looked it, Hannah thought, well-fed, when for many Germans the effects of the rationing brought in last year were starting to pinch. And yet, she mused, you would not know there was a war on, not really, save for the abundance of uniforms in the streets, swathes of gray and brown, the black and blood-red splashes of the swastikas above. Even children as young as ten wore their *Pimpf* or *Jungmädelbund* uniforms with pride, their goosestep as good as the Wehrmacht's.

The newspapers had continued to herald Hitler's seemingly unstoppable train of victories—Sudetenland, Austria, Czechoslovakia, Poland, Denmark, Norway, and most recently, France, its conquest heralded with parties and parades. The papers also boasted about the relentless bombing of England, claiming overwhelming successes that Hannah couldn't help but feel skeptical about. Still, it seemed as if no one could touch Germany, and for that, people were either intensely proud or wearily indifferent, depending, Hannah supposed, on how much they had to eat—or what they might have to fear from their glorious Reich.

"I have asked you here," Georg told her, drawing her thoughts back to the present, "because there is a small duty I require of you." He paused, his elbows resting on the carved wooden arms of his chair. "And one that I hope, considering our association and the kindnesses I have shown you in the past, you will undertake with both gladness and gratitude."

He met her gaze levelly, and Hannah managed a smile of polite inquiry. *Gladness and gratitude* was laying it on a bit thick, surely, although his words did pique her curiosity. What on earth could Georg want from her?

"What is this small duty?" she asked, keeping her tone pleasant.

He paused, and Hannah saw his fingers tighten on the arms of his chair, his knuckles whitening, making her wonder again what on earth this request could be. Then, drawing a breath, he continued carefully, "My son, Willi, requires treatment at a hospital for children. It is impossible for either his mother or I to accompany him, and so my hope was you would take that responsibility upon yourself." The gaze he gave her was unblinking, his hazel eyes boring steadily into hers, while Hannah could only stare back.

There seemed to be much he wasn't saying, so that she was unsure what question to ask first. "Where is this hospital?" she asked finally, when Georg had continued to gaze at her silently, waiting for her to respond.

"In Vienna. It is a new clinic specifically for children. I... I have only just heard about it." He pressed his lips together, as if to keep from saying more.

"All the way in Vienna," she remarked slowly. "I am surprised, when the Charité is right here."

"It is Professor de Crinis, at the Charité, who recommended this clinic in Vienna. He took over from Professor Bonhoeffer some years ago." When all the medical departments had been purged of Jews and their sympathizers, was what Hannah knew he meant. It was easy enough, then, to get the measure of someone like de Crinis, even though she'd never heard the name. Georg continued quietly, "Professor de Crinis is Austrian, as well. Perhaps it was that connection that inspired his suggestion."

"Perhaps." If de Crinis was like the other doctors who had been put in place by the Nazis, Hannah knew he would be a paid-up Party member, probably a rabid ideologist, as well. She was suspicious of anyone who embraced such maniacal devotion, but did her brother? Although Georg was in the Abwehr, she could not be sure where his sympathies truly lay. He did not discuss politics with her, and had, she sometimes thought, gone out of his way not to, but then didn't most people these days? Why say something that could get you in trouble, when you could choose to say nothing at all? Keep your head down and stay beneath anyone's notice? It was how she had always chosen to be. "Even so," she remarked, "that is quite far. Five hundred kilometers or more, at least ten hours on the train." And for how long? A few days? A week? Her half-brother had not said. Already she knew this was far from a so-called "small" duty.

"You can travel by car," Georg replied. "I will provide the car and driver myself, of course."

A car all the way to Vienna, in these days of petrol rationing. Hannah was reluctantly impressed, and even more uneasy.

"May I ask what this treatment is?"

"The clinic in Vienna is quite new," Georg replied, as if restating this was an answer to her question. "The treatments it offers are complex and innovative."

Hannah cocked her head, her gaze sweeping slowly over the man who in every way was her superior. He had wealth, power, status, privilege, far more of each than she could ever imagine having herself, and yet in this moment she thought he almost looked frightened. His hands were now clenched together in his lap, the skin around his tightly held mouth white. He met her gaze as steadily as always, but she sensed it took effort, and she felt a flash of sympathy for him, as well as a rising frustration that he wasn't being more honest with her.

"And how long will this treatment take?" she asked, feeling as if she had to draw every scrap of information from him, and reluctantly at that.

A long silence met this seemingly simple question, and then, with a squeak of leather, her half-brother shifted in his chair.

"Perhaps it is best if you meet Willi yourself," he said at last. "I thought you could stay for supper." Stay for supper! She must have betrayed her surprise for he continued with a strangely touching acknowledgement of their situation, "My wife is at a *Frauenschaft* meeting. They are arranging some refreshments for soldiers departing from Anhalter Bahnhof."

"How nice," Hannah remarked without expression. Of course his wife would not be present. Hannah was not sure the woman even knew she existed, but it was still a kindness on Georg's part to have her stay for a meal.

"Let me tell Elfriede that you are able to stay. That is, if...?"

She wondered if it was the first time he'd asked, rather than commanded her, presence. "Yes, thank you, Major Strasser," she replied. "I would be very glad to stay."

Something flashed across his face, twisting his mouth. Hannah could not tell if it was guilt or distaste. "Really, Hannah, we are related by blood. You must call me Georg."

"Of course," she replied, inclining her head. She had never before called him by his Christian name, but then she had never been invited to do so. Despite his generosities, she struggled to think of him as her blood relation—and yet he was. Why was he reminding her of it now? Simply so she would take his son to Vienna?

Georg rose to ring the bell on his desk to summon Elfriede as Hannah gazed at the dancing flames of the fire, her sense of unease deepening into something close to foreboding. There was still so much Georg wasn't saying—why?

Of course, in these times she knew as well as anyone else the wisdom of a closed mouth, a careful tongue, and eyes that managed not to see what was right in front of them. Anything for a quiet life, as Hilde used to say. That had been back during the dying throes of the Weimar Republic, when the police had marched in and killed thirty-three unarmed civilians in the streets of Neukölln during a communist-sponsored International Workers' Day Parade. Only seventeen years old and her mother just dead, Hannah had been living with Hilde, sleeping in the kitchen and getting temporary jobs charring, or typing if she was lucky. She'd stood watching as Hilde had closed and barred the shutters and they'd huddled inside until the fighting had died down and the streets had been empty of anything but blood.

But her half-brother, a major in the army's military intelligence, a man of prestige and status, someone to be feared himself... what could he possibly be afraid of now? What was making him seem so tense and cagey—and did Hannah, an absolute nobody in this ruthless Reich, really want to know?

Elfriede came to the door and Georg spoke to her quietly, asking to lay another place at the table. Hannah sensed the woman's annoyance, although she spoke politely enough. No doubt she felt superior to Hannah, a mere nurse who couldn't quite hide her humble origins—or her working-class accent. When the door had closed behind her, Georg turned to her.

"I will be glad for you to meet Willi."

Hannah suppressed the tart retort that had sprung to her lips, that he had never wanted her to meet any of his family before, quite the opposite. She hadn't even known he'd had a son before today. In the ten years of their association, they had only met in anonymous cafés over cups of coffee—not even a meal—and then only a handful of times.

Yet how could she begrudge him any of it, when he had arranged and paid for her nurse's training, as well as procured the position first at the Charité, and then at Heim Hochland? When he'd rescued her from destitution and poverty, and given her a way to live, a job that, for the most part, she enjoyed? No, she couldn't, of course she couldn't, and yet it was still a fact that had never stopped chafing at her, like a splinter under her nail, a thorn in her side. She would always be in his debt, and they would both always know it.

"And I will be glad to meet him, as well," she replied at last. "How old is he?"

"Eleven." There was a note of ringing pride in his voice, along with a touch of sorrow. "You will never meet a gentler boy."

Gentle, Hannah thought, was not a word applied to the hardy boys of the HJ, with their caps and daggers and willful sense of derring-do. She wondered just how ill Willi was.

Seeming restless now, Georg moved to the windows; the sun had already set, and night was drawing in, dark, chilly, and damp. He drew the curtains even more tightly across, cocooning the room in velvety warmth.

"It has been such a lovely summer," he remarked, his back to Hannah. "So very warm."

"So it has."

"The linden trees would have been glorious in blossom this year, if they had not all been cut down."

Hannah regarded him warily, for she knew as anyone else did that Hitler had had the trees cut down and replaced with swastika flags over five years ago, and in any case, linden blossoms were not nearly as spectacular as the cherry trees in the Tiergarten. Besides, it was autumn. Why was Georg mentioning the trees now? It almost felt like some sort of code, and one she decided would be wise not to try to understand.

Still staring out the window through the small gap in the curtains, he quoted softly, "I once saw many flowers blooming / Upon my way, in indolence I scorned to pick them in my going / And passed in proud indifference." He lapsed into musing silence while Hannah simply stared.

She knew the end of the poem, as others did, back when Heine was read and quoted by so many—*Now, when my grave is dug they taunt me; / Now, when I'm sick to death in pain, / In mocking torment still they haunt me, / Those fragrant blooms of my disdain.*

"Heinrich Heine," she said at last, unable to keep from naming the poet, wondering why Georg had quoted the Jewish writer, his books burned on Opernplatz seven years ago and now banned, his monuments removed throughout Germany. The *Völkischer Beobachter* regularly attacked and condemned the once much-beloved poet in its pages. For Georg Strasser, a major in the Abwehr and a devoted servant of the Reich, to quote him in these times was either dangerous or a trap.

"You know poetry?" he remarked, turning back to her, his face like a mask.

"I have always enjoyed reading," she replied carefully, for she did not want to be trapped into saying something about Heinrich Heine. She tried not to let the implication sting—that she, an uneducated girl from one of Berlin's poorest neighborhoods, who had quit school at twelve and gone on to work mainly as a skivvy, should barely be able to read, never mind know of Heinrich Heine. Not, of course, that she would quote him the way her half-brother just had.

Georg seemed as if he was going to say something more, and instinctively Hannah tensed. She did not think she wanted to hear whatever it was he intended to say, but in any case, he merely inclined his head as he gave a small, cool smile. "Shall we repair to the dining room? I believe Elfriede will serve supper to us shortly."

Hannah nodded, and as she reached for her suitcase, Georg gave a quick shake of his head. "You may leave that here."

"Thank you," she murmured, and then followed him out of the study, across the foyer with its floor of black and white marble, to a stately dining room, filled with heavy, mahogany furniture, the dark curtains drawn at both windows, the table that could seat twelve set for three at one end, with napkins of damask and cutlery of sterling silver, a porcelain tureen of soup in the center.

"Ah, and here they are," Georg said, sounding pleased, as a young boy came through the swinging door that led to the kitchen, a nanny or governess of some sort, dressed neatly in starched black with a white apron, guiding him by the shoulder.

At first, Hannah only saw the dark, glossy wing of hair lying across the high forehead, the bright hazel eyes that often seemed severe on the father but on the son glinted with gold and good humor. Then, with a jolt, she registered the slightly vacant stare in those eyes, the way his mouth hung open, the pronounced limp as he dragged his left foot across the floor.

She turned to face Georg and found him smiling with gentle sorrow as Willi clumped into the room.

"This," he said, his voice filled with quiet pride, "is my son Willi."

CHAPTER 3

"What did you think of Willi?"

The smile Georg gave her was both wry and sorrowful, as if he knew what she thought but was waiting for her to say it. And, in truth, Hannah did not know how to answer. She had expected Willi to be *ill*, of course, but not...

"He..." She hesitated, then stated carefully, "has disabilities."

"Yes." Georg's gaze remained steady.

It had been a painful hour, watching Willi dribble his soup, seeing with surprise the way Georg so gently wiped his chin. It had revealed a sensitivity and kindness to her half-brother that she'd had no idea he possessed, and it had stirred up an empathy as well as an absurd jealousy in her in equal measure—how could Georg be so gentle with Willi, and so terse with her? A ridiculous emotion, and she'd been annoyed with herself for feeling it. The situations were not in any way similar.

More than any of that, though, she felt fear. Did she not, as a pediatric nurse, know as well as anyone the difficulty of having a child like Willi in the Reich? Surely her half-brother knew it, too. Already she'd seen the scorn in Elfriede's eyes every time she looked at the boy, bent over his bowl, a napkin tucked into his collar stained with food he'd either dropped or dribbled.

"It is not hereditary," Georg informed her calmly. They were alone in his study, the nurse having taken Willi back to his room after their meal. Georg crossed the room to a small table with a decanter of schnapps and two glasses of cut crystal. French brandy by the look of it, Hannah supposed—black market or spoils of war?

"An accident at birth then?" she said as he poured the schnapps.

He nodded and handed her a glass. "A long and difficult birth. The doctors thought it happened then."

Although they could never be sure. Who was to say it had not happened in the womb? Hannah had seen it before, long labors that deprived the baby of oxygen and led to symptoms like Willi's—jerky movements, trouble speaking, drooling, limping, learning difficulties, even seizures.

Regretfully, she shook her head. "You must know that in these days it does not really matter which it was."

"It matters to me." Georg took a long swallow of his schnapps and then put his glass on his desk, the movement precise. "Willi is intelligent. He has trouble speaking and walking, it is true, but he is neither an idiot nor an imbecile. He has a condition, diagnosed when he was two years old by Oskar Vogt of the Kaiser Wilhelm Institute here in Berlin."

"And what is this condition?"

"Spastic cerebral palsy, caused by trauma at birth." Georg lifted his chin as he met her gaze, and Hannah wondered how he'd managed to secure such a confident diagnosis of it being non-hereditary. His military background, the medals he'd won in the first war? Or mere money? In any case, all the hospitals and institutes were stuffed with Nazis now; whoever had given the diagnosis was long gone, irrelevant, or worse, a liability. And so, sadly, was Willi, especially for a man like Georg, with his military career, his Nazi credentials.

"Do you know the nature of this treatment he will be having in Vienna?" she asked.

Georg hesitated, his gaze briefly sliding away from hers. "I have been told that there are some new therapies," he finally said, the words coming with reluctant care. "For movement and speech. Surgeries on individual muscles have had some success with similar cases..." He trailed off with a shake of his head. "I am not a medical man, so I cannot give you the information. You would undoubtedly understand far better than I do."

Another pause, this one weighty.

"My hope is that the care and treatment offered at this new clinic will be for Willi's betterment." He said the words heavily, as if they were a burden to be laid down.

Had he arranged the stay at the hospital, Hannah wondered, or had it been pressed upon him? Having a son like Willi might be seen as an embarrassment for a high-ranking officer in the Abwehr; better for him to be tucked away, taken care of far from Berlin. Perhaps that was behind the choice of going all the way to Vienna. The thought made Hannah bristle with indignation on Willi's behalf, as well as with Georg, for agreeing to such a thing.

She took a sip of the schnapps, the liquor burning its way down her throat. She could not remember the last time she'd had spirits, and already it felt as if her head were swimming—although perhaps it was just the nature of the situation she found herself in, and one she already knew she could not refuse.

"And how long is this treatment to last?"

"Indefinitely."

She paused, the glass halfway to her lips. "You mean—"

"I have arranged for you to have a position as a pediatric nurse at the clinic for the foreseeable future. I have already written to the *Lebensborn* home, terminating your position there."

Hannah knew she shouldn't be surprised—hadn't her half-brother arranged every aspect of her career so far?—and yet she was still angry and she struggled not to show it. "You had no right to act in such a high-handed manner," she told him, her fingers clenching around her glass. To arrange her career, her entire life, without even giving her a choice! She did not know a soul in Vienna. She had never even been out of Germany. And she did not want to work in some sort of asylum for the sick and disabled, a type of institution where she had no experience or interest.

"You would not be a nurse without my assistance," he reminded her, and her anger flared hotter, higher.

"Am I to be in your debt forever?" she asked, striving to keep her voice even. "Did you even consider whether I wished to move all the way to Vienna, to work in a hospital full of—" She swallowed down the unkind words she'd been going to say. "With nurses and doctors I don't know?" Her voice rose as she stopped to catch her breath. "I doubt my wishes even crossed your mind."

"I recognize I am asking you a favor," Georg replied, a quietly lethal note entering his voice that made Hannah's ire subside, replaced by a chilled wariness. "This is a renowned facility—Am Steinhof has been at the forefront of its field for nearly fifty years. In fact, you could consider this a promotion."

"Ha!" That was one way to dress it up, she thought, but she still did not want to go. While it may have been true she had started to feel uneasy at Heim Hochland, especially with the children arriving who cried at night, she'd still been comfortable, maybe even content, at least a little. She'd enjoyed caring for the children there, their arms around her neck, their easy smiles. The thought of going somewhere strange, filled with strange patients, nurses who might be the kind of fanatical Brown Sister she wouldn't be able to trust, doctors swaggering self-importantly... Besides, she had never nursed a child such as Willi before. She was not sure she would even know how.

And, she knew, while psychiatrists were held in high esteem, psychiatric nurses were not, and they had a decidedly lower status than that of a general nurse of her training and experience. You might as well shovel manure or scrub floors than haul insensible patients about with indifferent care, spooning them their soup and strapping them into their beds. Under the Nazis, psychiatric nurses hadn't even been included in their new, modern nursing initiatives. And Georg was asking her to become one, for what? So she could mollycoddle his son?

She didn't want to do it, not at all, and yet what choice did she have? Georg had already terminated her position at the maternity home; if she did not go to Am Steinhof, she had nowhere else to go, and she would most likely not be able to depend on him arranging a position for her in future. The truth was, she had no choice at all.

"And when am I to go?" she asked, the fight draining out of her as she considered her predicament.

"As soon as I can make the arrangements, hopefully within a week or two. In the meantime, I have booked a room at a modest hotel on the Kurfürstendamm."

"Not the Adlon?" Hannah quipped, naming the fancy hotel frequented by high-ranking Nazis. She was unable to hide her bitterness, although she knew it wasn't entirely fair.

Georg inclined his head. "However it may seem to you, Hannah, I am grateful."

At least he'd considered her lodging arrangements, she thought. She would not have to sleep on Hilde's floor, and for that she was grateful.

"And how long am I to work at this hospital?"

"For as long as required. It is my wish that you will take a kindly interest in Willi—indeed, my hope that you might enjoy doing so. He is a kind, intelligent boy, whatever his challenges."

That may be, Hannah thought, *but he is a stranger to me, and if you did not need me, I doubt I would have ever been allowed to meet him.*

"And what are my accommodation arrangements in Vienna?"

"There is accommodation at the hospital itself for those who do not reside in the city. You will have your own room."

Hannah could already picture it—somewhere up in the eaves, an iron bedstead, a thin, lumpy mattress, a few hooks for clothing, a pitcher and basin of old enamel on a rickety chest of drawers. Perhaps a braided rug on the floor if she was lucky, or a picture on the wall, most likely of the *Führer*, with his stern glare, bristling with affront every time she looked at him. Like every other nurse's accommodation she'd had; the thought of it almost made her laugh. Perhaps one hospital was just like another, after all, no matter who the patients were.

"Thank you," she said, and then, to her surprise, Georg grasped her hands quite suddenly and tightly with his own. It was, she thought, the first time he'd ever touched her.

"I do not ask you to love him," he said, his voice turning rough with emotion as he squeezed her hands, "but like him, perhaps. Look out for him. Keep him safe, if you can."

A lump of emotion rose in her throat as she met her half-brother's almost wild gaze. She'd never seen him look so moved, so *afraid*, and the disquiet she'd felt earlier returned in force, along with a sudden, deep sympathy.

"I... I will, Georg," she said, squeezing his hands gently in return. "I promise."

He nodded, holding onto her hands for another moment before he released them. "Thank you, Hannah. Thank you."

It was surely a nonsense, she told herself uneasily, to think a boy like Willi Strasser would be in any sort of actual *danger* of neglect at this hospital. He was the son of a major in the Abwehr, from a wealthy family, with a faultless Prussian background. At Am Steinhof, he would be treated well... unlike, perhaps, that little blue-eyed boy back at Heim Hochland, with his unwavering gaze and cleft lip. The thought of him still caused Hannah a wrench of regret. By the time she had left for Berlin, he'd already been taken to an orphanage somewhere, never to be talked about again. Even his own mother had been determined to forget him.

The next afternoon, Hannah made her way to Neukölln to visit Hilde, who had taken her in when her mother had died, and was someone she could call family as much as, if not more than, Georg.

As she alighted from the S-Bahn station Neukölln-Südring, she was surprised to realize how much she'd forgotten about her old neighborhood, things she had thought she would always remember—the smell of damp and drains, the way the tall, crumbling apartment blocks, elegant a century ago, seemed to leach the light from the sky. After three years of veritable luxury at Heim Hochland, the refuse-strewn streets and dilapidated buildings held the power to shock, or at least unsettle her. She'd become used to the comfort of the maternity home.

She had spent her entire youth here, knew these dirty streets like her own hand, and yet as she clutched her handbag tighter to her chest, she felt, in some small way, like a stranger— or perhaps it wasn't the strangeness, but rather the awful familiarity of it all, that made her feel an uneasy quaver of dread.

That sense of dread deepened as she came into the dank front hallway of her old apartment building, glancing upward at the single, naked bulb swaying on a bit of wire, before, as a visceral shudder went through her, she started determinedly up the stairs.

Her dread thankfully disappeared when Hilde threw open her door with a bellow of greeting and wrapped her in her thick, meaty arms for a tight squeeze of a hug before she released her so hard and fast Hannah nearly stumbled.

"Well, it's about time I saw you! Not too fancy for your old neighbor now, I hope, eh?"

Hannah smiled and shook her head. Throughout her childhood, Hilde had often been more like a mother to her than her own. "Of course not, Hilde."

"Come in, come in."

Hilde waved her into rooms that rushed up at her with their familiarity, with their walls of crumbling plaster and peeling wallpaper, black mildew creeping along their edges. The kitchen was crowded and dark, all of it the same as before—the table with its stained oilcloth cover, the rickety cupboard filled with mismatched dishes, the old metal basin where Hilde did all her washing-up; the tap and toilet were outside in the hall, shared by everyone on the floor.

"I've got coffee," Hilde told her as she filled a pot from a jug of water and put it on the stove. "But it tastes like dishwater, if it tastes of anything at all. I'm sure you're used to better, at your fancy hospital."

Briefly, Hannah thought of the rich, fragrant coffee she'd drunk at the Strasser table last night, while Willi had slurped his hot cocoa. "Ersatz is fine. I brought you something." She laid a pot of strawberry jam, filched from a cupboard at Heim Hochland, on the table. They wouldn't miss it, and Hannah knew Hilde would never be able to afford such a luxury.

"You shouldn't have," Hilde said, without any real sincerity, and then, with a quick grin, she whisked the pot out of sight, no doubt wanting to hide it from her husband, who would likely eat it all himself with a spoon, and give Hilde a slap or a shove if she protested. "So what brings you to Berlin?" she asked as she pulled out a chair. Hannah sat opposite her.

"Work. I've left the maternity home."

Hilde sucked her teeth. "What, did you swap one of those blue-eyed brats for a little Jew?" She let out a guffaw of laughter.

Hannah managed a small, tense smile at this seeming joke; there were certainly no Jews at Heim Hochland, and very few even on the streets of Berlin any more. Those who did venture out kept themselves to themselves and were forbidden from most hospitals, schools, or stores. "My father's son has arranged a place for me at a hospital in Vienna," she explained.

"Vienna! My." Hilde shook her head, as she sat back in her chair. "Look at you, the world traveler."

"So it seems." She gave a little shrug and a smile. "To tell you the truth, I wasn't given much of a choice."

"Well, as long as it sees you in work and fed."

The coffee began to boil, and Hilde heaved herself up from her chair to stir the sludge in the pot.

"So what will you be doing?" she asked as she strained the brew into cups and brought them back to the table. "No sugar, I'm afraid. Although they say we might get some soon from France." She smiled mirthlessly as she took a sip of what, Hannah quickly discovered, tasted just as Hilde had said—heated-up dishwater, with a bitter aftertaste.

"I'll be a children's nurse," she told Hilde. "The hospital is for... for sickly children."

"Sickly?" The older woman frowned. "Isn't everyone in a hospital sick?"

"Those with permanent conditions, I mean... who cannot be cared for at home."

Understanding dawned in Hilde's eyes. "So idiots and the like?"

Hannah shrugged uncomfortably, aware she'd said, or at least thought, as much last night. Hilde sounded matter-of-fact, but the words seemed unkind, or perhaps just dismissive. "So it would seem."

Hilde made a face. "Why has your brother put you in such a place? That doesn't sound nearly as nice as that maternity home must be."

"No, I don't suppose it will be. Georg's son... he had a difficult birth. He wants me to look out for him."

"You mean he's like the Hoffman boy?"

Peter Hoffman, Hannah recalled, had lived on the floor above. Most days, he'd sat in the stairwell staring vacantly at the people climbing up or down, sometimes speaking gibberish or screaming at random. No one had really minded him, but as he'd got older, he'd become harder to control; once, he'd attacked and hurt a little girl. When he'd been twelve or so, he'd been put in an asylum; his parents hadn't been able to cope any longer. Where, Hannah wondered, was he now? In a place like Am Steinhof?

"Something like that," she said.

Hilde sucked her teeth as she shook her head, a slow, disapproving back and forth. "Doesn't seem right, somehow. If he wants a nanny for his brat, he should hire one."

Hannah lifted her shoulders as she took a sip of coffee. "He seems a kind boy, and I suppose he has a nanny, in me. The boy will be treated well, I'm sure, with his connections."

Hilde nodded. "Well, you know what the world is like. Everything's easier if you have money." She spoke without rancor; it simply was the way things were. There was no point fighting or railing against it.

Hannah gave a little smile as she put her coffee cup down. "Yes, I know."

Hilde reached over and covered her hand with her own heavy, callused one. "Just do the job, Hannah, and don't be smart about it," she advised, dropping her jolly pragmatism for a moment. Her face looked old and bleak, with a spiderweb of broken veins across her nose and cheeks, a bruise fading on her temple, no doubt from a clout by her brute of a husband, Stefan, an ardent Nazi who was as drunk on his newfound power as the street's block warden as he was on cheap schnapps.

His position was one reason Hannah had previously been reluctant to return to visit her old friend—she was not brave enough to be a dissenter, but neither was she devoted to the Nazi dogma, and block wardens specialized in denouncing neighbors, as well as demanding money for the *Winterhilfswerk* drives. She preferred to avoid such a person if she could.

"This war will be over one day," Hilde continued stubbornly, "and you'll still have a life to live, away from your half-brother and his idiot son. Don't mess it up by protecting his child. He's not your concern."

"He's only a child," Hannah couldn't help but protest. "I can certainly see that he comes to no harm, and, in truth, I don't think that part will be very onerous. I doubt his father would have sent him there otherwise. I'm just insurance." Or so she'd decided last night, after leaving the Strasser home. As for the life she might live when the war was over... Hannah could not even begin to imagine that. It felt too risky, to dare to dream.

Hilde shrugged, pragmatic once more. "Well, then, it shouldn't be too bad, I suppose. As long as you have enough to eat."

"Yes," Hannah agreed after a pause, and they lapsed into silence. It seemed little enough to aspire to, but they both knew what hunger felt like.

In the days after the first war, when Hannah had been a baby and Hilde a young woman, hunger had been their near-constant companion. It hadn't been so bad at first; Hannah's earliest memories were of her father, coming to the apartment, bearing gifts—candied cherries, rich chocolate, a fat sausage. Once, he'd brought her a doll, the most beautiful thing she'd ever seen, with real blond hair arranged in cornsilk curls and blue eyes that opened and closed, a white porcelain face with a pale pink mouth, tiny little teeth.

When her mother had asked to see it, Hannah had presented it to her, trembling with childish ecstasy, hardly able to believe she was in possession of such a treasure. Her mother had picked up the doll, stared at it dispassionately for a moment, and then lifted it up and cracked it once, hard on the edge of the kitchen table.

Hannah had watched in horrified disbelief as the doll's porcelain head had shattered into a thousand jagged pieces. Her mother had handed her back the headless doll with its open, gaping neck with a grim smile. "Next time ask him for another sausage," she'd said.

Later, Hannah had overheard Hilde as her mother had related the story. "It seems a waste," she'd said with both a chuckle and then a sigh. "You could have sold it for a few marks."

"Who wants a doll like that these days?" Hannah's mother had returned. "And in any case, her life is going to be hard. Better she learns it now. That lesson's worth a few marks, to me."

And it *had* been hard, after that—her father had visited one day when she was about seven, seeming guilty and rushed, and although Hannah hadn't been able to hear what he'd said, after that there had been no more visits, no more cherries or chocolate or sausage, and certainly no more dolls.

Instead, thanks to the blockade at the end of the war, and then later the severe terms of peace as well as the ever-spiraling hyper-inflation, there had been nothing but years of grim survival—days spent scrounging for food or waiting to buy a handful of weevil-filled flour, dinner nothing but a moldy potato boiled in water with a little salt, and that if she was lucky. Her mother had become increasingly worn down and bitter, resentful of Hannah and the demands on her life, determined to prove to her in every way possible just how grim her existence could be.

Hannah had tried, with some kind of pointless self-preservation, to keep from going half-feral the way so many of the children on her street had, turning into thieves, stealing or worse for a bit of bread. She'd stayed at school until she was twelve, even though her mother had insisted there was no point and had been angry with her for wasting time when she could have been earning, no matter how little. She'd read as many books as she could from the local library, and she'd managed to buy a decent dress off a market stall for interviews when she was fifteen. She'd learned to type by memorizing the position of the keys on a typewriter in a shop window, and she'd practiced on the kitchen tabletop, determinedly impervious to her mother's sneers that no one would hire a girl like her, from the sewers of Neukölln, to type letters. She'd been determined to be different.

Still, that ambition hadn't been enough to get ahead, or really even to get by. She'd managed only a few temporary typist jobs, it was true, in addition to the more regular charring, and she'd dutifully given her mother her meager wages every week she was in work, but their existence had remained desperately hand-to-mouth, the wolf always at the door, the future entirely uncertain.

Then Hannah's mother had caught pneumonia when she was seventeen, and the fragile foundations of her life had collapsed completely. After missing work to care for her mother until her death, she was fired from her job, and, unable to pay the rent on her own, the landlord had kicked her out of the apartment. She'd become completely dependent on Hilde's generosity, dodging Stefan's groping hands and avoiding the leering bachelor across the hall who liked to keep the door open when he was in the toilet.

She'd spent days charring, nights huddled on the kitchen floor, doing her best to stay out of sight, to survive. It had been a wretched existence, and the only thing that had saved her from having to endure it forever had been the intervention of her half-brother.

"Well," Hilde said, heaving herself up from the table, "I'd ask you to write me from Vienna, but you know I can't read all that well." She let out another one of her guffaws of laughter, but Hannah sensed something weary and even despairing behind it. Hilde had had a hard life—two sons dead in the first war, one who'd only been sixteen when he'd joined up, just weeks before the Armistice, a husband who treated her with casual indifference when he was happy and beat her when he was in a temper, and drank much of their money away.

"I could send you a postcard," she suggested. "At least there would be a picture."

"That would be nice." Hilde smiled, and with the sunlight streaking through the dirty windowpane, touching her gray hair and turning it gold, she looked, Hannah thought, so very old, far older than her fifty-odd years. She had no idea when she would see her again. Even in this lull of seeming peace, the quiet confidence of Hitler's parade of victories, they were still at war, the future entirely unknowable and dangerously uncertain. Bombs fell, men came in the night, children wasted away. There were no promises for anyone.

"I will send one," she promised, and rose to hug the older woman.

Hilde clasped her in her arms tightly, and Hannah breathed in the familiar smell of cooking grease and sweat, cabbage and cigarettes as she returned the embrace. She thought of all the times Hilde had taken her in, the food she'd scrounged from her own bare cupboard, so Hannah could eat. The laughter they'd shared over this worn and rickety table, because choosing laughter had felt stronger than succumbing to tears.

"I will," she said again, her voice choking a little. "I'll miss you, Hilde. I'm sorry I haven't visited more."

"What, all the way from near Munich or wherever that fancy place was? Not likely." Hilde gave her one last squeeze before she released her. "Take care of yourself, Hannah," she entreated as she walked her to the door. "Who knows what it's like down there, what people you'll meet."

Hannah managed a small laugh even though she shared at least a little of her friend's unease. "It's a *hospital*, Hilde—"

Hilde nodded soberly. "Yes, but in these days..." She left the thought unfinished. "Just be careful," she said again, and Hannah touched her hand in a final farewell.

"I will," she promised. "And I'll send you that postcard. Vienna is meant to be beautiful, isn't it?"

"I wouldn't know," Hilde replied with an attempt at restoring her easy humor, "but I'll look forward to it all the same."

CHAPTER 4

BERLIN, NOVEMBER 1940

Ten days after she'd first spoken to Georg, Hannah stood in the drive of her half-brother's house in Grunewald, preparing to leave with Willi for Vienna. The day was cold and bright, the sky a hard blue, the trees stark and leafless.

Hannah had spent a rather pleasant week and a half in the city of her birth; in addition to arranging her accommodation, Georg had generously given her a small allowance, and although clothing was scarce thanks to rationing, she'd been able to buy a few books as well as a new hat. It had felt like such a luxury, to spend her days wandering the city, strolling along the frost-tipped paths in the Tiergarten or sipping coffee—such as it was—at one of the cafés on Kurfürstendam. She'd felt like a tourist, but also adrift, untethered to either time or place, a stranger in the city of her birth, knowing no one besides Hilde and Georg, yet determined to enjoy this surprising oasis of time and peace as much as she could.

A few days before, the air-raid sirens had screamed their warning as people had stirred groggily in their beds.

"It's just a drill," the hotel's staff had assured the guests as they'd trooped wearily down to the shelter Goering himself had insisted Berliners would never need.

Hannah had listened to two elderly, pragmatic men; dressed in overcoats and with blankets draped over their shoulders, they spoke of the war as they'd played chess; apparently there had been raids since the summer, although not too much damage yet.

"Ah, well," one of them had said as he moved his pawn. "Never mind, eh? The war will be over soon."

This was clearly a well-worn joke, for the other had let out a belly laugh, shook his head, and then captured his opponent's bishop.

A few hours later, the all-clear had finally sounded and they were able to emerge into the gloomy pre-drawn to go back to bed. Hannah hadn't seen any evidence of bombs or damage, but perhaps there had been somewhere else in the city.

Now she saw that Georg looked rather haggard and drawn as he rested one hand on his son's shoulder. His wife was nowhere to be seen; was that because of her presence here? Hannah couldn't help but wonder. Perhaps Frau Strasser still did not know of her existence, no matter what she was now doing for her son.

Willi was dressed neatly in flannel trousers and a collared shirt, his dark hair brushed back from his forehead. At first glance, he looked like any other boy, but Hannah knew it would only take a second glimpse to realize he was not. His mouth hung open and his gaze was unfocused. She was not quite sure how to address him; the children at Heim Hochland had been much younger and entirely different in situation and circumstance, but after a few moments' consideration, she decided to adopt the same cheerfully no-nonsense manner she'd used with her previous charges. Children were children, after all, whatever their capabilities or needs.

"Well, Willi, it will be a very long journey to Vienna," she said by way of greeting. "I hope you've brought something to occupy yourself. I would not like you to be bored."

He gave her a lopsided, drooling smile as he nodded and spoke, but the words were garbled, and she flushed, struggling to understand.

"He has a book," Georg stated quietly. "One of his favorites. He is a great reader. Like you are, Hannah, as you mentioned." He smiled with the same wry sorrow he'd shown earlier, his face downcast, and Hannah blinked, unsure how to respond.

She felt as if something had shifted between her and her half-brother, and she did not know how to treat him now. She had always been in his power, bound by his dutiful largesse, but for the first time, she sensed how beholden he now was to her. Was he worried for his son's health? His wellbeing? And yet how could she possibly make much of a difference to either? She was only a nurse, expected to obey without questioning, without murmur, and in any case, Willi did not even know her.

"I have a letter for the medical director of the clinic," Georg told her. "Dr. Erwin Jekelius. I hope you will introduce yourself to him immediately upon your arrival, make your position known."

"I shall do my best, of course." She took the letter, the name on the envelope written in black ink in Georg's elegant script.

The driver put their cases in the back of the Mercedes and then stood apart, waiting for the signal for them to enter the car. Hannah felt a sudden clutch of panic that she didn't entirely understand; this parting felt more significant, more permanent, than she wanted it to be. How long would she be gone? What would Berlin, Germany, life itself, be like upon her return?

Georg, his bearing as militarily straight and regal as ever, turned toward his son. "*Gott sei mit dir*, Willi," he said, his voice choking a little. God be with you.

Hannah found, quite suddenly, that she had to swallow hard and look away.

"*Auf Wiedersehen*, Papa," Willi replied, and though the words were mumbled, Hannah could understand them this time. She blinked rapidly.

Gently, Georg embraced his son, no more than a moment where he clasped the slight boy to his own solid frame. Willi grinned up at him and Hannah wondered how much he could understand. Then, with a lurch of something close to fear, she wondered how much any of them could understand.

Georg nodded to the driver, Klaus, who stepped smartly forward and opened the door of the car. He waved one hand in farewell, glancing meaningfully at Hannah, who took Willi by the hand. He was docile enough, a slight smile on his face that made her feel a sweep of uneasy sorrow. Did he not understand what was happening? Or did he, and he had simply reconciled himself to a future at Am Steinhof and whatever treatments or therapies there that might help him? Could he possibly know what it would be like? Could she?

As he clambered clumsily into the car, Hannah had her doubts as to both.

They drove away from the tall, elegant house in Grunewald, Georg standing in the drive, his hand raised in farewell until they turned the corner and were out of sight.

Hannah glanced at Willi, who had twisted around so his nose was pressed to the window, his palm flat on the glass.

"Papa," he said, and this time the word was clear, yearning. "*Papa*."

Having no words of reassurance, no promises to give, Hannah briefly touched his shoulder in sympathy and then looked out the opposite window as the buildings blurred by.

They drove in silence out of Berlin, and then through marshy fields and woodlands, the trees now bare of leaves, south toward Munich, where they would spend the night before crossing east to Vienna. Willi wriggled back down in his seat, sitting forward, a look on his face that was both vacant and expectant, as if he was ready for anything and nothing at the same time.

Hannah saw Klaus glance at Willi in the rearview mirror, his mouth twisting in derision. Then he caught sight of her looking at him, and he winked. She pressed her lips together and looked away.

After about an hour of silence in the car, Willi tapped Hannah very politely on the shoulder. She jerked, startled out of her blank reverie as she'd watched the wheat fields stream by.

"Yes?" she asked, and Willi spoke, the words painstaking yet unintelligible, and flushing, Hannah forced herself to admit, "I'm sorry, Willi, but I cannot understand you."

He took a breath, tried again. "What... what is your name?"

This time, Hannah understood, and she flushed all the more. "My name is Hannah." She paused, uncomfortably. Had Georg even told him that she was his aunt? Would he understand what that meant? It did not feel like her place to say. "I met you last week, do you remember?" she asked. "At supper."

Willi nodded slowly. "May I... may I call you Hannah?" he asked, with gentlemanly politeness.

Hannah had an urge to shift in her seat, to squirm. "Yes, of course you may."

He gave her that lopsided smile as he nodded slowly, a laborious bobbing up and down of his head. "*Danke*, Hannah."

She bit her lip and then nodded.

Another hour passed in silence, and Hannah tried not to feel twitchy. She wasn't comfortable ignoring Willi as she was doing, but the truth was, she didn't know how to talk to him and that made her feel both guilty and nervous. In any case, she told herself, Willi seemed happy enough in his own company.

Klaus, his hands encased in black leather gloves on the steering wheel, his gaze now firmly on the road, had not spoken once since the start of the journey, although he had whistled bits of Nazi marching songs—"*Horst Wessel Lied*" or "*Heil*

Hitler Dir!"—which was not all that surprising considering the Party pin on his collar. Hannah made sure not to meet his gaze again in the mirror.

Eventually, Willi reached down to the satchel by his feet and, with fumbling, painstaking effort, retrieved a book from within.

"What are you reading?" Hannah asked with both curiosity and an attempt to be friendlier to the boy.

To her surprise, Willi gave Klaus a rather sly glance from under his lashes, and then, jerkily but with obvious deliberation, pressed a finger to his lips.

Even more curious now, Hannah leaned forward, and Willi pushed the book toward her so she could read the title on the cover—*Wolfsblut*, or, in English, *White Fang*, by Jack London. A banned book.

She glanced up at him in surprise, and saw he was giving her his lopsided grin, this one more impish and knowing than before, and she found she was smiling, too. She nodded and pressed her finger to her own lips, and his grin widened as he nodded back.

"I like reading, too," she whispered. "I always loved going to the library, as a child." Novels had been her escape, when she'd been younger. In the pages of *Ivanhoe* or *Heidi*, she had been able to lose herself, far from the dank apartment, her mother's anger, her own longing and desperation, into a world of adventure, drama, possibility, *hope*.

Even at Heim Hochland, she'd found some needed respite from the comfortable yet sometimes dreary day-to-day in the maternity home's small collection of Nazi-approved books—American westerns by Karl May, or the blatant propaganda of Beumelberg's soldier stories or even worse-written romances. Still, they were better than nothing; fiction, Hannah thought, always provided an escape from the stark and unrelenting reality of life.

And didn't Willi need an escape from that, as well? Perhaps everyone did.

Gently, she pushed the book back toward him, hiding the cover from Klaus's sight with her hand. They shared one last smiling, conspiratorial look before Willi opened his book and Hannah turned to stare out the window, her mind in a welter of confusion. It seemed Georg was right about his son; he was a clever boy. The knowledge unsettled her; did a boy like Willi really belong in an asylum, even a comfortable one such as Am Steinhof was sure to be?

At midday, on Hannah's request, Klaus pulled off at a suitable sunny, grassy spot, the air chilly but clear. Elfriede had packed them a picnic; Hannah had not missed the flash of scorn she'd directed at Willi as she'd stowed the basket in the trunk of the car.

Now Hannah spread a blanket and unpacked the generous offerings—cold sausage, fresh bread, and slices of *Holsteiner Tilsiter* cheese, spiced with caraway.

As she'd seen Georg do the night she'd had dinner at his house, she cut up Willi's food into small, bite-sized pieces and tucked a napkin into his shirt collar, giving him a briskly encouraging smile before she turned to her own food.

Klaus sat a little bit apart from them, one booted foot crossed over the other, as he ate a hunk of bread and cold sausage, his eyes narrowed in silent speculation. Hannah continued to do her best to avoid that thoughtful, knowing gaze; she had no interest in interacting with such a man.

Willi ate slowly, with such laborious effort, so much of the food falling from his mouth, his hand scrabbling about the plate, struggling to clutch at any morsel. Once, Hannah caught Klaus's eye and saw how sneering he looked, and she felt a sudden, surprising bolt of fury. He must have seen something of it in her face, for he lifted his chin, his gaze turning cool, appraising.

"Here, Willi," she encouraged, putting a piece of cheese into his hand and closing his twisted fingers around it. He looked up at her with a kind of abject apology, which made her feel worse. There was no reason for him to be sorry, she thought fiercely. There was nothing for him to be sorry for.

"*Danke*, Hannah," he said, and thankfully he managed to get the food to his mouth.

After lunch, as Hannah tidied up the food and Klaus tapped his foot impatiently, Willi suddenly lurched to his feet, hands fluttering in agitation as he squawked out some words she couldn't understand.

"Willi, Willi, what is it? How can I help?"

He shook his head, gesturing with his hands, trying to say something, but the words were too much for him, and as he gabbled and gesticulated, Hannah stared at him in incomprehension and dismay, until she saw the wetness spreading on the front of his flannel trousers.

"He's pissed himself," Klaus exclaimed scornfully, and Willi stared at her in mute misery, his cheeks now flushed with shame.

"Never mind," Hannah managed as briskly as she could, determined not to show any concern or condemnation. "It could happen to anyone. We have a spare pair of trousers in your case. There's no reason to be upset." She threw Klaus a fulminating look as she added, "Please fetch his case from the boot."

Klaus huffed a response as Hannah led Willi a little bit away, to a small copse of trees, leafless now. He stood there mutely, his head hung low, as she hesitated, unsure whether she needed to help him undress.

After a few seconds, Klaus came forward with the case and dumped it unceremoniously at their feet.

"Now, then," Hannah said, and reached over to unbutton his trousers.

"I... I can do it myself." Willi spoke slowly enough for her to understand, the words filled with both dignified pride and miserable shame.

Hannah felt a rush of sympathy, a twinge of guilt. She wished she knew how to handle this better, how much help to give.

"Very well," she said after a moment, taking the clean trousers and underpants out of the suitcase and putting them within his reach. "Let me know if you need any help."

She walked a little bit away, toward the car, to give him privacy; Klaus was standing by the hood, smoking as he gazed out at the bright blue sky, a few white shreds of cloud on the horizon.

"And to think there's two of us, healthy and able, having to care for *that*," he remarked, and Hannah stiffened.

It was, she knew, no more than what most people would think, even if they didn't say it aloud in such a disgusted way; it was what one saw on the newsreels at the cinema, with their railing against the "useless eaters" who might cost fifty thousand Reichsmarks of taxpayers' hard-earned money to care for in the course of their miserable lives. Hannah hadn't thought too much about any of it, hadn't wanted to—out of sight, out of mind, she supposed, and it was probably the same for most people, happy enough to have such people tidied away in their asylums.

But here was Willi, right in front of her, struggling to pull up his pants; he'd been absorbed in *White Fang* for over an hour in the car, chuckling softly at some parts, gasping at others. Willi, with his fingers to his lips, or clasped tenderly by his father; Willi, a child, a son, a *person*.

"And we're both paid handsomely for it," she told Klaus

shortly, and he grimaced as he flicked the butt of his cigarette into the long grass.

"I could be operating a Panzer right now," he told her. "Or marching through Paris."

"Oh, and you think he's responsible for the fact that you're not?" Hannah returned with a short, mocking laugh.

He glared at her as she turned away, and she reminded herself to check her temper. She didn't want to make enemies, especially not of a man like this one, who hummed the *Horst Wessel* song, with a Party pin on his lapel.

Thankfully, the rest of the journey was uneventful. They stopped at a hotel in Munich; the *frau* at the front desk stared rudely at Willi, but Hannah ignored her, along with Klaus, who'd muttered something about wasting money on idiots under his breath as he parked the car.

The next morning, they were off again as soon as they'd finished breakfast, and over the course of the day, the air grew clearer, the sky a deeper blue, the landscape of jagged, snow-capped mountains and plunging valleys, lakes shimmering like mirrors in the distance, more majestic.

"It's so beautiful," Willi said, and Hannah smiled and nodded.

"Yes, indeed it is. I've never seen such mountains before. They look like something from a picture book. Have you read *Heidi*, Willi? It has mountains like this one."

He shook his head, and she smiled.

"Perhaps I can find a copy for you to read, once we get to Am Steinhof."

In the rearview mirror, she saw Klaus scowl.

· · ·

It was late afternoon by the time they had made their way into Austria, and then to the western side of Vienna, where the Am Steinhof Hospital lay, in the district of Penzing. Once part of Lower Austria, the district had been annexed to Vienna after the Anschluss, a gracious, park-filled suburb of the regal city.

As they turned to go through the hospital's imposing front gates, Hannah noticed a cluster of raggedy-looking women huddling together at the tram stop opposite, wrinkles of weariness and suffering etched onto their deeply lined faces. One stepped into the street, craning her neck to try to peer into the back of car. Another one shook her fist at them and shouted something, words Hannah couldn't hear.

"What are those women doing there?" she asked Klaus, who gave an indifferent shrug as he turned the car into the hospital's sweeping drive.

"How should I know?"

He showed their papers to the guard at the gate, while Hannah took in the sight of the high stone wall that ran all the way around the sprawling hospital complex, pavilion after brick-fronted pavilion, all set in rolling parkland, with gardens and trees, fountains and flowers. The church, its copper dome ablaze under the afternoon sun, was up a hill at the far end, the hospital's imposing reception, marked Administration, at the front, with an impressive clock tower standing sentry in front of it. All of it was as stately and elegant as any palace, and it both surprised and reassured Hannah. She'd certainly never been in a hospital as lovely as this. Even Heim Hochland had not been as well appointed.

Then she glanced up, and saw there were iron grilles on the windows of all the pavilions. To be expected, of course, in a psychiatric hospital, yet the sight of them still unsettled her, gave the whole place a slightly sinister cast.

She glimpsed a few patients strolling in the parkland—a man with crutches, a woman with a blanket over her knees, a nurse in starched blue and white pushing her wheelchair, no doubt from the part of the hospital still used for adults. The sight was soothing in its familiarity, offering a comfort Hannah clung to. No matter the grilles on the windows, this was, surely, a hospital like any other, a place of both healing and refuge.

Her half-brother must have known what he was doing, bringing Willi here. Surely, she told herself, nothing bad could happen in a place as gracious and beautiful as this.

CHAPTER 5

As Klaus drove the car up to the front of Am Steinhof's administration pavilion, a doctor in a white coat stepped forward smartly, opening the passenger door as soon as they had come to a stop by the clock, almost as if he were a valet, albeit with a clipboard and a frown.

"Papers?"

Hannah fumbled for the papers Georg had given her. "I have a letter for Dr. Jekelius—"

"Who is the patient?"

"Willi Strasser." She paused and then added significantly, "The son of Major Georg Strasser of the Abwehr."

Something flickered in the doctor's eyes, but Hannah couldn't tell what it was. His face was alarmingly impassive; it was impossible to know what he was thinking.

Clambering out of the car, she drew herself up. "I am Nurse Hannah Stern. Major Strasser has arranged my employment here, in particular to care for his son."

The doctor flicked his fingers, a gesture of dismissal. "You will have to talk to the matron about that."

He turned to Willi, who was coming clumsily out of the car,

dragging one leg behind him. The doctor's eye narrowed in instant assessment, and Hannah felt a sudden surge of protectiveness that she tamped down. This was what Willi was here for, after all. To be assessed, to be treated, and then to be cured, or at least helped.

Still, she felt an uneasy sense of helplessness as the doctor squinted at Willi, his manner brusque, and then wrote something down on his clipboard.

"Come with me," he said, steering Willi toward a side door. He barely glanced at Hannah. "The matron's office is through the front doors."

"Major Strasser would like me to—" Hannah began, and the doctor gave her such a scathingly quelling look that she fell silent. Who was she, a nobody nurse, to question a doctor? To insist anything be ordered differently? She had no right, not even with her brother's letter in her hand. She knew that full well.

"The matron will see you inside," the doctor informed her shortly, and then he marched Willi, who was limping badly to keep up, toward the unmarked side door.

Willi threw Hannah a panicked, pleading glance and she took a step toward him before she hesitated, wanting to follow him, knowing she couldn't. She wasn't his nursemaid, she reminded herself painfully, no matter what Georg had intended. She could not follow him around the hospital, even if right now she wanted to. She'd make sure to visit him as soon as she could; Hannah knew that was the most she could offer, the best she could do.

"I'll come see you when you're settled," she called after him, and then, as Willi disappeared with the doctor, she hurried up the front steps.

Inside the administration pavilion, her shoes made a loud clicking sound on the tiled floor of black and white diamonds. Windows high above let in the afternoon's fading light, but the spacious hallway felt cold, the soaring space empty and echoing.

The head matron stepped out of an office, her small, square hands laced together at her waist. "Ah, Nurse Stern. We've been expecting you. I am Matron Klara Bertha." Her manner was brisk rather than friendly, her eyes bright as a bird's, a knowing note to her voice that caused Hannah a wave of nameless apprehension.

"*Guten Tag—*"

"*Heil Hitler.*" It sounded like a rebuke.

"*Heil Hitler,*" Hannah murmured, and followed the woman into an office as small and neat as she was, the requisite photograph of the austere-looking *Führer*, his eyes a vivid, piercing blue, hanging on the wall behind her desk.

"So, you have been sent by Major Strasser," the matron said, pursing her lips as she sat down behind her desk and reached for a file, flipping it open and scanning the typed contents. She kept the file angled away from Hannah's gaze as she took her seat in the hard wooden chair in front of the desk, folding her hands in her lap.

"He is concerned for his son."

"You are not a psychiatric nurse," the matron replied without looking up from the folder, "and you have no experience of working in an institution such as this one."

"I have over four years' experience working with children," Hannah answered evenly.

"At a *Lebensborn* home?" The matron gave her a steely smile, touched with cold amusement. "You will find we are nursing quite a different kind of child here, Nurse Stern. Quite, quite different."

"I am a quick learner." It was an odd position to be in, she reflected, defending her position when she didn't actually want to be here at all, or at least she hadn't, but now she realized she felt a surprisingly fierce loyalty both to Willi and his father. She could not turn her back on them now, not in this unfamiliar place, even though she had once wanted to.

"You will have to be so," Matron Bertha remarked coolly. "Let us hope you are correct."

Hannah cleared her throat. "I have a letter from Major Strasser for Dr. Jekelius."

The matron held out her hand. "I will see it is delivered."

She hesitated, both cowed and irritated by the matron's officious manner, and then said politely but firmly, "My instructions from Major Strasser were to deliver it to Dr. Jekelius myself. He wished me to speak with him personally. I was hoping I could do so as soon as possible."

The matron looked amused rather than annoyed by her high-handed request, which felt worse. "You will find the medical director is a very busy man, Nurse Stern. In addition to running the clinic here, he works for the Main Health Office in the city, and of course he liaises with Berlin. He is not able to be here all the time, and in any case, he can hardly speak personally with every nurse who is hired, or who has an interest in a patient who happens to be a relative. We have hundreds of patients here, Nurse Stern, and dozens of staff."

"Willi is not—" Hannah began, only to stop suddenly as she realized afresh that, of course, Willi was a relative, her nephew, bound to her by blood. *Her family.* She had not considered the matter quite like that before; her relationship with Georg had been so unlike true family. Even though she called him her half-brother, she had never truly thought of him as such. She glanced down at her hands to avoid seeing the matron's smug stare, as if she'd just proved something to her. "Major Strasser will be very appreciative, I know, to hear that I have been able to speak to the medical director," she stated quietly. "He asked me to write to him as soon as I had done so, informing him of Willi's treatment, how he has settled here."

The matron was silent for a moment and Hannah glanced

up to see her gazing at her with a shrewd sort of indifference, her bright bird's eyes narrowed, her head cocked to one side. It made Hannah feel as if she were nothing more than an inconvenience to this woman, someone to be dealt with and dismissed, a complete irrelevance to the work that went on here, to anything at all.

Her relationship with Georg, the weighty way she'd thrown around the words *Major Strasser*, had absolutely no effect on this woman, or the doctor out front, or perhaps anyone at all in this entire hospital. She was, Hannah realized with an icy hollowing out of her stomach, a very long way away from Berlin. Had Georg had any idea of that, how unimportant she would be, or even *he* would be? What power did a major in the Abwehr have here, in these halls of psychiatric medicine, where decisions were made every day that had nothing to do with her —or her half-brother?

"When will I be able to see Dr. Jekelius?" she asked, her voice rising in a way that she knew would not help her cause. Still, better to seem assured rather than afraid.

The matron's mouth thinned. "You will find, Nurse Stern, that we do things as we see fit here at Am Spiegelgrund. Major Strasser is not a medical professional, and he has no idea of what constitutes proper care for a child like his son. Now." She closed the file and placed both hands flat on the table. "You will be serving in pavilion three, the hospital unit."

"Is that the pavilion where Willi will—"

"That is not your concern—"

"Major Strasser expected me to be nursing Willi," Hannah cut across her, and saw a flash of ire spark in the matron's eyes. "Indeed, that is why I came."

"I will have one of the nurses show you to your room," the matron replied, effectively ignoring everything she'd just said. "You will report for duty at seven o'clock sharp tomorrow morning." The matron inclined her head. "Good day to you, Nurse Stern. *Heil Hitler.*"

Hannah stared at her for a moment, feeling deeply uneasy about the whole, terse exchange, before she forced herself to nod and then stand. "*Heil Hitler*," she replied quietly.

Outside the matron's office, a young nurse was waiting to show her to her room; the matron introduced her as Nurse Franck. She looked to be only twenty or so, with a plump, pink-cheeked face and limp, curling blond hair, a slightly vapid look about her round, blue eyes.

"My name is Ida," she told Hannah shyly as they left the administration building.

Shielding her eyes from the slanting rays of the late-afternoon sun, Hannah glanced around the hospital complex, brick pavilions, their long, narrow windows all barred, stretching in every direction, amidst neat gravel paths. Where was Willi, in all this? In the distance, she saw a groundsman trundling a wheelbarrow, a white-coated doctor walking smartly toward a distant pavilion.

"You must call me Hannah," she told Ida, and with a small, childlike smile in reply, Ida turned left down the path, leaving Hannah to follow.

The afternoon was clear and cold, and as they walked along Hannah could almost imagine she was in a park or a pleasant neighborhood, taking the air.

Then she glanced up and saw a white, moon-like face appear like a ghost in a window in one of the pavilions, lips and nose pressed against the glass, turning the face into some sort of monstrous mask. She let out a little gasp and faltered in her step. Ida glanced at her in questioning curiosity, and Hannah gave an apologetic smile. She felt an urge to shiver that had nothing to do with the chilly autumn air. She glanced up again, but the strange moon-face was gone.

"The theatre and the kitchen are in the middle," Ida told

her, pointing to the wide avenue behind them that effectively bisected the complex into two. "And Am Steinhof, for the adults, is on the other side. All the pavilions on this side are part of Am Spiegelgrund, the children's clinic, save for the further ones that are part of the pulmonary clinic. You won't ever go there. We stay quite separate."

Hannah glimpsed a narrow railroad, almost like a fairground ride, trundling between the pavilions.

"For laundry and meals and such things," Ida explained, as she followed her gaze. "Here is pavilion three. There are four of us nursing here: two on each day shift and one at night. We manage all right." She stopped in front of the pavilion next to the one they'd just left, taking a set of keys from the pocket of her apron to unlock the front door.

Hannah glanced up at the tall, narrow windows, their panes glinting emptily in the sunlight. She didn't know exactly why she felt a strange sort of fear skittering along her skin, settling into her bones. Was it the doctor who had been waiting so officiously for them as soon as the car had driven up, barely meeting her gaze as he'd assessed Willi? Matron Bertha's smugly knowing manner, her indifference to Hannah and the mention of Georg? Or that anonymous face pressed up against the window, almost as if someone was watching her, warning her, even?

It was everything, she supposed, and nothing. She had never worked in a psychiatric hospital before, a place where they locked doors and barred windows, where patients had to be restrained, medicated, managed. Perhaps her unease was natural. She needn't get into a palaver over it. Working here would take some getting used to, that was all. She would find Willi, and all would be well.

"How long have you been at Am Spiegelgrund?" she asked Ida as the nurse opened the door and stepped into the hallway.

A smell of carbolic overlaid the rank yet sweetish smell of illness and disease.

"I'd been working with the adults at Am Steinhof for a year, and then I applied to be transferred to Am Spiegelgrund when they turned this part of the hospital into the children's clinic," Ida told her.

"Oh? Why did you wish to transfer?"

Ida gave her a wary look. "Well, they'd emptied it, hadn't they?"

"Emptied it?" Hannah repeated. "What do you mean?"

"The patients who were here before." Ida moved past her, a little more quickly. "Besides, children are so sweet, aren't they?"

"Yes, they are," Hannah agreed, although she felt as if there was more Ida wasn't saying.

"Our rooms are on the top floor," Ida told her, her voice instinctively dropping to a hush as they began to climb the open staircase in the center of the hall, wards of about a dozen beds each on either side.

Behind a set of glass-paned doors, Hannah glimpsed white metal bedsteads, the patients in each of them little more than unmoving lumps under the sheets. A single nurse, brown-haired and sharp-eyed, stood at the end of a bed, ticking something off on a chart. As they walked past, her dark gaze moved over them silently, without expression, and then dropped again. It was all eerily quiet.

"They're sleeping," Ida told Hannah, as if in answer to a question. "Many of them are recovering from surgeries or injuries... they're sedated, for their own good."

"I see," Hannah murmured. She had never been in a ward that was so quiet, so devoid of the usual life—patients asking for a glass of water or more medicine, or simply exchanging gossipy chatter with one of the nurses. Everyone here was silent, still.

They went up another set of stairs to the top floor of the building, underneath the sloping eaves. "There are three of us staying up here," Ida told her. "You, me and *Schwester* Margarethe. Nurse Bauer," she amended. "She used to be a nun."

"Used to be?"

"I'm not sure... I think she left the order." Ida shrugged. "I don't ask."

Ida unlocked the door to her room and then stepped aside so Hannah could enter first. As she gazed round the small space, she couldn't keep from letting out a huff of laughter, for it was all exactly as she'd imagined—the narrow bed, the lumpy mattress, the picture of a frowning, imperious Hitler hung on the wall, even the rug.

She turned to Ida, laughter bubbling on her lips, about to say how lucky she was for the braided rug on the floor—*makes for a bit of a change, hey*—only to stop suddenly as she realized, of course, the other woman wouldn't get the joke. No one would.

"Thank you, Ida," she said instead. "This looks very comfortable."

"It's not so bad. Hot in summer, cold in winter, but that's everywhere, isn't it?" Ida gave her one of her sweet smiles. "One of the porters will bring your suitcase, I think. Supper is in the staff room, downstairs. They bring the food from the main kitchen, so we don't have to cook for ourselves."

"Lovely," Hannah murmured, and ducking her head, Ida left her room.

Hannah let her breath out in a long, slow sigh as she looked around the small, bare room and then went to the one little window, to inspect the view. From her slightly crouched vantage point, she could see the parkland, the pavilions, the dome of the church in the distance, its greenish copper glinting under the fading afternoon light, surrounded by four pillars.

All of it looked perfectly pastoral, and yet it created in her an unexpected ache of longing, a homesickness for something she'd never had, a place she'd yet to discover, or perhaps a person she'd never known. Could you miss something you'd never had? Someone you'd never met?

Hannah never had let herself before, yet now, for a few seconds, the sense of loneliness she so often struggled against soaked right through her. Then her sigh trailed off in the stillness as dusk settled over the park, and slowly she straightened, squaring her shoulders as she turned away from the window.

CHAPTER 6

AM SPIEGELGRUND, NOVEMBER 1940

The next morning, Hannah reported to duty at seven o'clock, to a ward as quiet as she'd glimpsed the previous afternoon. She wore her new uniform of a plain blue dress, white apron, and cork-heeled shoes, her hair kept back with a kerchief. She'd eaten in the staff room last night with Ida; Margarethe, the other nurse who lived above the ward and had once been a nun, had been on duty.

Hannah hadn't asked any questions, and Ida hadn't made any conversation; already she had the sense that the children's clinic of Am Spiegelgrund was not like the other hospitals she'd known. There was a wary furtiveness to the place, in the way people hurried about their business, heads tucked low, not meeting anyone else's eyes, a sense of suspicion hanging in the air like a suffocating, invisible cloud. Or was she, in her unease, imagining it all, or at least some of it? Hannah couldn't be sure, but she wished she at least knew where Willi was. She was hoping to visit him after her shift.

"Ah, our new recruit," the pavilion's senior nurse, Helga Gruber, announced as she came into one of the two wards on the first floor, the staircase yawning in the middle. "All the way from Berlin." She gave her an appraising look, and Hannah bobbed her head in reply.

Helga was a large, cheerful woman with cheeks like apples and a glinting smile, her dark hair scraped back into a tight knob at the back of her head. She reminded Hannah a bit of Hilde, except cleaner and better fed, a shrewder look in her eyes, despite her jolly manner.

"What, cat got your tongue?" Helga exclaimed, with a booming laugh. "You'll soon get used to our ways here, Nurse Stern. It is Stern, isn't it? It's a quiet life we live here, isn't it, Nurse Franck? A very quiet life."

Ida, who was working the same shift, along with the nurse Hannah had seen last night, Nurse Schmidt, who had shifty eyes and a sour mouth, nodded quickly. "Yes, Nurse Gruber."

"Show Nurse Stern around," Helga instructed Ida. "I'm sure she'll get the hang of it all soon enough. She looks like a quick learner to me. Knows when to keep her mouth shut, eh?"

There seemed to be a warning in those words, and Hannah took it. "*Danke*, Nurse Gruber," she murmured, eyes suitably downcast.

"Yes, you'll see what it's like," Helga proclaimed with another loud laugh, and Hannah could not tell if her words were meant to be a promise or another warning.

She remained standing next to Ida as Helga moved off to greet a doctor who was coming through the door, white-coated and serious, and Nurse Schmidt gave them both a sour, suspicious look before tending to a patient who had begun to stir.

"I'll show you around," Ida told her, "although I don't know how much there is to see, really, besides the wards and the staff room, the supply cupboards and the sluice room."

One hospital ward, Hannah soon realized, was much like another, and her duties in pavilion three were not all that different than they'd been at the Charité, or even Heim Hochland. It was, she learned, the pavilion where patients from all the others came when they needed medical treatment for scrapes and burns, infections or fevers, or they were recovering from surgery, and in that sense, Hannah was able to perform many of the same functions she would have anywhere else, although without the small, simple pleasures of playing with children, giving them cuddles, making sure they were neatly presented, the way she had at the maternity home.

She spent the morning changing bandages, checking temperatures, and making the relevant notes on charts—finding a certain comfort in the familiarity of the mundane tasks she knew so well. Even the less pleasant tasks—rinsing out bedpans or washing dirty bandages—did not seem so onerous, for she was well used to both, and she was simply grateful that she knew what to do, that it was neither as difficult nor strange as she'd feared.

She laughed a little at herself, wondering what she was expecting, a tent full of circus freaks carousing about? The thought was both absurd and shaming. Really, these children were not all that different from the beloved, blond babies of Heim Hochland, and in any case, most of them were asleep or drugged with sedatives, due to their injuries or conditions, or perhaps both, so she barely interacted with them at all.

There was a boy of thirteen or so who had come in to recover from some sort of stomach surgery; a young girl with wispy blond hair and wide, staring eyes who had developed an infection; and a tiny slip of a girl, little more than a toddler, whose lungs rattled with pneumonia, and who had a tumor growing out of her shoulder, a great lump of a thing, to be sure. But Hannah had seen similar at the Charité, and when she'd taken the girl's temperature, she'd given her such a soft, sad smile that Hannah's heart had twisted painfully. To Hannah's eye, she and the others all looked, more or less, like any other children. When she scanned their charts, she did not see any mention of the types of diseases the clinic was meant to treat—spastic diplegia, epilepsy, idiocy.

"Why are they here?" she asked Ida when they were alone in the staff room, sipping ersatz coffee during one of their breaks.

Ida looked startled, guarded. "What do you mean? They're recovering—"

"No, I mean why are they are here at all?" Hannah cut across her, instinctively lowering her voice. "In this clinic. I was told it specialized in neurological ailments. My nephew..." She paused and started again. "What I mean is, what's... what's wrong with them?" She nodded toward the ward of children. "Most of them don't look..." She hesitated, not sure what word to use. She thought of Willi, and then she said, a bit hesitantly, "They don't look that different."

"That girl with the gargoyle perching on her shoulder certainly looks different," Ida replied with a little laugh.

Hannah thought of the girl's soft brown eyes, reminding her of old velvet, blinking up at her so slowly, and said nothing.

Ida subsided a bit guiltily. "Well, they're not all like *that* here, you know," she said. "Some are, of course, and naturally they're sedated in this ward, so you wouldn't notice their... their tendencies. But besides the clinic, there's a reformatory school on the site, for orphans and asocials and the like."

Asocials, the term for any child who was difficult, disobedient, or possessed the smallest drop of tainted blood. Hannah hadn't realized the clinic catered to that type, as well as children like Willi. Anyone, it seemed, who did not fit the Reich's idea of normality. Perfection.

"I see," she said after a moment.

"Yes, we get all sorts here, Nurse Stern," Helga said as she bustled into the staff room, making Ida jump and Hannah stiffen, wondering how much the ward sister had overheard—and if it mattered. "The idiots and imbeciles too, poor creatures.

There is no hope for them at all, absolutely none." She spoke without sympathy, her tone completely matter-of-fact. "The kindest thing we can do, of course, is to ease their suffering." She gave Hannah an expectant look, seeming to want a response.

"Yes, I suppose," Hannah replied after a moment.

"There is no 'supposing' about it, I'm afraid," Helga replied briskly. She turned to Nurse Schmidt, whom Hannah had yet to speak to, and who had crept into the room behind the ward nurse. She seemed the kind of person who was always skulking about, silent and listening, taking notes. "Isn't that right, Nurse Schmidt?" Helga finished with a pointed look for the shifty-eyed nurse.

She nodded, her mouth pursing up like a prune. "Yes indeed, Nurse Gruber."

Helga nodded, satisfied, like a schoolteacher who had been given the right answer by a star pupil. "They are completely beyond cure," she stated firmly. "This is the last place for them to find treatment. The end station, as it were." And she let out another one of her booming laughs, so this time Hannah jumped along with Ida, while Nurse Schmidt sidled back out of the room.

Was this Willi's last hope? Hannah wondered as she returned to the ward. Was that why Georg had been willing to send him so far away, for the treatments he'd mentioned? She had yet to discover what pavilion he was in, and she felt the failure of her duty with a surprising keenness. A few days ago, she had not wanted even to think of Willi; now she was acutely conscious of the fact that he was her nephew. Her family. She felt a responsibility to him, as well as an affection for him she hadn't expected. She did not want to fail him, or her half-brother, although she did not even know how to go about finding him in this place.

. . .

By the end of her shift, Hannah ached with tiredness; she'd forgotten how wearying it was, to always be on her feet, moving about the ward, hefting trays or bending down to make beds or remove bedpans. Life at Heim Hochland had been far easier, like living in a country house rather than on a hospital ward.

She'd tried to find out where Willi was, but Nurse Gruber had merely clucked her tongue and told her to see to her work, and no one else knew. As it was already dark, Hannah told herself she could leave it for another day.

As it was, when she sat down with Ida for supper in the staff room, she barely possessed the energy to spoon her soup to her mouth. And tomorrow she could look forward to doing the same thing all over again, and again the day after that, all her days marching toward an unseen horizon.

But after the war, things may be different. It felt like a faint hope, but she clung to it all the same.

"Ah, our new nurse!" A woman popped into the staff room, wearing the same blue dress and white apron as the other nurses, yet somehow she seemed more vibrant in it. The apron was cinched about her slender waist, and underneath her kerchief, her hair gleamed a deep, shining brown, the same color as her eyes that snapped with life and humor as she gazed at Hannah, a small smile playing about her wide, mobile mouth. "How are you finding it all? I'm Margarethe. Nurse Bauer, that is!" And she gave a jaunty, mocking salute that Hannah never would have dared.

Instinctively, she glanced around, looking for Helga, with her easy smile and shrewd eyes, or Nurse Schmidt, with her darting gaze and sly manner.

"Oh, don't worry," Margarethe said, "it's just the three of us here. Prune-faced Nurse Schmidt is on duty and the others have gone home. It's very quiet here at night, you'll find." She slipped into the chair next to Hannah's. "What do we have here?" she asked cheerfully as she reached for a bowl. "Potato soup? A hearty broth laced with cream and delicately seasoned with garlic and bay leaf?" She gave an appreciative sniff. "How delicious! We are spoiled here, are we not? Really, it's quite outrageous. What a life we lead, Nurse Stern! How fortunate we are, truly."

Hannah glanced down at the unappetizing bowl of tepid, watery broth with bits of potato and carrot floating in it and found herself smiling.

"Margarethe talks such nonsense sometimes," Ida said, as if it needed explaining.

"All the time, Nurse Franck!" Margarethe admonished severely. "*All* the time, thank you very much."

Hannah choked back a laugh, and Margarethe gave her a knowing, smiling glance. "If you can't laugh about it all, you'll go insane," she said, dropping her voice to a conspiratorial whisper. "And there's enough of that here already, isn't there? More's the pity." She popped a chunk of potato in her mouth. "Ah, delicious. Don't you agree, Nurse Stern?"

"A meal fit for a king," Hannah replied with a small smile. "Or in fact, a queen."

Margarethe gave a shout of appreciative laughter, and Hannah's smile deepened. Perhaps she would find a kindred spirit here, after all.

Later, when they were going up to bed, Margarethe wandered into Hannah's room, leaning against the doorframe as she eyed her speculatively, while Hannah stilled, her fingers at the sash of her apron.

"So is the gossip true?" Margarethe asked, her head cocked to one side. Being under her scrutiny, Hannah thought, felt both alarming and wonderful, like standing in a sunbeam. You basked in the glow, but eventually you'd seek to escape the glare. She had an instinctive liking for the other woman, but also a cautious wariness. "You came all the way from Berlin?"

"Yes, with my half-brother's son, who is a patient here. My brother wanted someone to look out for him."

"Did he now?" Margarethe replied softly, and Hannah tensed.

"Do you know something?" she asked.

"Do I know something?" Margarethe raised her eyebrows, spreading her slender arms wide. "What could I possibly know, Nurse Stern?" The question had the tone of a dare, laced with laughter, a hint of deeper darkness underneath.

"Willi has come here for specialized treatment," she stated slowly, not realizing until she said the words that they had the lilt of a question. "His father is in the Abwehr."

Margarethe let her arms fall as she shrugged, smiling. "And? So?"

Hannah continued to stare at her, unsure what she was really trying to say by mentioning Georg—or what Margarethe was, by her seemingly indifferent reply. There was, she realized, so much that she didn't know about this place—and she did not know how to go about learning it, or who to trust for the answers to her barely formed questions. "How long have you been working here?" she asked instead.

"Since the children's clinic opened, back in July."

"Ida—Nurse Franck said you were once a nun."

"They do like to gossip here, don't they?" Margarethe returned with a laugh. "No, I was not a nun, but a novice—I chose not to take my final vows."

"Why not?" Hannah asked, curious, although, in truth, Margarethe seemed as unlikely a nun as she could imagine—far too young and pretty and vibrant, with a seemingly irreverent sense of humor, a mocking gleam in her eyes. Hannah could not picture her with the white wimple, the pious, downcast gaze, the whiff of sanctimony as she recited her prayers.

"All these questions, Nurse Stern!" Playfully, Margarethe wagged her finger at her. "Don't you know you're not supposed to ask questions here?"

"Or anywhere," Hannah quipped before she could think better of it.

The other nurse's amused glance fell away as she gazed at her thoughtfully, and then a slow, knowing smile curved her generous mouth. "Yes, indeed," she replied, and she sounded strangely satisfied. "Or anywhere."

CHAPTER 7

A week passed of dreary sameness, with gunmetal-gray skies and fourteen-hour shifts as the weather grew bleaker and colder —Vienna's winters, Hannah learned from Nurse Schmidt, like Berlin's, were known to be cold and windy, and already in November, ice edged the windowpanes and frost rimed the hard ground of the parkland, the grass winter-brown underneath the fog-shrouded sky.

Hannah worked six and a half days straight, and then spent Sunday afternoon wandering through the hospital grounds, wrapped up warmly, determined to find some sign of Willi, having been reprimanded even for asking by Nurse Gruber several times. To both her frustration and her alarm, she was able to discover nothing; the staff whom she saw only shook their heads, tight-lipped and wary, when she asked about Willi, and when she went in search of Matron Bertha, determined to finally get an answer, she found the woman was doing rounds somewhere else, her office empty.

As she left the administration pavilion, she saw a row of orphans being led out of one of the further pavilions, raggedly dressed in green striped jackets and short pants, gaunt-faced and hollow-eyed as they marched toward the hospital's entrance.

"Where are they going?" she asked an attendant who was accompanying them, a big, beefy woman with arms like stone slabs, and a red, work-coarsened face.

She gave her an unfriendly look, not breaking her stride as she walked toward the gate. "They're getting their fresh air, *Schwester*," she replied, not even turning her head to call over her shoulder as they marched past. "Don't you know the benefits of fresh air? A daily walk of the walls, that is what these ragamuffins need."

Hannah watched them go, marching alongside the high, stone walls, two rows of twelve, all completely silent, shaved heads lowered against the chilly November wind, save for one tall boy, who glanced back and grinned cheekily at her, his face dimpling. Somehow that display of spirit heartened her almost unbearably, and she lifted her hand in what she hoped was a jaunty wave before setting off into Penzing in search of a chemist's to buy some hand lotion; already the harsh hospital soap had left hers red and cracked.

As she stepped through the hospital gates, she glimpsed a group of bedraggled women, like the ones she'd seen before, by the tram stop across the street. When they caught sight of her, they surged forward, almost as one.

"*Schwester, schwester!*" one woman called. "Tell me, do you know a boy named Friedrich Schumann? He is six years old, he was admitted two months ago, I haven't seen him at all—"

Another woman hurried across the street, dodging the icy puddles. She was wearing a pair of old work boots with cardboard peeking through the gaps in the soles. "My daughter," she said breathlessly, and Hannah breathed in the sour smell of cigarettes and schnapps. "Sophie Beitel. She is only two. I have written the director to ask for her back—she would do better at home, I am sure of it—" The woman grabbed the sleeve of her coat and Hannah only just kept herself from drawing away.

"I'm sorry," she said; in her discomfort, her tone came out terser than she'd meant it to. "*Entschuldige bitte.* I cannot help you."

She hurried down the street, pulling her coat about her, as the women watched her go. She heard one of them spit, another mutter under her breath, and she walked faster.

The unease that had been skirting her mind solidified into something heavy and hard, like a stone in her stomach. She could not answer those women's questions. She did not think she wanted to discover the answers, because what could she do about any of it? She already had Willi to worry about, and she had yet to find out where he was. Besides, everyone knew nurses did not dare to question their betters. They did not demand to see doctors. They did not involve themselves with patients beyond their immediate, necessary care, and they certainly didn't involve themselves with the parents of patients, especially ones who wore cardboard in their boots and smelled of schnapps. Good nurses kept their heads down and went about their business, and that was all.

And that, Hannah thought, reminding herself of Hilde's advice, was what she would do, as long as she remained at Am Spiegelgrund.

On the way back to the hospital, with her bottle of lotion wrapped in brown paper, Hannah crossed the street, keeping her head averted as she passed the women still huddled there, even though they had to know they would never get any answers, not from outside the gates, anyway.

As she passed the guard's gate, showing him her papers, she asked suddenly, against her better judgement, "Those women across the street? Why are they there? What do they want?"

The guard gave her a bland look as he returned her papers. "Their idiot children back, I'd say at a guess."

She stared at him for a moment, opened her mouth, closed it, and then walked on.

All around her, the hospital was a quiet hive of industry; she passed a groundsman pushing a wheelbarrow; the tiny tram line, like a toy train, trundled laundry and food and other supplies between the pavilions. Smoke bellowed up from the kitchen's chimneys, and she heard the sound of hammering coming from one of the workshops to the right of the central path that led up to the *kirche* on the hill. People were going about their business, but where was Willi?

Dispirited, Hannah headed back toward pavilion three, only to falter as a nurse walked smartly toward her, her caped coat billowing out behind her. It took her a few seconds to realize it was Matron Bertha, whom she had not seen since her first day a week ago.

"Ah, Nurse Stern," she called briskly. "I was just coming to find you. Dr. Jekelius has returned, and he wishes for you to call on him."

Hope and alarm both bloomed within her, equal in measure. *Finally—and yet.*

Hannah nodded as she put her parcel of lotion in the pocket of her coat. "*Danke*, Matron."

"You can come with me now." There was a steely note to the matron's voice that had Hannah tensing.

"I must fetch Major Strasser's letter first—"

"Very well." The matron's lips thinned. "I will wait."

"*Danke*, Matron," Hannah said again, and hurried toward the pavilion to retrieve the letter.

A few minutes later, back in the echoing administration pavilion, Matron Bertha led her to a wood-paneled door, knocked once, and at the commanded '*Komm*', she swung open the door, bid Hannah enter, and then walked quickly away.

Taking a deep breath, Hannah entered the study. The man who looked up from behind a large, mahogany desk was, at first glance, as elegant as a film star, with a sweep of thick, dark hair brushed back from a high forehead with a prominent widow's peak. His heavy, hooded eyebrows and lean, saturnine features were lightened by a ready smile, a deftness of movement as he straightened, one hand flung out in welcome.

"Ah, Nurse Stern. I am delighted to make your acquaintance. I apologize for the delay in meeting you."

Hannah swallowed dryly. She had not expected the medical director to be so handsome, to look at her with such interest. It was most disconcerting. "You are a busy man, *Herr Doktor*."

Dr. Jekelius made a little moue of acknowledgement. "There are so many demands on one's time, are there not? So many desperate children in need of care."

"So there are, *Herr Doktor*." Hannah took the letter from the pocket of her coat, willing her fingers not to tremble. Already, she felt overawed by this man, by the ease of his manner, the inherent confidence of his seemingly relaxed pose. His office was as well appointed as her brother Georg's study—a rich Turkish rug on the floor, heavy drapes at the window, framed diplomas on the walls. "Perhaps Matron Bertha mentioned that I had a letter for you, from my brother, Major Strasser of the Abwehr?"

A small smile played about the doctor's mobile mouth as his gaze moved over her. "I believe she did."

Trying not to betray her nerves, Hannah held it out. "Major Strasser wished me to deliver it to you personally."

"Did he?" Dr. Jekelius took the letter without any seeming interest. "Please, Nurse Stern, sit down." He gestured to one of the comfortable chairs in front of the desk.

Uncertainly, Hannah perched on the edge of one, her hands clasped in her lap, while Dr. Jekelius sat down in his own chair, searching among his papers for a silver letter knife, and then slit the envelope of Georg's letter, all with the attitude of someone opening a bill, or perhaps a leaflet advertising the latest charitable collection.

He had crossed one leg elegantly over the other, and he tossed the letter knife back on the blotter with a carelessness that somehow seemed affected.

"Tell me, how are you finding your time here?" he asked as he unfolded the letter.

"I... am learning," Hannah replied after a moment.

Jekelius gave her that small smile again, murmured "Very good" and then turned his attention to the letter, while Hannah waited, her hands still tightly clasped, wondering what would happen next. Outside, the evening was already drawing in, the sky the color of slate. Underneath a leafless tree, one of the groundsmen, in his shapeless gray trousers and coat, was pushing one of the covered carts Hannah had seen about the hospital—painted dark green, with a round, close-fitting lid so it was impossible to see what was inside.

She turned back to Dr. Jekelius, who was slowly stroking his chin with his forefinger as he finished reading Georg's letter.

Finally, after what felt like several endless minutes, he laid it down on the desk. "Major Strasser is your brother?" he asked, in a tone of polite interest.

"Yes." She was not about to go into the delicate complexities of just how she was related to Georg—his father's affair with the charwoman who had taken his passing fancy.

"His son..." He glanced again at the letter. "Wilhelm. Willi, he calls him. Are you well acquainted with the boy?"

Hannah swallowed, unable to look away from Jekelius's penetrating gaze. He looked at her as if he already knew, as if he had a file in his head of everything she'd ever done, never mind Willi or Georg. "Not very well, no," she said, and then, inexplicably, wished she hadn't.

"Major Strasser speaks very fondly of him. He says the boy is quite clever."

Hannah thought of him reading *Wolfsblut*, his finger pressed slyly to his lips, eyes dancing. "He is."

Jekelius cocked his head to one side, the look in his eyes turning almost gentle, his features softening in a way that gave Hannah a sudden, strange yearning to like him. To trust him, to believe in his kindness, that he cared not just about Willi and the children at this clinic, but even her. A ridiculous notion, and yet one she foolishly could not keep herself from feeling. "The boy has spastic diplegia."

"Yes, but it..." She licked her lips nervously. "I don't think it has affected his brain. His intelligence, I mean."

Jekelius raised his eyebrows in an eloquent gesture of silent skepticism; Hannah blushed, knowing how ill-equipped she was to offer a medical diagnosis, a professional opinion, and to someone with the esteemed credentials this doctor had. He should be lambasting her for daring to do so, and yet he remained silent, smiling slightly, almost as if to encourage her opinion, as if he understood why she needed to offer it.

Even so, Hannah struggled to think of what to say; her mind felt both racing and blank. She couldn't tell him that Willi had read *White Fang*, a banned book, or how he'd known to keep it secret from the Nazi driver; she couldn't explain that she'd seen humor in his eyes, or a touching dignity in his limping walk. She felt as if she were strangling in her silence, longing to blurt something out, and yet no words would come. She just shook her head helplessly, blushing, ashamed by her own ignorance and, worse, her cowardice.

Jekelius let out a little sigh, almost as if he were pained, and then he steepled his fingers together as he gave a sorrowful shake of his head. "What I so often encounter in my line of work, Nurse Stern, is the tragic and terrible delusion of the parents of the children I am called to treat. It is understandable, of course, and so very sad. Truly tragic." He paused, as if waiting for her to respond, and Hannah managed to force out through dry lips,

"Delusion, *Herr Doktor*?"

"Yes, indeed, I am afraid that is exactly the word for it, and admittedly it is one that is more commonly used with schizophrenics and suicidals, the criminally insane, and the like." He made a little grimace of apology. "I appreciate that in your previous nursing experience, these are not the types of truly unfortunate individuals with which you have come into contact. You were formerly a maternity nurse, were you not? At a *Lebensborn* home? Quite a different environment there, of course. Completely the opposite, in fact."

Was she imagining the kindly yet disparaging note in his voice? The smile he gave her was almost whimsical, full of that gentle understanding that Hannah was afraid to trust—and yet she wanted to, more than she liked to admit, even in the disquiet of her own mind. She wanted to believe he could be kind, was genuine.

"I was," she confirmed, and then fell silent again.

"You have only been here a short time, Nurse Stern, but perhaps you have already seen some of the kinds of lamentable unfortunates we are dealing with. Children utterly without any hope, any hope at all, of treatment or cure." He shook his head, a slow, mournful back and forth.

He sounded so much like Nurse Helga that Hannah wondered if the nurse had parroted him on purpose. Were they taught to say such things? And yet it had to be true, or at least *mostly* true. Many of the children in this place were, for one reason or another, in a lamentable state.

"I must admit, *Herr Doktor*," she finally said, "I do not believe I have seen many such children in pavilion three." She thought of the little girl with the tumor on her shoulder, but surely it could be removed? Even if it couldn't, Hannah had doubts as to whether the condition would affect her brain, her intelligence. She was not necessarily beyond hope the way the doctor seemed to suggest.

"Of course you are more sheltered there," Jekelius agreed readily enough. "The children who come to pavilion three are being treated for the more usual ailments, infections and fevers and the like, and in any case, many of them are from the reformatory school... We have taken in *those* poor children, Nurse Stern, to educate and reform them for society. A thankless task, you will appreciate, for many of the children are very nearly beyond educability, and are disobedient, defiant, and sly, as well. Yet it is such an important endeavor, for the good of the Reich." He took a breath before resuming, "But the unfortunates in the children's clinic, those with definitive, incurable neurological conditions..." He paused again, with dramatic deliberation, a frown marring his handsome features as his gaze turned distant. "Hopeless cases, truly hopeless, and yet the parents don't see it at all. They can't, of course. It takes a professional to offer an objective opinion, to speak into such a miserable situation, and offer the truth—a terrible panacea, as it were, but so very necessary."

"Willi Strasser is not..." Hannah paused to summon her courage. "He is not without such hope, *Herr Doktor*. As I said, he is quite lively. Quite intelligent."

Dr. Jekelius stared at her for a long moment, his handsome, mobile face turning still and expressionless, as if the very life had drained out of it. Without the lightness of expression, the brightness flaring in those dark eyes, his face looked slack and dull; Hannah could see a nick on his jaw where he must have cut himself shaving.

Straightening, she met his gaze as evenly as she could, trying to school her features into an expression of both placidity and determination. She offered a faint, inquiring smile, although inwardly she trembled. She did not know what to make of this man; she still had an inexplicable desire to trust him, even to like him, and have him like her in return, and yet she could not deny that sitting in his office, watching him watch her, she felt, suddenly and certainly, afraid.

"Take this case," he said finally, springing to alertness, the vividity flooding back to his face as he reached for a file on his desk. "Ilse Wagner." He flipped open the file and scanned the typewritten pages inside. "Born 1930, weighing a healthy thirty-two hundred grams. In all appearance, a normal, happy child."

He gave another one of his deliberate, dramatic pauses, and Hannah shifted in her chair, wincing at the loud creaking sound of the wood.

As if somehow satisfied by her response, Dr. Jekelius continued, "The sixth of ten children, born into an impoverished family. In 1934, the father was arrested and detained for antisocial behavior. The mother was hospitalized for pericarditis and rheumatism. The financial circumstances of the family became increasingly dire."

Another pause, just as significant.

"By the time Ilse was eighteen months old, it had become apparent she exhibited both mental and physical difficulties. She could neither sit up nor stand, never mind speak or walk. She would never be a productive member of society, and she would always need debilitatingly extensive care."

Another pause, his gaze sorrowful and steady on hers.

"The father, in desperation, sent her to a day nursery, where she was, quite rightly, diagnosed with *schwachswinn*—feeble-mindedness. As her parents could not care for her appropriately, she was transferred to the Alsterdorf Asylum, near Hamburg, where she remains today, with no hope of a useful life, incapable of work, of pleasure, of any kind of enjoyment. She has been recommended to come here, to Am Speigelgrund. Her family have had no choice but to surrender her to the state.

The state has no choice but to care for her." He stopped abruptly, and Hannah felt as if a silent question hovered in the air, expecting an answer, but she did not know what either were meant to be.

"A tragic situation, to be sure, *Herr Doktor*, just as you have said," she murmured after a moment.

"You see?" he demanded, almost jubilantly, as if she had just proved whatever point he was making. "You see? These parents are consumed by guilt. They have not been able to care for their child. They invent stories, complete fabrications, without even realizing they are doing so, as if these delusions can somehow assuage their guilt, their sense of responsibility for the miserable child they have brought into the world who has no hope whatsoever of one day becoming a productive member of society."

The miserable child. But Willi was not miserable. She wondered how many of the children in this institution would be so miserable, if they had families to love and care for them in their own homes, instead of being sent to asylums, looked after by nurses, only some of whom would show any kindness or tenderness. She did not, however, feel she could say any of this to the good doctor.

Jekelius had leaned back in his chair like a lawyer who had both presented and rested his case, waiting for her verdict.

"I... I'm not sure I understand," she said at last.

He clucked once, impatiently, between his teeth, making Hannah feel as if she were being deliberately obtuse. Perhaps she was, because she did not want to follow where Jekelius was, so elegantly and persuasively, trying to lead her.

"These children are hopeless cases, Nurse Stern. Quite, quite hopeless. They will never live independently. They will never work productively. They will never enjoy relationships, families, a book or a song or a play. They will never do anything but lie helpless and insensate in their beds, silently begging for release." He paused, stared at her hard, his eyes dark and yet burning into hers, making her long to look away. "Do you understand?"

"I... I am not sure," she replied hesitantly, feeling her way through the words, not truly wanting to think about what he might mean. *Release?* Did he mean treatment? Sedation? Or simply being kept away from the rest of society, in a place like this? Hannah did her best to rally, straightening in her chair, meeting the doctor's dark, blazing look. "What about the parents of these children, *Herr Doktor?* What are you saying about them?"

Another cluck, more like a hiss, as if he was starting to suspect she was wasting his time. Hannah had an urge to apologize, but she kept herself from it. "They delude themselves, Nurse Stern. They convince themselves their children are healthier than they ever actually were, that they are in possession of their senses, useful, even beloved, and then," he continued in a tone of rising incredulity, "sometimes they even demand them back. Can you imagine? They don't want them back, of course, not even one bit. If we released these unfortunate creatures to their parents' care, they would have no idea what to do with them. They would be resentful, helpless, *angry* that their children were once again their responsibility. It would, quite frankly, be a complete disaster." He let out a short, sharp sigh. "But that is how they manage their guilt, for releasing them to us in the first place. Perhaps you have seen the women who cluster at the gate?"

Hannah thought she heard a sly note in his voice, and she had the unsettling suspicion that he already knew she had seen them. Perhaps he even knew she had asked the guard about them. How much, she wondered, went unnoticed in this place? She suspected very little.

"I have," she confirmed quietly.

"They beg for their children back, but do they actually *want* them? No. There is one mother, a most determined woman, so difficult and stubborn, nagging day and night about her little Sophie, a girl who cannot so much as lift her misshapen head from her pillow. She wants her back, she says, we 'cannot keep her like this, locked up like a criminal'." He adopted a high, falsetto voice, a cruel mockery of the woman in question—the woman who smelled of schnapps and had grabbed Hannah's sleeve—before dropping it with a tired laugh that edged into despair and almost made Hannah want to like him again. Why did she feel so *confused*? "As if that is what we do, Nurse Stern! As if any child is 'locked up', or cannot be released into the care of capable parents. Do they think we are monsters? Do you?"

Startled, Hannah realized he was waiting for a response. "No, of course not, *Herr Do*—"

"So, of course," he cut across her with a flourish, "we often usher Frau Beitel into the hospital. We allow her to visit her little daughter, lying there in her crib, unable even to take in the world around her, never mind her own distraught mother. And what do you think we see then, Nurse Stern? Does this wretched woman fall on her daughter and embrace her with weeping and rejoicing?" The smile he gave her was hard, a glittering light in his eyes. "No, she does not. No, instead she gasps and backs away in horror. Horror, Nurse Stern, is what she feels when she looks on the lamentable, unworthy creature her daughter has always been. *Horror*."

He fell silent, breathing heavily for a moment, while Hannah simply stared. She thought of Frau Beitel, grabbing her sleeve. She had not seemed horrified then; she had seemed quite desperate to see her daughter. Was Jekelius lying, then? Or had he convinced himself this was the truth? She had no idea what to make of any of it.

"That is very sad, *Herr Doktor*," she finally said, the sentiment sincere and yet sounding so very trite, and he nodded heavily.

"Very sad, Nurse Stern, very sad indeed." He sighed again, looking at her with dark, liquid eyes that seemed to hold all the pain of the world, and, bizarrely, made her want to comfort him. Her hand twitched at her side, as if to reach out in supplication, and she laced her fingers together tightly to keep from doing such a ridiculous thing. "I do not hold the position of medical director lightly, Nurse Stern," he told her quietly, "and you may tell Major Strasser so. Indeed, I entreat you to do so. My responsibilities weigh on me heavily, very heavily, indeed." He sighed, the sound a great gust of sorrow as he leaned back in his chair. "Very heavily indeed," he repeated softly, almost to himself.

Hannah stared at him, touched by his emotion, mesmerized by the charisma that surrounded him like an electric force, a magnetism she could not help but be drawn to, even when she felt so confused. She wanted, she realized, to believe in all that he'd said, the emotions he grappled with, the burden he bore. She *needed* to believe that a man who held the lives of so many in his hands had a sensitivity of feeling toward the patients he treated, as, in this moment, Dr. Jekelius seemed to.

"I will tell Major Strasser so," she said after a moment, the words stilted. "*Danke, Herr Doktor.* But..." She paused, again needing her courage, seeing the way Jekelius's expression had turned alert once more, in a way that made her nervous. "Willi is not like Sophie Beitel, though. He is quite in command of his... his thoughts, even if his speech and movement are both admittedly somewhat compromised."

Jekelius nodded soberly. "So we would like to think, Nurse Stern."

"Has he been assessed?" she asked, her tone rising just a little. Jekelius's eyes narrowed. "For surely, if a thorough assessment was carried out, you would come to the same conclusion yourself. Indeed, I am sure you would, you would see he could read, read books—"

"Naturally, all the patients in our clinic are thoroughly assessed, Nurse Stern."

"Major Strasser wished me to discover what treatments would be carried out," Hannah persisted, keeping the doctor's gaze with effort. She knew she was crossing a line that would have most doctors giving her a thorough dressing-down. "He is not a medical man himself, of course, but he hoped I might be able to enlighten him."

Jekelius stared at her for a long moment. "As you do not have a professional background in either psychiatry or neurology, I fear you would understand as little as Major Strasser," he answered after a moment, his tone final and, for the first time, turning cool.

Hannah stared at him helplessly; he was sitting back, one leg crossed neatly over the other, his elbows resting on the arms of his chair, his fingers steepled together once again. In his dark suit and white doctor's coat, he was the epitome of loose-limbed elegance; he almost looked as if he were posing for a photograph.

"May I see him?" she finally asked, knowing she could not possibly press the matter further, at least not right then.

Jekelius sprang to attention as he leaned forward, his face transformed into an expression of almost eager lightness. "Of course, Nurse Stern, of course! Why, did you think you could not? I assure you, you may visit him whenever you wish. The pavilions are locked—of course, you understand the necessity of such a measure. But if you knock on the door, one of the nurses on duty will let you in, without question." He smiled at her, with a strange tenderness that made her both ache and want to recoil. "He is in pavilion five. You may visit him right now, if you so wish, and then you can report to Major Strasser on how you find him."

"*Danke, Herr Doktor.*" With a nod of thanks, she rose from

her chair while Dr. Jekelius watched her with that same small smile on his face, as if he were amused by her, by it all.

As she turned toward the door, he spoke again.

"Oh, and Nurse Stern? Please understand I appreciate how different and strange, unsettling even, things might be for you here. In perfect honesty, it is neither an easy nor pleasant place to work for any of us, although, of course, the work we do is so very important. But it can be distressing for some, especially for those who have not before had experience working with the poor unfortunates whose only hope is this asylum. I do hope you feel that if you have any questions or concerns, you can come to me. I will always be happy to speak with you."

She glanced at him uncertainly, his gentle, paternal tone a surprising comfort. Did he mean what he said? She wanted him to, just as she'd wanted to believe him before.

"*Danke, Herr Doktor,*" she said again, and he nodded graciously as he gestured toward the door.

"I hope you find your nephew in good spirits, all things considered."

"*Danke—*"

"And, Nurse Stern," his tone was casual, almost offhand, "it goes without saying that matters in this hospital are entirely confidential, as they relate to the security of the Reich. Any discussion of such matters, with anyone outside of this hospital, would result, unfortunately but understandably, in me having to take necessarily severe disciplinary measures." He smiled at her, while Hannah simply stared, noting the flintiness in his eyes, the ease of his smile. "I am quite sure you understand the situation," he finished, and with his nod, she knew she was dismissed.

CHAPTER 8

The first thing Hannah noticed about pavilion five was the noise. The orderly who opened the door to her was a big, bluff man with thick, blond hair, bright blue eyes and a round, reddened face whose features were softened by an easy smile.

"I am Nurse Stern, I am here to visit my nephew, Willi Strasser," she began, and then stopped abruptly, as the chaotic noise of the pavilion crashed over her.

Somewhere in the building, a child was screeching, the sound like a siren—rising to a deafening screech and then down again, before rising once more, in a way that made Hannah struggle not to wince.

"That's Ernst," the orderly told her with a huff of laughter. "He never shuts up. Willi, you say? He's on the first floor."

He turned toward the stairs, and Hannah followed him, shocked by how different pavilion five was, in every possible way, to the quiet and controlled atmosphere of the hospital unit in pavilion three. Children wandered about freely, not confined to their beds or even their wards; in the dayroom downstairs, a boy of about seven or eight was banging repeatedly on an old, out-of-tune piano, without either rhythm or seeming enjoyment, staring blankly in front of him as he hit the keys with methodical indifference. A young woman of fourteen or fifteen was swaying silently in the corner, her head thrown back, her eyes closed, her painfully thin arms stretched out.

As Hannah followed the nurse up the stairs, a tiny, elfin girl in a ragged nightgown was bumping her way down the steps, her brown hair in a dirty tangle about her face. She was humming to herself, quite lost in her own world, until Hannah brushed past her, and she let out a sudden growl and lunged at her legs.

With a startled gasp, Hannah jerked back, nearly falling down the steps, her heart racing as much from the threat of such a dangerous tumble as the girl now clawing at her legs, growling all the while.

The orderly stepped quickly behind her, his large hands on her shoulders, his big body close to hers as he steadied her. Hannah stiffened, conscious of his warm breath near her ear, the smell of him, soap and sweat. Then he released her and turned to the girl still clinging to her legs and shrieking.

"Enough, Liesel," he said, and, as calmly and efficiently as if he were merely picking off burrs, he plucked the girl from Hannah's skirt and bundled her under one arm like a parcel, marching her upstairs while she howled all the way, kicking and flailing.

Hannah stood where she was on the stairs for a moment, one hand clutching the bannister, feeling quite faint. Was this how the children acted? Were treated? It all seemed horrible, even wrong, and yet she suspected an asylum anywhere else would be no better, with no more sense of order or care.

The man glanced back at her, a small smile curving his mouth; she could not tell if it were sympathetic or scornful, perhaps a little of both. "Welcome to the madhouse," he told her. "You get used to it, after a while."

"These children aren't *mad*," Hannah replied, but he'd

already gone up to the ward. She followed him on unsteady legs up the stairs.

The ward the man led her to was in just as much chaos as anywhere else in the pavilion. A few children were wandering aimlessly around the room; one was curled up in the corner, like a cat. A small boy stood by the window, banging his head against the glass, until a nurse directed him away from it, distracting him with a wooden ball attached to a string. Hannah watched as the boy, happily enough, began to drag the ball along the ground, and the nurse turned away to deal with another patient.

Several children were lying in bed, glassy-eyed and lethargic, seeming hardly aware of their surroundings, so Hannah could only wonder what drugs they had been given, and how much. The air smelled strongly of carbolic, underlaid by the unpleasant, acidic tang of both urine and sweat. Swept by a sudden dizziness, she reached out one hand to brace herself on the doorframe, until a nurse clucked at her to move out of the way. She murmured her apologies as the nurse swept past with a clean bedpan.

"Willi," the orderly said, having deposited Liesel in one of the beds by the window, "you have a visitor."

"Hannah!"

Hannah blinked, barely recognizing the boy who had called out to her from a bed in the middle of a row, for he seemed so terribly different from the boy with whom she'd driven from Berlin just one week ago. His head had been completely shaved and was now as pale and bald as an egg, and even after such a short time, he looked thinner, the plump cheeks of childhood already turning lean and haggard. He wore the same shapeless nightshirt that all the children wore; it had ragged cuffs and a dirty hem, and his feet were bare.

"Willi." She swallowed down her horror at how much he'd changed as she started toward him, going to sit on the edge of the bed. She clasped his fingers in hers as she tried to smile. "I'm so sorry I was unable to visit you before now. How have you been?"

The question seemed absurd, offensive even, in light of his situation. How could he possibly be, in such a place? Surely Georg could have had no idea it would be like this, and yet what had he expected? Or had he known, and that was why he'd asked her to come?

Her mind whirled with questions, even as she realized there was nothing she could do about any of it.

"Where's... Papa?" Willi asked, and for once the words were heartbreakingly clear.

Gently, Hannah squeezed his hands. "Your father is back in Berlin, Willi. Remember, you said goodbye? We drove all that way in the car?" She smiled encouragingly, but he shook his head, as if to dismiss her words.

"Papa?"

"He's not here, Willi." She spoke as kindly as she could, willing him to understand and accept the hard truth. "He's back in Berlin, at your home. Remember? He'll write to you, I'm sure. Perhaps we could write him a letter, together—"

"Papa!" His voice broke on a cry, his expression hardening into something stubborn and desperate.

"*Willi.*" To her shame, Hannah couldn't keep from sounding a little stern. "Willi," she said again, gentling her tone once more. "Your papa is not here. He's back in Berlin. We'll write him a letter. How would that be? You can tell him..." She stopped abruptly, realizing there was nothing about his current situation that either she or Willi would wish to tell his father. "We'll tell him about our journey here," she said instead. "Remember the mountains? They had snow on top, so pretty, just like in *Heidi*... Remember how I told you about *Heidi*... If I can find a copy, we could..." She trailed off as Willi simply stared at her, shaking his head, a monotonous back and forth that unsettled her; she'd never seen him act this way before.

"Papa," he said again. "Papa. Papa. Papa."

Hannah released his hands, trying to hide how alarmed his stubborn insistence made her. Where was the clever, funny boy who had shown her the cover of *White Fang*, who had pressed his finger to his lips with a sly glance for that odious driver, Klaus? "Willi, where's your book?" she asked, trying to sound cheerful rather than desperate. "Have you been able to read? You know how much you like reading." She stooped down to open the small metal cupboard by the side of his bed. There was nothing in there but a toothbrush, a piece of flannel, and a bar of hard, gray soap. "Where are your things?" she asked sharply, while Willi continued to stare at her, still shaking his head, back and forth, back and forth. Surely Georg hadn't realized it would be like this.

"Papa," he said again. "Papa. Papa. Papa."

"Let's find your book, Willi. We'll read it together." Hannah took a deep breath as she straightened, turning around to look for the orderly who had let her into the ward. He was, she saw, crouched on the floor by the window, playing a game with the boy with the ball; he'd push it toward him and then the boy, chortling, would pull it away by the string. He caught her eye and slowly stood up.

"*Schwester?*" he asked politely.

"Where are my nephew's things?" Hannah tried to moderate her strident tone. She felt panicked by Willi's chanting for his father, the lack of his belongings, the way he seemed to have regressed, how awful everything was. He didn't belong here; *surely,* he didn't belong here. "He came here with a suitcase," she said. "Clothes, books, a photograph of his father, some toys..." Her throat thickened and to mask her distress she glared at the orderly, innocent bystander though he might be.

"None of the children have any of their things in here, *Schwester*," he told her.

"Why not?" Now she sounded shrill.

He gave her a look of mingled pity and exasperation, as if he thought she was stupid but he felt sorry for her all the same. "Because they could be stolen."

"*Stolen—*"

"By another child or..." He shrugged. "You get all sorts in here, *Schwester*, haven't you noticed?" He rolled his eyes and she pretended not to see.

"He had a book," she stated firmly. "A book he enjoyed reading. He should have it with him. It would provide him with some entertainment, help him—"

The orderly shrugged. "I don't know where it is."

"Then I will find it," Hannah retorted. "What do they... they do, with all their things?"

"Most of the children don't come here with much. Those that do..." He hesitated, and then said more quietly, "Look, it's gone, okay? It's all gone. He's not going to get any of it back, I can tell you that much."

She stared at him, a fear of something even more terrible than she'd already seen gnawing at her insides, hollowing her out. She had an urge to grab this big, bluff man by his shirt, shake him till his teeth rattled. She clenched her hands into fists instead. "But he likes to read."

"There are some books in the dayroom," he replied on a sigh. Now he most certainly sounded exasperated, as if she were being as difficult as one of the children. "You can give him one of those."

Downstairs in the dayroom, the selection of stories was pitifully small—a handful of battered books, most of them Nazi tracts or blatant propaganda masked as children's books, as well as a few classics that had somehow slipped through the censors. In the corner of the room, the boy was still banging away at the piano. Hannah's head ached, along with her heart. She took a copy of *The Time Machine* by H.G. Wells and hurried back upstairs; in the ward, the noise was just as loud as before.

Another child had suddenly started screaming from her bed, one that resembled a cage with high bars and a net of metal mesh over the top. She shrieked as she pressed her face against the bars and rattled them like an animal in a zoo; the comparison, Hannah feared, was dreadfully apt. The orderly was nowhere to be seen, never mind a nurse or a doctor. The other children ignored her, and Hannah suspected this was a regular occurrence. She glanced at the girl, trying to offer a smile, but she was beyond noticing such things, and so Hannah turned to Willi.

"Here you are, Willi," she said as cheerfully as she could. "*The Time Machine*. Have you read this one?"

He took the book and glanced at its cover listlessly before flipping it open and scanning the pages without any real interest.

"It's not *White Fang*, I know," she told him, "But it's still an adventure story. I think you'll like it very much."

She sat next to him on the bed, her arm around his shoulders as she turned the page to the first chapter, willing him to start reading, to show something of the enthusiasm he'd had before, the boy he'd been just a few short days ago.

He glanced down at the book and then said in a quiet, sing-song voice, "The land itself was a desolation, lifeless, without movement..."

Hannah frowned and looked down at the page, the first words of a chapter. *The thing the Time Traveller held in his hand was a glittering, metallic framework, scarcely larger than a small clock...*

She looked back up at Willi. "It's about a time machine, Willi," she said, pointing to the page. "See? Why don't you read it? I would so enjoy hearing you read."

He gave her his familiar, lopsided smile that made her heart ache all the more. "There was a hint in it of laughter," he continued in that same, sing-song voice, "but of a laughter more terrible than any sadness—a laughter that was mirthless as the smile of the sphinx, a laughter cold as the frost and partaking of the grimness of infallibility. It was the masterful and incommunicable wisdom of eternity laughing at the futility of life and the effort of life. It was the Wild, the savage, frozen-hearted Northland Wild..."

Hannah sat back, stunned. He was quoting from *White Fang*, she realized. *Why?* Did its familiarity comfort him? "Willi —" she began, just as a bell rang, and the children, trained to the sound, all began to shuffle toward the ward's door.

The girl in the caged bed shrieked louder.

"Supper," the orderly told her as he came to stand at the end of Willi's bed. "Come on, Willi."

Tossing *The Time Machine* aside, Willi clambered up from the bed. Hannah watched as he took the nurse's hand and limped from the room. The other children filed out; the girl in the caged bed lay down again, defeated, listless, and woefully ignored.

Hannah sat there for a moment more, listening to the noise of the children tramping downstairs, the shouts and screeches, the sudden burst of laughter, a single, protesting wail. Slowly, she reached over and picked up *The Time Machine*. She closed the book and put it in the metal cupboard, next to Willi's toothbrush and soap. Then she rose from the bed, pausing to smile down at the girl in her cage, who stared at her with blank eyes before she turned her head away.

Hannah walked quietly downstairs, past the busy dayroom now full of children eating their meager supper of soup and black bread, and outside to the blessed silence of a dark night.

. . .

Later, after she'd had her own supper, Hannah slipped out to the enclosed courtyard behind the pavilion, a small, concrete space where children could go for fresh air, if they were well enough, although in pavilion three they usually weren't. It was empty now, and dark, the stars shining coldly high above, looking so very distant, impossibly out of reach, the world around her stretching out in bleak silence.

Hannah lit a cigarette and smoked silently, staring into space, trying to keep her mind empty. *Don't think. Don't think. Don't think...* Don't think about Willi, and how changed he was, or any of the other children, their circumstances so desperately sad. Don't think about where Willi's belongings had gone, or why that orderly had told her just to accept such a thing. Don't think about Dr. Jekelius's sly manner, or Nurse Gruber's booming laugh. Don't think about any of it, because if she did, she would start to ask herself questions, and she did not want to discover the answers.

"You do get used to it, you know."

She whirled around, nearly dropping her cigarette. "You." It was the orderly from pavilion five, standing in the open doorway, smiling easily. He took a step into the courtyard and closed the door behind him. "What are you doing here?" Hannah asked.

"Someone bumped into little Liesel during dinner. A bowl of soup fell into her lap. She has burns on both her legs." He explained all this with a shrug. "I brought her over here to be treated."

"Will she be all right?"

"Oh, she'll recover." He took a step toward her, into the darkness. Hannah stiffened. "He can't read, you know."

"What?" she said, her tone blank, although she knew what he meant.

"That boy, Willi. He can't read." He took out a cigarette and lit it, cupping his hand around the match's flame before he flicked it out and tossed it onto the ground. "He's memorized some book someone read to him once maybe, and he keeps reciting bits of it. About a dog or something."

Hannah stared out into the night, closing her eyes against the darkness. Fabrications, Dr. Jekelius had said. Delusions. *They convince themselves their children are healthier than they ever actually were, that they are in possession of their senses, useful, even beloved...*

Was that what Georg had done? What *she* had? If Willi couldn't read, if he didn't actually understand things... what did that even mean? For him, for this place? For everything Dr. Jekelius had said? Her temples throbbed. She felt the threat of tears behind her lids and she willed them back, not even sure what—or whom—she was weeping for.

"Are there any treatments?" she asked, opening her eyes.

The man let out a huff of sound, something too tired for a laugh. "Treatments?" he repeated, as if it were a word he hadn't heard before.

"Treatments for the children like Willi. Surgeries on the muscles, to help with mobility, therapies to help with speech and coordination..." She spoke with an increasing hopelessness as understanding thudded through her. Of course there weren't. There were never going to be any *treatments*. Not here. Not for Willi, and most likely not for any of these children. Had Georg known that? Surely he wouldn't have sent Willi here if he had? If he'd known it was just an asylum like any other, nothing more than a holding place, a *prison*, without any hope of treatment, healing, release?

And yet Dr. Jekelius had spoken of release. What had he meant, if not treatment, healing, *hope*?

The man drew hard on his cigarette, then slowly blew out a plume of smoke into the frosty air as he spoke. "If there are treatments," he said without looking at her, "you don't want him to have them."

Hannah stiffened. "What do you mean?"

He shrugged. "Just trust me on that one."

She stared at him, his features barely visible in the dark, just that plume of smoke, curling toward the sky.

"Remember what I said?" he told her, his tone gentling. "You'll get used to it."

"Maybe I don't want to get used to it." She dropped her cigarette and ground it beneath her heel as he shrugged and took another drag on his own. "Why aren't you fighting on the Front?" she asked abruptly.

With a smile, he tapped the side of his head. "I'm deaf in one ear. From a fever during childhood. Too bad, eh?"

"Lucky," she retorted, and he shrugged, good-natured. She let out a sigh that felt as if it came from the depths of her being, dragged something out of her and left her feeling weary and wrung out. A few weeks ago, she hadn't even known Willi existed. Why was she letting herself care so much about him now? That wasn't the way to get through this war. That wasn't how you survived, especially not in a place like this, that clearly had secrets. *Keep your head down. Just get through it.* One day this war would be over, and like Hilde said, she wanted to make it to the other side, whatever that could be. And yet... was life nothing more than survival? Didn't she want more for herself than that, more for Willi?

"Next day off," the man said, his tone easy, "why don't we go out? I'll take you to Schönbrunn."

She stared at him, completely nonplussed by the invitation, the whole idea of it. She had not had many such invitations before. "Schönbrunn?"

"The palace? With the gardens?" He laughed. "I forgot, you're not from Vienna."

"I'm from Berlin."

"With the brother who's a bigwig. Right."

"You've heard about me?"

He laughed again. "Haven't you learned by now everybody gossips here? We all know each other's business. What else is there to do, after all?"

"Everyone gossips," Hannah replied, "but no one talks."

He nodded, understanding exactly what she meant. "That's about right."

A gust of wind blew through the courtyard, causing dry leaves to scuttle across the ground, the sound skeletal, like fingers scrabbling on concrete. Hannah shivered.

"Well?" he asked, flicking the butt of his cigarette onto the courtyard. It glowed briefly and then winked out. "How about it?"

Hannah wrapped her arms around herself. "I don't even know your name."

"Karl."

"Karl?"

"Karl Muller." He paused, a smile in his voice when he spoke again. "And you're Hannah Stern, sister to Major Strasser of the Abwehr."

"You sound as if you know everything about me."

"Just that." He dug his hands into the pockets of his loose uniform trousers. "Well?"

She stared at Karl, with his thick blond hair, his round face and blunt features, the powerful body that would one day likely run to fat. She felt as if she had seen a thousand men like him— men from Neukölln, men in brown shirts or gray uniform, or even HJ boys who swaggered down their street, fingering their daggers. Men who could be charming when they chose and brutish when they didn't.

Although, she allowed, perhaps she was being unfair. She recalled Karl playing with that little boy and his ball; he hadn't had to do it. Perhaps he was really kind, and she was just cynical, suspicious, because everything about this place was making her hackles rise, her stomach hollow out.

"Well?" he said again, and now his voice was, very slightly, edged with impatience.

Hannah pulled her coat more tightly around her as she stared back up at those faraway stars. She felt numb inside, battling a hopelessness that threatened to sweep right over her. "All right," she said.

CHAPTER 9

Another week passed where Hannah did nothing but work. When she worked, she didn't have to think, and she longed not to think—not about Dr. Jekelius, or Georg, or even Willi, or any of the unfortunate children she nursed, who looked up at her in either mute supplication or sedated indifference, and made her feel a clutch of terror she was frightened to examine too closely.

The ward was busy enough, with several cases of pneumonia, a boy recovering from abdominal surgery, another with rickets, and a girl who had been stabbed by another patient with a pair of scissors.

"Terrible, that a child was able to get their hands on a pair of scissors," Nurse Schmidt had said, clucking her tongue. "And right in the thigh! Good thing it wasn't her stomach, or she wouldn't be here. They really are little savages, these asocials."

Hannah had learned from Ida a bit more about the reformatory school housed within several of the pavilions, collecting what was deemed the detritus of society—orphans, illegitimate children, gypsies and those with "Semitic traits"—children who had been passed along like unwanted parcels, and ended up here, as something, Hannah suspected, of a last resort.

"They come here to see if they can be educated," Ida had told her placidly.

"And if they can't?" Hannah had asked, after a pause.

Ida had lifted her round shoulders in a shrug. "Then they go to the orphanage in Mödling, or one of the youth work camps, I suppose." She spoke as if it was not her concern, and Hannah supposed it wasn't hers, either, although she couldn't help but wonder about the children she'd seen, marching out in raggedy rows, barely dressed despite the near-freezing temperatures, their heads shaved and their faces gaunt, eyes like dark holes. One had wolf-whistled at her, only to be smacked hard on the ear by one of the wardens; another had stared at her hungrily, almost as if he would eat her. It was only after they had passed that Hannah had realized she'd been holding a loaf of bread she'd fetched from the kitchen for their supper. She'd almost torn a chunk off to give to one of the boys in the back row, a tall boy with bright, hazel eyes—eyes like Willi's—but she suspected she'd only make it worse for him, and so she'd smiled at him instead. He'd smiled back, a wry, whimsical grin that made her like him, for being able to smile at all, in such a place as this.

As they'd marched off, she'd wondered where they were going, whether they had parents to visit them, family who wrote them letters or wanted them back. She thought of her own mother, cracking her doll's head into a thousand pieces. She knew she was lucky not to have ended up in a place like this as a child; if the Nazis had been in power then, perhaps she would have. The knowledge made her feel a rush of hopeless sympathy for them, a futile wish that she could help them in some way.

Each night after her shift was over and supper eaten, she went up to her bedroom to huddle under her blankets, for the icy wind rattled through the spaces underneath the window-panes, and although it was only late November there was already talk of snow. She thought about what to write her half-brother, and had begun a letter half a dozen times before putting it aside each time, annoyed with herself for wasting ink and paper, yet the words simply wouldn't come.

Hannah knew she had to write something to Georg about Willi, although when it came to what she was actually able to say, she was at a loss. She had to be careful, that much was certain, for she had no idea who might open and read her letter between there and Berlin, or what amount of information might get her into trouble. Writing anything about the hospital at all, as Dr. Jekelius had told her, would be dangerous, both for her and for Willi, and maybe even for Georg.

Why had he sent Willi here? she wondered uselessly, time and time again. Had he had no choice? Had he wanted to be rid of him, the way Dr. Jekelius had intimated so many parents did? She recalled the way Georg had clasped Willi to him, the raw throb of emotion in his voice. Surely, *surely*, he hadn't wanted him to go. He'd told her Willi could read. Did he believe that himself, or had he simply been trying to trick her, to paint a picture he thought she would be more willing to accept, of a boy who was gentle and clever despite his disabilities? What, Hannah wondered hopelessly, was she meant to believe about anything?

Finally, she penned a brief, pointed letter:

Sehr geehrte Georg, Willi and I have arrived safely at the Spiegelgrund Clinic at Am Steinhof. It is a very beautiful hospital, with parkland and many buildings. As I am working in a different pavilion from Willi, I am not able to see him very often. When I do see him, I think of him playing under the linden trees you mentioned, that were so beautiful. It is his hope and mine that you may be able to visit soon. Your sister, Hannah.

As she sealed the envelope, she wondered if Georg would

realize what she'd dared not say. Would he make the connection with that offhand remark he'd made about the linden trees, how they'd been cut down, and Willi's current predicament? She had no other way of telling him she feared for Willi's wellbeing in such a place as this.

When she managed to slip away after her shift the next day, Willi seemed even less himself—paler, thinner, more agitated, constantly asking for his papa.

A nurse she didn't recognize spoke sharply to him, when his voice rose as he demanded yet again to know where Georg was.

"Your papa's not here, can't you get that through your thick head?" she snapped, and Hannah bristled, her arm around Willi's shoulders.

"There's no reason to speak so," she told her coldly. "Can you not afford a little kindness in a place like this?"

The nurse looked at her as if she were speaking a foreign language. She harrumphed and walked off without replying, while Willi shrugged off Hannah's arm. She feared her visits did more harm to him than good, and yet she could not stay away. If she did, she would be leaving Willi to languish alone in the asylum, confused, neglected, forgotten.

Surely, she told herself, *surely* Georg would come and take his son from this wretched place. She thought of how tenderly he had wiped Willi's chin, how proudly he'd spoken of his son. If he'd truly understood what an asylum like Am Spiegelgrund was like, he never would have sent him to such a place.

"I'll come back soon, Willi," she told the boy as she rose from the end of his bed, her voice wavering, because she couldn't bear to come back and see him like this, or worse yet. She looked in his cupboard and the book she'd put there was gone; she feared he did nothing but lie in bed or wander the ward, asking for his father, losing his memories one by one, as they were subsumed by the dreary emptiness of days locked in the pavilion with children in an even more lamentable state than he was.

As she hurried back to pavilion three, her head tucked low against the freezing wind funneling down from the Church of St. Leopold, high on its hill above the hospital, she felt someone put a heavy hand on her shoulder.

She let out a gasp as she spun around, jerking away from the unknown grip with an instinctive, deep-seated alarm.

"Hey." Karl held both hands up, grinning. "It's just me. I have this Sunday off. If you do too, what about going to Schönbrunn?"

Hannah stared at him for a second, the sudden terror at being so accosted still juddering through her body. She hadn't forgotten about his invitation, but she'd wondered if he had.

"Well?" he asked and, suddenly feeling shy, a little nervous, she nodded.

"All right, this Sunday. I have the afternoon off."

"*Gut.* I'll meet you at the clock in front. At one?"

She nodded, as a small, wary pleasure unfurled inside her. She'd had precious little romance in her life; working as a nurse had prohibited much of a social life, and the only men she'd met were medical students who thought just about any nurse was good for a grope, or the leering men from her apartment block, whom she had, through bitter experience, learned to dodge. A date with a man like Karl Muller—decent enough and perhaps even truly kind—was a rare thing indeed.

"See you on Sunday," he said and, whistling, went off to pavilion five.

"How do you know Karl Muller?" Margarethe asked when Hannah came up the stairs of pavilion three. She was standing at the top of the staircase, looking slender and pretty in the nurse's uniform that made everyone else, Hannah thought, look frumpy and old. Her head was cocked to one side, her dark eyes bright with curiosity.

"He works in pavilion five, where my nephew resides."

"And what is he talking to you about, I wonder? I saw the two of you outside, heads close together." Margarethe's tone wasn't exactly sharp, but something in it still made Hannah feel a little bit uneasy. She sounded almost suspicious, and of what? They'd merely been chatting.

"We're going to Schönbrunn on Sunday."

Margarethe nodded, her hands on her hips, her eyes alight and her lips pursed. "Ah, a date! Of course."

"How do you know him?"

"Oh, everyone knows everyone here, you'll see," she replied, and moved away, making Hannah wonder. She had yet to get the full measure of Margarethe, with her bright eyes and knowing manner, the way she laughed so easily, and glided around the ward almost as if she were at a party, graceful and light. Helga had told her, with one of her booming laughs, that Margarethe had left her nun's order because of a doomed love affair; Hannah had not been able to tell whether she was serious or not.

She could almost imagine it, with Margarethe so full of life, often almost deliberately impious, daring to tease in a place that felt deathly serious. How was she not affected by the poor children she saw here, or the indifference of so many of the staff? Yet she seemed not to be, and Hannah wondered if that was the only way to survive in such a place as this.

"So Schönbrunn with Karl Muller," Margarethe said later that evening, popping her head around the doorway when Hannah was getting ready for bed. It was already late; through the wall, she could hear Ida's snuffly snores. Nurse Schmidt was on night duty, a silent specter drifting through the wards. "Such beautiful gardens. The Marionette theatre is such fun! I suppose he'll try to steal a kiss by the Angel Fountain?"

"I don't think so," Hannah replied before she could think better of it.

Margarethe raised her eyebrows. "You almost sound as if you don't like him."

"I don't know him," Hannah replied, "and I certainly am not angling for a kiss from him. Not the first time we step out, anyway."

Margarethe let out a bark of laughter and then, to Hannah's surprise, flung herself on her bed, stretching out languorously, as if she intended to stay awhile. "If he heard you!" she said on another laugh that faded into a sigh. "Oh, the Karl Mullers of this world," she remarked, a slight edge entering her voice. "Always angling for a kiss."

Hannah, who had been in the middle of untying her apron, shrugged it off and then pulled a cardigan on. "Do you know many Karl Mullers, then?" she asked, curious now. Perhaps Helga's gossip of a doomed love affair held some truth.

"Oh, don't we all?" she replied, lifting her head from the bed. "Every fresh-faced boy in the HJ, every goosestepping soldier. They're all the same, these earnest, awful boys, so eager to prove themselves, to get what they can." Margarethe flopped back on the bed as she stared up at the ceiling, her lips pursed in thought. "Karl's not as bad as some," she added after a moment. "Although he's not as good as some, either, to be sure."

"Helga said you had a doomed love affair," Hannah remarked, hugging her arms around herself. The room was freezing, but Margarethe seemed unbothered by the cold, stretched out on her bed, arms flung out almost as if she were posing for the cover of a magazine. She was too striking to be beautiful, with her wide mouth and large eyes, a nose that fit her face but was far from pert, and yet she had the kind of features, Hannah thought, that were hard to look away from. She was so unlike all the other nurses, so vibrant and vivacious, her manner mocking and strangely conspiratorial. Hannah was fascinated by her, and yet she also knew she didn't understand her at all.

"A doomed love affair?" Margarethe glanced at her, her lips curving into that old, mocking smile before she stretched again, arching her body with catlike grace. "Oh, if only! Was it with a prince? A count at least, I hope. Some kind of nobility, surely. I've always wanted to be a countess."

Hannah shook her head, smiling, yet still unsure how to respond to her levity.

Margarethe rolled onto her side, propping herself up on her elbow, one slender hand bracing her head. "I left the order because I knew I couldn't keep my vows. Not those of chastity, although I suppose I'll find those difficult eventually, if I ever meet a man worth my notice—hasn't happened yet! But those of obedience."

Hannah perched cautiously on the edge of the bed, her hands clasped in her lap. "What was it that you could not obey?"

"Everything and anything, if it was blindly, which it had to be, because that's the whole nature of it, of any order." Her gaze turned both distant and inward, as if she weren't seeing Hannah at all, or even thinking of her. "I meant to make my vow to God, a sacred and solitary thing, but it felt as if I were making flimsy promises to mere humans—to the mother superior, to the other nuns, to the *idea* of the convent, perhaps, but not the idea I had in my head. In the end, I realized I could serve God better out of a convent than in it."

A pause as she seemed to consider what more to say.

"The mother superior was particularly weak-willed, when it came to bowing and scraping to the Reich. She didn't want any trouble—who does?—and so she said yes to all the demands. We prayed for our *Führer* every night, and that, dear Hannah, was the least of it. The very *least*." Her eyes flashed in challenge, as if daring her to say something.

And what could she say? Margarethe had just, in effect, uttered complete treason. If Hannah reported her remarks, she would be fired, arrested, perhaps even sent to a camp, simply for saying as much as that. Hannah had seen it back in Neukölln, and even at Heim Hochland, with the ferociously fanatical Brown Sisters, always listening, waiting to pounce on the slightest remark and report it. It didn't even have to be about saying something bad; displaying a lack of fervor could be just as dangerous. They both had to know the truth of it—so why had Margarethe said such provocative things now? Was it a test —or a trap?

Hannah stayed silent and Margarethe's eyes narrowed, a small smile curving her mouth.

"You don't object?" she asked.

"To what?" Hannah tried to keep her tone bland.

Margarethe cast her eyes to the ceiling. "Oh, let me see. To what I just said, which you could report if you had a mind to, although I don't think you do." She slid Hannah a speculative, sideways glance. "Or maybe, just maybe—to what happens here?"

She paused in a way that felt as if she were holding her breath, or perhaps Hannah was. From next door, she heard Ida let out a loud snuffle of a snore, and she turned abruptly from the bed, going to the little window to draw the curtain across the icy pane, her back to Margarethe. She heard the other woman move, her feet hit the floor. A silent tension reverberated through the room. Hannah pulled her cardigan more closely about her.

"You have nothing to say?" Margarethe asked, her tone caught between gentle and just a little jeering. "Your nephew is a patient here, is he not?"

"You know he is."

"Aren't you curious?"

"About what?"

"About what happens here."

Hannah turned around to face Margarethe; she was sitting up now, looking alert, watchful, her eyes as bright as a bird's, her body thrumming with a tangible tension although she didn't move. She looked, Hannah thought, arrested, electrified. If she touched her, there would be a spark.

"I know what happens here," she said, feeling as if she were on more sure ground. "I've seen Willi myself, with all the other unfortunates on his ward, and no doubt every other ward in this place. I've seen what it's like. They wander around, they bang their heads on windows, they live like... like animals in a zoo, and nobody even seems to care, or try to improve their conditions." The words burst out of her, making her tremble as she realized the terrible truth of it all over again. "Some of the staff are worse than indifferent," she continued, her voice turning hard. "They're callous, cruel, and they have no reason to be. If you cannot find pity in your heart for ones such as these..."

"But that's no different from any asylum, ever," Margarethe replied calmly, seemingly unmoved by Hannah's agitated recitation. "It's the same in Lainz, in Graz, in Berlin, even. It's an asylum, after all. What did you expect?"

"I don't know." Hannah clutched the folds of her cardigan together at her throat, shaking her head. "I've never nursed in such a place before. I don't think I ever truly realized..." *How terrible it was.* How hopeless. She left it unfinished, knowing it didn't need to be said. She'd been deliberately naïve, obtuse about all of it, back in the cosseted safety of Heim Hochland. *Out of sight, out of mind.* But that was impossible now, when she saw these children every day. She could not dismiss them. She would not.

"Lucky you, then," Margarethe remarked with a small smile.

"Yes, I suppose," Hannah agreed shakily. "Where were you working before coming here?"

"I was at a sanitorium in Graz, with the Sisters of the Cross."

"You have always worked in such places?"

"Such places?" Margarethe teased. "What places do you mean, Nurse Stern?" Her voice rose, her eyes widening in pretend innocence as she shook her head slowly. "What are these places like, I wonder, to which you refer?"

Hannah blushed, although she didn't really understand her joking. Surely Margarethe knew what she'd meant, what they'd just been talking about. "Sanitoriums and asylums and the like."

"Yes, I have." Margarethe was silent for a moment, her gaze distant as she dropped her mocking look as easily as a mask she'd picked up and could put down again. "The Sisters of the Cross ran their own sanitorium, before it was emptied out."

"Emptied out?" Ida, she recalled, had said something similar about Am Steinhof.

"The patients were transferred here, to Am Steinhof." Margarethe eyed her narrowly, her head tilted to one side, a smile flitting about her lips as if she were almost amused by her ignorance. "And then they took them from here to Hartheim Castle, along with many others—do you know it? Built in 1600, a wonderful example of Renaissance architecture," she explained, as if reading from a guidebook, planning a holiday. "Prince Camillo Heinrich Starhemberg kindly donated it to the Upper Austria Charity Organization about forty years ago, for a psychiatric institution. An 'Idiot's Institute', they called it, back then. Not very nice, but there you are."

Hannah eyed her uncertainly, unsure what Margarethe was trying to tell her. She felt it was something, the way her gaze burned into hers, that strange little smile playing about her mouth.

"Why transfer all the patients there, to Hartheim Castle?" she asked at last, the words coming with reluctance.

"Oh, it has facilities there they don't have anywhere else,"

Margarethe told her, her tone turning positively airy. "Quite state of the art. You should go have a look sometime—it's just outside Linz, not all that far on the train. Well worth the visit, I assure you. You can see its smoke in the sky, all the way from the station, on any given day."

Hannah shook her head slowly. "I don't understand you."

"No?" Margarethe sighed. "I'm not surprised. Perhaps you don't want to understand."

"Well, I can't if you speak in riddles," Hannah protested, stung even though she recognized the truth of the other woman's words. She didn't want to ask any more questions, and yet some awful part of her felt compelled to ask, perhaps even to know.

"What do you think I am saying?" Margarethe asked. "With my riddles and hints? Do you know what really happens here, Hannah? Do you have any idea at all? Do you *want* to?"

"What happens here? I told you, I saw—"

"What? A ward run like a madhouse? Children banging their heads, crawling on the floor, while nurses look on, wearily indifferent because some of them are cruel, yes, but what can they really do? How can they help?" Hannah didn't reply and Margarethe let out a weary laugh. "That's nothing, Hannah. *Nothing*."

She spoke with such grim certainty that Hannah instinctively recoiled. It wasn't nothing to her, to Willi, to any of these children. It was utterly awful. Why was Margarethe able to dismiss it all so easily? Because it was the way it always had been? Because these children didn't care about their circumstances, didn't *matter*? Most people would say so, certainly.

She could almost hear Dr. Jekelius's gentle voice, filled with both sorrow and certainty. *They are as good as insensate, Nurse Stern, like dumb animals. They do not have thoughts or emotions as we do. They cannot feel pleasure or pain.* Yes, he would surely say something like that. Many doctors would. But Margarethe?

Hannah had thought she was different, kinder, even though she still didn't understand her.

In confusion, she gazed at the other woman, saw how her face was twisted into something both ugly and despairing. She seemed to be in the grip of a powerful emotion, something between grief and anger. Then Margarethe took a deep breath, gazing down at the floor, and when she looked up, her face was back to its usual lines of, if not good humor, then at least determined placidity.

"If you won't go to Hartheim," she said, "Then visit pavilion fifteen. See what it's like there. Then come back and tell me what you think. I'd be interested to know."

Hannah shook her head slowly. "How is pavilion fifteen different?"

"Go and see. Find out for yourself."

"I can't just walk into a pavilion without a reason—"

"No? You walked into pavilion five easily enough."

"Dr. Jekelius gave me permission—"

"Oh, you want permission?" Margarethe raised her eyebrows.

"No…" Hannah heard how half-hearted she sounded. What could possibly be in pavilion fifteen? She didn't think she could bear to learn something even more distressing when what she already knew was so difficult to bear.

"I think you could come up with some pretext," Margarethe said, more kindly now, "don't you? You've probably noticed how chaotic things can be here, patients coming and going, and such patients as they are. You could find a way, if you really wanted to. If you really wanted to know." She paused, her gaze blazing into Hannah's while her mind continued to spin. "The question is," she continued, her voice hardening, "do you?"

CHAPTER 10

NOVEMBER 1940

The Sunday of Hannah's outing with Karl was cold and bright, with a sky of deep blue, the sidewalks rimed with frost, the air so icy, every cleansing breath hurt her lungs. They took the 47 tram from outside the hospital gates, standing a little apart from the usual ragged cluster of women who waited there, muttering among themselves, along with a man in peasant's clothes. He looked as if he'd come from the country, without any of the city's polished gloss.

"Poor fools," Karl said, without any real sympathy, as he glanced at the crowd. "They should just give up."

"Why won't the hospital give their children to them, if they want them back?" Hannah asked in a low voice.

Karl shrugged, uninterested. "They were taken away once already, weren't they? There had to have been a reason for that. There usually is."

Hannah thought of Peter Hoffman, or even of herself, as a child. Once again, she was uncomfortably aware that she could have easily ended up in a place like this, with a little less luck. Would her mother have been waiting at the gate, begging for her back? She doubted it.

She caught the eye of the man, and he took a step toward her as if he was going to ask her something, but before he could —or she could think how she might reply—Karl reached for her hand.

"Come on," he said as the tram rattled down the street toward them. "We have an afternoon away from this godforsaken place. Don't worry about those poor *sauen*." He jerked his head toward the women, before, tugging on her hand, he helped Hannah up onto the tram.

It was both odd and exhilarating, to be out of the hospital's grounds on this cold winter's day, the whole city opening up before them as the tram took them down through Baumgarten and then across Hadikgasse. Hannah glanced at the people going about their business—walking down the street or into shops, talking, chatting, laughing—and she was reminded, with a jolt, that there was a whole world out there, away from the confines of the hospital—a world at war, yes, but one that did not smell of carbolic and infection, that existed beyond the black and white tiles and the moans and shrieks, the suspicious silences and covert looks of the Spiegelgrund wards. Being out in it felt like taking a deep breath of fresh air, or perhaps giving one of relief. She felt herself start to relax in a way she hadn't in the weeks since she'd first come to Am Steinhof.

"What is Schönbrunn, exactly?" she asked Karl, and he gave her a teasing smile.

"You really don't know Vienna, do you?"

"I'd never been here before now."

"You'll see."

She felt both apprehensive and excited; when was the last time she'd had any sort of adventure?

Her heart gave a funny little skip as Karl helped her off the tram at Schloss Schönbrunn, opposite the main entrance of what Karl informed her was the city's most impressive palace, built as a summer residence for the Hapsburgs two hundred years ago.

Hannah gazed up at the enormous edifice in amazement; it was the largest building she had ever seen, and considering some of the Reich's recent grandiose architecture in Berlin, that was, she knew, saying quite a lot. Made of mellow yellow brick, it stretched seemingly endlessly in every direction, rising up in front of them, a behemoth beneath a blue sky.

"It's the gardens we'll visit," Karl told her as he reached for her hand again. "They're free."

The gardens were just as magnificent as the palace, a great parterre of twisting paths and ornate flower beds, bare but no less beautiful in winter, interspersed with fountains and statues and leading up to a hill on which perched an imposing, ornamental gloriette, with colonnaded arches, topped by an imperial eagle, from which one could look out over the grounds.

"You grew up in Vienna?" Hannah asked as they strolled along the paths, their breath creating frosty puffs of air. There were only a few other visitors in the gardens on this wintry day —a smart-looking man in an SS uniform with a simpering blond on his arm; a couple of girls giggling and walking together, wrapped up in coats and scarves.

"Yes, in Favoriten," Karl answered. "My father worked in the brickyards there."

"And your mother?"

"Died when I was small." He shrugged. "I don't remember much about her, except that she cried a lot. My father wasn't a very nice man. He certainly didn't mind giving me a clout about the ear when the mood took him." He let out a huff of laughter, seeming more bemused than bitter. "I was raised mostly by my grandmother, my father's mother. She didn't much like him either. We all lived in a couple of rooms, pretty shabby. I couldn't wait to get out of there."

Hannah nodded slowly. His story could have been told up

and down the streets of Neukölln: families living together in crowded, squalid rooms, working all hours for a crust of bread, growing either angry or resigned by their depressing predicament. No wonder the Nazi Party, with all their promises of prosperity, had become so popular. They'd provided people with bread; they'd given them hope, misplaced as it might have been.

"How did you end up working in a hospital?" she asked.

"There was a job going when I was sixteen, at the sanitorium in Lainz. It wasn't much fun—the patients weren't kiddies there, let me tell you, some of them were bigger than I was. It could get pretty rough. But it was work, and I seemed to be good at it, or good enough, anyway, and so I kept at it. It's a job, isn't it?"

"Yes, I suppose so."

He slid her a speculative, sideways look. "What about you? With your brother in the Abwehr? How come you ended up here?"

"He's my half-brother, and he's the reason I'm here, or a nurse at all." She hesitated and then admitted cautiously, "I'm illegitimate. My father was an economics professor, and my mother a charwoman. They had an affair, brief as it was, and she ended up with me. He gave her money and visited me on occasion, but then disappeared when I was seven or so, I'm not sure why. Maybe it had all become too expensive. Or maybe he just stopped caring. In any case, I never saw him again."

They had been wandering down the Schönbrunn merry-go-round, the many circular paths winding through the garden, and now Hannah stopped in front of a fountain of naiads—a spirit of the sea bending toward a plump, angelic-looking child, his face upturned in wonder. She stared blindly at the statue, doing her best to swallow past the lump that had risen in her throat. She didn't usually tell anyone of the circumstances of her birth; no matter how many unwed mothers they welcomed into the *Lebensborn* homes, in society at large, illegitimacy was considered a stigma, a shame, and one she still felt keenly.

"Sounds like he was the real bastard to me," Karl said, and she let out a choked laugh of surprise, averting her face so he couldn't see the emotion written on it. "What does your half-brother have to do with any of that, though?"

"He approached me at our father's funeral, some years ago. I hadn't been invited, of course, but I went anyway. I'd read of his death in the newspapers. Georg knew who I was, even though we'd never met. I've never asked him about that," she reflected slowly. "How he knew me at all, but he did. He even knew my name. Yet we'd never spoken." Had she been the dirty secret everyone knew about but no one spoke of?

"And he paid for your training?" Karl surmised.

She nodded. "Yes, out of duty. He was generous, I can't say he was anything but that, and more than fair—"

"But he let you know how much he was doing for you," Karl finished with a huff of cynical laughter. "I know how that goes. Rich people always think you should be so grateful for their castoffs and crumbs." He shook his head, the chilly wind ruffling his blond hair. "They're all the same."

"Maybe." She could not begrudge Georg anything, not now. She understood why he'd wanted her to come here, to care for Willi. She wondered if he had received her letter—and what he would do about it.

"Come on," Karl said, reaching for her hand once again. "Let's warm up with a coffee. There's a café by the marionette theatre."

After their coffee, they continued to stroll through the gardens, up toward the gloriette, the wind on the hill cutting right through them as the evening drew in, the bright blue sky turning violet at its edges, like ink soaking through paper, even though it wasn't yet four o'clock.

It had been remarkably pleasant, to wander down such lovely paths, to chat about anything and nothing, to have someone listen and maybe even understand—and to not have to think about Am Spiegelgrund, or Dr. Jekelius, or any of it. At a kiosk, Hannah bought a postcard of the palace for Hilde, and by the gloriette, Karl took her hand and she let him, even though the feel of his gloved hand in hers, solid and grasping, felt unfamiliar, a bit forward.

This was what young women did, Hannah told herself, although she never had. They strolled in gardens, they chatted with their sweethearts, they stole kisses by fountains, just as Margarethe had teased. Why shouldn't she? Why shouldn't she want to?

As the shadows lengthened, Karl glanced up at the ornate clock, topped by a golden swan, above the palace. "We ought to think about getting back," he said, "if we want to catch the tram."

The park had already started to empty out as the air had become more bitter, an icy bite to it that had Hannah burrowing deeper into her coat. She nodded in agreement, even though the thought of going back to the hospital, those gates closing behind her, and then into the pavilion with its smell of sickness and antiseptic, a bowl of soup, her freezing room, the knowledge of Willi, alone and unhappy... It filled her with nothing but deep sorrow as well as dread.

"It's not so bad," Karl said, as if reading her mind, and Hannah forced a smile she didn't remotely feel.

"Like you said, it's a job."

He cocked his head. "Are you worried about your nephew?"

"Yes. I feel responsible for him." She hesitated, her gaze on the palace now half in shadow. "I don't think my half-brother could have had any idea what it's really like here. I'm sure he wouldn't have sent him, if he had known."

Karl let out something close to a snort, and Hannah frowned.

"He thought Willi would be having treatments here," she told him. "Surgeries, therapies. Ways to get better, or at least improve his condition—"

"Sure he did." Karl shook his head. "Trust me, most parents know exactly what they're sending their kids to here." He tucked his chin toward his chest, his hands burrowed in the pockets of his coat. "It's not exactly a secret, is it? The way we're supposed to think? You must have seen the newsreels, the posters."

"Yes, some of them." The government was relentless with its propaganda—Jews had hooked noses and greedy, slavering mouths, all of them out to steal your money; someone like Willi was pictured as a sniveling, pathetic wretch costing a blond, brawny man—a man much like Karl—his entire working life. But like Karl had said, it was a job. Who was to say it wasn't a worthy one? "No, it's not a secret," she stated slowly, and then asked with sudden recklessness, "What's in pavilion fifteen?"

Karl stilled for no more than a second before he reached for a cigarette from the crumpled pack in his breast pocket. "It's just the children's ward," he said, and Hannah could hear how his tone had changed. His disinterest sounded feigned, calculated.

"Aren't they all children's wards?" she asked. "Am Spiegelgrund is a children's clinic, after all."

He lit his cigarette and then blew out the match. "Infants, I mean, the ones with the most serious conditions. Braindead and the like. No-hopers."

Just like Dr. Jekelius and Nurse Helga had both said. *Utterly without hope.*

Hannah shivered and Karl reached for her hand. He'd been

doing that a lot this afternoon, and she wasn't sure how she felt about it—the possessiveness of it, as if he had some claim on her, but also the comfort of being wanted.

"Hey," he said, tugging her toward him. "Why are you asking about pavilion fifteen?"

She shrugged, his hand still gripping hers. "I don't know. People were talking about it."

"Margarethe?" Karl guessed, his eyes narrowing as he took a puff of his cigarette and blew out a plume of smoke. "You don't want to get involved with the likes of her."

Hannah stiffened. She liked Margarethe, more, she thought, than she liked Karl. "What do you mean?"

"She's trouble, that's all. Nosy."

"Is she?"

"Just keep your head down," Karl advised. "And do your job. The doctors don't like you asking questions, trust me."

"Why not?"

"Questions about pavilion fifteen and the like. I mean it, Hannah."

There was a warning note in his voice that she resented. "And I'm to obey your every command?" she said, and he let out a huff of laughter.

"No, just take my advice. I'm looking out for you, that's all." A sleepy kind of smile curved his mouth and he dropped his half-smoked cigarette on the ground, grinding it beneath his heel. Then, before Hannah could realize what he was about, he'd tugged her even closer, and then he leaned forward to kiss her.

She froze, shocked by the feel of his fleshy lips against hers. He tasted of cigarettes and coffee, and she stood there, completely still, adjusting to the unfamiliar sensation, a flicker of pleasure chasing through her, ephemeral and distant. Then he stepped closer so she felt the bulk of his body against hers, and a wave of some half-forgotten fear crashed over her, shocking her with its suddenness.

With a gasp, she wrenched herself away, took a few steps back as she wiped her mouth with the sleeve of her coat.

Karl noticed the gesture, his eyes narrowed, his lip curling. "What are you," he asked in a tone somewhere between surly and hurt, "frigid?"

"No," Hannah replied, her voice shaking, vague, half-formed memories suddenly thudding through her in a blur of sound and color—shoes on dark green tile, her head hitting the stairwell hard, the dim glow of the bare bulb hanging from the ceiling above her, swaying slightly in the breeze from the open door. She pushed them away. "I just like to be asked before I'm kissed."

"Oh, with a please and thank you, too?" he said, the words caught between a joke and a jeer. "I suppose having a half-brother in the Abwehr can make even a bastard like you act all jumped up."

Hannah stared at his disgruntled expression, the curl of his lip, for a few taut seconds before she whirled around and started walking blindly out of the garden, toward the tram stop in front of the palace.

She heard the sound of gravel kicking up as Karl ran after her, and then tried to grab her arm. She shrugged him away, walking faster, while he let out an exasperated huff of laughter.

"Don't be angry," he called after her. "I'm sorry. I didn't mean it."

"Didn't you?" she replied, her voice choking as she walked faster.

"Oh, Hannah, for the love of...!" He blew out an impatient breath. "You acted as if you were kissing a pig when I'd barely touched you! My pride was hurt, I'm sorry."

"I suppose it would have been too much to ask you to behave like a gentleman," she replied stiffly.

"A gentleman!" He gave another huff of laughter, this one scornful. "Is that what you think I am?"

Hannah didn't bother replying as she kept walking toward the tram station. Muttering under his breath, Karl followed her.

They both rode in silence all the way back to Am Steinhof; hers an affronted one and his resigned. By the time they came to the stop opposite the hospital gates, the day had grown dark and the huddle of women at the tram stop had dispersed. The journey back hadn't lessened Hannah's anger, but it had turned into something more despairing.

Perhaps she had overreacted; God knew, most men—and women—would think she had. *What's so bad about a little kiss, eh?* She could imagine Margarethe saying it, with one of her teasing laughs, an arch of her eyebrow. And yet, Hannah knew she could not change her reaction, or herself. Or her memories —ones she couldn't bear to think about it, even as they continued to flash through her mind, like broken pieces of a puzzle, bits of shattered glass.

As they passed through the gates, Karl made another half-hearted attempt at an apology. "I had a good time," he told her awkwardly, "and I thought you did too, at least at the start?"

"At the start," she agreed woodenly, and he let out a little, hopeful laugh.

"You're like one of the statues at Schönbrunn," he said with a crooked smile. "How can I warm you up?"

Perhaps he meant to make her laugh, but she felt closer to tears, furious with him, with herself, with the once-pleasant day that had now been ruined. She didn't respond as she kept walking, past the clock tower and the administration building, toward pavilion three.

"Hannah," Karl called in exasperation as she reached the door. "Come on. Don't be stupid."

She didn't answer as she unlocked the door to the pavilion and hurried inside.

CHAPTER 11

"So how was your big day out?"

Margarethe stood in the doorway of Hannah's bedroom as she fumbled with the buttons of her coat. After leaving Karl, she'd gone straight upstairs, blinded by her own anger and foolishness, fighting off a soul-deep sorrow she didn't want to feel, not about this. There was already enough to feel sad about here, without having to fight off old memories.

"You skipped supper," Margarethe continued when Hannah didn't reply. She closed the door behind her. "And it was so delicious! Bread as hard as rock and yet more soup—do you think they close their eyes when they decide what to put into it? A potato, a carrot, the sole of a boot? No, surely they wouldn't want to waste good leather. Or even cardboard, as it happens."

Hannah made some sound; it was meant to be a laugh, but it came out too choked. She shook her head, her back to Margarethe.

"Hannah." Margarethe crossed the room to lay her hand on her shoulder. "My dear. What happened?"

"Nothing, really." Hannah drew a breath and finally

finished unbuttoning her coat. "The stupid *dummkopf* kissed me, and I didn't want to be kissed."

"Ah." Margarethe dropped her hand and Hannah heard the creak of rusty springs as she went to sit on her bed. She took a deep breath and pressed her hands to her cold cheeks before, feeling composed enough to turn around, she took off her coat and hung it on the hook by the door. "And I thought I was meant to be the nun," Margarethe remarked as she regarded her closely. "What was so bad about a kiss?"

Just what she'd expected her to say, and Hannah had no answer. She shrugged, unwilling to put what she'd felt into words.

"I admit, I'm no admirer of Karl Muller, or any man like him. But what are you upset about, really? A kiss... or something else?"

Hannah folded her arms and went to the window. The first stars were coming out in an indigo sky, distant glimmers of light. "I was attacked," she said quietly. "Back in Berlin. A long time ago, I can't recall exactly when. When I was fourteen, fifteen, maybe? I must have left school, because I remember I'd been coming home from work. A neighbor, someone from my building, I didn't even know his name..." She drew a quick breath, fighting against the tide of memory that threatened to swamp her. "I didn't remember it, not entirely, not until..." She drew a shaky breath, kept her gaze on the stars.

"I'm sorry," Margarethe said quietly. "That is a terrible thing to have to bear."

"It wasn't as bad as... I fought him off before he was able to... well, you know. And then someone came in, and he ran off. But kissing Karl made me remember it all..." She paused, her gaze on the glittering stars while she recalled the dim glow of the light bulb swaying above her head as she'd been sprawled on the stairs, her back pressed into the edge of the step, his hands fumbling under her skirt. "It's so strange," she continued after a moment. "I think I always knew it had happened, deep down, but I never, ever thought about it. I acted as if it hadn't, even in my own head." She pressed her hands to the side of her head, hard enough to feel the pressure, to hurt in a way that felt almost comforting, or at least necessary. "I have so many things in my head I won't let myself think about," she whispered. "My head is empty, and yet it's full. It's so *full*."

"Perhaps you need to think about some of them, then," Margarethe replied. "Perhaps then it will get better." Her tone was gentle, but Hannah still heard a hint of challenge.

She turned around as she dropped her hands from her head. "I can't."

"You can," Margarethe corrected, her voice still gentle, "but I think you don't want to."

Hannah knew they weren't talking about Karl or that man back in Berlin anymore. "Margarethe..." she began, and it came out like a plea. She couldn't think about any of that now—the children here, the mothers by the gates, pavilion fifteen, not with these old memories still haunting her, as well.

Margarethe's level expression changed suddenly into something softer, and she rose from the bed. "Wait here," she said, and she walked quickly out of the room.

With a ragged sigh, Hannah sank onto the edge of bed. She felt, quite suddenly, utterly exhausted. Her eyes fluttered closed just as Margarethe came back into the room.

"What on earth is—" Hannah began as she opened her eyes, straightening.

"What do you think it is?" Margarethe answered with a laugh. She was carrying a wind-up gramophone, set in a wooden box with a brass handle. She put it on top of the bureau with a flourish. "And now for some music. A lovely little concert sponsored by yours truly."

"Music..." Hannah said wonderingly. She could not remember the last time she'd heard anything but a Nazi marching song on the *Volksempfänger* at Heim Hochland. She had not known anyone with the means to possess a gramophone. She watched as Margarethe took a record from its paper sleeve and placed it on the gramophone with the kind of reverence normally reserved for the sacraments.

"Do you know classical music?" she asked, an expectant look in her dancing eyes.

Hannah shook her head. "We never had a radio."

"Well, you won't hear this on the radio now," Margarethe told her with a laugh, and Hannah felt a frisson of alarm—as well as of excitement. Banned music, then. What was it? Jazz? Swing?

But, no. It was something far lovelier. There was a crackling hiss as Margarethe placed the needle on the record, and adjusted the volume so it played quietly—a swell of violins, followed by a single instrument playing a mournful yet determined tone. Margarethe sat back, her eyes closed as the music wound around their souls, the violin building in desperate crescendo, the other instruments of the orchestra taking up its tune. There were no words, and yet the music spoke of so much —of pain and determination, of striving and falling, and then rising again, and always with the single violin catching the tune, leading the orchestra on, with both urgency and courage.

Hannah found herself closing her eyes as well, letting the music breathe into her. She felt as if it were taking her over, carrying her along on the waves of its melody, to a distant, unknown shore, as the violin continued with its slow, mournful lament, causing unexpected tears to prick her eyes as a feeling of loss overwhelmed her, an ache not for what she'd once had, but for what she'd never known. For the welcoming home, the tender smile, arms around her, *laughter*... a world she'd always longed for but had never found.

Then, quite suddenly, the music sped up to an almost frenzied pace, faster and faster, so Hannah was hitching her breath, her heart racing, everything in her tensing as all the instruments drew into a terrible, troubling crescendo, the last notes ending with an ominous finality that reverberated through her very bones.

She opened her eyes, feeling shaken, as if she'd learned something, or traveled somewhere. It was almost a surprise to see her shabby little room all around her, the same as always.

"Mendelssohn's Violin Concerto in E Minor," Margarethe said quietly as she removed the needle from the record. "The first movement."

Embarrassed, Hannah found she had to brush at the corners of her eyes. Why, she wondered, did beauty hurt so much? "Why is it banned?" she asked. "It *is* banned, isn't it?"

"Oh, yes, certainly." Margarethe put the record back its sleeve. "Mendelssohn was a Jew."

"Oh." Hannah was not sure how to reply; she had never really known any Jews. There had been one Jew in her apartment building, back in Neukölln, Lena Goldbaum. She'd had several dark-eyed children; her husband had died in the first war. They'd left long ago, when Hitler had first come to power. Hannah couldn't recall anything about them except that they'd kept to themselves, but Lena had always given her a quick, shy smile when they'd met in the hall.

There had been a few Jewish nurses and doctors at the Charité, when she'd first been training, but they'd all gone by the time she'd begun working, in 1933. And then, of course, at Heim Hochland, there hadn't been any Jews at all. The only Jews she saw, really, were the ridiculous caricatures in the newspapers, and those depictions were hardly accurate.

"Are you shocked?" Margarethe asked, a humorous note in her voice, as if Hannah's disapproval would amuse her.

"No." She paused and then said, rather recklessly, "I don't know why they would ban such music, even if it is by a Jew. It didn't even have any words."

"Well, you can't have a Jew making anything beautiful, can you?" Margarethe replied, unfazed. "That would ruin everything."

Hannah stared at her, her dark eyes full of mischief, the corners of her wide mouth turned up. "Thank you," she said after a moment, her voice full of sincerity. "That was beautiful."

"I thought you needed cheering up, although, to be honest, I don't think that music is very cheering. Moving, perhaps, but not cheering." She let out a little laugh that ended on a sigh. "Still, we need to remind ourselves there is something beautiful in this world, don't we? Because it can be so difficult to find it in this place. We must work together, to remind ourselves. There is always beauty, even here."

"Thank you," Hannah said again. She glanced down at her work-roughened hands in her lap. It almost seemed like a waste, to make something that was beautiful rather than useful, only to be enjoyed, without any practical purpose. Normally, she knew she would dismiss such things—music, art, a lovely dress or a china doll. *Next time ask for another sausage.* What was the point in a song for a song's sake? And yet, right now, with those last notes still quivering through her, she felt better for it. Stronger, or perhaps richer. She was glad, fiercely so, she'd heard the concerto, never mind that it had been banned.

A sigh escaped her, a quavery sound, and to her surprise, Margarethe leaned forward, cupping her face in her hands, shocking her with the gentle, motherly touch. Hannah opened her mouth to say something—what, she didn't even know—but then Margarethe leaned forward and kissed her on the forehead.

"There," she said as she eased back. "You've had one bad kiss and one good one today. At least now you're even."

Hannah gave a trembling laugh; she found she had to brush at her eyes again. She, who out of necessity had hardened herself to such things, being undone by a little kindness...! The music must have affected her more than she realized.

"Well, I should put this away," Margarethe said with a nod toward the gramophone. "Wouldn't want it to get confiscated."

"Why aren't you worried I might report you?" Hannah asked. Listening to banned music would result in not just the gramophone's confiscation, but certainly a warning, maybe even an arrest, and that was without considering the other things Margarethe had said.

Margarethe gave her a smiling look. "I can get the measure of someone quite quickly, I think," she replied. "And you, Hannah, are no Nazi."

The words were given like a compliment, and one that warmed Hannah, even as her heart fluttered a little in fear.

"I worked in a *Lebensborn* home," she felt the need to remind her. "I follow all the rules."

"All the same," Margarethe replied with a wink, and she hefted the gramophone.

As she headed out of the room, Hannah had the urge to say something more, but she didn't know what it was. When Margarethe had left, the door closing quietly behind her, Hannah felt a sweeping sense of loss, of loneliness, crashing over in a wave of longing. She wished the other woman hadn't gone.

Two days later, while Hannah was changing a little boy's bandage, Dr. Jekelius swept onto the ward, accompanied by the two doctors who tended to the patients of pavilion three, although Hannah hardly ever saw them there. As soon as the door opened, a tension tautened the very air of the room; even the children, most of whom were sedated, seemed to stiffen a little in their beds, as if connected by a current or jerked by a string.

Jekelius looked as handsome as ever, with his dark hair swept back from that saturnine face, the hooded eyes and heavy eyebrows giving him a sleepy, languorous look. He moved with an easy, loose-limbed grace, almost like a dancer, or at least an actor, in his crisp white lab coat, gesturing with his long-fingered hands as he spoke to his impassive-faced colleagues.

"*Herr Doktor.*" Helga marched over to greet him, clicking her heels like a soldier as she bowed her head in practiced humility.

"Greetings, Nurse Gruber." The doctor's smile seemed both kindly and condescending. "I am here to examine the patients."

"Very good, *Herr Doktor.*"

Hannah watched, caught between curiosity and apprehension, as Jekelius began to move down the ward, pausing at the foot of each bed, flanked by the two silent doctors.

At each bed, he would glance at the patient's chart, flicking over the notes with a speed that bordered on unconcern, or perhaps just a surfeit of knowledge, before giving the two doctors his pronouncements.

"Patient suffers from epileptic convulsions and continued muscular spasms." He flicked the sole of the girl's foot with clinical detachment. "Babinski and Rossolimo reflexes present." He glanced up at one of the accompanying doctors. "The child shows a marked degree of idiocy."

For some reason, Hannah glanced at Margarethe, who was standing on the other side of the ward. Her hands were clasped sedately at her waist, her expression entirely impassive.

"Nurse Stern!"

The sound of her own name, spoken in a tone of enthusiasm bordering on joy, had Hannah startling, turning quickly from Margarethe back to Dr. Jekelius, who was smiling at her as if she were a long-lost relative or dear friend.

"Dr. Jekelius," she said, her voice little more than a whisper.

Why was he looking so thrilled to see her? It filled her with embarrassment, as well as a sense of gratification she tried to hide. And, beyond that, a flicker of fear. The way he looked at her made her feel as if she were on display, exposed.

"I have been wondering how you were," the doctor continued in a jovial manner. Hannah glanced at Nurse Gruber, who had a determined expression of placidity, although her eyes were watchful. "Have you heard from your half-brother, in the Abwehr?"

Hannah kept her expression neutral with effort. She had never told the doctor Georg was her half-brother rather than her full brother, and neither had she informed him she'd written to him. The knowing tone was deliberate, she was sure; he was letting her know how much he knew about her circumstances. Had he read her letter? Had he wondered about the linden trees?

"Not yet, *Herr Doktor*."

"Well, you must let me know what he says. I hope he finds our care of his son is sufficient!" This said in a tone that suggested any other outcome would be quite, quite laughable.

"Indeed I will, *Herr Doktor*."

"You must call on me when you do," he instructed. "I am sure your half-brother wishes to make sure you're looked after, along with his son."

Hannah bowed her head, willing the man to move on. As much as she had initially appreciated his attention, right now it felt excruciating. After a few seconds, he finally did, to Inger, the girl with pneumonia and the tumor on her shoulder. Her lungs had begun to recover, and she'd offered Hannah a small, weak smile when she'd checked on her just that morning.

"Patient exhibits signs of tuberous sclerosis, with accompanying epilepsy." Dr. Jekelius paused as Helga leaned in to whisper a few words in his ear.

Hannah glanced again at Margarethe, who looked as impassive as ever and yet alert—yes, Hannah realized, alert and watchful, her dark eyes snapping.

"Impaired intellectual development almost certain," Dr. Jekelius continued, his tone caught between matter-of-fact and mournful. "A degree of idiocy has already been displayed."

A degree of idiocy? How could Jekelius possibly know? All Inger had shown to Hannah were heartbreaking smiles.

She opened her mouth to object, and then promptly closed it. She could not defy a doctor in such a setting; it was not to be thought of. She went cold just imagining the outrage and derision doing such a thing would cause; it would be cause enough to be disciplined, perhaps fired. In any case, no one even looked at her as Dr. Jekelius resumed his summary.

"Considering the nature of the ailment, I would normally recommend a lumbar puncture, followed by a cranial X-ray." He let out a sigh, a sound of sorrow, as he glanced down at the tiny girl with her velvety eyes. "But, on further reflection, considering her age, as well as her general state of debilitation, I do not think such procedures would be very useful." He turned to Helga with a significant glance before pronouncing, "I recommend the patient for further treatment."

Further treatment? For a second, Hannah's heart leapt with hope—there were treatments to be had, after all!—and then she felt a sudden, inexplicable frisson of alarm, even dread. She thought of Karl, blowing smoke up at the darkened sky. *If there are treatments, you don't want him to have them.* She glanced again at Margarethe; her eyes were brighter than ever, her body completely still.

"Very good, *Herr Doktor*," Helga murmured, and Jekelius moved on.

"So you know the good doctor," Margarethe remarked when, a short while later, she came into the sluice room where Hannah was washing out bedpans.

"I don't know him at all," she replied. "I only met him once."

"Still, he seemed quite taken with you."

Hannah knew she could not deny it. "I don't know why," she confessed.

"Because of your illustrious brother, perhaps?"

"Half-brother—"

"Ah, yes, Jekelius made that point clear, didn't he?" Margarethe nodded sagely. "He never misses a trick, that man."

"I suppose not." Hannah kept her gaze on the stream of cold water. She felt shaken, an unease creeping along her skin and settling deep in her bones. She kept thinking of Willi, of Inger now recommended for further treatment, of Jekelius's sweeping, imperious manner.

"He invited you to call on him in his office," Margarethe remarked thoughtfully. "You might not realize how unusual that is."

"To tell you the truth, I'm not sure I want to see the man again." Even if part of her still wanted to like him, despite her unease, her fear.

"No? Not even for your nephew's sake?"

"What will he do about it?" She fought against the sense of helplessness that threatened to sweep over her once more. "I am coming to realize," she stated slowly, "that Willi's only hope is for my half-brother to come and take him from this place."

"Do you think he will?" Margarethe asked, her tone diffident.

"I don't know." Hannah let out a huff of sound, something alarmingly close to a sob. Her chest felt tight and her eyes smarted. "I thought he could read," she whispered wretchedly.

A second's pause while Margarethe absorbed this admission. "And he can't?" she surmised quietly.

Hannah shook her head. "No, he's only memorized the one book. Georg must have read it to him many times. I don't know if he's fooled himself, or just fooled me, that Willi is smarter than he seems, but he *isn't*." The sob came then, a choking sound. "The poor boy. I thought... I thought he was clever."

"And?" Margarethe asked, and now her voice was cool. "So?"

Hannah turned to her, bewildered. "*So?*"

"What difference does it make that he can't read? That he's not a clever little boy trapped in the body of an idiot?" She took a step toward her, her face blazing with the force of her feeling. "What difference does it make, Hannah, to anything?"

Hannah shook her head slowly, not understanding. "I... I don't—"

"Is it only the ones who can read who should be saved from their wretched lives here?" Margarethe asked. "Only the ones who seem clever enough? What about Inger, with the tumor on her shoulder?"

Hannah stiffened, unsure what point Margarethe was trying to make. "What about her?"

"What do you think of her *further treatment*?"

"I don't even know what that means," Hannah protested. Why was Margarethe sounding almost angry with her? None of this was her fault, even if she felt guilty. "I don't even know what treatment he is recommending."

The other woman's lips twisted. "And you don't want to find out. You don't even want to *think*, because if you did, even for one moment, you'd know what I was talking about. You'd have to." Margarethe fell silent, and Hannah simply stared at her, knowing she'd disappointed her, wishing she hadn't... and yet still she did not ask. "Mark my words," Margarethe stated in a low voice, "they'll send someone to take her to pavilion fifteen tonight."

Hannah hesitated, everything in her cringing because she did not want to hear Margarethe's answer, and yet she knew she had to ask the question. "And if she is?"

"I thought you didn't want to know," Margarethe replied before whirling around and marching out of the room.

CHAPTER 12

Hannah woke up suddenly, bolting straight up in bed as her eyes adjusted to the moonlit darkness and her breath came out in ragged gasps, as if she'd been running. Or dreaming... dreaming of blurred shapes, a sense of mounting panic as she'd moved through narrow, twisting corridors, walking faster and faster, searching for something—or someone...

All around her, pavilion three stretched in icy, silent darkness, as if the whole world was holding its breath. It had only been a dream, after all. A nightmare of half-forgotten memories, vague yet palpable fears. Her breath began to slow, and then—

The creak of a door, as loud as a shout in the tense stillness. In bed, her blankets rucked about her knees, her heart starting to race again, Hannah stiffened, everything in her straining to hear, to know.

The quiet click of a door shutting. Footsteps, light and hurried, down the hall. It had to be at least two o'clock in the morning, judging by the moon.

As silently as she could, Hannah slipped out of bed. She crept to the door and opened it a scant few inches, peering into the gloom of the hall. She held her breath as she watched

Margarethe hurry past; in the silvered glow of the moon, the expression on her face was one of elation—and surprising fury. Her hair, Hannah saw, was falling down from underneath her kerchief, and her cheeks were flushed as she smoothed down her crumpled uniform.

Margarethe slipped into her own room, shutting the door behind her, and after a second's taut pause, Hannah closed her door and crept back to bed. She lay there huddled beneath the blankets, trying to get warm, ears still straining, but all was silent. After a few minutes, she closed her eyes and willed herself to sleep.

The next morning, Margarethe was as cheerful as ever as she moved about the ward, taking temperatures and changing bandages, checking charts and smoothing blankets. Hannah watched her out of the corner of her eye, looking for some clue that would tell her what last night had been about—and yet she thought she could guess, if she let herself think about it for a moment the way Margarethe had challenged her yesterday.

The bed where Inger had lain was empty, its sheets stripped, its mattress bare. The other nurses moved around it as if the little girl with her soft eyes and misshapen shoulder had never been there at all. Of course, patients came and went from pavilion three all the time—back to their own wards when they'd recovered. It was no odd thing, to have an empty bed, and yet... there seemed something more conspicuous about Inger's absence, something unspoken yet very much present.

A few days after Inger was taken from the ward, Hannah finally had a letter from Georg. Her heart lightened with hope as she took the envelope, only to see, quite plainly, that it had been opened, read, and resealed. She unfolded the letter with apprehension, her heart weighing all the more heavily as she read the few lines:

> *Dear Hannah, Thank you for your letter, giving me news of Willi. I trust he is in good care, at the hands of such esteemed medical professionals as I know there are at Am Spiegelgrund. I regret to write I will not be able to visit in the foreseeable future. Yours, Georg Strasser, Major.*

She looked up from the single page, her gaze unfocused as she considered what her half-brother had meant. Had he not understood Willi's situation—or had he understood it all too well? In any case, the result was the same—he would not be coming, and Willi would not be rescued from the life he had here.

It was clear, too, that Dr. Jekelius must have already read the letter when he'd addressed her on the ward—that knowing, almost laughing tone, when he'd asked if she'd heard from Georg. He'd known what the reply had been, and he'd been smug in his certainty that either Georg did not care about his son, or he was compelled not to care.

And why, Hannah wondered with a sudden spurt of bitterness, should she think it was the latter? Why give her half-brother the benefit of the doubt, when he'd sent Willi all the way to Vienna easily enough?

She was the only one who cared about Willi now, if caring was to be measured in actions, and not just words. She was the only one who could help to ameliorate his situation in whatever small way she could, to love and tend to him in a way his father could not. And that, Hannah decided with a sudden blaze of certainty, was what she would do.

.　.　.

On her next afternoon off, she went directly to pavilion five, full of determined cheer. She'd become used, if not completely inured, to the noisy chaos of the ward; a boy was once again banging at the piano in the dayroom and Liesel, recovered from her burns, was huddled on the stairs. This time, Hannah gave her the necessary wide berth.

Upstairs, Willi was lying in bed, slack-jawed and sleepy-eyed, making her suspect he had been sedated. She was glad, at least, not to see Karl anywhere, as she knew she wasn't ready to encounter him quite yet. She had not seen him since the day they'd gone to Schönbrunn, and she didn't particularly want to.

"Willi, it's so good to see you." She touched his hand, smiling as Willi gave her a sleepily indifferent glance from beneath lowered lids. He looked as gaunt and unkempt as ever, dressed in his ragged nightshirt, dozing back against a lumpy pillow. "I thought you could use some fresh air." Like all the other pavilions, there was an enclosed courtyard behind the building where patients could stroll or play, if the nurses could be bothered to unlock the doors.

She turned to look for a nurse, and found one coming down the ward, her face set into suspicious, discontented lines.

"I am taking my nephew to the courtyard," she said, a statement rather than a question. "His father, Major Strasser, wishes him to take the air as often as possible. It is good for his health."

The nurse shrugged, unimpressed, and Hannah wondered how long she could bandy about her brother's name as if it meant something. That currency, she feared, had already been spent, if it hadn't been counterfeit in the first place.

Willi was compliant but sluggish as Hannah helped him from his bed, watched by a few other children, some with interest, others with bored indifference.

"It's a beautiful day," Hannah told him bracingly, "although cold. Where's your coat?"

Willi simply stared.

Hannah looked around for the nurse again; she was at the other end of the ward, leaning against the wall and flicking through a tattered copy of *Wiener Illustrierte* with a bored air, ignoring the children around her who lay in their beds or wandered about, silent or screeching. Frustration boiled through Hannah. Surely some of these children could have used her attention, her care.

"*Entschuldigung*," she called sharply. "Where is my nephew's coat?"

The nurse looked up from her newspaper, uninterested. "A coat? He doesn't have one."

Hannah thought of Willi's warm woolen coat that she'd buttoned up herself during their journey here.

Pressing her lips together, she turned back to Willi. "Come on, then," she said cheerfully. "We'll find you a coat. Will you unlock the door?" she demanded of the nurse, who shrugged and tossed the newspaper aside.

Downstairs, she took a man's overcoat from the staff-room cupboard and bundled Willi into it. He gazed up at her in dazed wonder, and the sight of his lopsided smile both heartened and touched her. Here was a glimpse of the boy he'd been, the boy he *was*.

"Come on, then," she said again, nodding to the door to the courtyard that had been opened by the now-surly nurse. She'd retreated upstairs with a dark look for Hannah that she'd determinedly ignored. "Let's walk awhile and take some air."

Outside, the walled courtyard was devoid of any grass or trees, nothing but an oblong of concrete whose perimeter they could stroll, even with Willi's limping walk, in just a few minutes. Still, it was better than having him in his bed, staring into space or begging for his papa. The sky was blue and the sun was shining, and the air was as fresh as a drink of water. Yes, Hannah thought, this was much better.

She did her best to keep up a steady chatter, although there was little enough to talk about. Hannah told him about Schön-brunn Palace, and the fountains she'd seen, and the marionette theatre that had been closed for winter but which perhaps she could take him to sometime—a futile wish, she feared, but she spoke of it anyway, because perhaps *one* day it would be possible. One day, in a different world.

After a few minutes, Willi tugged on her sleeve, and Hannah turned to him. "Yes, Willi?" she asked kindly.

Grinning, he pointed up to the leafless branch of a tree stretching out above the courtyard's high wall.

"Yes, Willi? What is it? What do you see?" Hannah squinted to see the tree in the glare of the afternoon's light.

"Bird," he said, and then she saw it—a robin, tiny and bright-eyed, with a vivid red breast. It was perched on the branch, head cocked, eyeing them quizzically.

"Yes, you're right, it's a robin," Hannah said, squeezing his hand gently and smiling at the simple sight. "Isn't he lovely?"

The little bird was, she thought, the only thing of beauty in this cold, empty space of cracked concrete and cruelty, and yet Willi had found it.

Laughing a little, she tilted her head to the sky as they both gazed at the robin, before, with a cheerful twittering, it rose on outstretched wings and flew away.

Maybe *that* was what she could do, Hannah thought with a sudden lurch of hope, wild and fierce. She would help Willi to find the beauty, even in a place like this, just as Margarethe had with her Mendelssohn. For surely it was such beauty—whether it was a bird or a song—that would keep them sane in such a place as this, no matter what their state when they'd come in? Otherwise there was no hope at all, not for someone like Willi, and not for someone like her.

But if she tried, if they both did... perhaps, just perhaps, they could survive. Survive Am Spiegelgrund, and survive this war. And as for after... who knew what might happen? Perhaps, when there wasn't a war to fight, the attitudes toward children like Willi would change. They'd be softer, more accepting. For a second, Hannah let herself envision a vague future, something warm and pleasant, with Willi in it, although she didn't let herself get further than that, not yet.

"It's good to see him up and about."

Hannah tensed at the sound of the familiar voice, turning to see Karl standing in the pavilion's doorway, his mouth curved in a crooked smile. Hannah stared back, unsure what to say, or even how to school her features. Emotions churned through her in an unsettling mix—embarrassment, anger, a tiny fluttering of hope.

"What are you doing here?" she asked finally, knowing the question to be a stupid one. He worked here, after all. "I didn't see you up on the ward."

"I was in the staff room." He nodded toward Willi, who was grinning at him. "He's wearing my coat."

"Oh." Hannah fought a flush. Of course she would have taken Karl's coat out of half a dozen. "I'm sorry."

"Don't be. I don't mind." He lowered his gaze briefly before returning it resolutely to hers. "I'm sorry about before. I shouldn't have said what I did. My pride was hurt, that was all, but I still shouldn't have said it."

Hannah gave a little shake of her head, unsure how to respond, or even what to feel. Karl's apology both confused and gratified her, and she half-wished he hadn't given it. It would have been easier that way.

"I should get Willi back inside," she said. Despite the heavy coat, the boy was starting to shiver.

Karl nodded, stepping to one side so Hannah could pass, into the pavilion.

Back inside, Hannah took Willi to the dayroom, determined that he would not spend so much time in his bed. The boy at the piano had thankfully stopped with his banging, so the room was mercifully quiet, empty save for a small child sitting on the floor, drawing circles in the dust.

"Shall we read a book, Willi?" Hannah suggested, and the boy's face lit up.

"*But there* was *life*," he proclaimed excitedly, tugging at her hand, "*abroad in the land and defiant. Down the frozen waterway toiled a string of wolfish dogs. Their bristly fur was rimed with frost...*"

He was quoting *White Fang* again, she realized.

She turned to the bookshelf with its pathetic collection of tattered books, only to pause. Why *shouldn't* Willi quote from *White Fang*? She doubted anyone here would recognize it as a banned book, and it occurred to her for the first time, what an incredible accomplishment it was, that he could remember such complex passages. If he was able to continue quoting them, perhaps it would ground him in a better reality—the one formed from his memories, when he'd been settled in a home, happy and loved.

There was *life, abroad in the land and defiant...*

Slowly she drew away from the bookcase, and turned back to Willi. "Go on," she encouraged him. "I want to hear more."

His smile widening, Willi settled himself on his chair and continued, his voice growing in confidence and volume with every syllable. "*Their breath froze in the air as it left their mouths, spouting forth in spumes of vapor...*"

Hannah nodded her encouragement as he continued to quote from the book.

"*The sled was without runners. It was made of stout birchbark, and its full surface rested on the snow.*" His voice had taken on a mesmerizing, singsong quality that had once unsettled Hannah, but now she found it comforting. He continued to spin the story, reciting every word without a single hesitation. "*On the sled, securely lashed, was a long and narrow oblong box...*"

. . .

The light was fading from the sky by the time Hannah took Willi back up to his bed. He'd quoted from *White Fang* for an astonishing hour with barely a pause for breath, amazing Hannah with his memory, before he'd finally begun to wilt, turning a little fractious as tiredness claimed him, batting her away when she put her arm around him.

"You've done so well, you know," Hannah told him as she helped him from his chair. "You speak so beautifully, Willi, and your memory is so very good. I'm sure you're hungry for your supper now." The boy looked far too thin, but she realized she could help him there, too. If she brought food herself, and watched him eat it to make sure he did, that it wasn't taken, like so many other things had been, his book and his coat...

Hannah was feeling as fatigued as Willi as she led him by the hand upstairs, and yet she was exultant, as well. She couldn't rescue him from this place, it was true, the way Georg might have done if he'd been willing, but perhaps she could save him all the same, with food and fresh air and, most of all, attention. *Love.* Something she'd never truly felt for anyone, she realized, because there had been no one to feel it for. But now there was Willi, and she wanted to give it. It was all she had to offer, and perhaps, *perhaps*, it would be enough.

As she came up the stairs, Hannah saw the little girl, Liesel, was still huddled on the middle step, her hair tangled about her forlorn face. Had she been there all afternoon, lost in her own lonely little world? Did no one care about her at all? The answer was all too obvious. Hannah gave her a small, encouraging smile as she passed.

Back in the ward, she surveyed all of the other children with a sudden, awful dismay—the girl in her crib with the metal mesh above, the boy who banged his head against the window, the girl who danced to a song only she heard, head thrown back and eyes all closed. They were all *doomed*, she realized with a terrible, sinking feeling. Doomed to live out their days in this awful place—neglected, half-starved, perhaps even abused outright; Hannah had already seen a few careless slaps or shoves. They were all in desperate need of love, just as Willi was. Yet how could she care for them all? She was merely one person, and she knew she had to think of Willi first. He, she thought with a sorrow bordering on grief, was the only one she could truly save.

"There you are, Willi," she said as she brought him back to his bed. "It will be supper soon." He looked up at her in sudden alarm, sensing her departure, scrabbling at her arm. She patted his hand, trying to comfort him. "I'm sorry, Willi, but I must go. I'll come back as soon as I can, I promise—"

"Hannah," Willi said, in the same pleading tone he'd said Papa. "*Hannah*."

"I'll come back, I promise, Willi." She bent to kiss his forehead, just as Margarethe had kissed hers, and then she walked quickly from the ward, unable to bear looking back to see Willi's desperate face.

She was opening the front door of the pavilion when she heard quick footsteps coming down the stairs, and then Karl came forward to lay a hand on her arm. She flinched a little, and he dropped it with a grimace.

"It's good you came," he told her in a low voice. "For Willi's sake."

Hannah nodded jerkily as she thought of the way the boy had pleaded with her. "I know."

"I don't mean just that..." He hesitated and then said, "Come as often as you can, if you can."

There was something urgent and meaningful about his tone, the same mysterious sense of import that she'd heard in Margarethe's voice.

"What do you mean?" she asked.

"Just come as often as you can. They'll notice. It will help."

"Help how, exactly?" she pressed, her voice sharpening.

"Just do it," he said, and now he sounded annoyed. "Take a bit of advice from someone who knows, eh? And don't ask so many damned questions."

With Hannah still staring, he turned and walked quickly away, back up the stairs.

CHAPTER 13

DECEMBER 1940

All through December, Hannah did her best to visit Willi as often as she could, stealing away to pavilion five after her shifts or on her afternoons off. Sometimes they strolled in the courtyard, Willi swathed in Karl's coat; other times, when it was quiet, they sat in the dayroom and she listened to him recite *White Fang*, amazed by his seemingly limitless memory. If he was willing, she read to him from one of the books there, although he had less patience for those than for his beloved Jack London.

It was inevitable that, along with getting to know Willi better, she came to know some of the other residents of pavilion five, as well. Not only Liesel, who seemed to tolerate her a bit better, but Leon, the boy who banged the piano, and Elsa, the girl who swayed to music, arms flung out and eyes closed. Johann, who liked to play with the ball and string; Anni, the girl who screamed and rattled the bars of her crib; Emil, a boy with beautiful blue eyes who lay in his crib utterly silent and still, barely stirring.

It was both strange and wonderful, Hannah reflected, how one could become *used* to things, to people, to their ways and quirks, their likes and dislikes, even—*especially*—children like these. Despite their various physical and mental conditions, they were, she recognized, children like any other, like the plump, blond, blue-eyed babies of Heim Hochland, like the boys and girls she sometimes saw in Penzing, walking to school in their smart uniforms, or the raggedy children of the reformatory school marching along the walls, chivvied on by their stony-faced wardens. All of them were, simply and completely, children.

As the weeks passed, Hannah learned that while Liesel couldn't bear to be touched, she liked to be talked to. Leon liked to bang on the piano, but he hated to have anyone singing. If you stood by her crib long enough, Anni would turn her head to look at you, blinking her big brown eyes slowly. It almost felt as if she were speaking a silent language that Hannah yearned to understand.

Most of all, she came to know Willi. Willi, who couldn't read a single word, but could quote the entire two hundred and ninety-eight pages of *White Fang*. Willi, who grinned joyfully at the sight of a robin, and made sure not to step on cracks in the concrete, and no longer asked for his papa, which saddened Hannah more than when he once had. Willi, who could be cheeky, after all, throwing a snowball at Hannah when the courtyard was dusted with the winter's first fall, and chortling gleefully as she blinked in icy surprise, and then let out a laugh herself.

It was impossible, of course, to avoid Karl, now that she was spending so much time on pavilion five. He'd insisted on Willi using his coat, and sometimes he'd pause in the doorway of the dayroom to say hello, chatting to Willi or Leon or any of the others with an ease Hannah knew she did not yet possess, no matter how she tried. It made her wonder if she'd misjudged the man, if Karl had more kindness than she'd given him credit for. Yes, he could be blunt, a bit brutish, even, but he had a patience with the children that she couldn't help but admire.

"Maybe we could go the cinema one day," he suggested one evening, jangling the keys in his pocket as she put on her coat to return to pavilion three. "That new film *Falschmünzer* is playing at the Admiral Kino."

Hannah stared at him helplessly, caught between a desire to do something as simple and fun as going to the cinema, and a lingering distrust not just of Karl, but also of herself. Perhaps, she'd thought more than once, she wasn't made for romantic relationships.

"What do you say?" he pressed, keeping his voice light. "I'll even buy popcorn."

"Maybe," she allowed reluctantly.

"You're playing hard to get now, are you?" Karl asked with a little laugh as she walked past him to the door.

Hannah gave him a chilly glance. "Hardly."

Karl blew out an exasperated breath. "Are you still cross about what I said at Schönbrunn? I told you, I didn't mean it. You don't need to make an elephant out of a mosquito, you know."

"I'm not," Hannah replied, although she wondered whether that was exactly what she was doing—and yet didn't she have a reason to? Karl had shown his true colors, and she hadn't liked them. "I must go." She slipped through the door, digging her hands deep into the pockets of her coat, her head lowered against the icy wind as she walked back through the oncoming darkness to pavilion three.

In mid-December, a great tree went up in front of the hospital's lecture theatre, for Christmas. In Berlin, the Reich might insist on *Julfest*, but here in Vienna Christmas was still celebrated with glad determination.

A few days before Christmas, the nurses and orderlies were instructed to tidy the pavilions' dayrooms and wards. Hannah watched with aggrieved frustration as toys and books she'd never seen before suddenly came out, clean sheets were put on beds, and everything was polished and dusted, swept and mopped, so the air smelled of beeswax and lemon polish rather than carbolic and sweat.

"It's for the visitors," Margarethe explained one evening as they ate supper, although Hannah had not actually asked a question. Somehow, Margarethe had known the question was there, lingering on her lips, unwilling to give voice to it because she knew the answer anyway. "Parents or foster parents, anyone who is visiting over Christmas. We've got to look respectable, you know. Keep up appearances." There was an acidic note to her voice that Hannah did her best to ignore.

Since she'd decided to spend more time with Willi, she had, out of instinct rather than deliberate decision, spent less time with Margarethe. With Willi, she'd found a fragile equilibrium —not happiness, not quite, but perhaps an approximation of it— and she was reluctant to have the other woman's enigmatic remarks challenge it, even though she missed her company. She let herself be content simply to go about her duties in pavilion three, to spend her spare moments in five, and to search out what small pleasures she could give to Willi—a postcard of the mountains they'd seen on their journey to Vienna; an orange she'd bought in Penzing, and watched him eat bit by juicy bit, smiling as he licked the sweetness off his fingers.

She had never, Hannah knew, asked or expected much of life; she'd learned not to, starting from the moment her mother had cracked the head of her doll against the table and she'd watched the shattered fragments fall to the floor. And so now she was content to enjoy these small pleasures and do her best not to be affected by all the rest—Margarethe's challenging stare; the disappearance of Inger; the way the nurses would ignore Anni's desperate screams, or bundle Liesel under an arm like a pile of dirty washing, or open the parcels meant for the children and take whatever they liked for themselves.

If I can just have this, Hannah thought as she closed her eyes at night and willed sleep, and not dreams, to come, *I won't ask for anything else.*

And she wouldn't ask any questions, either, even if she had to swallow them down, so they burned all the way down her throat.

At Christmas, the visitors came—the women who waited by the tram stop, as well as parents and grandparents from further afield, relatives who peered cautiously into the wards, flinching as their glances skated away from the other children, or even their own. Perhaps Dr. Jekelius wasn't entirely wrong, Hannah thought, wishing it were otherwise, but neither was he completely right. She saw too many happy reunions, mothers weeping over children they held in their arms, kissing their poor, beloved faces, to think they'd all bid good riddance to their sons or daughters. And yet perhaps some had, because for every child who had a visitor, there were at least three who did not.

For Willi, no one came to visit, but there was a parcel from his parents, with a precious box of chocolates, a pair of knitted woolen socks, and a copy of *Gulliver's Travels*, which was, Hannah had heard, a novel Hitler himself approved of. The parcel had been addressed to her, making Hannah suspect that Georg had known it would be opened and disposed of if sent to Willi directly.

When Hannah had, rather sharply, questioned a nurse who was unabashedly dipping her finger into a jar of raspberry jam meant for Elsa, she'd simply shrugged and laughed. "Do you really think she'll eat it? Why should I let it go to waste?"

Hannah had opened her mouth to say that it shouldn't

matter whether the girl ate it or not, it was *hers*, but then she'd stopped herself. She wouldn't be able to keep the nurse from taking it, and at least she'd made sure Willi had his candies; he'd eaten them, his face smeared with chocolate, with delight.

"And you keep the socks on," she'd told him, a bit severely, for she knew all too well how things disappeared, and not just the food. One of the orderlies on pavilion three had been wearing a pair of warm woolen gloves that Hannah had never seen before, and had almost certainly been a present for one of the residents. "It's cold out, Willi, and you want to stay warm." She'd touched his cheek with a tenderness she wasn't used to feeling and even now she wasn't entirely sure she wanted to. It was frightening, Hannah realized, to care about someone this much. It left you open to the kind of hurt and heartbreak she'd kept herself from all her life, even as she'd yearned for the deep connections that could provide it. It seemed almost absurd that it was *Willi*, of all people, who had finally cracked open the tightly sealed door of her heart, and yet he had. He'd flung it wide open, to sunlight and sorrow and a fierce gladness that she had at last been changed. As much as she struggled with the impulse to slam that door closed again, for safety's sake, she knew she never would.

Hannah was given two days off for Christmas; not enough time to return to Berlin, and so, with both trepidation and a flickering excitement, she agreed to see *Falschmünzer* with Karl at the Admiral Kino in Burggasse.

As promised, he bought the popcorn, and Hannah let him hold her hand as they walked back to the tram stop. He didn't try for a kiss and, all in all, it was a more pleasant evening than she'd expected.

"Another date with Karl?" Margarethe exclaimed as she

met Hannah outside her bedroom. "And here I was, thinking you weren't charmed by the oaf!"

"The oaf?" Hannah repeated, raising her eyebrows. "The last time you spoke about him, you said he was better than most."

"And worse than some," Margarethe flashed back, before the defiant spark faded from her eyes and the corners of her mouth turned down, making her look mournful. "I thought you didn't like him."

"I don't know if I do. We just went to the cinema, Margarethe." Hannah gave a shrug as she moved past her toward her bedroom. "Why do you care so much?" she asked, meaning to sound dismissive, but Margarethe took the question seriously.

"Because you're different, Hannah. I care about you. And I don't want you to be hurt."

Touched by the admission, Hannah's irritation melted. "Thank you," she said. "I will heed your warning."

She went into her room, and Margarethe followed her, undeterred by the door Hannah was already trying to close.

"Just be careful," she pressed.

"Be careful?" Hannah repeated as she took off her hat and flung it, restlessly, onto the top of her little chest of drawers. The windowpanes rattled in the icy breeze, their thin glass rimed with frost. "Be careful of what, exactly?"

"Just... everything." Margarethe seemed to choose her words with care, her voice quiet rather than querulous with her usual spiky challenge. "Hannah, don't you want more out of this life than a man like Karl? Someone who will undoubtedly drink his pay away and give you a slap if he's angry? Oh, he may not be as bad as some, it's true, but in the world we live in, the people we see, what does that even mean? He's certainly not *good*." She looked at her earnestly, her fingers pleated together. "Don't you see?"

Hannah shook her head slowly. She'd never heard Margarethe sound so impassioned, even when talking about the hospital, the children, the dark hints of what Hannah still wasn't ready to learn. As for Karl... "I'm not going to marry him, you know. Far from it."

"Then why step out with him at all?"

With a sigh, Hannah sank onto her bed. "I don't know. I don't even like him, not really. I suppose I just want to feel like any other young woman for a little while, as pathetic as that may sound. To go to the cinema, to eat popcorn, to hold someone's hand, even if it's Karl's. Is that so wrong?" She glanced up at Margarethe in appeal, and the other woman came to sit next to her on the bed.

"No, not so wrong," she said quietly. "It is the small pleasures in this life that make the rest bearable." She let out a sigh of her own as she put her hand over Hannah's. "I cannot begrudge you that, certainly, but... be careful. That's all. For my sake, as well as yours."

Hannah gazed down at their joined hands, touched by Margarethe's concern. "I promise," she said. She wasn't all that eager to see Karl again, anyway. "And what about you? Is there a man you'd like to step out with?" She tried to sound teasing, and Margarethe let out a scoffing sound.

"I certainly haven't found one yet, and I doubt I will in this place. One day, maybe, when things have changed."

"If they will ever change," Hannah replied on a sigh, and Margarethe grimaced her agreement.

On Christmas Day, when they'd walked together, they had seen the children of the reformatory school lined up, shivering, outside the theatre for the one acknowledgement of the holiday —a shriveled apple each. What had been even worse was seeing how each child had desperately fallen upon the fruit, feasting on its wizened flesh as if they'd been given a delicacy. Hannah had recognized the tall boy with hazel eyes; he'd met her gaze and given her the same wry smile. It had compelled her to take one of the oranges for Willi from her pocket and slip it to him.

"*Danke, Schwester*," he'd said, so politely that Hannah's eyes had smarted. That any child could retain such courtesy in a place like this had seemed like a miracle.

"Why does it have to be like this?" she asked Margarethe, not quite meaning it as a question, but she felt the other woman's fingers tighten briefly on hers in response.

"Like what?" she asked, her tone so very careful.

Hannah took a deep breath and then looked up at her. "What is it you want me to know so much?" she asked baldly.

Part of her wanted to claw the words back as soon as she'd said them, and yet, with a sense of inevitability, she knew she could not. Would not, not now, because of all she'd seen at this place—and because of Willi. If she truly cared for him, how long could she keep closing her eyes to whatever evil Margarethe hinted at? Even if it would be so much better for her not to know.

Margarethe gazed at her steadily, saying nothing, until Hannah felt a flicker of impatience, even irritation. She'd finally asked—and Margarethe wouldn't even tell her? It almost made her want to laugh, or at least shrug and dismiss it all. *Fine, you don't want to tell me? Good.*

But, no. She wouldn't close her eyes again. "Well?" she asked.

"Have you seen the covered green carts the groundsmen push about?" Margarethe finally remarked, after such a long silence that Hannah had thought she wouldn't say anything at all.

"Yes, of course." She shrugged, more of a twitch of her shoulders, as if to say, *what of it?*

"Have a look at their load," Margarethe replied. She slipped her hand from Hannah's and rose from the bed. "Have a look, when no one is about, lift the lid and see, and then come and tell me what you think."

She moved about the room, chafing her hands, restless and uneasy, in a way Hannah had never seen before. She almost seemed afraid, or at least distressed.

"And then?" Hannah asked eventually.

Margarethe turned to face her. "And then you will have to decide what to do about it." She reached for Hannah's hands. "I'm glad you asked, Hannah. I knew you would. I knew you'd care."

Hannah opened her mouth to reply, then closed it again, not knowing what to say. She did care, even if she'd fought against it, even if part of her still wished she hadn't asked. She had, and soon she would know... whatever it was Margarethe wanted her to discover.

It was two weeks before Hannah was able to do as Margarethe had asked. Two weeks of bleak gray January weather, the earth as hard as iron, an unforgiving wind sweeping down from the Wiener Hausberge, settling into every crack and crevice, into her very bones.

Whenever Hannah was outside, she walked with her head tucked low against that icy wind, hurrying to get to whatever warmth she could. There was no time to look under covered loads, to creep and sneak about like some sort of spy. And, she acknowledged, she did not particularly regret that fact. Away from Margarethe, from the glitter in her eyes and the urgency in her tone, Hannah was able to let her days relax into a familiar routine, with both work and Willi, with little time to think too much about anything else.

She had been reading to Willi from *Gulliver's Travels* and, much to her gratification and joy, he was absorbed by the story. She had written to Georg to let him know of his progress, making sure not to mention anything that could be seen as either a warning or criticism of the hospital.

Then, one day in late January, when she went to visit Willi, she saw that Anni was not in her crib. She'd become so used to the girl's noise, her desperate screams and rattling of bars, only to fall back into a dejected silence, that the lack of it felt shocking, an unnatural stillness.

Hannah paused by the empty crib, glancing around the ward, as if Anni might be found there—by the window, perhaps, or on the stairs, but of course she wasn't, because, as far as Hannah knew, the girl never left her crib. She couldn't climb out on her own and no one ever bothered to move her.

"Where is Anni?" she asked Nurse Scholz, the one who had dipped her finger into the pot of jam.

Her expression was flat as she shrugged and moved past her. "Gone."

"*Gone*? Where?"

The nurse gave her a look that was mingled exasperation, unfriendliness, and scorn. "Pavilion fifteen, for further treatment."

An icy unease trickled through Hannah's veins, left her rooted to the spot, while Nurse Scholz moved on, hefting a bedpan, mindless of the drops that spilled and splattered.

Hannah glanced down at the empty crib, stripped just as Inger's bed was. Gone, just as Inger was gone... for further treatment.

If there are treatments, you don't want him to have them.

Hannah took a deep breath, let it out slowly. Nurse Scholz had gone to the sluice room with the bedpan and the ward was now empty, save for the children; from his place by the window, Johann stared at her silently, his eyes wide and somehow knowing, his skinny arms wrapped around his knees.

Hannah turned to Willi with the brightest smile she could

and said, in a voice that trembled only a little, "*Guten Tag,* Willi! Shall we walk outside today? Finally, the sun is shining!"

Dusk was nearly falling, the pavilions lost in shadow, when Hannah finally slipped out of pavilion five, still disquieted by Anni's absence. The sky was almost indigo, the first few stars glimmering on the horizon. The air held a bitter chill, even though just a short while before, the wintry sunlight had felt warm when she'd been strolling the courtyard with Willi.

Hannah was halfway back to pavilion three when she saw it —one of the green-covered carts resting by a tree, its bearer chatting with another groundsman a dozen or so meters away, both of them smoking. It seemed eerily providential, to come upon it like that. It would surely only take a moment, a few seconds at most, to lift the curved lid and see whatever it was underneath that Margarethe so wanted her to see.

Hannah glanced at the groundsmen; they were oblivious to her, standing in the shadows. No one else was about. She could do it quickly, lift the lid and shut it again, it wouldn't be hard at all, and yet—

Quite suddenly, with a certain dread that came upon her as a deep, roiling nausea, she knew she did not want to lift that lid. She had not let herself think about what could possibly be underneath; if she'd spared a few seconds, she would have assumed—what? A load of logs? Broken branches and grass clippings? Or, damningly, the clothes and belongings purloined from the children? But if it was only one of those, why would the carts be covered so tightly? Why would Margarethe insist she see whatever it was they held? And why, right now, would Hannah be feeling such a terrible sense of dread, her stomach near to heaving?

She glanced again at the groundsmen; they were still oblivious. If she didn't lift the lid now, she never would—and she would never know.

But I don't want to know.

And yet she had to know. For Margarethe's sake, and even for her own. Here was her chance; she had to take it. Quickly, Hannah reached for the lid, surprised when it swung up easily, without much effort. In the gathering shadows, it was difficult at first to see what lay beneath; it looked, she thought, like a bundle of withered sticks, except they were the color of old ivory, a yellowing white...

Then realization slammed into her, and her narrowed, horrified gaze picked out the forms of several children, their bodies all heaped together—the claw-like fingers of a hand, the bony knobs of a spine, a limp shock of hair, an open mouth like a dark hole...

With a gasp, she stumbled back, and the lid clanged down onto the cart, making the groundsmen turn.

"Hey," one of them called, sounding angry. "What are you—"

But Hannah was already turning away blindly, stumbling down the path toward pavilion three, going faster and faster until she was running, slipping on the icy patches, the freezing air searing her lungs, running, as if she went fast enough, she could somehow escape the damning truth she'd just left behind.

CHAPTER 14

Hannah burst into Margarethe's room as if she were being chased, hunted down by an unseen, mortal enemy, but the room was empty. She let out a gasp that ended on a sob, and then whirled around, hurrying back out to the hallway, only to stop, completely still, and realize she needed to think.

She could not rush about this place like a madwoman—*a madwoman!* Another choked sob escaped her and she pressed her fist to her mouth. And they thought the *children* were the mad ones... the children, tumbled in the cart any old way, legs like spent matchsticks, their *faces*...

No, she had to remain calm, just as Margarethe did. Yet how could Margarethe laugh and toss her head and make jokes about their watery broth, when all the time she'd *known*?

Hannah couldn't understand it at all.

Taking another even breath, she lowered her hand from her mouth and then slowly went downstairs. The ward was quiet, Nurse Schmidt gliding between the beds, the children sleeping or sedated. Night had fallen, and outside the long, narrow windows, the world gleamed blackly under a sliver of rising moon. The other nurse gave her a sharp-eyed glance as Hannah came down the stairs, each step as careful as if she were step-ping on thin, cracking ice, heading to the staff room for supper.

"Ah, Hannah! Just in time for our delicious repast!" Margarethe's voice held all the old, irrepressible humor, her eyes sparkling, her wide mouth curved into a smile that invited Hannah to share the joke, and suddenly she couldn't bear it.

"Don't," she said quietly, and Margarethe leaned forward to look at her closely.

"What's wrong, *liebe*?" she asked, her attitude of gaiety instantly dropped to be replaced by one of tender concern, but Hannah could only shake her head. She glanced at Ida, who was placidly slicing a loaf of black bread, oblivious.

"Don't," she said again, and pursing her lips in understand-ing, Margarethe gave a little nod.

The meal felt interminable. How could she sit here, spooning soup into her mouth, while children were loaded into carts, a tangle of naked limbs, as if they were no more than the pile of logs she'd once thought might be underneath those dreadful lids? It was unbearable, and yet it *was*. And she could not possibly be the only one who knew; in fact, Hannah thought it likely she'd been one of the only ones who hadn't.

But perhaps she was being melodramatic, she thought with a sudden lurch of desperate, drunken hope. Of course she was! This was a hospital after all; patients died. She knew there was a morgue to the right of the main path, beyond the workshop. Children who died on the ward of whatever ailment or illness they'd suffered from would have to be taken there—why not in the covered carts? She was being silly, to think it was anything more malevolent than that. It was simply a fact of life, sad but utterly unavoidable. Death came to all of them, and that's all it was, all it had to be...

She glanced up, and saw Margarethe was watching her shrewdly. Ida was eating her soup with a methodical, machine-like regularity. Hannah had the wild urge to knock the spoon out of her hand, to upturn the tureen, to shove all the dishes onto the floor, *anything* to relieve this growing frenzy inside her, like a howl of anguish and anger and fear that she could never give voice to.

Because of course it *wasn't* just that. Hannah knew it as surely as she knew her own hand, her own face. At any other hospital, when patients were taken to the morgue, it was on gurneys, their limbs neatly arranged, a sheet respectfully draped over their supine bodies. It wasn't *hidden,* secret, bodies dumped in a tangle together like so much rubbish, pulled by indifferent groundsmen who spat and smoked as they bore their terrible, murderous loads.

Murderous...

A little gasp escaped her and she shook her head, as if she could convince herself that the dark alleys her mind was racing down were nothing but nightmarish fantasies. It couldn't be that, it simply couldn't, not at a hospital of all places. A place of healing...

She pushed her bowl away, unable to manage a single mouthful.

A hard gleam, something strangely like satisfaction, entered Margarethe's eyes as she turned back to her soup, and the meal continued in insufferable silence.

"Well?"

Margarethe's voice was quiet as she closed Hannah's bedroom door and leaned against it, her arms folded, her face watchful.

They had just finished supper, although Hannah hadn't managed to eat anything. Ida was downstairs in the staff room, writing a letter home, while Nurse Schmidt was still on duty, the patients sleeping. The whole world felt both hushed and weary.

"I looked." The two words fell into the stillness as if she'd tipped them out of a bucket. "I looked in one of those carts."

Margarethe nodded slowly, unsurprised. "And?" she asked after a moment.

"Why?" The question burst out of Hannah, demanding an answer she could accept. "Why do they... pile them like that?"

"Why do you think?"

Of course Margarethe wouldn't give her a simple answer. She never did, making Hannah draw the conclusions herself, state the facts.

"I don't know," Hannah replied stubbornly.

"I think you do. I think you know very well, Hannah Stern." Margarethe's voice sounded gentle, and it was that which undid her.

Hannah sank onto her bed as she dropped her head into her hands, rocking back and forth. "I don't want to know," she whispered, the words coming out in a moan of anguish. "I don't want to know, I don't want to know, *I can't*..."

Margarethe's voice was steady and strong. "Tell me what you think happens here, Hannah."

She kept her face in her hands, her shoulders hunched as if a weight had settled there—a weight of knowledge she would never, ever lift. She would never *not* know anymore; she would never be able to claim ignorance, never be able to tend to a child or read to Willi and claim she didn't know, *she didn't know*...

Now she would know, she would always know, and knowing meant making a choice. Wasn't that what Margarethe had said? *Then you will have to decide what to do about it.* Yet how to live with such knowledge? How to breathe in and out, dress and wash and sleep, work and play, think and dream? *How?*

"Tell me," Margarethe commanded, and now her voice sounded hard.

"They..." She couldn't say it. She wouldn't, because just

like with the knowledge, there would be no unsaying. It would always be between them, Margarethe would know she knew— oh God... *God,* where was He, here? In this? How could this happen? How could any god let this happen, how could people *do* such things? "They kill them," Hannah whispered. "They kill them, don't they?" The words thudded through her, and with them came absolutely no surprise. She realized, dully, that she had really known all along. How could she have not? And yet still it shocked her to her core with its horror.

Life unworthy of life. The useless eaters. Helga, with her booming laugh: *the end station, as it were...*

And more, so much more. The further treatment, the covered carts, *utterly without hope...*

Just like with the attack she'd suffered on the stairs so many years ago, Hannah had both known and not known the reality of it. She'd suppressed the knowledge, the memory, because acknowledging it had been too hard, too painful, even while that knowledge had informed every single choice she'd ever made. Just as this had. How could she have been so blind? *Why, it's easy, all you have to do is close your eyes.*

Slowly, everything in her aching as if she had, in mere moments, become an old woman, Hannah lifted her head. "I'm right, aren't I?"

"Yes." Margarethe spoke tonelessly. "You're right."

Hannah dropped her head back into her hands. Why did she now feel so burdened by this knowledge, when it did not come as a surprise? When she had known, she *must* have known, somewhere, somehow, even at Heim Hochland, perhaps...

A sudden thought, too terrible to absorb, assailed her. That little baby boy, with his cleft lip...! The matron had said he would go to an orphanage. Hannah had let herself believe it... had she suspected the truth, somewhere deep down, suppressed it completely and yet—had she known? Had he been killed—like Anni, like countless others?

Dear God! She scrunched her eyes shut tight, the sight of his innocent, unblinking face burned into her consciousness. Had he been thrown into the back of a cart like a bundle of old rags? Was she complicit in his *murder*?

Bile rose in her throat and she doubled over, trying not to either retch or sob. *Dear, dear God...* yet what else could she have done but make that awful report? Even as she asked herself the question, another answer came to her—relentless, right. She should have gathered that poor innocent child up in her arms and run off into the night, saved him somehow, no matter what the cost... if she'd actually known.

But she hadn't let herself know.

"Tell me," she commanded Margarethe, her voice coming out in a hoarse rasp. "Tell me everything."

Margarethe regarded her in cool appraisal. "Are you sure you want to know it all?"

No, not even one bit. "Yes," she said stonily. "I must, now."

Margarethe nodded once, and then she began. "They emptied Am Steinhof out first, all the adult psychiatric patients. Bundled them in blacked-out buses to Hartheim. *Charitable ambulances*, they called them."

"Hartheim." She recalled Margarethe's mocking words: *Oh, it has facilities there they don't have anywhere else, quite state of the art.* "Why Hartheim?"

"Because they have the space there to gas them—and yes, that is what they do. They pile them into sealed chambers and then they pipe in the gas. Carbon monoxide, I believe. They call it disinfection, or so I've been told. And then they burn the bodies." *You can see its smoke in the sky, all the way from the station, on any given day.*

Hannah shot up from the bed, rubbing her arms as she paced the little room, her mind racing, longing to escape

Margarethe's unrelenting words, but, of course, there was no escape. She had to face this, finally. "How do you know all this?" she asked.

"I've made it my business to know."

And she had tried to do the opposite. "And here?" Hannah turned around to face her. "What happens here? How do they —" She couldn't say it, but Margarethe knew anyway.

"They give the children the barbiturate Luminal, dissolved in raspberry juice or hot cocoa, so they'll take it, a *treat*. And then the children slide into a coma, their organs fail, and eventually they die. Sometimes it takes hours. Other times days or maybe even weeks."

Hannah shook her head slowly as she stared at Margarethe, who was looking so calm, so fierce, her arms folded, her chin tilted at a determined angle. It was all so monstrous, utterly monstrous, and yet she realized she was still not surprised. "How do they choose the children to...?"

"Ah, now that is the question." Margarethe took a step toward Hannah, her lips parted, her expression now one of avidity. "How *do* they choose? We don't know exactly, not yet, but we suspect the decision must come from Berlin. We have reason to believe Jekelius receives the names in the post from some committee, and then goes to see the patients himself."

"And recommends them for 'further treatment'," Hannah finished heavily. Just as Karl had tried to tell her. The horrible irony of it all, the evil... She thought of Inger. *Anni*. How many others?

"At the moment, it's no more than three or four children a month, or so we think," Margarethe said, and Hannah realized with a jolt she must have spoken the question out loud. "The children who are killed are always first recommended for further treatment, and then transferred to pavilion fifteen. After that..." She blew out a breath. "It is as if they never even existed."

"We," Hannah repeated slowly, acknowledging the word for the first time. So Margarethe didn't act alone. There were others... how many others? "*We?*" she said again, a question.

"Yes," Margarethe stated firmly, a challenge to the word. "We."

Hannah made no reply. She did not want to know about any others; she had too many secrets to keep already. Too much to bear, too much to somehow learn to live with. She could not yet see how. "And the doctors keep it all secret," she surmised after a moment. "Or pretend to." The covered carts, the weighted words, Dr. Jekelius's significant pauses—and yet surely the nursing staff knew. Many of them, anyway. Most of them, perhaps. "From the parents, too?"

"Of course from the parents. They are sent a letter, saying their child died of pneumonia, or an infection, or perhaps appendicitis."

"How do you know such things?" Hannah demanded, longing to cast even just a flicker of doubt over Margarethe's blazing certainty, a chink of light in this unrelenting darkness.

"I've seen such a letter." She paused, and then continued more quietly, "One of the first children killed, back in September, Gerhard. He was only eighteen months old."

"How did you—"

"One of the women at the gate showed the letter to me. As it happened, I remembered the child, because he'd come through pavilion three. They said he died of pneumonia, but he'd been on the ward for a burn. He never had pneumonia, not that I saw. Not that *anyone* saw." The last words were said with a quiet, bitter grief that tore at Hannah, even though she'd never known the boy. "Of course I'd already begun to suspect," Margarethe continued, her voice steady now. "Because of all the Am Steinhof patients. And even before that, in Graz. That's why I came here, you see. Because the Mother Superior at Graz was sent a letter with orders to empty the entire sanitorium.

Every single patient to go to Am Steinhof, and then onto Hartheim. Well, it's hard not to wonder, isn't it? To guess. Unless, of course, you don't want to."

And Hannah hadn't wanted to, not at *all*. But there was no going back now, that she knew full well. She did not know what the future could hold, not yet, but it would be a changed place.

"And why do you stay?" she asked. "Now that you know what happens here? How can you bear it?"

Margarethe lifted her chin another notch. "I stay so I can do what I can. Save those whom I can."

Hannah nodded, unsurprised, yet still fearful. How much was Margarethe risking? Her very life? "Inger?" she guessed.

Margarethe nodded. "She's safe."

A breath escaped her in a lonely gust of both relief and sorrow.

"Anni?" she pressed, and this time Margarethe shook her head.

"I'm sorry. I can't save them all, Hannah. No one can. I don't even know who Anni is."

"*Was*," Hannah corrected softly. "Who she was."

Margarethe bowed her head in silent acknowledgement, and Hannah sank back onto the bed. She couldn't bear anymore, she thought, she *couldn't*, not without screaming, clawing at her skin, going *mad*—or else becoming numb to the horror. Was that how the other nurses managed? The mothers? How else could you possibly survive, except by inuring yourself to such terrible, terrible things?

And wasn't that what Hilde had told her do? Survive the war, get to the other side. *Just do your job and don't be smart about it. One day this war will be over, and you'll still have a life to live.*

That was all she had wanted—a life to live. The small pleasures of a child's smile, Willi's hand in hers, an evening at the cinema, maybe even a kiss. Somehow, in this wretched, godforsaken place, she'd found a little happiness, just a little, and it had become so very precious.

And Willi! More than ever, she had to keep him safe. That was why she was here, for Willi... and, in any case, what could she do for these children whose lives were doomed anyway? *Children utterly without any hope, any hope at all, of treatment or cure.* Dr. Jekelius was right, that *was* what they were... because he had made it so.

"So." Margarethe spoke into the stillness. "Now you know."

"Now I know," Hannah agreed. She ached with weariness, and she longed only to curl up on her bed, close her eyes, and sleep and sleep. Maybe then, for a few minutes at least, she would forget. Except she knew even then she never would.

"Are you going to be like all the others, Hannah?" Margarethe asked with a quiet, pulsing intensity. "Are you going to turn a blind eye because it's easier?"

"Is that what everyone else does?"

"Oh, not everyone. Some of them are simply sadists. They enjoy it, the petty power they wield over the helpless."

Hannah flinched, and Margarethe continued, her voice stronger.

"Surely you can tell. Some of the nurses—the way they torment their patients, how they enjoy it. Nurse Scholz in pavilion five, for one... I know you must have seen her. And there are worse things than that... worse things than even I know."

"Don't—"

"The pitiable children in the reformatory school, for one. There have been whispers about what happens to them, how badly they are treated, and not just neglect, not just the occasional pinch or slap, either. And as for those with neurological conditions, those like your dear Willi..." She fell silent, and Hannah half-rose from the bed, her fists clenched, filled with something close to fury.

"What?" she demanded. "What happens to those like Willi?" What could be worse than what Margarethe had already told her? Dear God, *what*?

"I have heard that Dr. Jekelius and some of the other physicians conduct experiments on them," Margarethe replied steadily, her dark gaze burning into hers. "For research purposes, into the brain, the nervous system. They inject oxygen into their brain, or sulfur into their legs... it's extremely painful, and some of the children have died as a result. I suppose, because it's all for research, Jekelius thinks that makes it worthwhile. Their lives aren't worth anything, anyway, are they? Not to someone like him."

Hannah let out a sound, something caught between rage and grief, and shook her head, putting her hands up to her face. "Don't," she implored as she pressed the heels of her hands into her eyes until the world blurred and brightened, the darkness exploding into stars—cold, distant, unreachable stars. "Don't tell me any more, please. *Don't.*"

Margarethe was silent and Hannah kept her hands to her eyes, pressing and pressing as if she could blot out the whole world, as if she could somehow, *somehow*, forget it all if just for one blessed moment.

"Fine," Margarethe said. "I won't. I don't think I need to. You know enough. You won't forget."

I want to forget, Hannah thought desperately. *Please, please let me forget.* If only she could go back—back to before she looked in the cart, before she met Margarethe, before she stood in Georg's study and he told her what he wanted.

Georg! Did he know about this? Could he possibly guess at the monstrous enormity of it all? Perhaps he had suspected, at least a little of it. She thought of how tenderly he'd held his son, the odd brevity of his letter. If he knew, if he even suspected, how then did he bear it?

How would she?

She let out a soft moan of anguish.

"So now you know," Margarethe stated heavily. "But the question remains, just as before," she continued, her voice hardening a little as if she'd just read Hannah's mind, read it and judged, "now that you know, Hannah, what are you going to do about it?"

CHAPTER 15

JANUARY 1941

What are you going to do about it?

For nearly a month, the question hammered Hannah relentlessly, even as she struggled to find an answer. She felt as if she were in shock, her body seemingly separated from her mind. Sometimes she felt as if she were floating; other times as if she were invisible. She worked on the ward, she sat or walked with Willi, watching over him as much as she could. She ate, she slept, and one bright afternoon in mid-January, she even agreed to go to the Wurstelprater fairground with Karl, because she was so tired of the despair that covered her like a shroud.

On top of the *Wiener Riesenrad*, he stole a kiss, and this time Hannah allowed it, although she didn't enjoy it overmuch.

He eased back with a crooked smile, his bright blue gaze scanning her face as if looking for clues. "That wasn't so bad, was it?" he asked.

"No," she replied after a second's pause, glancing down at the wintry world stretched out before them, the parkland cloaked in frosted white, the grand boulevard, the Hauptallee, bisecting the slate-colored Haustadtlwasser lake. "Not so bad, I suppose." Not so good, either, but at least she'd been distracted, for a little while.

To her surprise, Karl let out a shout of laughter and put his arm around her, and this made Hannah smile, more in surprise than pleasure or humor. She didn't like him, not like that, and she doubted if she ever could, considering what she knew of him, of Am Steinhof, everything. But it felt nice to smile, a moment of relief.

Later, she walked with Karl down the Hauptallee, the chestnut trees that lined the road now leafless under the bright blue sky, and tried to anchor herself in the beauty of the moment, the sunshine sparkling on snow. If she just didn't *think*... didn't think about any of it... except she *was* thinking about it all the time. She could not keep herself from it. Even on top of the *Riesenrad*, part of her mind was back behind the gates of Am Steinhof, wondering what names Jekelius had received, what innocent children had been marked for further treatment, wheeled to pavilion fifteen, ignorant of their death, their doom...

Twice a week, she wrote letters to Georg about Willi, letting him know all the little bits of news—how they were reading *Gulliver's Travels*, about the pleasure Willi had had in the box of chocolates or a stroll outside. It felt both important and necessary, to remind Georg about Willi, to reassure him that she was caring for him, and perhaps reassure herself, as well. And, she hoped, Dr. Jekelius would see the letters going out, and know that a Major in the Abwehr had a continued interest in the welfare of his child.

Maybe it could be enough.

For now that she knew the truth of what happened at Am Spiegelgrund, she saw the signs and symptoms everywhere, as much as she tried to close her eyes to it all, for the sake of her own sanity. She watched out of the corner of her eye as Nurse Helga carefully locked the cupboard with its rows of bottles of

Luminal, and, with a secretive little smile, deposited the key in her pocket. She felt the awful indifference with which Nurse Schmidt regarded her patients, picking up a child's arm to change a dressing or take a temperature with the same sort of weary boredom as if she were handling a piece of wood. There was nothing warm or real or *human* about the exchange, and it chilled Hannah in a way she had not let herself be affected in before, because she knew, she *knew* Nurse Schmidt, along with so many others, did not think these children were really human, worthy of kindness, of dignity, of life itself.

One afternoon in late January, when the snow on the ground was hard and crusted and the sky was the color of flint, winter's death grip unrelenting on all of Vienna, Hannah came onto the usual noisy chaos of pavilion five to find little Emil lying miserably on top of his urine-soaked sheets.

"Nurse Scholz!" she exclaimed sternly as the nurse who had once stolen the jam slouched up to her with a surly expression. Johann was crouched in the corner of the ward, watching them both with wide eyes, and from the dayroom, the discordant sounds of the piano echoed. A new patient had taken Anni's bed, a boy of about four years old who lay on his side and sang to himself quietly, unceasingly, his unfocused gaze never wavering from the bars of his crib. "What is the meaning of this?" Hannah asked as she pointed to Emil's bed. "His sheets need to be changed. They're positively sodden."

"I just changed them an hour ago," Nurse Scholz answered with a scowl. "And straight away he pissed himself again."

"If he is incontinent," Hannah replied evenly, "then there should be a rubber sheet on the bed. Why isn't there one?"

The other nurse simply shrugged, uncaring, and Hannah had to hold onto her temper with effort. How had she not noticed such indifferent incompetence before? Or had she simply not wanted to acknowledge it, as with so many other things?

"Change the sheets," she commanded shortly. "It's inhumane to leave a child like this."

Nurse Scholz's expression twisted into something ugly. "You're not the ward sister here, you know," she told her. "You can't tell me what to do."

Hannah would have transferred to pavilion five if she'd been allowed, but Matron Bertha had merely shaken her head when Hannah had suggested such a thing.

"If he's left like this," she persisted, "he'll develop bedsores that will become infected—"

"Why should I care?" Nurse Scholz spat.

Hannah clenched her palms to keep from giving the woman a good slap. "You are a *nurse*, remember," she stated quietly. "Your duty is to care and to heal—"

"Oh, *halt die klappe*," Nurse Scholz replied irritably as she turned away. Shut up. "He won't be here that long anyway." She leaned over Emil's crib; he was gazing up at them mutely, his beautiful blue eyes filled with misery, his thin, wasted body prone and helpless on those sodden sheets. "Will you, you little brat?" she asked in a voice of awful, sugary sweetness. "You're not going to last much longer. Look at the state of you, all skin and bones. Not long for this world, I'd say. Not long at all." She jerked her chin in a satisfied nod as she straightened. "Well, it'll be nothing but a relief, won't it?"

"Stop it," Hannah demanded in a low throb of feeling, caught between rage and a terrible grief. "How can you be so cruel? He's just a child."

"He's an idiot."

"That—" Hannah's mouth worked as she tried to sort her thoughts and speak calmly. "That doesn't matter."

Nurse Scholz shook her head slowly. The twisted ugliness of her expression had slackened into something more like pity. "If you think that way, you don't belong here, Nurse Stern."

"And I could say the same to you," Hannah replied, her

tone severe, although her hands were shaking. "What kind of nurse treats the patients in her care with such... such needless, casual cruelty?"

If she'd been expecting so much as a flicker of remorse from the other nurse, she was to be disappointed. Nurse Scholz just let out a laugh that ended on a sigh and then walked away.

Hannah changed the sheets herself.

Would she have dared to have such an exchange before she'd seen that cart? she wondered as she lifted a soaked and stinking Emil from the bed. He was as light as a handful of twigs in her arms, his head lolling back on his neck like an apple on a stem. If the children here weren't killed by a dose of Luminal, they would likely die slowly from starvation, cold, and neglect—especially children like Emil, whose parents had surrendered him to the state when he was just a baby, unable or unwilling to care for a child with such needs.

"There you are." Hannah tucked the blanket around Emil while he blinked up at her silently. She touched his cheek, aching for him, seething at the impossibility of his situation... and hers.

Margarethe was risking her life to save these children. Hannah did not know the particulars, but she was sure of that much. Was she not willing to do the same?

And yet there was Willi. Willi, who depended on her, who needed her. If she risked her life for other children, if she lost it, what would happen to him?

She turned away from Emil to see Willi sitting on the edge of his bed, waiting for her with an alert expression, the copy of *Gulliver's Travels* held in his hands. He'd already begun to memorize it, reciting passages with an ebullient joy that filled Hannah with both pleasure and gratitude. *My father had a small estate in Nottinghamshire: I was the third of five sons...*

"Shall we read, Willi?" she asked, and he nodded eagerly.

Hannah slipped her hand into his as she took him downstairs, now well used to his limping walk, adjusting her pace accordingly. In the dayroom, Leon was still banging methodically on the piano; Elsa was swaying in the corner, eyes closed as she murmured to herself. Accustomed to both, Hannah settled herself on the sofa with Willi at her side, her arm around his shoulders as she opened the book.

"*My gentleness and good behavior had gained so far on the emperor and his court,*" she began to read, "*and indeed upon the army and people in general, that I began to conceive hopes of getting my liberty in a short time. I took all possible methods to cultivate this favorable disposition...*"

Half an hour later, the light was fading from the sky and Willi was becoming restless, turning the pages before Hannah had finished them, drumming his feet against the floor. "We'll stop for now, shall we?" she remarked with a smile and Willi nodded. She closed the book as she gazed around the room; Leon had stopped playing the piano some time ago and now lay with his head resting on top of the keys. Elsa had wandered out of the room, humming softly to herself, and for a second it felt, if not entirely peaceful, then at least quiet.

The anxiousness that had been constantly seething under her skin since she'd looked in that cart settled for a few moments and she simply sat there, her arm around Willi as the room slowly darkened about them, the corners dissolving into shadows. She could almost imagine they were somewhere else— Georg's house, perhaps—and there was a fire crackling in the grate, dinner about to be called. They would eat rich soup and good bread at his plentiful table, and then she would tuck Willi into bed with another story... simple pleasures, and yet she ached for them. Ached for things to be different, for this world and this war to dissolve into shadows just like the light in this room, as if they'd never been.

The bell for dinner clanged, making them both jump a little, and the hazy vestiges of her daydream vanished as quickly as the ghostly shreds of a morning mist as Hannah got up from the sofa, reaching out one hand to Willi.

"Time for me to go and for you to have supper," she said as cheerfully as she could. "But I'll be back tomorrow. We'll read chapter four."

"Hannah... come?" he asked haltingly, and she nodded, used to this ritual now, his need to check and double-check her return, his one anchor in these wild waves of uncertainty.

"Yes, I'll come, Willi. Tomorrow afternoon. I promise."

The corners of his mouth drew down, his fingers tightening on hers. "Hannah... stay?"

"I'm sorry, Willi, I can't stay." Gently, she squeezed his hand, her heart aching. "But I promise I'll come tomorrow, when my work is finished. Come on, now. You don't want to miss your supper."

Slowly, his face full of resignation, he nodded, and Hannah led him to the dining room as the other children trooped down the stairs. She watched him find his place at the table as one of the orderlies passed down plates and cups and the children, some noisy, some silent, clambered to their places.

She stayed for a moment, watching Willi turn to talk to Johann, and then she saw Elsa laugh at something another child had said. Such small things, and yet signs of life, of happiness, even in this wretched place. They heartened and hurt her in equal measure, because every moment that she simply stood by and told herself she was doing enough by caring for Willi, who knew what was happening elsewhere? Who knew whether a child's name had been written on a list, ticked for further treatment?

Even in this very moment, an orderly might be carrying a child out on a stretcher, taking them to pavilion fifteen, administering the lethal dose of Luminal. How long, Hannah wondered, could she keep trying to close her eyes to such horror?

No, she knew, she had to do something. The question was, what?

CHAPTER 16

FEBRUARY 1941

A week passed as January slouched into February, cold and gray and wet. Willi was fractious and had developed a rattling cough, and Hannah brought medicines from Penzing to help him, cough syrup and lozenges he liked to suck. It seemed like so little, and she knew it *was* little.

Every time she saw Margarethe on the ward, the other nurse raised her eyebrows in silent query, and Hannah knew what she was thinking. Asking.

What are you going to do about it?

In the middle of February, Hannah finally decided to do something—she would speak to the medical director himself. The idea had come upon her when, one evening, Margarethe had told her about a nurse who had protested the removal of patients in Am Steinhof back in the summer.

"Her name is Anna Wodl. She works at the General Hospital here in Vienna and she has a disabled son. When she heard about the removal of patients, she staged a protest outside the hospital, before you came, with hundreds of people present. Even more people wrote letters of protest to Berlin—'by the basketful', or so it was reported—it's part of the reason why they stopped the whole program. At least, *officially*." She'd rolled her eyes, but Hannah had been seized with a sudden conviction—and hope.

If public protests could halt one part of the program, why not another? Anna Wodl's protest had spurred other people to act similarly, and that had *changed* things, if only a little. Why not again? Hadn't Jekelius invited her to bring her concerns to him? His solicitous attention to her must mean that Georg still held some sway, if not as much as she had once thought; perhaps she could use that to her advantage. To the children's advantage.

Stopping the program completely would surely be better than saving one or two lives, as worthy as that was. And who could object to a measured discussion between professionals? Of course, she knew it was not as simple as that, but if she could risk Jekelius's displeasure, invoke her brother's name...

Hannah knew that doing so would be a risky proposition, not just for her, but for Willi, perhaps even Georg. Yet Jekelius had not been angry with her before; he had been, surprisingly, almost eager to answer her questions. Would he be so again? Did she dare...? She would have to, Hannah decided, for the sake of the children.

"Nurse Stern!" Dr. Jekelius's smile was ready and welcoming as Hannah opened his door after he'd bid her to enter. "How delightful to see you. I trust you are well?"

"I..." To her horror, despite all her determination, her voice wavered audibly, and the doctor's expression softened in a fatherly sympathy.

"Are you finding things difficult, Nurse? Come, sit down."

His kindness was almost too much to bear.

Taking a steadying breath, Hannah moved to sit down in the same chair she'd sat in before, while Dr. Jekelius elegantly sank into his own seat behind the desk, fingers steepled underneath his chin as he smiled thoughtfully at her. For the first time, it occurred to Hannah that this man was a trained psychiatrist, that he could no doubt analyze her every movement, every flicker of feeling across her face. She had always considered herself to be pragmatic rather than emotional, but right now, with everything she'd learned and seen at Am Spiegelgrund still so fresh, she felt painfully raw, and underneath Jekelius's compassionate gaze, as good as naked.

"Do tell me what is the trouble," he invited.

She took another breath, unsure how to begin. Come right out with it, or be discreet, diplomatic? What would Jekelius respond more kindly to? The answer, Hannah feared, was neither. And yet she *had* to try. Except, now that she was here, under Jekelius's seemingly kindly yet still shrewd gaze, she did not want to, as much as she had back in the safety of her room.

"I have learned of things that happen at this institution that distress me, *Herr Doktor*," she stated, and thankfully this time her voice did not waver.

Jekelius nodded, unsurprised, sympathetic. "Yes, I imagine you have, Nurse Stern, I imagine you have. And it must have been very distressing indeed. For that I am truly sorry."

His ready sympathy unsettled her even as it gave her a hot, bright flare of hope.

"It has been," she replied after a few seconds' pause. "And I am glad for your concern. I confess, I don't understand how such things can happen, in an institution devoted to the care of individuals…" she trailed off meaningfully, while Jekelius nodded along, as if he were agreeing with every word she said.

"Exactly so, Nurse Stern, exactly so. Did I not say what a tragedy this was, when we first spoke? And how heavily these burdens weighed on me?" He held both hands out in appeal, his eyes so big and mournful Hannah was caught between sympathy and a sudden rage. What, she wondered, had she expected him to say? And what was she to believe, now that she knew what really went on here?

"At that time, I had no idea what these burdens were," she returned evenly. "I did not realize that children were being—" She hesitated, caught on the precipice, wanting to claw her way back to safety even now. Then she thought of Inger, of Anni, of Willi. "Dr. Jekelius, is it true you are authorizing the killing of children who are meant to be receiving treatment in this institution?" The words fell into the stillness, settled there, starting tremors. Hannah could feel their reverberations throughout her body; she clenched her hands in her lap to keep them from trembling. There would be no going back now. Dear heaven, why had she come? Why had she dared to be so bold, so *stupid*?

Dr. Jekelius stared at her for a long moment, his eyes so large and dark, and yet now they didn't look mournful, but alert. Watchful, yet with no guilt.

Hannah sat back in her chair, her hands still clenched in her lap, as she waited for his reply.

"What is it you think I am doing here, Nurse Stern?" he finally asked in a tone of curious inquiry.

Hannah opened and closed her mouth before she managed to answer, "I... you, that is, I think you are killing the children entrusted into your care."

He nodded slowly, his fingers steepled once more under his chin. "And why do you think I would do such a thing?"

She stared at him helplessly, not knowing how to respond. Had she really thought her single, pathetic protest, the simple mention of her brother's name, would change this man's mind? Had she let herself believe, as she'd so wanted to before, that he cared for these children? "I don't know why you do such a thing, *Herr Doktor*," she finally answered.

"Because I am a monster?" he suggested, his tone one of gentle whimsy. His heavy, dark eyebrows rose above his liquid eyes, and a tiny smile played about his lips. "An evil sadist who enjoys torturing and killing small, vulnerable children? Is that it?"

"I..." Was he goading her? Or could he actually offer some explanation, something she hadn't considered before? Nothing, Hannah knew, could ever make sense of what happened here. *Nothing.* "There are some nurses here, *Herr Doktor*," she told him, "and no doubt some doctors as well, who would answer to that description."

"Ah." He sat back in his chair, crossing one leg over another. "Indeed, I fear that is true. It is so very difficult to get decent staff these days."

Hannah let out a choked sound, and he nodded as if she'd made some salient point.

"Of course, that is not the only reason. There are some who are... fanatical in their devotion, and this gives them an excuse for their cruelty. That is abominable, make no mistake. Of course, one must be sincere in one's convictions. I, am, naturally, a loyal servant of the Reich. Even so, one need never be cruel."

"And is it not cruel, to kill these children?" she asked quietly.

"Is it?" he returned gently. "Is it really?"

Hannah simply stared. She thought of Inger, of Anni—how many others? Dozens? More? Margarethe had said three or four a month, maybe more. How many was that, in total? "It must be," she answered, and to her shame, she heard a tiny, twanging note of doubt in her voice, the lilt of a question she had never meant to ask, had never meant to *think*.

"Must it?" Jekelius returned, rousing himself a little, although his expression was still gentle. "We make assumptions, Nurse Stern, without even realizing we are doing so. 'It is wrong to kill another human being.' Of course, that seems like a perfectly right and moral assumption. Naturally it does! And yet... must it *always* be wrong?"

"You are playing tricks with your words," Hannah protested. Already, her mind felt tangled up, her thoughts hopelessly twisted. She'd come here to make a protest, not have her mind changed. "It *is* wrong to kill an innocent child."

"Then is it wrong to put an innocent child out of its unrelenting and truly miserable suffering?" he countered. "For in the case of the patients at this institution, they are one and the same."

She simply shook her head, even more at a loss. If Margarethe were here, Hannah was sure she would have a quick answer, a ready argument. She would be able to see the deep and terrible flaw in the doctor's sorrowful words; as it was, Hannah could sense it, like some shadowy thing brushing her fingertips yet still out of reach, and she was not sure she wanted to make a grab for it.

"They do no harm..." she began after a moment, far too feebly.

"They are in pain, Nurse Stern."

Hannah thought of Inger, with her velvety eyes, of Anni, so resigned in her crib. "Not all of them—"

"If they are not in pain," he cut across her, his tone kindly but matter-of-fact, "then they are virtually insensate, unable to walk, talk, or even think. Unable to function as human beings, as God made us to be."

"How can you know?" Hannah protested. "How can you possibly know how much goes on in their minds?"

The smile he gave her was that familiar mix of pity and scorn. "I am a neurologist, Nurse Stern."

"Even so—"

He leaned forward, the gleam of an evangelist in his eyes. "What exactly are you protesting against, Nurse Stern? The tender, compassionate easing of another human being's suffering?"

Hannah thought of the bodies tossed in the back of one of

those wretched carts, the disdain with which Nurse Scholz had gazed down at Emil, as if he were nothing, *less* than nothing. "That's not how it is," she said. Again, she realized how woefully uncertain she sounded. She was practically begging him to convince her—why? Why did she have to be so *weak*?

"Isn't it? You should see Nurse Katschenka, when she administers a dose of the medicine we must give. How tenderly she holds a child as they sip their juice! How sweetly she strokes their hair and lays them back on their pillow, whispering endearments all the while, until they fall asleep, and are finally, thankfully, rescued from this body of unimaginable suffering. Why, were you to see it, Nurse Stern, you would say it was far from cruel." He leaned forward a little more, so he was half over his desk, his eyes blazing with fervent certainty, while Hannah could only gaze at him mutely. "I daresay," he pronounced, "you would think it the kindest act imaginable. A noble sacrifice, to be willing to do such a thing, to see it to its sorrowful end. It is not for the faint-hearted, Nurse Stern. Not at all."

"And what of their parents?" Hannah asked after a moment. Her mind was seething with insidious and newfound doubts, and she wished she hadn't come.

But what if you came for exactly this? that sly voice inside her insisted. *Not to make some grand protest, oh no, but to be convinced? To have your conscience salved, because then you can rest more easily? It is only too bad that you are resisting the process.*

"What of their parents?" Jekelius replied with a dismissive wave of his hand. "I have already told you about them. They pretend dismay and wring their hands and are only too glad to be rid of the burden that we take on willingly, difficult as it can be to bear. And it *is* difficult—"

"Only to dispose of it as soon as you can!" The words bubbled indignantly from Hannah's lips, but Jekelius did not look annoyed by her outrageous presumption.

He gave her a tolerant smile, the look of a parent to a tantruming child, or perhaps one who still believed in fairy tales. "Do you imagine, Nurse Stern, that I make any decision here lightly?" he asked. "In fact, they are not even my decisions to make. It is a specialist committee in Berlin, a committee with far more experience and knowledge than you or even I possess, that decides which children have reached the lamentable point that forces us to take the action that we do."

Just as Margarethe had suspected. "A committee that hasn't even seen the children in question?" she asked, hardly able to credit her daring.

"They are completely informed by my reports." He spread his hands with a rueful twist of his lips. "There is, of course, another dimension to the decision-making which must be considered, and that is a financial one. As disagreeable as it can be to think about such things, it is, alas, the reality. The care of children such as these is, understandably, very expensive—"

"Is it?" Hannah interjected, bitterly. She thought of the shriveled apples for Christmas, the raggedy nightshirts all the children wore. Even the meals the staff were provided were meager, their accommodation poor.

"It is," Jekelius stated firmly. "There are hundreds of children here requiring specialized care. It does not come cheaply, I assure you."

"So the children are killed simply to save money?" she demanded in ringing tones. She had forgotten her fear; Dr. Jekelius's tone of utter reason had ignited a new fury, and a deeper courage, inside her.

"How very reductionist of you." He gave her another smile, this one edged with irritation. He had, Hannah realized, expected to win her over by now, by both his charm and his logic. And she wouldn't let herself be swayed, even though part of her was still tempted.

"Is it not that simple then, *Herr Doktor*?" she challenged.

Jekelius paused, his gaze distant before he swung around to face her, his expression now cool and firm. "Every able-bodied man who serves here as an orderly or a nurse is not on the Front, defending our country. Every Reichsmark spent sustaining the life of a child in this institution is one not spent on a healthy child just as, if not more, deserving of food, clothing, education. One who will grow up to learn, love, marry, work, unlike *any* of the children here." He spread his hands, a cold glint in his eyes now. "There is only so much money to go around, Nurse Stern, and we are a country at war. Difficult decisions must be made every day."

Hannah was silent, knowing for her own sake, and perhaps even Willi's, she should drop the whole subject. Jekelius was not going to change his mind. The idea that her protest would somehow convince him to drop an entire program directed by Berlin was horribly laughable. But had she come here expecting that, or simply needing to make a stand?

In any case, Jekelius had humored her insubordination far more than she had ever imagined he would; most doctors would have shouted her down at her very first protest. She deserved to be disciplined, even dismissed. Perhaps it was only her connection to Georg that had the doctor humoring her, but she sensed he would do so no longer.

"What of Inger?" she asked quietly, daring to push one last time.

"Inger," Jekelius repeated, and she could not tell if he knew exactly whom she was talking about, or he had no idea at all. She did not know which would be worse.

"She had a tumor on her shoulder. There was nothing else wrong with her. She was a happy child—"

"Oh, my dear." Now the doctor's voice was rich with something almost like amusement, although his expression remained serious. "She had tuberous sclerosis. Her condition was too poor to attempt a lumbar puncture or cranial X-ray, but there was little doubt, very little doubt indeed, that there were tumors throughout her whole body, including the brain. Since diagnosis, her condition had only deteriorated, and the single possible conclusion to draw was that her intellectual ability was severely impaired, along with her mobility. She was likely to die, slowly and painfully, of bronchopneumonia or renal failure." His chin lifted as he gave her an appraising look. "Her death, Nurse Stern, was a mercy."

"But..." Hannah found she couldn't go on. Would Inger have died in such a way? She was safe now, although how or where, she had no idea. And what of Anni, trapped and enraged in her crib? Could there have been any better life for her, away from this place? Yet who would have cared for her? Like Dr. Jekelius had said, she hadn't been able to talk, or walk, to learn, maybe even to love...

And yet she smiled when she looked at me, sometimes.

Hannah sat back in her chair, her gaze on her lap. That fury she'd felt so hard and fast was already fading away, replaced by a weary confusion. She felt as if she didn't know anything anymore. The bodies in the carts, Jekelius's smooth words... which was the truth? Or was it somewhere in between?

"You see?" he said, and his voice wound its way around her like a vine. "We are not monsters here, Nurse Stern."

"No," Hannah said slowly, the word drawn from her as if she'd been asleep and was just waking up, or perhaps it was the other way round. She felt, quite suddenly and overwhelmingly, exhausted, filled with a despair deeper than any she'd known before. "No, I see that now."

A silence stretched between them, settled there. It felt almost like relief, but Hannah knew it was defeat. *I understand now*, she told herself, and the worst part was, she knew she did. She could not change Jekelius's mind. She could not change what happened here. She could only learn to live with it somehow—and save Willi.

"Naturally, due to the extremely sensitive nature of our discussion, I must demand for your complete silence on this matter," Jekelius said after a moment, while Hannah simply sat there, staring at her lap. "These are official matters, Nurse Stern, and if you were to speak on them, on government policy... well, the matter then would be quite out of my hands."

"So you have said before," she replied tonelessly.

"Indeed, but our rather frank discussion requires something a bit more official. There is a document you must sign, for the good of the Reich." She heard him opening a drawer, and she looked up to see him placing an official-looking piece of paper on the desk. Silently, he handed her a pen and she took it with nerveless fingers.

Why, she wondered, must she sign such a thing if the killings were a mercy, as Jekelius claimed? But she did not ask the question. She signed her name.

Back in her room, Hannah moved about slowly, numbly, feeling as if she were deaf and blind, the world an unfamiliar place that she could not make any sense of. Eventually—she did not know after how long—she sank onto her bed and simply stared into space as the minutes ticked past.

The sun was starting to set, the light leached from the sky, when someone rapped on her door and then Margarethe came into the room, her footsteps light and quick. "It's time for supper... what's wrong with you?"

"I don't know," Hannah said slowly.

Margarethe placed her hands on her hips. "Well, then get going before the soup cools. It's even worse when it's cold. Practically inedible."

Hannah turned her head to blink up at her. "I spoke to Dr. Jekelius."

"Oh?" Margarethe was immediately alert. "About what?"

"About the children. The killings."

"You didn't!" Hannah couldn't tell if she were irritated or impressed; perhaps both. "Well, well. What did he say?"

"He said they were a mercy." She suddenly startled to wakefulness, leaning forward, her arms wrapped around herself as she gazed up at Margarethe, pleading for her to understand, to accept. "They are, aren't they, at least in a way? Couldn't they be? Little Anni... what a miserable life she led! She couldn't talk or walk, stuck in her crib, there was no hope for her at all..."

"Oh, so she should be killed, then?" Margarethe retorted, her voice sharp with sarcasm. "Overdosed with barbiturates and then left to waste away, because she's not quite up to par? Tell that to one of our veterans, why don't you? One in a wheelchair, or with half of his face melted off from mustard gas. He might think a little differently about it."

"But Anni and the others... they couldn't think the way a veteran can," Hannah persisted, a desperate, stubborn note entering her voice. "Who knows how little goes on in their minds? They're not like us, Margarethe—"

"Or how *much* goes on in their minds," Margarethe returned with an impatient shake of her head. "They're *exactly* like us, Hannah, and you know it, too. I know you do, but I understand why you might try to believe otherwise. You can bear it that way, can't you?"

"But if they have no hope of doing anything but lying in a crib?" Hannah continued, her voice rising on something close to a sob, "Their whole lives, miserable and alone, without any hope of any sort of real life—"

"What does it matter, Hannah?" Margarethe cut across her. "Either a human being is worthy of life, or they aren't. You cannot make a list of conditions, tick them off one by one, because then who gets to decide? Little Peter's life is worth something, but Anni's isn't. Is that how it is—and why? Because

Peter can talk? Or maybe because he can *read*." Her voice twisted along with her lips as she stared at her knowingly. "Because if he couldn't read, if he can't make something useful of his life, then, well, what's the point? It's time to take out the Luminal. Really, it's a *mercy*. If you can't read a book or walk across a room, why bother living? And if you don't agree, well, never mind, because someone else will decide for you, and since they get to make that list, who knows who will be on it? Maybe you will be, one day. Maybe we will all be."

As her voice rang out, Hannah put her hands up to her face. "Don't," she whispered, her voice catching on a sob. "Willi might not be able to read, but he *feels*..."

"They *all* feel," Margarethe cut across her. "And if you think they don't, you're lying to yourself. And if you believe Jekelius's lies, it's because you want to. I know how that goes."

Hannah closed her eyes. She'd been numb in Jekelius's office, defeated by both shock and despair, willing to sign her name because she saw no way out. Now she was startled to an awful, jarring wakefulness; she felt as if she were naked and raw, every nerve exposed, every sense twanging. That baby boy at Heim Hochland... he'd never even had a *chance*. And she'd had something to do with that, even if she hadn't known. She'd filled out the form, she'd been ignorant and yet complicit... "What can I do?" she whispered. "I can't do anything..."

"You can," Margarethe returned with force. "We can't save all the children selected for further treatment, because we don't know who they are. And we don't know because we don't have the list, so we just have to listen and wait and hope. But if we had the list..."

Hannah opened her eyes. "What list?"

"The list from Berlin, with the children on it who are going to be killed," Margarethe replied. "I know that's how it happens. Jekelius has said enough, so has Nurse Gruber, for that matter.

She can't keep her mouth shut. She loves knowing all the secrets too much, loves rubbing our faces in it."

Hannah thought about how the head nurse had joked about Am Spiegelgrund being *the end station*, Jekelius's talk of the committee in Berlin. "How could I do anything about that list?" she asked.

"Jekelius spoke with you this very afternoon. I've never said two words to the man, lowly nurse that I am. He won't even look at me. But you... he listens to you, perhaps because of your brother. You could get into his office, find the list—"

"Get into his office!" Hannah stared at her, aghast. "And go through his drawers while he smiles on? Margarethe, don't be stupid—"

"I'm not being stupid," Margarethe returned with heat. "As if I'd suggest such a thing! No, you go when he isn't there, of course. Sneak in and have a look around, find that list. He's too arrogant to lock his files up. I know his type, he likes leaving things around, just because he can. I think he even likes people knowing, because he thinks they can't do anything about it. He probably enjoyed telling you today. No doubt it gave him a smug feeling of power."

Hannah knew the truth of it was in her face and Margarethe shook her head.

"You could do it, Hannah. No one will look twice at you knocking on his door, while they'd demand to know why I was even in the administration pavilion at all! You might not think you have special status, but you do. It's just a matter of whether you're willing to use it or not."

"I... I couldn't," Hannah whispered. "Margarethe, if I was caught..."

"You'd be sent to a work camp, yes, I know. You think I haven't thought about that before?" Margarethe took a step toward her, everything about her blazing. She was beautifully incandescent, on fire with her fury and certainty, and she made Hannah feel both ashamed and afraid. "That first time, when I took a little boy named Josef in my arms, I ran out into the corridor with him, right out into the night. I didn't think about what I was doing. I just knew I had to save him." She paused. "Karl saw me then."

"Karl? He helps?" Hannah heard the surprise in her voice along with the eagerness. If Karl helped...

"Oh, he helps," Margarethe replied, a bitter, sarcastic edge to her voice. "The only reason he's involved, is because he has to be." She wagged a finger at Hannah. "Don't think he's doing this out of the goodness of his heart, because he absolutely isn't."

Hannah blinked at her. "But—"

"But with Rosa, and Paul and Walter and Inger, it was different. Yes, there have only been five in total. Five children whose lives we have saved, and their names are written on my heart. For all the other times, I thought it through. I sought help. And we saved them, Hannah. We *saved* them. How many more could we save if you helped us? How many?"

Hannah closed her eyes. "I... I can't," she whispered. The words slipped from her in something close to a moan.

"You won't."

Hannah didn't reply, her eyes still closed, as if she could block out the whole world.

"Tell me," Margarethe asked in a different, more diffident voice, "do you believe in heaven?"

Hannah opened her eyes. "*Heaven?*"

"Yes, heaven. A life after this one. A place where there is no sorrow or pain, where God wipes away every tear from our eyes." The smile she gave her was gentle, touched with sadness. "Do you believe in that, Hannah?"

Hannah shook her head, confused. "I... I don't... I haven't thought..."

Margarethe nodded in resigned acceptance. "Well, then, I understand your reservations. If this life is the only hope you have, then naturally you cling to it. But what a poor hope it is." She met her bewildered gaze not with the expected censure, but with a deep compassion.

"I've never asked for much," Hannah whispered.

"But what you have, you want to keep. Yes, I understand." Margarethe let out a weary gust of a sigh as she came to sit next to her on the bed and put her arm around her, drawing her against her side, so if she chose, Hannah could lean her head against her shoulder. "If our hope is only for this life, what hope is it?" she asked quietly. "If we stay silent and meek so we can say on our deathbed that we planted a few flowers, we made someone smile... is that really all there is?" She turned to Hannah, the look in her eyes both pleading and defiant. "If there is no after, what is the point to anything?"

"I..." Hannah shook her head. She had not thought of such things before, at least not much; if she believed in God, it was as some distant deity who took little interest in the events of this earth, because, considering all of them in their horror, what other god could there possibly be? And yet... she envied Margarethe's quiet certainty. "Are these children in heaven?" she asked quietly.

"Yes," Margarethe replied fiercely. "Yes, such innocents as these? They are very near the throne room of heaven. Very near indeed." She paused, and then turned to face Hannah. "So will you help?" she asked after a moment, as if she already knew the answer.

"If I did such a thing..." Hannah said, feeling her way through the words, "Margarethe... if I risked it, if I were caught... what would happen to Willi?"

Margarethe met her gaze calmly. "I don't know."

The honest admission made Hannah shake her head, certain now. "Then I can't. For Willi's sake, Margarethe—"

"Oh, it's for Willi's sake, is it?" She sighed and shook her head, slipping her arm off Hannah's shoulders, making her miss her. "Never mind. We'll manage without you."

She rose from the bed and started toward the door without looking back. Hannah felt as if she'd not just disappointed, but failed her. And failed herself, utterly. And yet, for Willi...

For *Willi*, she would do almost anything. For Willi, she would risk her own life. She would, Hannah thought suddenly, get him out of this hellish place. If Margarethe could rescue Inger, she could save Willi. Somehow...

And then realization crystallized inside her, with a hard, glittering certainty. She would go to Berlin. She would tell Georg everything, no matter what it cost her—discipline, arrest, even death, for spilling the secrets of Am Spiegelgrund. And then he'd come and get Willi, and they could leave this dreadful place and never look back.

CHAPTER 17

BERLIN, MARCH 1941

It had taken over fourteen hours to get to Berlin from Vienna, thanks to delays, missed connections, and endless waits as trains bursting with troops trundled past. For most of the long journey, Hannah had simply stared out the window, watching wintry fields flash by, letting her mind go blessedly blank.

It had taken nearly a month for her to be granted the necessary three days' leave to travel back to Berlin. Part of her had been surprised it had been granted at all, but when she'd seen Dr. Jekelius in passing, he'd given her one of his liquid looks full of sympathy and said, "I hope you enjoy your visit with your half-brother, Nurse Stern. He will be eager to hear from you, I am sure." The words had been kind enough, but the import he weighed them with had chilled her. Did he know what she intended, to tell Georg everything? Did it even matter?

She trusted that her half-brother's position would keep Willi safe in her brief absence, and she'd entreated both Margarethe and Karl to keep an eye on him while she was gone. Karl had agreed readily enough, although with some bemusement.

"You really care about that kid," he'd remarked with a shake of his head, as if he couldn't quite understand it.

Margarethe had merely nodded tersely; Hannah knew she remained a disappointment to her, choosing Willi over all the other children as she had done, and yet how could she have done anything else? Still, the closeness she realized she'd come to depend on had cooled into something merely polite. Even so, she trusted Margarethe to watch out for Willi.

As the train headed north, Hannah was half-hoping she might never see the imposing gates of Am Steinhof again. She imagined Georg galvanized into action, rushing to Vienna immediately to rescue his son. She'd never have to see those brick pavilions lined up in rows like blank-faced soldiers, never see one of those terrible, covered carts. She would never see Margarethe, or Karl. She felt a twinge of regret for Karl, nothing more, but an ocean of grief for Margarethe. She was the closest friend Hannah had ever had, even if she'd disappointed her so grievously. If she didn't return to Am Steinhof, Hannah vowed, she would write to Margarethe, at least, explain why she had left. Perhaps, in time, her friend would come to understand.

The longer Hannah considered the matter, the more likely it seemed she *wouldn't* have to go back, for surely Georg would not let her, once he knew what happened at that forsaken place. He would go himself, at once, to rescue Willi, and bring him back to Berlin, and all would be well. She even imagined, in a hazy sort of way, that Georg might employ her as Willi's nurse. He wouldn't have to tell his wife they were related; she wouldn't mind pretending they weren't, as long as she could stay with Willi. A warm house, enough food, and Willi to care for were all she needed.

These happy, hazy dreams gained clarity, their edges honed to a determined sharpness, as she alighted from the train at Grunewald Bahnhof and then walked, through a chilly dusk along Grunewald's parkland, winter having not lost much of its grip on the frost-tipped ground, the leafless trees, to Georg's gracious home on Douglasstrasse.

She had written to tell him when she would be arriving, and had had a brief reply in return, yet as she knocked on the door, she realized she was not entirely sure of her welcome.

The sight of a scowling Elfriede turned back the clock to when she'd first been summoned there and made her heart sink to her toes.

"*Guten abend.* I'm here for Major Strasser."

"Hannah."

Georg stood behind Elfriede, his expression weary and resigned. He didn't look well, Hannah thought, with a ripple of shock; his once jowly face was slack and he needed a shave, his clothes disheveled.

"You may go, Elfriede."

With a dark look for Hannah, the maid disappeared, down the hallway to the kitchen in the back of the house. Georg gestured to her to come in.

"You were expecting me?" she asked as she stepped across the threshold, for the sight of him looking so much less than his usual immaculate form had surprised her, making her wonder if he'd forgotten her visit.

"Yes, yes, of course. You must stay with us while you are here. I have arranged for Elfriede to make up a room."

"Stay with you..." Hannah had not been expecting that, although she was grateful for the invitation, as she had not been sure whether she would have to beg a bed with Hilde, or try to stay in one of the more modest hotels in the city. Her purse would have stretched to a night or two, but only just. "That is very kind, but... what about your wife?"

Georg stared at her for a moment, nonplussed, seeming a little dazed. "What about her?"

Hannah kept his gaze as she answered, "I was under the impression she was not aware of my existence."

"She knew of you," he replied after a pause, "but it is true she would not welcome you under our roof. That is of little concern to me, however, as we are now leading almost completely separate lives."

"Oh." She paused, absorbing this news. "I'm sorry." She wondered what had changed since she'd been here in October, a mere four months ago, even if it felt an absolute age. A lifetime. *Too many lifetimes.*

Georg turned toward his study. "Come and get warm."

The room was just as cozy as Hannah remembered, a fire crackling in the grate, the velvet curtains drawn against the night. She sank into one of the chairs by the fire and closed her eyes, suddenly so very grateful that she was here, that she was safe. But now she had to tell him the truth about Am Spiegelgrund, about Willi, and she had no idea how even to begin. She had intended to be completely honest, sparing Georg nothing and forcing him to act, but as she watched him move to the side table and pour himself a generous measure of schnapps, she realized afresh just how dangerous doing such a thing could be.

She had, after all, signed a paper, an official-looking document that would very much be both binding and incriminating. She'd been in too much of a despairing daze to pay attention to its severe language at the time, but it had been clear—very clear —that to speak of the things covered by that document, and to someone in the Abwehr no less, would constitute a crime, perhaps even treason. And if she thought she was safe from prosecution at her brother's house, well, she should really know better than that; no one was safe in this country, not the Jews, not the gypsies, not even the *Führer*'s closest friends, and certainly not the children of Am Spiegelgrund. Suspicion was everywhere, like a dark miasma they all breathed in, poisoning their minds, polluting their lives. The only difference between here and Vienna was that it was a shorter distance to Prinz-Albrecht-Strasse.

"You are well?" she asked eventually when her half-brother did not seem inclined to speak. He was standing with his back to her as he raised his glass to his lips and drained half of the spirit in one long swallow.

"As well as can be expected," he replied. He moved to his desk and sank into the chair behind it, giving every indication that he was a man exhausted and almost defeated by life. As he lifted his head to meet her gaze, she saw such sober knowledge in his hazel eyes that she had a sudden, jolting suspicion that she would not have to tell him anything, because he already knew it all. But, no. That had to be impossible. He would not have sent his only son there if he had known, surely.

"You haven't asked about Willi," she said.

"Your letters have been so wonderfully informative." He placed his glass on his desk, his gaze now on the glinting, amber liquid. "I must thank you, Hannah, most sincerely and deeply, for your care of my son. You cannot begin to know how much it means to me."

"Georg..." She hesitated, longing to tell him the truth and yet holding back, yet again, out of fear. That bravado she'd felt a month ago now, when she'd decided she would tell Georg everything, was swiftly slipping away in the cold clarity of this moment. She didn't actually *know* what his response would be, or how fervent his devotion to the regime. What if he reported her? She thought of that one, brief letter he'd sent. *I regret to write I will not be able to visit in the foreseeable future.* Why should she not take the terse sentiment of that letter at face value?

He lifted his head from the inspection of his glass to look at her once more, his gaze already bleary from the drink. "Yes, Hannah?"

"I am concerned for Willi." She took a quick breath and then continued carefully, "The hospital... Am Spiegelgrund... I don't think you can be aware of the conditions there. The... the policies."

Georg fumbled for his glass and then drained it. "I am perfectly aware of both the conditions and the policies," he informed her tonelessly. "And I always have been. Why do you think I sent you with him?"

"But..." She licked her lips, her mind frozen with shock at such a blatant admission. "Why did you send him there at all, then?"

"I had no choice." He set his glass back on the desk as he gave her a weary, cynical smile. "I am a loyal servant of the Reich, after all."

"I do not think you realize just how serious it is." She leaned forward, trying to communicate the force of her feeling through her strained gaze, the throb of her voice. "It is... not a normal asylum, with the usual unfortunate deprivations. It is—"

"I know, Hannah." He cut her off quietly as he returned her urgent gaze with a levelness that shook her. "I know."

Hannah sat back in her chair, her mouth agape for a few seconds. "You *know*?"

He nodded.

"But then you must realize Willi could... could be in danger."

"I do not think," Georg stated slowly, "that they will go that far. Not when they know whose son he is, and when you are there, watching him."

"That may be, but... it is still a terrible place, Georg!" She leaned forward again, her hands clenching. "The food, the clothing, the lack of care. Most of the staff are indifferent, but some are cruel, truly cruel, sadists even, delighting in their abuse and neglect. They took all of Willi's belongings, he lies in bed half out of his mind with sedatives—there is nothing good for him there, nothing!"

Georg smiled faintly. "You've come to care for him, then."

"Yes." The word burst out of her, deflating her as she sagged back in her chair. "Yes, I have," she said quietly, "even though I didn't expect to. I even didn't want to, not at the beginning. But I have. Very much."

Georg nodded slowly, his chin bobbing to his chest. He was only fifty, but he now looked old. "I understand."

"You have to save him," she stated with quiet force. "He could die in that place. If... if not one way, then another. The neglect, the abuse—"

"Hannah, I can't."

For a second, she could only stare; her half-brother had once again shocked her. She had not expected such a flat refusal; she knew then just how much she'd let herself believe that Georg would charge to the rescue, even when every indication had been that he would—or could—not. The fact that he'd been willing to send Willi in the first place, his indifferent letter, Dr. Jekelius's smug knowledge. Of course Georg was never going to save the day. Of course he wouldn't save Willi.

"Why can't you?" she whispered. "Children can be withdrawn, you know." A few children had left the asylum since she'd begun there, but only a very precious few. "They're allowed visitors sometimes, and if the parents can prove they have a stable home, an income, they may be granted permission to take them out..." She trailed away because Georg was shaking his head. "Why not?" she demanded, her voice rising in agitation. "He's your *son*—"

"I know that!" Georg rose from his desk in one abrupt movement, and the anger flushing his face made Hannah press back against her chair. He prowled toward the window, driving one hand through his hair so a dark lock of it fell against his forehead. "Do you think I don't know that?" he asked, his back to her, one hand braced against the window frame. "That I don't live with the knowledge of what I've done every day? But I had no choice, Hannah. I tell you, I had no *choice*."

"But you're a major in the Abwehr," she insisted, her voice low. "Surely you could have arranged something." She'd heard the gossip, how Goering had smuggled some Jewish friends out of the country; why, Goebbels had a limp! *One rule for them, another for us,* Hilde might say with a shake of her head, more pragmatic than bitter, but surely then Georg could bend the rules? Break them, even?

"Which is why I have had to show my loyalty and devotion," Georg replied. "Hitler has always had his suspicions about those in the Abwehr, and in particular my superior, Admiral Canaris. The SS have resented the military intelligence, the power and knowledge we have, and they make sure we're closely monitored. My house is undoubtedly watched, as well as all my movements. I wouldn't be surprised if one of my servants was an informer." He smiled humorlessly. "Elfriede, perhaps. We should lower our voices."

A tremor of terror shuddered through Hannah, but Georg seemed indifferent to the potential danger he was in, or perhaps just used to it.

"I'm sure it was Himmler who first reported Willi to the Office of Hereditary Diseases," he continued, his voice hardening. "And I know who told Himmler." He paused, his throat working, before he continued, "He's always had such an obsession with racial purity and perfection." He shook his head, the disgust and pain audible in his lowered voice.

"I know that full well, from working in a *Lebensborn* home," Hannah replied quietly. "He orchestrated the whole, despicable program." She hesitated as her mind began to make new connections. "Why *did* you find me a position there?"

"It was a comfortable place, was it not?" He turned around. "You had no complaints."

"That is beside the point."

"I wanted to establish your credentials," Georg admitted. "The nurses at the *Lebensborn* homes have tended toward the fanatical. No one would question your devotion if you worked there, which would make it easier if and when the time came that I needed you elsewhere."

"And you thought you would?"

"It became clear soon enough what kind of society Hitler wanted to build," Georg replied, his voice low. "And where Willi would—or wouldn't—fit into it. I might have admired the man at the start, it is true, but I soon came to my senses."

His senses? Hannah was shaken by her brother's flatly given statements; they were both treason and truth. "If you think my position will keep Willi safe," she told him quietly, "I am afraid you might be mistaken."

"Your position and mine." He moved to the chair opposite her and met her gaze directly. "Do you think Willi is in danger?"

"Every child in that godforsaken place is in danger," Hannah replied, her voice cracking. "Georg, you *must* rescue him."

"I told you, I can't." His voice was flat, his tone final. "If I take him out of there, it will be known immediately. I am watched, Hannah, all the time I am watched! Himmler, even Hitler himself, will question my loyalty—"

"So to save your own skin," she cut across him, not bothering to hide the scorn she felt, "you will sacrifice your son's."

"I would gladly die for Willi," Georg returned, his voice a low throb of heartfelt dignity. "Gladly, this very moment, if it would save him. But it won't, Hannah. If I brought him back here, he would not be safe. They would hear of it and they would take him from me, simply because they could. As it is, they hold him over my head, the child I save only by staying the course and doing as I am told. Don't you see? They won't touch him as long as they believe I am loyal."

The meaning of his words reverberated through her. "But..." She dropped her voice to a whisper, conscious of

Elfriede lurking somewhere in the house, able to eavesdrop. "*Aren't* you loyal?"

Georg did not answer for a long moment, and he did not meet her gaze. Hannah waited, a shudder of horror rippling through her, that she'd asked the question at all. If anyone heard this conversation, even a few seconds of it... it would not be Willi who needed saving.

"We are not going to win this war," Georg stated, so quietly that Hannah strained to hear him, and even then, when she realized what he had said, she struggled to believe it.

"But... but there have been so many victories," she whispered. The newspapers were always trumpeting the successes of the Wehrmacht and Luftwaffe—why, only last week Buckingham Palace itself had been bombed, and there had been decisive victories against the British in North Africa. Poland, Denmark, Norway, France... they'd all fallen. No one could resist the might of the Wehrmacht. No one.

Georg was still staring off into the distance, his expression set. "Nevertheless."

"Why do you say such a thing?" she demanded, keeping her voice hushed. "What is it that you know?"

Resolutely, he shook his head. "I cannot speak of what I know, and in any case, it won't become apparent for some time, perhaps years. Indeed, Germany is sure to have many more victories—in North Africa, in Yugoslavia, in Greece. We will celebrate our victories, but we will not win the war." He was silent for a long moment and then he looked up at her, his expression so bleak, Hannah had to bite her lip to keep from making some small sound of fear. "And I am afraid that that is something the *Führer* will never accept. He will die trying for total victory, and he will take everyone down with him, right down to the very grave."

He averted his gaze, his expression shuttered, and for several long moments they were both silent, the only sound the settling of embers in the grate, the tick of the clock on the mantle.

She had not, Hannah realized, reflected very much about whether Germany would win or lose the war; she had only thought about it finally being over. But in just a few devastating words, her brother had painted such a grim picture of the future that everything in her resisted thinking of it as a reality—the inevitability of defeat, the country nothing but rubble and ashes, perhaps even taken over by a regime worse than the one they knew, a never-ending prospect of ruin and despair.

"You cannot be sure," she finally said. "No matter what it is that you now know."

He turned back to face her, lifting an eyebrow in weary cynicism. "And do you think it would be better for us, if Germany wins this war? Better for Willi? *Mein Gott*, Hannah, it will be hell. *Hell.*"

Shaken, Hannah looked away. To live in a country always ruled by fear, for Willi never to be safe. For *no one* to be safe. There was no way out, she thought hopelessly. There was no way forward. No wonder her brother looked so haggard and bleak.

"You are speaking treason," she stated after a moment.

Georg let out a tired laugh. "We have both spoken treason tonight, as you very well know." He leaned forward, dropping his voice to barely a whisper. "And I am *thinking* treason every moment of every day. I am living and breathing it, Hannah, so it seeps out my pores, so it *consumes* me. If there is any way I could..." He let the words trail off, while Hannah stared at him in dawning, horrified realization.

"*Georg...*"

"Let us not speak of it anymore." He spoke tersely, rising abruptly from his chair as he passed a hand over his face. Hannah saw his fingers tremble. "Have you eaten?" he asked. "I will ask Elfriede to prepare you something. Some soup, perhaps, and bread. I think there is some cold meat."

"And what of Willi?" Hannah returned. Her thoughts were jumbled, seething. Treason, defeat, *death*. Georg had spoken as if they were all distinct possibilities, certainties. *Right down to the grave.*

"You must return to Vienna, to Am Steinhof," he told her, straightening the cuffs of his smoking jacket. "You must continue caring for Willi, encouraging him, loving him. God willing, that will be enough to see him safe."

"But for how long?" She thought of the way he had spoken. "The war could go on for *years*—"

"Indeed, it most certainly will."

Hannah gave a vehement shake of her head. "Every day in that place is a living death for him, Georg. A waking nightmare. I try my best, but I cannot—"

He gave her a tight, bleak smile as he held up one hand to forestall any further protests. "Then that is all I ask."

CHAPTER 18

That night, Hannah slept deeply, despite her troubled and jumbled thoughts. The soft bed, the warm room and peaceful quiet all conspired to have her sink into a thankfully dreamless sleep, and then wake more refreshed than she'd expected, although her conversation with Georg slammed through her mind the moment she opened her eyes.

We are not going to win this war.

He'd been so quietly, bleakly certain—why? From everything Hannah saw and read, Germany was a nation brimming with victory. You only had to listen to a few minutes of one of the ranting radio programs listing all the ways in which the Fatherland was triumphant to be sure of that. Of course, Hannah knew neither the radios nor the newspapers told the whole, unvarnished truth; most people received those ringing pronouncements with rolled eyes, even if they didn't dare say anything against them.

But to *lose* the war? What would that even mean? Hannah tried to imagine it—Hitler toppled, all the swastika flags torn down, the country transformed and overrun by—whom? The

British? The Soviets? Faceless soldiers waving guns, even more violence...

And yet... Hannah stared at the sliver of morning's blue sky visible through the crack between the curtains. Perhaps it would provide a chance for children like Willi to live without fear. For *everyone* to live without fear. Or, she acknowledged as she turned her head away from the sunlight, it could be even worse.

Either way, it was impossible to imagine now. Germany had just marched into Greece and made a pact with Bulgaria. No one, absolutely no one at all, was standing in their way. America, it was said, didn't want to get involved in a European war. Britain was already on its knees. How could Germany possibly be defeated?

The thought should have brought some relief, but it didn't, only more disquiet. The future loomed in front of her, more uncertain and unknowable than ever.

Trying to banish such futile worries from her mind, Hannah dressed and did her hair, washed her face and brushed her teeth.

As she came down the stairs, Elfriede met her at the bottom.

"You'll eat in the kitchen," she told her, the smugness in her voice betraying the satisfaction she felt at having Hannah put in her place. She may have been given a guest bedroom, but she was not quite a guest. Not at all, perhaps. "And next time you should use the back stairs," Elfriede added over her shoulder as she headed down the hallway, back to the kitchen.

Hannah did not bother to reply, keeping her head held high as she went back to the kitchen, where the cook, Marta, a comfortably plump woman with an easy manner, set a cup of coffee and a plate of bread, cheese and sliced sausage in front of her. Thanks, no doubt, to Georg's position, as well as the Wehrmacht's many victories, the portion was generous. She hadn't even had to hand over her coupon cards.

"So," Marta said as she poured herself a coffee, then leaned against the stove and subjected Hannah to a long, speculative look, "you're the Major's sister."

"Half-sister," Elfriede put in, pointedly.

"It seems there are no secrets here," Hannah remarked before setting to her breakfast.

"Oh no, no secrets," Marta replied comfortably. "Not down here, leastways. We've known about you for ages."

Hannah swallowed a lump of bread and cheese, curious to know more, even though, under Elfriede's beady stare, she was hesitant to ask questions. "Oh?" she finally said neutrally, and Marta nodded with cheerful conviction.

"Oh, yes. The Major and his lovely wife had quite the set-to about you, didn't they, Elfriede?"

Elfriede just shrugged, and Hannah merely raised her eyebrows, sensing Marta needed little encouragement to keep talking.

"He told her he was putting you through nurses' training," she said. "She didn't like that much, I can tell you."

"That was eleven years ago now." Hannah had had no idea that Frau Strasser had known about her for that long, right from the beginning.

"Yes, about that, wasn't it?" Marta paused musingly. "It was back when they were in and out of hospitals, for the boy's sake. But, of course, you haven't been talked about all this time, have you? She won't have your name even mentioned."

"Or maybe she forgot," Elfriede chimed in waspishly. "It's not as if you're anyone important."

"Oh, she didn't forget, not for one minute." Marta ignored Elfriede's surly glare. "She's the kind who remembers everything, especially something like that."

Hannah kept her face neutral despite the chill she felt at hearing her half-brother's wife so described. "She must not like having me here, then," she remarked after a moment, taking a sip of her coffee.

"Why do you think you're in the kitchen?" Marta let out a laugh while Elfriede glowered. "Of course, the Major doesn't care what she thinks, not since..." She trailed off, her round, wrinkled face collapsing into sadness for a moment before she banished the emotion with a pragmatic shrug and sipped her coffee.

Hannah glanced between Marta, who still looked thought-ful, and Elfriede, who looked as if she could spit.

"Since...?" she prompted warily.

"Since he left," Elfriede stated derisively. "The idiot child."

"Elfriede," Marta protested in quiet reproof. "He was a good boy."

"He was an idiot."

"They argued over Willi?" Hannah asked, determined to ignore the maid's hostility.

Marta and Elfriede exchanged glances.

"You could say that," Marta replied, and then she hefted herself from her position by the stove to go to the sink, her back to Hannah as she started on the dishes. Elfriede smirked.

Hannah turned back to her breakfast, determined not to ask any more questions, even though she was desperately curious. Had Frau Strasser not wanted Willi to go to Vienna? And yet, from what Marta had intimated, she was a hard woman. Had she been ashamed of Willi? The thought made everything in Hannah burn. For a mother to reject her child...! But hadn't she seen it, time and time again, at Am Spiegelgrund? Even if there were other parents, parents like Georg, who loved their children...

"She was the one who sent him away," Elfriede said, clearly bursting to tell the news. She smiled smugly as Marta gave her a quelling look over her shoulder.

"Enough, Elfriede."

"It's true."

Slowly, Hannah put down her coffee cup. "She did? But Major Strasser told me it was Himmler..."

"The mistress was the one who told Himmler," Marta said heavily. "After Willi had gone, they argued terribly about it."

"Broke a whole set of Meissen figurines," Elfriede chimed in with a grin. "They'd belonged to the Major's mother. The mistress threw them all onto the floor."

Hannah's stomach cramped at the thought, and she felt a sudden rush of pity for her half-brother. To be betrayed in such a way, and by his own wife. And for Willi, to be betrayed by his mother...! Suddenly she couldn't bear to see Elfriede's awful gloating, or even Marta's careless pity.

"Thank you for breakfast," she told the cook as she rose from the table.

Marta frowned. "You've barely eaten anything—"

"I'm sorry, I'm not hungry."

"Stuck-up piece, aren't you?" Elfriede remarked as she snatched a piece of sausage from Hannah's plate.

She walked blindly from the kitchen into the hall, her mind swamped with misery. Had Willi ever known his mother's love? Perhaps he *was* better off at Am Steinhof, even with its deprivations. If she could just keep him safe...

It was only when she reached the foot of the stairs that she remembered she was meant to use the servant stairs in the back. She turned around, stopping when she heard Georg's voice from the doorway of his study.

"*Guten morgen*, Hannah. I trust you slept well?"

"Yes, although I didn't expect to." She tried to smile, but it felt as if her lips couldn't work properly. *Poor Willi. Poor Georg.* "I'm sorry," she said, "I know I should have used the back stairs."

"What?" Georg's heavy brows came together in a scowl. "That is nonsense. No doubt my wife said something of it to

Elfriede. You may use whatever stairs you like, Hannah. You are a guest in this house."

Sudden tears pricked Hannah's eyes and she blinked them back. "I've always had the feeling you resented me," she said quietly. "And that you had helped me only with reluctance, out of duty." Admitting as much now felt a relief; she saw the guilt that flickered across Georg's face.

"It is true I might have acted so in the past," he admitted quietly, the words laced with regret. "Hannah, there is much I would like to tell you. Shall we walk?"

Hannah stared at him in surprise. "Walk?"

"It is chilly out, but there are signs of spring. Grunewald is lovely at any time of the year."

After a second's pause, she nodded. "I'll get my coat."

They walked along Koenigsallee into the park, the faraway glint of the Havel visible through the leafless trees, the tiny, bright heads of crocuses pushing up through the hard ground. The air held the chill of winter with only a hint of spring, the pale sunlight warm on Hannah's face, even though the brisk breeze made her burrow deeper into her coat.

"I'm sorry," Georg said, "for my wife's treatment of you."

"She has not treated me in any manner," Hannah replied, "as I have never even met her."

"And she would always have it so." He turned to gaze out at the park, his eyes narrowed against the glare of the sun. "She is very set in her ways."

"What is it that she has against me?" Hannah asked after a moment. The only sound was the crunch of their steps on the gravel path, a bird chirping from a branch somewhere above them. All around them, the park stretched in stark, wintry silence. "Is it the lowness of my birth?"

He let out a huff of something that was not quite laughter.

"It is rather the supposed *highness* of your parentage that upsets her. She cannot bear any reminder of my father."

"What!" This, Hannah had not expected.

Georg nodded soberly. "I don't know how much you know—"

"Only that he was a professor."

"Yes, a professor of economics. Our family is Prussian, with military service stretching back over a century. We are related to princes, if only distantly, and my father was a great proponent of the Kaiser. When he fell from power, my father was distraught—almost as distraught as he was at the loss of my brothers during the war."

"I knew they had died," Hannah replied quietly. "I'm sorry."

"Yes, Wilhelm at the Somme, Ernst at Passchendaele." He let out a short, tired sigh. "In any case, my father was no admirer of Hitler's, or his regime."

"But he died before Hitler even came to power—"

"Indeed, but my father was always outspoken in his politics. He wrote several articles about Hitler quite early on, decrying him as an ill-mannered upstart, and his brownshirts no more than jumped-up bully boys. He also humiliated him in public, when he refused to acknowledge him at a dinner party."

Hannah shook her head slowly. "I had no idea—"

"He died of a stroke some months after the economic crash. He'd lost many of his investments. All in all, a sad end to his life."

"I'm sorry," she said, meaning it. "All I remember of him are a few visits. They stopped when I was still a small child."

Georg nodded in understanding. "Yes, after the war, my mother gave him an ultimatum, not to visit yours. And things were challenging for us financially, as I'm sure they were for you."

Hannah managed a tight-lipped nod. As much as she was

gaining in sympathy for her half-brother, she suspected things had not been nearly as *challenging* for him and his family as they had been for her.

"I always knew about you," he remarked. "I was twenty-two when you were born, just before the war. I remember my parents arguing about it. My mother was not a woman to stand by and quietly bear such an insult." He glanced at her. "My father must have loved your mother very much."

"I don't know about that." Hannah's memories of her mother were of a sour-faced woman beaten down by a difficult life. She struggled to think of how her father must have been charmed, and yet he must have been, surely.

"In any case, I am sorry that I was not able to help earlier. With my father, it would have been impossible. He had determined to act as if you had never existed, and he would not change his mind. As it was, I never told my mother that I was in contact with you. She died a few years ago now, God rest her soul."

"But your wife knew," Hannah said, her gaze on the ground. Georg's plain speaking didn't hurt her, not exactly, and it certainly wasn't anything she hadn't already known or at least suspected, and yet... it *did* sting, to know how thoroughly her father had turned his back on her. From being petted and coddled and given expensive presents to... nothing. Less than nothing. She supposed he hadn't been that *charmed*, after all. "And it was because of your father she has disliked me all this time?"

"My wife is an ardent admirer of the *Führer*'s," Georg stated quietly, in the manner of a confession. "As was I, in the early days. I did not share my father's skepticism. I loved Germany, and ten or eleven years ago, I thought Hitler and his party might be the answer to its many problems. It is true that they ushered in an era of prosperity and national pride. After the humiliation of the war and the treaty of Versailles, both were a balm to my battered soul. It was only later that I realized they came at a cost, and what a cost it has been. I daresay we cannot even imagine the enormity of the price, not yet." He pressed his lips together as he shook his head.

It must have been his wife's political fervency that had compelled her to give up her own son. Hannah felt nothing but disgust for such a woman, and pity for her brother, for marrying her.

Georg stopped on the path, his hands dug into the pockets of his woolen greatcoat as he glanced at the parkland stretching in front of them, all the way to the river. "We should head back. I'm sure you're hungry, and this time you can eat at the dining-room table." He gave her a smile of genuine warmth. "How do champagne and oysters sound? Neither are rationed now, you know."

Hannah smiled back and they turned around, the wind now at their backs, as they headed back toward the house on Douglasstrasse in a silence that almost felt companionable.

The next morning, Hannah stood on the drive outside her half-brother's house, ready to depart for the station and Vienna. It had been such a brief visit, and yet her head was still spinning with all she'd learned, and her heart was both heavy and full. She knew she would need time to sort through this new knowledge, as well as her own feelings about it.

To her surprise, Georg embraced her tightly. "God go with you, Hannah." He stepped back, his hands on her shoulders as he gazed soberly into her face. "When you first went to Vienna, I made arrangements for there to be a bank account in your name, with Deutsche Bank," he told her in a low voice. "There is enough in it to see you comfortable for some years. When this war ends, if, for some reason, I am unable to care for Willi..." His voice wavered as Hannah stared at him in shock.

"*Georg...*"

"If," he continued more steadily, "then I ask you use the funds to care for him."

"Yes, of course," Hannah whispered numbly. "But—"

"Perhaps nothing will happen," he replied with a small smile that did not reach his shadowed eyes. "In any case, the money is yours. I should have given it to you far sooner, I know. Forgive me."

"There is nothing to forgive," Hannah whispered, both shaken and moved.

Georg nodded soberly and stepped back. "Take care of him, Hannah," he said, his voice choking a little. "As best as you can. For both our sakes. Please."

"I will, I promise." She swallowed past the lump forming in her throat. "I promise, Georg," she said again, and with tears blurring her eyes, she turned and started down the street, toward the station.

By the time Hannah arrived at Am Steinhof, it was nightfall, and the sight of those tall, forbidding gates, the clock tower pointing starkly to the sky, pavilion after pavilion stretching away in the darkness, made everything in her wilt. As eager as she was to see Willi, she did not want to be back in this terrible place.

A sense of claustrophobia made her skin crawl as she entered pavilion three, breathed in the scent of carbolic and infection, felt the horror of the institution press down on her so it hurt to breathe.

She put her things away in her room, glad for the quiet. She was not ready for Margarethe's knowing gaze or sharp questions, Helga's booming laugh or Nurse Schmidt's sly glances. She couldn't bear any of it, and so she hurried back down the stairs, avoiding even looking into the wards, and headed toward pavilion five, wanting to see Willi.

The pavilion was quieter than usual as an orderly, one she didn't recognize, unlocked the door for her, the children already getting ready for bed. Hannah hurried up the stairs, her heart tripping in anticipation as well as that ever-present anxiety.

She came into the ward and then stopped in the doorway, her shocked gaze trained on Willi's empty bed. The sheets had been stripped, the mattress bare—just as it had been for Inger, for Anni...

She whirled around, looking for a nurse, but the ward was empty, save for the orderly, a pimply-faced boy, barely older than the children, who scratched his ear as he gave her an uninterested look.

"Where is the boy who was in that bed?" she demanded, her voice shaking. "Where is Willi?"

The orderly shrugged. "I only started here yesterday. The bed was empty then."

The room began to sway and Hannah grabbed hold of the doorframe to steady herself as panic choked her, made it hard to speak, to breathe. "No..." she whispered. "*No.*"

"You're looking for Willi?" Nurse Scholz came onto the ward, grinning. "He was taken yesterday morning. For further treatment."

CHAPTER 19

It felt as if the world had fallen silent; as if Hannah had clapped her hands over her ears to blot out the noise, even though she hadn't moved. She stared at Nurse Scholz's leering face for a few stunned seconds before she shoved past her, hitting her hard in the shoulder, making the nurse cry out in pain and irritation, and Hannah's own shoulder throb. Hannah didn't care about any of it.

She ran down the steps, tripping in her haste and nearly falling, having to fling one hand out to the bannister to steady herself, before running the rest of the way and wrenching open the door. She sprinted out into the night, with no plan, no thought, except to get to Willi. She would get to him, and she would save him, it was as simple as that. It had to be.

She had walked by pavilion fifteen many times but had never dared to go inside, despite Margarethe's challenge; from the outside, it was just like any other, made of brick, bars on the windows, looking both stately and sinister. Hannah hammered on the door, heedless of the commotion she was making, unable to think clearly or even at all, save for Willi.

Willi...

"*Schwester!*" The nurse who answered her knocking had a smooth, round face, her glossy dark hair kept back by a kerchief. Her tone was reproving, although her expression remained placid. "Such noise. What is the matter?"

"There has been a mistake," Hannah rasped. "A terrible mistake. Willi Strasser was taken here from pavilion five for further treatment and he should not have been."

"I have heard of no such mistakes." Somehow the nurse's tone sounded both kindly and implacable. She had taken a step to stand in the doorway, preventing Hannah from entering.

Hannah glanced up at that smooth, placid face and saw something chilling in its utterly untroubled countenance. She squared her shoulders and straightened, keeping the woman's steady gaze.

"I assure you," she stated coldly, "there has been a mistake. A grievous error, in fact. The patient in question is the only child of Major Strasser of the Abwehr. If he were to find out that his son has been treated in error, he will be *very* displeased, and he will make his dissatisfaction known in the highest circles." She took a breath and repeated pointedly, "The *very* highest circles."

The nurse's gaze remained steady, but Hannah saw the flicker of hesitation in her dark eyes, and it was enough to embolden her to push past her, up the stairs.

"*Schwester*," the nurse called after her, in deep disapproval. "I must first speak to Dr. Jekelius about this matter, or at least Matron Bertha—"

"They are aware of the situation," Hannah snapped. She took the stairs two at a time, her heart thundering in her chest as she reached for the door to the ward, peering through the glass panes, searching for Willi.

She barely caught a glimpse of the children who lay supine and silent, many of their beds covered with mesh netting like

Anni's had been, most of them too feeble even to stir or turn their heads as Hannah started to open the door.

"He's not there," the nurse said from behind her, her tone flat. "If he came yesterday, then he's in the gallery."

"The gallery?" Hannah turned and her heart, which had been racing so fast, suddenly seemed to stop, suspended in her chest, as she took in the sight of three or four beds that had been set up in a shadowy alcove off the landing.

The world seemed to slow down, every second trickling like sand in an endless hourglass as Hannah walked numbly toward the beds. The children who lay on them all looked near death, their bodies motionless, their eyes fluttering or closed, as if their souls had already begun to slip away. Their breath, if it could be seen, barely lifted their thin chests and rattled through their lungs.

Willi was in the bed closest to the wall.

A soft cry slipped from Hannah's lips as she ran toward him, dropping onto her knees by the side of his bed. His eyes fluttered open and he stared at her glassily for a moment, a flicker of recognition sparking there—or was she being fanciful, because she longed for it so much?

"Willi..." She pressed her lips to his forehead, her hand to his cheek. "Willi, Willi." Could she force him to vomit up the phenobarbital he'd been given? Even as she frantically asked herself the question, she knew the answer. It was too late; he'd been given it yesterday. Already his skin had gained the waxy pallor she knew meant death was looming closer.

But he did not, she thought with sudden, savagery, have to die here, in this godforsaken place, without love or comfort. Acting on deep-seated conviction as well as reckless desperation, Hannah scooped Willi up—he was light, so light!—into her arms. From behind her, she heard the nurse draw a shocked breath.

"What are you doing!"

"I am taking him away," Hannah replied, her voice shaking.

"You cannot save him." The nurse's tone was matter-of-fact. "He is too far gone."

"Then it doesn't matter if I take him," Hannah retorted.

"I will have to make a report—" the nurse warned as she followed Hannah down the stairs.

Hannah turned to her, her gaze narrowed. "What is your name?" she asked with icy politeness.

The nurse pursed her lips and then, after a pause, she answered, "I am Nurse Katschenka."

Nurse Katschenka, the supposedly saintly woman whom Jekelius had said held the children in her arms and wept as she ushered them gently into death.

"Remember," Hannah told her coldly, "this boy's father is a major in the Abwehr. I trust you will need to make no report." She turned away from her, dismissing her completely, concentrating entirely on Willi.

Her arms were aching as she left the pavilion and marched toward pavilion three, heedless of the few people about who glanced at her in curiosity before quickly looking away again, not wanting to know. As she came into pavilion three, she stayed close by the wall, avoiding being seen by anyone in the wards. Upstairs, she laid Willi, whose breath was rasping through his chest, down on her bed.

His eyes opened again, flickering so Hannah could see their glinting hazel, and he let out a tiny breath of sound. She held his hand between his own.

"It's Hannah, Willi," she told him, keeping her voice steady with effort. "It's Hannah, I'm here, I'm here. I won't ever leave you, *lieb*, I promise."

Was she imagining the way his fingers tightened on hers, that imperceptible touch that signified he was still there, he could hear her? She sat on the bed next to him, murmuring to him in a low, soothing voice, willing him to live even as she felt him slip away, second by second, breath by breath.

She told him about the crocuses that were pushing up through the ground, the robins that would soon be building their nests. "It's been as cold as the Yukon, Willi, hasn't it? But it's getting warmer. It's getting warmer, and soon it will be spring." She squeezed his hands as his eyelids fluttered closed again and she felt the snap of another fragile thread that bound him to this life. "I saw your father, Willi," she continued, "your dear papa. How he loves you! And I love you, Willi." Her voice choked and she bent her head, closing her eyes against the tears that crowded hotly beneath her lids. "I love you, dear boy. So much. So very much."

Hannah didn't know how long she sat there, as the night grew cold and dark, speaking life to Willi even as his own ebbed away. After some time—a few minutes, an hour—she heard a quick, light knock on the door and then Margarethe stood there, her startled gaze taking in the sight of Willi on Hannah's bed, before clearing in immediate understanding.

"When was he given it?" she asked in a low voice as she came toward Willi and gently laid one hand on his forehead.

"Yesterday, I think." Hannah blinked back tears as she kept her gaze on Willi.

"I'm so sorry, Hannah. I checked in on him yesterday morning, before my shift. They must have..." Margarethe's breath came out in a slow hiss. "The bastards."

"It's all right." Hannah managed a trembling smile as a tear slipped down her cheek and she dashed it away. "It's not your fault. And at least he's here with me, he's as comfortable as he can be." She glanced up at Margarethe, pleading. "Is there anything else I can do for him?"

The other woman's face was drawn in stark lines of grief as she shook her head. "Just talk to him. Stay with him."

"I will," Hannah promised. "To the end."

The end, she knew, was not far off.

Margarethe gave Hannah a swift, hard hug before she hurried back down to her duties on the ward.

Hannah gathered Willi in her arms and whispered to him about the robin and the sunlight and the spring that was coming one day, a day when they would be able to walk in the warmth and see the fragrant blooms, just as Heine had written.

Willi's fingers were slack under hers, and then his eyelids stopped flickering, his long lashes fanning his pale, pale cheeks. Still she spoke, telling him how much she loved him, how she would never let him go... even as she knew she had to. She already was.

Then his breath came in one last, long gasp that ended on a soft sigh of surrender, and his body, so slight and so small, slackened, his fingers slipping from hers. Hannah gazed down at him, knowing he was gone. She hoped, with sudden ferocity, that Margarethe was right, and there was a heaven, because if so, then Willi was surely there now, dancing and free.

She gazed down at his beloved face, knowing she would never again see the spark in his eyes, that mischievous smile. *Oh, Willi.* She pressed a kiss to his forehead and closed her eyes, willing the tears back yet again. After another few moments, she rose, aching, from the bed, knowing what she needed to do.

Back at pavilion five, Hannah rapped sharply on the door. The same young orderly answered, looking sullen now.

"What is it this time? It's two o'clock in the morning, you know—"

"Where is Karl Muller?" Hannah cut across him, her voice flat and hard. "He works as an orderly in this pavilion."

The boy shrugged. "Off duty, I guess."

Hannah had never been to the male staff quarters, a block of cottages on the far side of the complex, but she went there now. She marched with cold, clear determination, forcing down the wild grief that threatened to burst out of her, consuming, overwhelming, drowning out everything else. She would have time for that later. For now, she had one last job to do, for Willi.

"Hannah!" Karl rubbed his eyes blearily, having answered her determined rapping. "You're back from Berlin." He frowned. "What on earth is it?"

"Willi is dead."

Hannah watched him closely, saw how his expression froze for a second before he said, just a little too late, "I'm sorry."

"You knew." It was a statement; she felt no doubt.

"Hannah—"

"Don't lie to me, Karl. There's no point."

He sighed heavily. "Yeah, I knew. I was off duty yesterday, and they took him then. When I came onto the ward this morning, he was gone."

"And you didn't think to do anything?" The question was cold rather than angry. Right then, she felt past rage; she was numb with grief, and yet, for the first time, so very focused.

"What could I do?" Karl protested, with a hint of that old annoyance. "I was a day late. He would have been dead by then—"

"No, he died only a few minutes ago, in my arms."

Karl tried to hide his grimace of distaste, but Hannah saw it. "Well," he told her, "it still would have been too late."

The icy numbness she'd been cloaking herself in suddenly shattered as the grief she felt reared up, spilled out. "I *asked* you to take care of him," she cried, the words torn off on a sob as she hit him hard in the chest with the flat of her hands, so he was forced to take a few stumbling steps back. "I *told* you!"

"Hannah, I'm sorry." Karl captured her hands in his, drawing them down. "I'm sorry, truly. There was nothing I could have done. We can't save them all."

"You don't care about saving any of them." She thought of what Margarethe said, about not trusting him. She'd been right about that, hadn't she? "I thought you *liked* Willi, at least."

"I do. I did," he amended. "They must have taken him yesterday, because they knew I wasn't there. I'm sure that's it, Hannah—" His tone had turned pleading, in his desperation for her to believe him.

"But why?" Hannah cried. "*Why?* His father—"

"There is no why." He squeezed her hands again. "I am sorry, Hannah."

She drew a steadying breath, but then it collapsed inside her as grief crashed over her in a wave and she could not keep the sobs from escaping, doubling over as if she could somehow contain them.

"Hannah... Hannah..." Karl put his arms around her, drawing her to his chest. Hannah didn't want to go to him and yet she still craved comfort, even from him. He smelled familiar, and his arms were warm and strong. She wept into his nightshirt, wept for Willi, and all the other children who hadn't had to die.

"None of them..." she choked out as the tears slid down her face. "*None of them.*" Not Anni, not Willi, not a single one. They'd all been innocent and worthy of life, just as Margarethe had said. No one else got to choose.

Karl made soothing noises as he stroked her back, and after a few moments, Hannah pushed herself away and wiped her face. She would not let herself be so weak again.

"Do you forgive me?" he asked, and she let out a short, humorless laugh.

"Do you care?"

He looked hurt. "Yes, I do. I care about you—"

"Fine, then. I forgive you."

The pout of his lips turned sulky. "You still blame me—"

"No." She could not blame Karl for what had happened to Willi, she knew, but even so, she saw little to admire in him. Still, she needed him now. "I need you to bury Willi," she told him, watched as his eyes widened first in shock, then in dismay.

"If you care about me at all, then you will do this for me. I won't have him carried away in one of those carts—*I won't!*" Her voice rose shrilly and she took a calming breath. "You can bury him, a proper burial."

"Hannah, where?" Already, Karl was shaking his head. "There's no cemetery here, I can't just dig up some corner, and in any case, the ground is as hard as iron—"

"*I don't care.*" She grabbed him by his nightshirt, bunching her fists in the old cloth. "He can't be tossed aside like any old rubbish. He *can't.*"

"All right, all right." Karl wrapped his hands around hers and slowly she unclenched her fists from his nightshirt as her breath shuddered out of her. "I'll take him to the mortuary myself. I'll make sure it's done properly, Hannah, I promise. I know some of them who work there. It'll be done as well as it can be."

With aching grief, she knew this was the best she could hope for. Slowly, Hannah nodded her reluctant acceptance. "All right, then. Thank you."

He nodded back, and then turned to go inside. "Let me just get dressed."

It was nearly dawn by the time Hannah walked back toward pavilion three, the sun glinting over the tops of the trees, having seen Willi to the mortuary with as much dignity as she could possibly give him. He was gone. There was nothing more she could do, and yet she felt an emptiness all the way through her.

Back in pavilion three, she went straight upstairs, past the wards. She knocked once, quietly, on Margarethe's door; it was opened immediately.

"Willi...?" she asked, and Hannah gave a terse nod.

"We took him to the mortuary, after."

"Oh, Hannah." Margarethe took her in her arms and

Hannah hugged her tightly, allowing herself that comfort before she pulled away and wiped at her damp cheeks.

"I was wrong, Margarethe, before. I was wrong, so wrong, to have refused to help you." She shook her head slowly, amazed that she could have been so short-sighted, so selfish. "I thought I was saving Willi, but I couldn't even do that. And it isn't just Willi, is it?" She stared at her helplessly, yet with growing determination. "It's every single child here. They all need saving."

"Oh, Hannah..." Margarethe's face was soft with sympathy, suffused with tenderness.

"I'll do it," she stated fiercely. "Whatever it is I need to do. Sneak into Jekelius's office, find the names, carry the children myself." Her voice thrummed with passion, and her eyes blazed with both sincerity and defiance. "Whatever it is," she promised, "I'll do it. For Willi, and for all the children here."

CHAPTER 20

"Wake up, sleepyhead!"

Hannah opened her eyes, blinking the morning light into focus as Margarethe came into her bedroom. She'd slept somehow, even though she hadn't thought she would, and yet as she woke now, just a few short hours later, she felt weak with an exhaustion that sapped both her spirit and strength. It was as if a weight were pressing down on her and she couldn't move, could barely breathe.

"Come on. You're already late for breakfast, you know."

Margarethe, already neatly dressed in her uniform, moved to the window to draw open the curtain. Hannah watched her from the bed, still unable to move.

Margarethe turned to her, a sympathetic smile twisting her lips, her dark eyes shadowed. "I know it's hard, Hannah, but you've got to get up, get moving. If you don't, your porridge will be cold, and just like the soup, it's even worse when it isn't warm. Like eating sludge."

"How do you do it?" Hannah asked. The words came slowly; it was a struggle to form them. She felt as if, in a matter of hours, she had turned into an old woman.

Margarethe didn't pretend to misunderstand. "Because I'm no use to anyone if I let myself be mired down in grief and sorrow," she stated. "Those who let themselves be overwhelmed by the horror never actually act. They just wring their hands and cluck their tongues. I won't be like that. Neither will you."

Hannah closed her eyes. "That's how I was, though, wasn't I?"

"No, Hannah." Margarethe came to sit next to her on the bed, resting one cool hand against her cheek. "You fought, which showed me you had spirit. It was why I pushed you so hard. Because I knew you had it in you to fight not me, but them."

Hannah was silent, and Margarethe stroked her hair.

"Are you having second thoughts?" she asked gently, without censure. "I know how brightly the fires of indignation burn, and how quickly they can die out."

Hannah opened her eyes and stared up at her. "I'm not having second thoughts."

"Good."

"I am just wondering how you survive it, Margarethe." Her voice choked and she drew a quick breath. "How you can keep being so cheerful, knowing what you do. Seeing it every day. How does it not..." She shook her head as tears slid from the corners of her eyes and trickled into her hair. "How does it not kill something inside of you?"

Margarethe was silent for a long moment, and Hannah turned her head so she could look up in her face. Her expression was both pensive and drawn, and something resolute entered her eyes as she answered quietly, "It does not, Hannah, because I died before I came here."

Hannah simply stared and Margarethe continued, her tone turning gentle.

"That's part of taking vows, I suppose, entering a convent. You die to self in a way most people never do, never need to."

She pressed her lips together and her eyes gleamed with unshed tears before she added, her voice growing stronger, "And when I saw what happened to so many, the injustice, the utter *needlessness* of it all... I knew then that I would die for them. For this. At least, I would be willing to." She let out a little laugh, the sound tired and yet with a touching hope, as she stroked Hannah's hair again. "Now, before I sound far too noble, understand that in my stubborn stupidity, I try my hardest to resurrect myself every day! Why, when Ida took the last potato last night, I was *quite* put out, let me assure you." She smiled before subsiding into a sigh. "It's hard, Hannah, it will always be hard, and in truth, it's likely only to get harder. But the alternative—to do nothing—is worse than death. Far worse."

She lapsed into silence, and from far below, somewhere in the ward, Hannah heard Helga's booming laugh.

"I'm not afraid," Hannah said, and realized as she did so, it was true. *I died before I came here.* That may have been so for Margarethe, but Hannah, or at least that part that had hoped for some small happiness, the part that *had not asked for very much*, had died last night, with Willi.

"Good," Margarethe replied as she rose from the bed. "Because there are things we can do, plans to make. With your help, Hannah, it is my hope that there will be many more children we can save."

For the first time that morning, Hannah felt a flare of energy, a flicker of hope. "Good. When can we get started?"

Margarethe pursed her lips. "First there is someone you need to meet."

Hannah did not have a chance to meet whoever it was Margarethe wished her to for several weeks, at the end of the month. She had been working flat out, or Margarethe had, and their days off had not overlapped. Hannah had been grateful for the slight reprieve being busy gave her from her grief. When she did have a spare moment to think, to feel, it threatened to overwhelm her, swamping her with a paralyzing despair that reminded her of Margarethe's words. *Those who let themselves be overwhelmed by the horror never actually act.* She didn't want to be like that, and yet there was nothing, at the moment, that she could do, except wait and watch.

And she did watch; she watched the administration pavilion, and noted who came and went, and at what times. She followed the white-coated doctors with her eyes, eavesdropped as they murmured over patients' charts. She learned the names of the orderlies from various pavilions and smiled and chatted with them, just in case any of it helped. Information, she knew, was knowledge.

"When can we meet this mysterious person?" she asked Margarethe one day when they were both on the ward. Outside, the tulips and daffodils grew in bright clusters under the trees, and there were clouds in the sky like wisps of cotton wool. Willi had been gone for three weeks, and Hannah felt his absence in every empty moment, a physical pain she carried with her. Only that morning she'd spotted a robin chirping from its perch in a tree and grief had lanced through her, yet again.

"You've got the fire in your blood now, I know," Margarethe told her with sympathy, "but we have to be careful. We can't go haring off into the night with a child in our arms—"

"Isn't that what you did with the first one?" Hannah interjected.

"Yes, and it was very foolish and costly of me," Margarethe replied, her tone sharpening.

Hannah looked at her in confusion. "Costly? But he was saved—"

"Yes, but... Oh, never mind." She shook her head. "You must meet my contact first. He is the one who makes it possible to save any children at all. Until he is able to meet us, there is no point to any of it. I wish there was."

"But meanwhile children are dying," Hannah protested, her voice catching as she thought of those children, of Willi. She had not heard of any children who had been recommended for further treatment, as none had been in pavilion three, but she had seen the green-covered carts. She knew it must have been still happening.

"I know, Hannah," Margarethe told her, "and it pains me greatly, but the terrible truth is, we cannot save them all. In truth, we have only been able to save a very few, although I am hopeful that will change. But even one life saved is better than none." She smiled bleakly. "Patience, please. I know it is hard."

Everything was hard, Hannah thought. Every day she woke up and stared out at the blue sky, the fleecy clouds, a breath of spring in the air, and she felt leaden inside—not just for the loss of Willi, but for the utter hopelessness she felt about the future. More and more, she thought of Georg's words, the terrible finality of them. *We are not going to win this war.* Whatever happened, whatever future loomed in front of her, it was going to be unimaginably challenging.

It had been bad enough having to write Georg about Willi's death, keeping the letter painfully brief as she knew she had to, for it would surely be opened and read, if not by Jekelius, then by someone in the Abwehr or the Gestapo, perhaps by Himmler himself. Georg had said he was being watched, after all.

She'd steeled herself to see Dr. Jekelius, to ask him how Willi's death had been written down, for she knew an official letter would come from the clinic declaring death caused by pneumonia, or appendicitis, or heaven knew what else, and her letter to Georg would have to be consistent with the official cause of death.

She didn't think she could bear to see the affected pity in those dark eyes, the little moue of sympathy he would give as he made one of his mellifluous yet barbed remarks. She thought she might either fly at him in a rage or break down weeping; she did not know which would be worse—or more dangerous.

In any case, when she went to the administration pavilion a few days after Willi's death, it was to find Jekelius absent. It was Matron Bertha who informed her, with pursed lips and a disapproving expression, that Willi had died of pneumonia. "It happens in so many of these cases," she'd told her without even a pretense of sorrow. "Their bodies are simply too weak to withstand it. The winter is always hard."

That's because you starve them half to death and keep the windows open so the wards are freezing, Hannah thought, biting her lips to keep from saying the words out loud. *In any case, a fatal dose of Luminal hardly helps.*

"Thank you, Nurse Bertha," she'd replied stiffly, and a small, cold smile curved the nurse's thin lips. She'd given a nod of dismissal and Hannah had turned and walked away, trying to keep her hands from clenching into fists, her body vibrating with fury.

Later, while sipping coffee and keeping to herself in the staff room, she'd overheard the reason for Jekelius' absence; Helga had hardly been able to wait to spill the latest gossip, juicy as it was.

"The doctor is courting Fraulein Hitler, isn't he?" she'd announced, lacing her hands over her wide stomach. "Far greater matters to attend to than pushing papers here."

"Fraulein Hitler?" Hannah had repeated, unable to keep from showing her curiosity. "You don't mean—"

"Yes, the *Führer*'s sister, although, in truth, she goes by the name Wolff." Helga had nodded, smug in her knowledge. "No doubt he hopes to marry her. Wouldn't that be a promotion!" She had let out one of her booming laughs, while Nurse Schmidt gave a small, mincing sort of smile and Hannah had stared blankly into space.

For Dr. Jekelius to marry Hitler's sister...! She could not even imagine the power he'd have, the access. Would he leave Am Steinhof, or would he enforce even worse measures upon it and the children here?

"Did you know about it?" she'd asked Margarethe later, when they were getting ready for bed.

Margarethe had shrugged as she took down her hair. "Like others, I've heard the gossip, but that's all. I can imagine someone like Jekelius pushing for such a match though—he's ambitious, can't you tell?" She'd let out a harsh laugh.

"You're not scared of him?" Hannah had ventured. "Of what he knows?"

"I'm more concerned with what he doesn't know, and must never know."

"But what if he finds out—"

"He won't." Margarethe had turned around briskly, her dark hair tumbled about her shoulders. "He's hardly here anymore, it'll be even less if he's really courting that precious *fraulein*, and you've seen yourself how chaotic things are— patients coming and going between pavilions. It will be fine. The real trouble," she'd added as she undid her apron, "is finding somewhere for these children to hide. To live."

"I met Nurse Katschenka," Hannah had said slowly. "In pavilion fifteen. She seems as if she knows exactly what is going on there."

"Oh, I know of Nurse Katschenka. Everyone whispers about her. I think she's half in love with Jekelius herself, little good that it will do her. I've heard she runs the pavilion with an iron fist—which is why the children we save must never *get* to pavilion fifteen." She'd turned to Hannah, her expression serious. "You've seen what it's like there, as I did, months ago."

Wordlessly, Hannah had nodded.

"We both finally have a day off together next week," Margarethe had told her, reaching over to squeeze her hand.

"Then you can meet the man who helps us. Patience for just a little while longer, Hannah."

That Saturday, they walked through the gates of Am Steinhof, Margarethe with a jaunty step. She was wearing a dress of green sprigged muslin, nipped in at the waist and flaring out about her shapely calves. Hannah, in one of only two off-duty dresses, this one of dark blue wool, felt mousy and plain in comparison.

The usual huddle of women was by the tram stop, and Margarethe kept her distance from them as they waited for the tram.

"Don't you feel sorry for them?" Hannah asked in a low voice, and Margarethe shot her a sharp glance; it was only then that Hannah realized she'd sounded accusing.

"I do, very much," Margarethe replied, "but sadly there is nothing I can do for them, and were I to be seen as sympathetic, someone would be sure to notice, and then I would be under suspicion. I do more for their children by pretending those women don't exist." She sighed as she pulled her coat more tightly around her. Although it was just turned April, the breeze was still brisk. "We all have to make choices, Hannah."

The tram came down the street, and Margarethe hopped nimbly onto a tram, while Hannah scrambled to follow.

"Where is it that we are going?" she asked as they took their places on one of the wooden benches that ran the length of the vehicle.

"Questions, questions!" Margarethe wagged her finger at her. "When will you ever learn?"

Hannah gave a rueful smile in return, glancing around the passengers on the tram with a wary unease. It was only half full and most were looking weary and haggard even though it was only mid-afternoon, their chins drooping toward their chests.

Still, she knew one could never be too careful. "Margarethe," she asked in a low voice, "do you ever worry... do you ever think you might be followed, wherever it is you're going?"

Margarethe gave a little laugh as she tossed her head. "Who would want to follow a simple nurse like me?"

"Jekelius seems like he knows so much," Hannah continued, dropping her voice even lower. "I know you said you weren't worried about him—"

"I'm not."

"I'm sure he's read my letters."

Margarethe shrugged. "Good thing I don't write any, then."

Her tone was as insouciant as ever, but Hannah was taken aback. "Don't you?" she asked. "What about your family?"

She shrugged. "My mother died when I was little more than a child and my father is a loyal party member. We haven't seen eye to eye for years."

"I didn't realize."

Margarethe pursed her lips and glanced out the window as the tram rattled eastward, into the city. "He was a petty little bureaucrat back in Linz, who, after the Anschluss, became an aide to the gauleiter, thanks to his devotion. I was glad to leave his house, when I entered the convent at eighteen."

"Do you have any brothers or sisters?"

"One brother. He's older than I am, by a few years. He's fighting in Greece." She paused, her gaze still on the grimy window. "He's cut from the same cloth as my father."

It sounded terribly lonely, as lonely as her own childhood. "And what about your friends? The sisters from your convent?"

"Nuns don't write each other letters," Margarethe told her with a laugh. "We are meant to forsake all worldly things, including friendships. But you needn't feel sorry for me, Hannah. I've never minded being a solitary creature." Her smile turned impish, yet still sincere. "You're the closest friend I've ever had, you know."

"And you are mine," Hannah replied with just as much sincerity. She had not had many friends in her life; she'd never really had the chance. Willi was, she knew, the first person she'd really loved.

Margarethe's expression softened. "That means a great deal to me, you know." She reached over to cover Hannah's hand with her own. "A great deal." The tram's bell clanged and Margarethe half-rose from her seat to peer out the window. "Ah, we're almost there."

"There" was the northwest suburb of Währing, a leafy district that was as pleasant as Penzing, with handsome houses edging the *Wienerwald*, the Vienna Woods. Margarethe marched briskly down the pavement, leaving Hannah no choice but to follow, until they reached Bischof-Faber-Platz in Gersthof, and Margarethe stopped in front of a large, brick church with a tall, pointed spire.

"Here we are," she said under her breath, and then, with an air of solemn purpose, walked up to the church's doors and slipped inside.

The dim and hushed atmosphere fell on Hannah like a cloak as she breathed in the ancient, unfamiliar scents of candle wax and incense.

Margarethe walked quickly over to one of the confessional booths to the side of the nave, made of dark wood with a curtain drawn across. She went into the booth before she gave Hannah a quick, pointed glance.

"Go into the other," she whispered.

Uncertainly, Hannah glanced at the darkened booth, then walked across, drew the curtain aside, and slipped into the small space. She fumbled for a few seconds in the dark before she found the small, built-in bench and perched on it uneasily, her heart starting to thud.

She'd never been in such a booth before, had hardly been in a church. Her mother had had no faith, only cynicism, and

Hannah knew she was more like her than she cared to admit. She shifted on the bench, having no idea what to do or expect, when she heard the sound of someone sitting down opposite her, hidden by the latticed screen. A silence stretched on; she could hear the man breathing.

"My daughter?" he finally asked, and startled, Hannah realized she was meant to say something, but what? To confess her sins, and yet she barely knew what that meant.

I've failed Willi... and that little boy back at Heim Hochland...

"I..." she began, helplessly, surprised to realize tears were gathering under her lids, only to have a door on the other side suddenly open and then Margarethe was pulling her out, into a small room.

The priest emerged from the other half of the booth, dark-eyed and serious, although a small smile played about his lips.

"I take it you've never made confession before?" he asked wryly, while Hannah could only stare dumbly.

"Hannah," Margarethe said, "This is Heinrich Maier."

CHAPTER 21

Heinrich Maier was a vigorous man in his early thirties, with closely cropped dark hair, penetrating dark eyes underneath equally dark, heavy eyebrows, and a restless, charismatic energy about him that reminded Hannah of Margarethe. In fact, she thought as she glanced between the pair of them as they sat around a small table in the kitchen of the church's rectory, they could almost be brother and sister.

"I haven't seen you for quite some time, Margarethe," Heinrich remarked. "I am glad we were able to arrange a meeting today." While he sounded friendly enough, Hannah thought she heard a slight underlying coolness to his tone, almost as if he'd been glad of her absence.

"As you know, it is not always easy to act," Margarethe replied. "But I am hoping things will be different now, with Hannah here."

"Oh?" Heinrich gave Hannah an appraising glance, and once again she had the sense he did not entirely welcome their visit. A shiver of apprehension went through her; could he really be trusted? "And why is that?"

"Hannah's brother is a major in the Abwehr," Margarethe

began, and Heinrich turned to her, his eyes narrowed, a new alertness adding to his energy.

"Oh?" he asked, interest sharp in his voice. "Is he sympathetic to our cause?"

Before Hannah could even think how to reply to that, Margarethe broke in, "The point is, his position has elevated Hannah's—she may have access to Jekelius's study."

"I see." He sounded, Hannah thought, disappointed.

"Do you?" Margarethe leaned forward, her face alight with determination and zeal, her fingers knotted together. "Heinrich, this means we could discover the names of the children before they are designated for further treatment. We'll have time to arrange their escape properly, for you to find a place for them. Think how many more children we can save—"

"Do you really think so?" Heinrich sounded weary now. Hannah had the sense he had not been thinking about the children at all; that it was Margarethe's passion, not his. "Surely Jekelius will notice if every child goes missing right as he's about to send them to death? How long do you think you'd escape notice, with such a plan?"

Disappointment flickered across Margarethe's features before she schooled them into a more complacent cast. "Of course, I have always known we can't rescue them all," she replied with dignity. "But some of them, at least. A precious few. You can't understand how chaotic the hospital can be, Heinrich, with patients being pushed here and there, moving between pavilions all the time. Jekelius is only there one day out of four, if that."

"He is not the only one you have to worry about," Heinrich remarked quietly.

"That is true, but I can bluster my way through with the others, and the records they keep are shoddy at best, and for a reason—to shroud everything in secrecy. It would be easy enough to say a child has already died when they come to collect for further treatment. Indeed, that has happened often enough as it is." Her lips twisted and her tone hardened. "Let me worry about the hospital side of things, Heinrich. All I ask is that you are there to receive the children and find them a place to stay."

"How does it actually work?" Hannah asked, flushing a little at the presumption of her question. She felt woefully ignorant and entirely out of her depth, and yet she still blazed with a determination, a *need*, to help. To save.

Heinrich and Margarethe exchanged glances before she offered an explanation. "As I told you before, we have only been able to help the children whom I know are being sent to pavilion fifteen. When that happens, Karl has taken the child from whatever pavilion they're in, before another orderly comes to collect them for pavilion fifteen. In the usual mayhem, no one has ever objected. Sometimes I wonder if they even notice."

"It is hard to imagine that they don't," Heinrich interjected quietly, "Or won't one day."

"They haven't yet." Margarethe turned back to Hannah. "Instead of delivering the child to pavilion fifteen, Karl brings them to me. Then I hide them somewhere safe—there is an old potting shed out by the orchard, that I've used before. It's not ideal, especially in winter, but it's the best we can do, and God willing it's only for a few hours. In the past, I've sent a message to Heinrich, or, if I have had time, I have gone myself. He arranges for someone to meet us by the wall, in the night. There is an apple tree in the orchard that is easy to climb and has branches extending over the wall. We use that, and we pass the child over."

"And then I arrange for them to be transported to a safe place," Heinrich finished. He turned back to Margarethe with a pointed look. "But it is not easy, as you know. These children have many needs, and they are difficult to hide, even for those who are devoted to hiding them."

"They are *children*," Margarethe returned fiercely. Hannah could tell this was an argument they'd had before, in one guise or another. "They deserve to live."

"I would never argue that point, Margarethe," Heinrich replied quietly. "You know that very well. But we must consider the bigger picture. We must create a world where children like those at Am Spiegelgrund are welcomed in this world and treated with dignity. We must, in some cases, sacrifice the individual for the sake of the greater good—that of winning the war and destroying the Nazi regime forever."

Margarethe's gaze remained unwavering as she replied softly, "As our Lord Himself said, 'In as much as you have done it to the least of these, my brethren, you have done it to me.'"

Hannah gazed at her in confusion, not recognizing the words, but Heinrich looked away, abashed, although Hannah thought she saw a flicker of irritation mixed in with the guilt that colored his face.

"I don't mean to sound unfeeling," he said after a moment, "but surely you can see what's at stake?"

The words, she thought, could have been coming from Georg. Her brother had, in effect, sacrificed his own son for the greater good of trying to defeat Hitler, although Hannah had no idea how he might do it, and didn't want to know. *I am living and breathing treason every day.* No, she most certainly did not want to know about that. She had enough secrets to keep.

"I don't see why one has to be to the detriment of the other," Margarethe replied. "The sisters are willing, Heinrich."

"I know they are." He glanced at Hannah with a small smile. "The Franciscan Sisters of Christian Charity call Margarethe the 'Angel of Vienna.' They are more than glad to shelter the little ones she is able to save."

The Angel of Vienna. Yes, Hannah thought, Margarethe *was* like an angel—spreading her wings over the innocents, guarding their lives, and yet both fierce and fearsome in her certainty and zeal.

"Then why are you reluctant?" Margarethe demanded of Heinrich.

He hesitated and then stated quietly, "My priorities must be the defeat of Hitler and the restoration of Austria as a free and independent nation." He glanced at Hannah. "That is why, when I heard your brother is in the Abwehr, I had hoped he might be sympathetic. We could use good intelligence."

Hannah remained silent, not wanting to say anything about Georg.

Heinrich turned back to Margarethe. "I have already contacted others throughout the country who share my aims. We have the potential to affect the outcomes of battles, Margarethe, of the war *itself*—"

"By what?" she interjected. "Blowing up a railroad? Passing on the location of an armaments factory?"

Heinrich looked startled and she let out a hard laugh.

"Don't think I don't know what you might be up to, and I *understand*, of course I do, but don't you realize, Heinrich, if you turn away from the most helpless, unloved and innocent children in this world—*the least of these*—because you think what you are doing is more important..." She shook her head helplessly. "Why, then, you are turning away from our Savior Himself."

Heinrich glanced down at his large, square hands placed flat on the table, as if to brace himself. "Do you think I haven't searched my conscience about this?" he asked quietly. "Many times?"

"Then search it a little more," Margarethe answered. "At the moment, it's four or five children a month who are marked for death. No doubt it will increase eventually, since they're getting away with it. Jekelius grows bolder by the hour." Her words were spiked with bitterness. "But, in the meantime, if we can save only one or two of those... one or two a month, Heinrich, perhaps three! A few precious lives saved from a terrible and unnecessary death—from murder. Surely you cannot deny your help?"

He let out a tired sigh as he slowly nodded, his gaze still on the table. "Very well. I will not deny it... not yet. In truth, I don't want to, but there might come a time, Margarethe—"

"And we'll spoon that soup out when we have to," she cut across him with a sudden, impish smile. She reached over to cover his hand with her own. "Thank you, Heinrich. I know I am asking for much. I will send a message as soon as I can, when we have seen the month's list."

Hannah's stomach cramped. When *she* saw the list, she knew Margarethe meant. When she'd somehow managed to sneak into Jekelius's office, riffle through his papers, and find out what children he was meant to kill—all without being caught. How could she possibly do it?

And yet she knew she would try.

They left soon after, with Heinrich's assurance that he would respond as needed to whatever message Margarethe sent.

"I didn't expect him to be so reluctant," Hannah remarked as they headed back to the tram stop on Gentzgasse.

"Oh, they all are," Margarethe replied. "Everyone wants to do something so *important*. Saving a child, and a seriously ill one at that, is lowest on their list." She shook her head. "But no, I'm being unfair. Heinrich is a good man. He would give his life for the cause, I know it, and in a heartbeat." She sighed. "But sometimes I feel as if I am the only person who cares about these little ones. The little ones that no one else even seems to see."

"I care," Hannah stated quietly.

"I know you do!" Margarethe turned to her with a quick,

blazing look as she held her hands in hers. "I think I knew it from the first, even before you knew it, or wanted to. I saw it, Hannah, like a light shining out of you."

Hannah let out an embarrassed laugh. "That's a bit much, surely," she managed.

"It isn't." Margarethe reached for her hand, clasping it briefly between her own. "It isn't."

"How do you know Heinrich, anyway?" Hannah asked after they'd gone on a little while longer, the sky darkening at its edges, the air possessing a bit more of a chill.

"One of the nuns with the Sisters of Charity mentioned him to me. There are a few among the convents and monasteries who resist the regime. We make sure to know each other's names."

"I didn't realize how much Karl was involved," Hannah ventured after a few moments. "Collecting the children as he does. You trust him, to do that?"

Margarethe pressed her lips together. "I have to," she replied shortly.

Hannah frowned. "Why?"

She hesitated, and then said repressively, "Because he knows, and he's willing. But he could change his mind as soon as it suits him. Anyway, it doesn't matter," Margarethe answered as she quickened her step. "Look, here's our tram."

As they alighted outside the gates of Am Steinhof, Hannah realized she did not feel the usual wave of dread, the tightening of her stomach muscles in grim anticipation of all that lay ahead. She felt a determination, a strengthening of resolve that was similar to what she'd felt when she'd decided to protect and care for Willi, but this was harder, cleaner. She would not let the evil horror of this place endure, whatever it took. Whatever it cost.

As if she could sense something of what she was feeling, as they walked toward the hospital gates, Margarethe whispered, "'The gates of hell shall not prevail against them.'"

Hannah gave her a fleeting smile. "No," she agreed softly, "they won't."

"Excuse me... *bitte*... do you work at the hospital?"

Hannah stiffened instinctively as Margarethe turned to face the man who had addressed them. He was a rough-looking sort of fellow, although with kind, droopy eyes and a pleading expression. He held a worn cap in his hands and his face was unshaven. His clothes shabby but clean—loose trousers tied with rope, and a peasant-style shirt with a battered coat. Hannah thought she recognized him from other times she'd left the hospital; he'd been in the crowd of mothers, standing by the gate, looking like he'd just come from the countryside.

Margarethe glanced around covertly and saw that no one else was about. "Yes, we are," she said quietly. "Can we help?"

"My son... he is in this hospital, but they do not let me see him."

Hannah sucked in a quick breath, but Margarethe only smiled in sympathy. "Your son, what is his name?"

"Hedji."

"Is he unwell?"

The man frowned in confusion. "Unwell? No. I traveled to Vienna from Budapest for work, but there has been no work." Margarethe nodded in quick, silent understanding and he continued, "When I got here, they told me I could not keep Hedji with me, without a fixed address. But I cannot find a place to live! I had a cousin, but she has no room..." He shook his head, both impatient and abashed by his situation. "I am sorry, you do not need to know these things. But I have work now, good work. A home for Hedji... at least I will, soon." He grimaced, embarrassed by his own lack. "But they will not even let me see him. They said they could care for him, here at their school, but I want to see him." He shrugged his shoulders help-lessly. "Why do they not let me see him?"

"What is your name?" Margarethe asked the man.

"They call me Lash."

"I am a nurse at the hospital, Lash. There is a school attached, and it might be that Hedji is there. I will see if I can find your son. They should let you visit him, at least once in a while."

His worn face creased into a smile of desperate relief. "Thank you—"

"Come here tomorrow night," Margarethe instructed. "Seven o'clock, if you can. I will give you news then."

"Yes." He nodded, overcome. "Yes, I will."

Briefly she clasped his work-roughened hands between her own. "Try not to worry. I will look out for your son."

"Why did you talk to that man but not the women by the tram stop earlier?" Hannah asked quietly once they'd gone through the gates, leaving Lash behind, looking after them with a hungry sort of yearning.

"Because I do not like to be a hypocrite," Margarethe replied frankly. "I am angry with Heinrich for seeing only the big picture, and not the individuals so desperately in need of care. And yet I did the same thing in refusing to talk to those women earlier today." She shook her head. "God forbid I lose sight of each precious little one." She pressed her lips together. "And heaven help his son, stuck in that school."

"Why was he taken? Just because the man had no address?"

"Because he is Roma." She glanced at her. "Couldn't you tell?"

"No." Hannah had not seen many gypsies in her life. She recalled how, for the Olympics held in Berlin in 1936, the gypsies had all been rounded up and taken to a camp out in Marzahn, between a cemetery and a sewage dump. Like so much else, they'd been kept out of sight and therefore out of mind, hers included, although she'd seen them being herded away.

"You know the Roma are included in the race laws?" Margarethe asked, and Hannah nodded.

"Well." Margarethe let out a gusty sigh. "It won't bode well for little Hedji, to be a gypsy in a place like this. It's just about as bad as being a Jew."

"What... what will they do to them?" Hannah realized she had only considered what they did to the children who were ill or disabled, not the ones who were perfectly healthy but still seen as undesirable. Those bald and skinny scarecrows that marched around the parkland, dressed in rags, shoulder blades like chicken wings, that tall boy with hazel eyes and the polite manner... what happened to them?

"I don't rightly know," Margarethe replied. "But I know it's nothing good."

"And how will you find Hedji?" The children in the reformatory school were entirely separate from those cared for in the hospital pavilions, guarded by their stony-faced wardens. Hannah had only seen them in passing, when they were marching out.

"I don't know," Margarethe admitted. "But I will."

They'd reached pavilion three, its brick bulk shrouded in darkness. Around them, Am Steinhof stretched out in a cold, dark silence, and the resolve Hannah had felt when she'd seen the gates came back, even fiercer this time. They would find Hedji. They would rescue those who could be saved. Somehow, she promised herself, she would bring good out of this place, or at least freedom.

CHAPTER 22

MAY 1941

While spring melted the hard ground and brought out flowers all through the hospital's parkland, the apple trees in Am Steinhof's orchard now in full, frilly bloom, Hannah tried to find a way into Jekelius's office. She had always known it wouldn't be easy; indeed, she'd feared it to be quite impossible, and yet she'd allowed her resolve to buoy her, as if her own determination would provide the necessary key, when, in fact, it proved only to be a source of frustration.

Three times over the next month she ventured to the administrative pavilion, walking briskly down the black and white tiled hallways as if she had a right to be there, the letter from Georg in her hand, in the hope that it would provide a pretext to enter Jekelius's study. The brief letter had, she suspected, already been opened and read, most likely by Jekelius himself, although she could easily pretend otherwise if she had to.

In any case, each time she didn't get very far. The first time, Matron Bertha met her on the steps, and, with her palm held out, crisply informed her she'd hand the letter over to Jekelius herself. When Hannah had blustered about needing to speak to the medical director privately, the head matron replied wither-ingly that Dr. Jekelius was a very busy man, currently on impor-tant business in Berlin. Talking to Hitler about his sister, Hannah had wondered, or perhaps discussing the fate of his patients with the shadowy committee that decided such things? Either way, it didn't matter; she was forced to murmur a polite thanks and walk back to pavilion three.

The second time she attempted to enter his study, she found the administration pavilion blessedly empty but his door locked. She rattled it uselessly and foolishly, for the sound echoed through the high-ceilinged hallways, before turning around, dispirited.

The third time she nearly bumped into one of the doctors from the children's ward, Marianne Türk, whom she recognized but had never spoken to, right on the front steps. The doctor gave her a quelling glance, her dark hair pulled back into a neat bun, her expression severe as she pushed past her. Hannah had been about to enter the pavilion when Dr. Türk called out sharply.

"Where are you going, *Schwester*? Surely you have duties elsewhere?"

"I wish to speak with Dr. Jekelius—"

"He is not available. I advise you to see to your duties."

Hannah had no choice but to turn around and walk back to pavilion three.

Meanwhile, she thought hopelessly, children were surely dying.

When she could, she kept watch from the window of pavilion three, to see if any orderlies were taking patients in the direction of pavilion fifteen, or if any of those wretched green carts were being pulled by groundsmen, and at various times, she saw both, knowing she could do nothing about either, not yet.

Margarethe, at least, had been able to locate Hedji; Hannah

had been walking with her toward the kitchen when they'd seen a dispirited line of raggedy boys emerge from pavilion seven, their hard-eyed warden leading the way, the tall boy she'd seen before in the back.

"*Bitte*," Margarethe had called, her tone ringing out in imperious authority. "Who here has the name Hedji?"

The warden had paused mid-stride to glower at her. "Who wants to know?"

"His father," Margarethe had returned in a clipped voice. "He is about to make a complaint to the city's youth welfare office, because he has been kept from seeing his son. You know the medical director is already in trouble with them, don't you?"

The warden's scowl had deepened and she'd glanced back at the boys, some of whom were following this exchange with a bright-eyed avidity, while others had simply stared at the ground, too weary and worn down to be anything but indifferent.

The woman had jerked her head, and the tall boy in the back stepped out of the line. "Please," he'd said with quiet dignity. "I am Hedji."

Hannah had stared at the boy in surprise—it had been him all along!—while Margarethe had smiled at him. "Your father will be glad I have spoken to you, Hedji. Are you being treated well?"

The boy had glanced wordlessly at the warden and then nodded.

Margarethe had turned back to the warden. "I will make a full report," she'd said warningly. "The man must be allowed to visit his son."

"That has nothing to do with me," the warden had replied, and the children had marched on, toward the hospital's garden, where they were to spend the day hoeing and weeding. As Hannah had watched them go, Hedji had turned back and waved at them both, smiling. Heartened, Hannah had waved back.

"I've seen him before," she'd told Margarethe as they'd walked on to the kitchen. "Only in passing, but he always seemed... strong. As if he wasn't letting this place change him, at least not too much."

"Good," Margarethe had replied grimly, "because he needs to be strong, to survive the reformatory here. I'm glad I can tell Lash I have found him. Perhaps there will be a way for him to visit him, or take him out in the city. Such things have been allowed, for the children in the school."

"Did you mean what you said, about the welfare office?" Hannah had asked. "Is Jekelius in trouble with the officials there?"

"I have heard rumors of complaints, and I am not surprised. Jekelius has always had a high and mighty view of himself, but even he has to answer to the welfare office—for those at the reformatory school, anyway. The ones in pavilion fifteen have no one to advocate on their behalf."

"Except us," Hannah had returned feelingly, and Margarethe had given her a quick smile.

"Yes," she had agreed, "except for us."

Toward the end of the month, Hannah finally got her chance. It was a glorious spring day, the parkland full of birdsong and blossom, so even surly Nurse Schmidt's mood had lightened. Everyone was talking about Rudolf Hess, and how he had, without any instruction or advice, flown solo to Scotland on an apparent peace mission, and parachuted into Eaglesham when he'd run out of fuel, before being promptly arrested by the British police.

Everyone seemed to find the episode highly amusing, and Hitler had duly stripped him of his title and declared him mentally incompetent. There had been jokes about him being sent to Am Steinhof, if he ever made it back to the Fatherland. Still, it had given Hannah a flicker of hope, that someone so close to Hitler had actually tried to sue for peace. Perhaps the war would be over sooner than any of them thought. But, in the meantime, she needed to act.

Margarethe had already spoken to Lash several times, assuring him that Hedji was well, and twice Hannah and Margarethe had gone together to the pavilion that housed the reformatory boys, and checked on Hedji.

Hannah had been horrified by the careless cruelty of the school's matrons, even worse than that of the nurses she knew, clouting a child as he passed, or, as Hedji had told them in a low voice, shaming and beating the children who wet their beds at night.

"It's all right if you just keep your head down," he'd told them, adding with a rueful smile, "I don't always."

"Don't let them break your spirit," Margarethe had said, and Hannah had slipped him a chunk of black bread that he ate in two bites.

Now, as she headed once more for the administration pavilion, she realized she had no firm plan, just a burning determination to finally get in the medical director's office. And this time it did seem as if her sense of purpose provided the key, or perhaps it was Providence, for she slipped through the empty hallways without seeing anyone.

When she arrived at Jekelius's door, she knocked once, softly, her heart starting up a hectic beat, and when she heard no response, she tried the handle and found, both to her terror and joy, that it turned.

She stepped quickly into the medical director's office, breathing in the scent of leather and paper, as well as the faint, lingering aroma of his expensive aftershave. She closed the door behind her; already her palms were damp, and they slipped on the door's knob, so it closed with a louder click than she'd intended, and which sounded like the crack of a gun to her ears, the blood pounding through them making her feel faint and sick.

She stayed still, taking a few careful breaths, straining to hear the click of heels on the tiled floor outside, but there was nothing. Slowly, as if in a dream, she moved toward Jekelius's desk. She saw the silver letter knife he'd used to open Georg's first letter, with such careless grace, and a pile of papers that looked, upon a further glance, nothing more than bills from local suppliers.

Her gaze moved slowly around the desk's wide surface, past a photograph of a dark-haired, dark-eyed woman—was that the *Führer*'s sister?—and another pile of correspondence that looked as innocuous as the first. Was she not to find anything? But, no. She had to.

Hannah moved to stand behind the desk, resting her hands lightly on its burnished surface. Her heart was racing so hard and fast she could feel her pulse through her whole body, like a ticking clock. She opened the first drawer, and saw nothing but fresh sheets of stationery, blank medical forms. Another drawer held a selection of pens and ink. Another was locked.

No, no, no. She bit her lip, her gaze swinging wildly around the room. Margarethe had seemed so sure that she would find something, that Jekelius would be careless and arrogant enough to leave such important papers lying about, for anyone to see. It seemed ludicrous now, and yet she could not go away empty-handed. She simply could not.

Then she spied a wooden tray on top of a filing cabinet, with several mailing envelopes in it, each the size of a sheet of paper. She walked toward it on unsteady legs, and then took the first from the top. The address stamped in the corner was Tiergartenstrasse 4, Berlin—an innocent enough address, and yet... *Berlin.*

Could it be? Did she dare?

She glanced around and then, knowing she was being reckless, reached for the silver letter knife and loosened the sealed flap along its edge, as carefully as she could. Her heart thundering more than ever, her fingers damp and trembling, she eased the few papers out. They were medical forms, typed on yellow paper. She scanned the first one quickly, taking in the usual details—a patient's name, the date of birth. Then she took in the benchmarks listed—responsive, reflexes, docile, educable. Next to each one was simply typed *nein*.

She scanned down further, and felt her stomach tighten. *Entafflung: Nein.* The patient would not be discharged. And then, on the very last line, was typed one simple, stark word. *Unbrauchbar.* Useless.

In the bottom left corner of the form, someone had scrawled some illegible notations in red ink, followed by a bold red cross, or plus sign. What did it mean?

And yet already Hannah knew. This had to be a patient marked for death. Sara Barth, aged only three.

Quickly, Hannah went through the rest of the forms; there were four in all. In addition to Sarah Barth, there was Leo Weiss, Oskar Weber, and Ilse Koch. Hannah whispered the names to herself, committed them to memory. Sarah, Leo, Oskar, Ilse. She felt as if she already knew them, as if she'd recognize them when she saw their faces, for here were the children she could save. *Finally.*

Except, she realized almost at once, she did not know in which pavilions they resided. How to find them in time?

Outside Jekelius's office, she heard the murmur of voices, the brisk click of heels. Hannah froze, the incriminating forms still gripped between her nerveless fingers. If the door opened, she knew she would have no excuse. No escape.

The voices moved on, and releasing a slow, careful breath, Hannah slipped the forms back into the envelope and pressed the flap down, in a fruitless attempt to reseal it. There was nothing more she could do, she knew. Perhaps Jekelius would assume the letter had simply become unsealed; perhaps he would suspect. At least she had the names. *Sarah, Leo, Oskar, Ilse.*

She glanced around the office, making sure she left no mark. The letter knife she put back where it belonged, even going so far as to wipe it with the hem of her skirt. As if Jekelius would dust for fingerprints! And yet she knew she could never be too careful.

She went to the door, straining to hear anything, but all was silent. Taking another careful breath, she opened it and slipped out into the hallway, closing it quickly behind her. She walked briskly down the hallway toward the front door, her chin held high. As she reached the doors, she heard footsteps behind her.

"Nurse Stern! What are you doing here?"

Hannah turned around to see Nurse Bertha frowning at her.

"I was looking for Dr. Jekelius," she replied in as quelling a tone as she dared. "My brother is eager to convey his regard."

"The medical director is elsewhere—"

"So I see. I will try another time." She turned back, walking quickly down the steps without waiting for the senior nurse to dismiss her.

Back in pavilion three, Hannah did not risk telling Margarethe her news until the end of the day, when they were both upstairs, getting ready for bed.

"I found the names," she said quietly, and Margarethe's face glowed.

"You did? In his office?"

Hannah nodded and Margarethe clutched her hands.

"Good girl! Were you seen at all?"

"Nurse Bertha saw me as I was leaving the building, but I don't think she suspected."

"So no one will know you were there?"

Hannah thought of the unsealed envelope; it was not impossible that Nurse Bertha could tell Jekelius of her visit, and he could draw the necessary inferences, but that was surely something Margarethe didn't need to be troubled with now. "I don't think so."

"Well done, then! Very well done." Margarethe squeezed her hands. "And now we must act."

"Jekelius has been away," Hannah offered. "So we have a little time, I should think, to plan."

"Yes." Margarethe nodded, her brow furrowed as she began to pace the room in thought. "Yes, I think it is best if he does his visits as usual, so there is no suspicion. But we will have everything in place, so we can move quickly as soon as he has come."

"I don't know what pavilions the children are in. It wasn't on their forms—"

"Leave that to me."

"And then we'll move them? We'll save them?" Hannah heard the eagerness in her voice, and her face fell as she saw Margarethe shake her head.

"You have done enough, Hannah, you must leave the rest to me."

"But—"

"It is too dangerous, to have us both skulking about in such a way whenever we are not on our shifts. Dear Helga would certainly start to suspect!" She reached for her hands once again. "You have done so well, and shown so much courage. You need not risk anything more. Not till next time, anyway." Her eyes flashed with an attempt at humor, but Hannah could not summon a smile.

"Please," she said quietly, "let me help."

"You already have—"

"Why won't you let me with this, as well? Two of us are surely better than one—"

"Not in this instance. For the sake of the children, we cannot risk it."

"But—"

"I understand why you want to," Margarethe said gently, "considering Willi. I'm truly sorry, but it must be this way. Otherwise it really is too dangerous."

Knowing Margarethe would not be moved on the subject, Hannah nodded reluctantly. The last thing she wished was to endanger the lives of the children they meant to save. "What will you do, then?" she asked. "At least tell me how it happens."

"Much as I told you before, when we were with Heinrich. Once Jekelius has visited the patients, we will see about moving them before anyone else does."

"Karl will do it?"

"That is my hope." Margarethe's tone was acidic, making Hannah wonder yet again what had happened between the two of them. She had continued to avoid Karl as much as she could, and although he'd seen her in passing, he'd done nothing more than smile ruefully at her, and once had given her a wink that Hannah had chosen to ignore.

She'd felt a tug of sorrow for the friendship they'd had, such as it had been. She knew it had been faint and fledgling and barely anything at all, yet she found she still missed it.

"And you will contact Heinrich?" she pressed, trying to envision how it would all work. "And he will meet you at the wall and take the children?"

"Yes, God willing."

"Where will they go?"

"To the Franciscan Sisters of Christian Charity. They take them in, hide them in their convent or move them to families who are willing to care for them."

Hannah nodded slowly. "You will tell me?" she asked. "How it goes? When they're safe?"

"Of course." Margarethe put her arms around her, hugging

her tightly. Hannah clasped her back, grateful for the gesture of affection, realizing in that moment how much she needed it. In her arms, Margarethe's body was wiry and strong, warm and alive. "Thank you, Hannah," she whispered. "You have done so much, more than you know. Thank you, for being so brave."

Margarethe released her with a quick, sorrowful smile, and then hurried back to her own bedroom, leaving Hannah alone.

She undressed slowly, gazing out the window at the spring night, the trees in blossom, the world reborn. *I helped,* she thought, with a tremor of wonder, a thrill of fear for what still might come to pass. *I helped to save those children, God willing. God willing.*

She closed her eyes, offering a wordless prayer to the god she didn't entirely believe in, even as, for the first time, she wanted to. *If you really do see 'the least of these', then save them. Save them.*

She opened her eyes and gazed out at the dark night for another long moment, a sliver of moon sending long, silvery beams across the shadowy ground. It was a night as peaceful as any, even though bombs fell in Berlin on an almost daily basis, and just this last week both Hamburg and Bremen had been badly hit.

Here they were safe... as those children would be, once Margarethe rescued them. With that thought like a promise in her heart, Hannah turned back to her bed.

CHAPTER 23

Three days after Hannah had crept into Jekelius's office, Margarethe gave her a quick, meaningful nod as she passed her on the stairs. Hannah bit her lip to keep from asking an inopportune question, and Margarethe hurried on. *It was happening*, she thought with a thrill of wonder. It was finally happening.

For the rest of the day, she could barely think; she spilled a full bedpan all over the floor, much to Helga's irritation, although she found it amusing enough to see Hannah on her hands and knees, scrubbing up the mess. At dinner, she toyed with her soup, staring down at the usual watery broth, her stomach too clenched with anxiety even to think of managing a mouthful.

Upstairs in her room, she tried to read a book she'd bought at a shop in Penzing, a silly romance that had her tossing it aside in frustration after just a few pages. She stared out at the night, straining to listen, but there was nothing to hear. Had Karl collected the children? Had Margarethe moved them? Was Heinrich even now waiting by the wall? She had no idea about any of it.

An hour crept past, each minute seeming to last an age.

Hannah paced her room, her mind flitting between imagining what might be happening somewhere in the darkness, and memories of Willi—in the garden, with his book, her arm around him. If only he was clambering over the wall tonight! If only she had been able to save him.

What if you caused his death instead?

It was a prospect she could not bear to consider, and yet it still burrowed into her consciousness, filling her with corrosive guilt. If she hadn't gone to Berlin, if she hadn't tried to help in a way that had seemed safer for her, perhaps Willi would still be alive. Perhaps Jekelius would not have acted on that terrible order, knowing how Willi had been protected by both her and Georg.

In her more practical moments, with the vestiges of her old pragmatism, Hannah knew this could not really be true. Neither she nor even Georg were powerful enough to counter-mand shadowy orders from some committee in Berlin. And yet she would never know for sure, and the uncertainty tormented her, when she let it.

Another hour passed, and Hannah lay on her bed and closed her eyes, although she knew she would not sleep. From the ward below, she heard a child call out, and then the brisk, answering heels of Nurse Schmidt.

Eventually, she must have fallen into a doze, for suddenly she found herself springing to alertness, blinking in the gloom as she heard the sound of a door closing, then light footsteps. A few seconds later, Margarethe came breathlessly into her room, her cheeks flushed, her hair half falling down from underneath her kerchief.

"It is done," she said, and Hannah clasped her hands to her heart, overwhelmed.

"All the children? They're safe?"

Margarethe's glowing expression faded a little. "They're safe, yes, but only two."

"Only two!" *Sarah, Leo, Oskar, Ilse.* She'd wanted them all safe. She'd *needed* them to be. Hannah couldn't help feeling crushed, and sounding it, as well. "But why—"

"The little one, Sarah, was too ill. And the boy Oskar..." Margarethe sighed and shook her head. "He was too old and unruly. He wouldn't have come willingly, and we couldn't have managed him. He might have given it all away."

"Couldn't you have given him a sedative—"

"And lug a fourteen-year-old across the park and over the wall?"

"If I'd come too—" Hannah protested.

"It would have been too suspicious. It was hard enough, arranging it as we did. I wondered if old Katschenka suspected when she was told they'd already died. But we saved two—two precious lives, more than we ever have in one evening before!"

"Yes." Hannah tried to smile. *Oskar and Ilse.* They were alive. She would always remember that, remember them, even if she'd never seen them.

Margarethe straightened her dress, shaking out the cuffs and then tidying her hair as she took a deep breath and let it out slowly. "It is done," she said, and her voice sounded heavy in a way Hannah didn't understand.

"Did Karl help?" she asked, and Margarethe looked up, her eyes suddenly flashing.

"Karl, this! Karl, that! Why do you care so much about Karl?"

Stung by her suddenly waspish tone, Hannah retorted indignantly, "I don't!"

"Good," Margarethe replied, "because he's not worth caring about. He helps, yes, but only just." Quickly, she embraced Hannah. "We've done it, that's all that matters. And, God willing, you will find the list of names for next month, as well. You'll have a few weeks' reprieve, at least, before then."

"Yes," Hannah replied, returning the embrace and trying to smile. "A few weeks."

But it did not feel like much of a reprieve. Now that she was involved, Hannah was constantly on edge, always feeling the need to tread carefully, to look over her shoulder. The hospital's environment of surly suspicion and deep disquiet had calcified so that managing every moment felt near impossible. How to school her expression, how to keep her hands from trembling, how to look unassuming, uninterested, as she waited for another month of names, another opportunity to go into Jekelius's office? She admired Margarethe's adopted attitude of insouciance, a mask she slipped on, a well-worn costume Hannah did not have the strength to don.

And yet somehow the days marched on, and she got through each one, waiting for her next opportunity. May was a glorious month of blue skies and lemony sunshine, the windows open to the fresh air, so after the cold, damp winter, the wards were full of warmth and light. At least once a week, Margarethe met with Lash outside the hospital gates to inform him of Hedji's progress. Together Hannah and Margarethe had managed to keep tabs on the boy, often stopping the warden when she marched the boys out, speaking a few words to Hedji whenever they could, slipping him bread or an apple or potato if possible.

"I don't know if it gives him trouble, to know he's being watched," Margarethe told Hannah on a sigh. "That warden is an absolute ogress. Those are the true sadists in a place like this. But we must do what we can."

"I'm sure his father appreciates it," Hannah replied. She had begun to notice how Margarethe's cheeks would pinken whenever she talked about Lash. She'd told Hannah already that he was a carpenter by trade, originally from Debrecen, but he had made his way east in the hope of finding a place where the Roma people were more accepted. In Vienna, at least, he'd found work, but he was sleeping on the floor of a distant relative, and had not yet been able to acquire a suitable set of rooms for him and Hedji.

"But he will one day," Margarethe told Hannah, almost fiercely. "I'm sure of it."

"Will he be allowed?" Hannah asked dubiously. In the last few months, she'd begun to hear rumors and whispers of deportations of both Jews and gypsies, along with anyone else the current regime deemed undesirable. Hannah didn't know much about it, except that they were headed east. Out of sight, out of mind yet again, but perhaps there would be more opportunity for them there, considering all the restrictions that had been forced upon them in Vienna and elsewhere. She could only hope such a thing were possible, although she had her doubts.

Meanwhile, children came and went through pavilion three, with their fevers and infections, pneumonia and rickets, and Hannah did her best to treat them with as much gentleness and care as she could.

Then, at the end of May, she found another opportunity to slip into Jekelius's office. Once again, the corridors were quiet, the man himself on business in the city. Once again, Hannah found the envelope, almost as if it were waiting for her. This time it had, thankfully, already been opened, and she scanned the forms in seconds, committing the names to memory. *Freya, Friedrich, Anna.* Once again, she told the names to Margarethe, and two days later it was done.

"All three were saved, Hannah," Margarethe told her, her face flushed, her eyes defiant. "All three!"

"Tell me about them," Hannah begged. She longed for details to put to the names.

"Anna was in the reformatory school. Eleven years old, strong and intelligent, but too defiant for them, it seemed. She was transferred to seventeen and we got her then. Freya is little more than a baby, and Friedrich is about six—she was in pavilion five, he was in seven. It was almost easy, how we were able to do it with them." She shook her head. "The orderly came and they were already gone. We said they'd died already—he didn't even care."

"Will they suspect, though?" Hannah asked anxiously. "If we save them all?" Yet how could they sacrifice a single child, whose name they knew, whose life they could save? *Oskar. Ilse. Freya. Friedrich. Anna.* The names were written on her heart.

"I don't care," Margarethe replied. "Let them suspect. What are they going to do about it?"

Hannah nodded slowly, because what other answer could there be? If they could save children they would, of course they would. There was no other choice possible.

The war went on too, marching with the days; rumors swirled of an imminent invasion of the Soviet Union, Germany's erstwhile ally. On the morning of the twenty-second of June, the staff on duty gathered around the *Volksemptfänger* in the staff room to hear Goebbels read out the *Führer*'s proclamation. "German people! National Socialists! After long months when I was forced to keep silent, despite heavy concerns, the time has come when I can finally speak openly..."

Hannah looked up to meet Margarethe's pointed glance. To think Hitler himself struggled in the way they did! It was both ludicrous and obscene.

She pressed her lips together as she continued to listen to the Minister of Propaganda's strident claims—how Hitler had brought Germany out of starvation and poverty, how Germany alone in all the world had created a "true people's community." She glanced at Margarethe again, who rolled her eyes. Despite the seriousness of the moment, Hannah had to suppress a sudden urge to laugh—wildly. The man could justify anything, she thought. Anything at all, with his lies. Did no one else see it?

She glanced around the room and saw Helga looked suitably serious; Ida was gazing out the window, as if daydreaming. The doctor on duty had his hands in his pockets and was staring at the radio with a furrowed brow; Hannah had once heard him talking about his brother on the Eastern Front.

"Now," Goebbels continued, "the hour has come when it is necessary to respond to the plot by Jewish-Anglo-Saxon warmongers and the Jewish rulers of Moscow's Bolshevist headquarters. German people! At this moment, an attack unprecedented in the history of the world in its extent and size has begun."

Again Hannah glanced up; no one was smiling. This was not, she realized, good news for anyone, not even an ardent National Socialist like Helga. A war with the Soviet Union, with its vast armies and endless terrain... it did not bode well at all.

"The purpose of this front," Goebbels finished, "is no longer the protection of the individual nations, but rather the safety of Europe, and therefore the salvation of everyone. I have therefore decided today once again to put the fate of Germany and the future of the German Reich and our people in the hands of our soldiers. May God help us in this battle."

After a second of staticky silence, Helga leaned over and turned off the radio with one quick twist of the dial. "Back to work," she said brusquely, and everyone filed out of the staff room without speaking.

"What do you think this will mean?" Hannah asked Margarethe later, when they were having a coffee, just the two of them in the staff room.

Margarethe shrugged as if it were of little consequence. "Germany will lose the war, of course."

"Margarethe!" Hannah glanced around quickly. "It is treason to speak so. You know that as well as I do."

"So is everything I say, do, and think," Margarethe replied, "but in this case it is no more than the truth that is staring everyone in the face. Did you see Helga? She looked like she'd swallowed a lemon. Her nephew is in the Wehrmacht, I believe, in Lithuania."

"But Germany's weapons are so much more advanced," Hannah pointed out. It was what she'd read in the newspapers, which were assuring everyone of victory, instant and absolute. That might not be true, but that didn't mean the opposite was, either.

"And the Soviets have ten times the manpower," Margarethe returned. "It might take time, but it will happen all the same." She gazed out the window as she pronounced softly, "Hitler has signed all our death warrants."

"Don't say such a thing!" Hannah suppressed a shudder.

"Well, you don't want Germany to win, do you?" Margarethe replied, raising her eyebrows. "Imagine the Nazis in charge forever? I can think of nothing worse."

"Yes, but if they lose..." It was the same dilemma she'd faced when talking with Georg. Either outcome was, in its own way, disastrous. And yet... "Of course they must lose," Hannah said, almost to herself. "I know that. I just don't know what it will look like."

"I don't think any of us want to imagine such a thing. But, God willing, these little ones will be safe. Safer, anyway. If it is only for this life we have hope, we are to be pitied," Margarethe told her quietly. "It is what St Paul wrote, and as I have said before, it is what I have always believed. It can be a comfort, when you consider the way the world is."

I never asked for much. And she would not get even that, it seemed. Yet she could not drown in self-pity, Hannah knew; she was better off than many, maybe even most, and there was still so much to be done. So many children to save. *Oskar. Ilse. Freya. Friedrich. Anna.* And more. Many more, God willing.

Hannah straightened, squaring her shoulders. "I can't think about the future," she stated firmly. "It will take care of itself. Isn't that somewhere in the Bible?"

Margarethe laughed and clapped her hands. "Very good! Each day has enough trouble of its own, which is true enough."

"Indeed it is."

Margarethe laid a hand on her arm, her expression turning serious. "It is almost the end of the month."

Hannah swallowed. "I know."

"When...?"

"Soon," she promised. "As soon as I can."

Margarethe squeezed her arm. "Today would be better," she replied.

That afternoon, as the sunlight was turning to the deep, glinting color of syrup, streaming through the leafy trees and creating warm, golden pools on the ground, Hannah headed for the administration pavilion for the third time. She walked with a swing in her step, a set to her shoulders, compelled by something deeper than desire, stronger than fear.

As she slipped past Nurse Bertha's office, she heard her speaking on the telephone, her tone clipped and irritated. Hannah hurried to Jekelius's study, knocked once, and then, holding her breath, opened the door. Empty again. It almost felt too lucky.

In fact, the whole scenario felt surreal, for just as the last two times, the envelope was in the tray, and again it had already been opened. Hannah slid out the papers, memorized the three names printed on them, the damning plus sign in each corner. *Helga. Franz. Otto.* She whispered them as she returned them to the envelope, feeling exultant. Jekelius really was as arrogant as Margarethe had said.

Hannah glanced around the study to make sure she hadn't disturbed anything, and then hurried out, closing the door behind her. She'd only gone half a dozen steps when Dr. Jekelius himself rounded the corner, affecting an expression of pleased surprise.

"Ah, Nurse Stern! It has been some time since I have spoken to you, I believe."

"Indeed it has, *He-Herr Doktor*." In her nervousness, Hannah stammered slightly, but Jekelius only looked amused.

"Come in, come in," he invited as he stepped past her to open the door Hannah had just closed. "I presume you have some word from Major Strasser, for you to be by my study?" He threw the question over his shoulder as he came into the room, tossing some papers carelessly onto his desk.

"Yes, of course." Hannah wiped her damp hands on the sides of her skirt. Her mind felt both whirling and blank; she could not think of a single thing to say. She knew she must not seem suspicious.

Jekelius dropped gracefully into his chair, crossing one leg over the other, steepling his fingers together, just as he had the last time Hannah had spoken to him. It was a pose, she knew now, and he was nothing more than an actor.

"And?" he asked in that same amused tone, one dark eyebrow arched. "What is it that Major Strasser wishes to say to me?"

Hannah touched her tongue to her dry lips as she slowly sat down opposite him, the blood rushing in her ears. She knew Jekelius must read Georg's letters, so she could say nothing that wasn't already in them. "He wishes to thank you for the... the assiduous care of his son," she finally managed, quoting practically verbatim from her brother's letters, and Jekelius's mobile mouth curved into a sly, knowing smile.

"Does he indeed? Perhaps the man has more political prowess than I gave him credit for."

Hannah stared at him for a few seconds before she inclined her head in acknowledgement, deciding to play along. "Perhaps he does."

Jekelius smirked, pleased she'd agreed with him. "I can only assume that what happened to your nephew was a warning to your brother." He pressed his fingers to his lips. "*Half*-brother," he corrected. "Forgive me. If his position did not protect the boy, then there must have been a reason."

Hannah felt a chill creep through her, an icy horror she tried to keep from her face. *I am watched, all the time I am watched! Himmler, even Hitler himself, will question my loyalty...* Could it have been Georg's activities, rather than her own absence, that had caused Willi's death? The news did not bring any relief, only more sorrow—and rage at the evil she saw all around her. Still, she did her best not to show it.

"I assure you, Dr. Jekelius," she said as politely as she could, "that my brother is loyal to the Reich."

"As you say." He inclined his head. "It has nothing to do with me, of course. I merely carry out orders, Nurse Stern. That is all I do."

"Indeed, Dr. Jekelius, I know what a burden those orders are for you." She forced a small, sympathetic smile, and he leaned back in his chair, his chest puffing out, enjoying this little bit of praise.

"I am glad you realize it, Nurse Stern." He paused while Hannah wondered how she could reasonably excuse herself. "Was there anything else you wished to say to me?" Jekelius asked, in such a knowing tone that for a second Hannah was horror-struck, thinking he knew what she was doing, where she'd been. She forced herself not to glance over at the envelope still lying on top of the filing cabinet. "From your brother," he prompted, and a shuddery relief rushed through her.

"No, *Herr Doktor*, thank you, that is all."

"Very well." He gave a nod of dismissal and Hannah rose from her chair on shaky legs. She started toward the door, only to be stopped by that light, seemingly insouciant voice. "Oh, and Nurse Stern?" he called, almost lazily, and she froze, her hand on the doorknob. "Be careful."

Jerkily, Hannah nodded and then hurried from the room.

"He can't know," Margarethe stated definitively when Hannah told her about the conversation later that night. She sat on her bed, her hands tucked between her knees, as she tried not to give in to the terror that threatened to sweep over her at the mere thought of Jekelius knowing what they were up to. "Although, in truth," Margarethe mused, "he might suspect, considering... Still, there is no proof, and I really do believe he is too arrogant to believe someone would dare to spy on him in such a way. He's too busy courting Fraulein Hitler, anyway!" She dropped her scornful tone as she turned to Hannah. "But you will have to be careful, now more than ever. Perhaps we should wait a month before we try again."

"And consign children to death?" Hannah demanded.

Margarethe gave a small smile. "My goodness, but you are beginning to sound like me!"

"He enjoys toying with people," Hannah stated, as she remembered that little smile that had played about Jekelius's lips. "And teasing them. It's all a power game to him, isn't it?"

"Almost certainly, but people who indulge in such games usually end up losing them. The Vienna Youth Welfare Office is already most displeased with him, I hear, and Helga let it drop that our *Führer* might be, as well. It seems he may not want his dear sister consorting with the likes of a jumped-up doctor. It almost makes me wonder if Jekelius is long for this place—or even this world."

"You mean he'd be fired?"

"Fired, arrested, shot, killed?" Margarethe raised her eyebrows. "Who knows?"

"And who will take his place?" Hannah wondered out loud.

"Someone even more devoted, no doubt." Margarethe dropped her indifferent tone to give her a long, level look. "We will save these three children this month, and who knows how many again? Perhaps you are right, Hannah, and you should act while you can, for we don't know how long we have."

CHAPTER 24

JULY 1941

In the middle of July, when the days were baking hot and the pavilions had become nearly stifling, Margarethe announced that Lash had, at long last, been allowed a visit with Hedji. Although he still had not found a place to live, and so couldn't take Hedji out of the school, a visit was the next best thing.

"Don't think they granted it out of the kindness of their hearts," Margarethe told Hannah. "Oh, no. It's just that they've got to look as if they're reasonable, don't they? Otherwise the Youth Welfare Office might become concerned—not that they'd do anything to help, either. It's all just lip service, but at least it means Lash can see him. He's permitted to take him out for the day, and I thought we could all go." Margarethe's tone was exultant. "We'll take a picnic, and our swimming costumes, and for five hours at least we will pretend this wretched war doesn't exist."

"All of us?" Hannah said with some surprise, and Margarethe reached for her arm. "Yes, all of us! You, me, Hedji, and Lash. Why not? Let's have fun, Hannah. Let our cares slip away for a while. I've already spoken to Ida, and she'll swap shifts with me, so we'll have the same day off. Everything's arranged, all you have to do is agree."

"Oh, my." As Hannah considered the idea, she felt a warmth spread through her that she realized was pleasure.

A day without cares, in the company of friends... it sounded almost too good to imagine, too wonderful to be true, and even more so when she saw what Margarethe was packing for their picnic—tinned ham, fresh cheese, bread rolls and a pot of jam.

"Where did you get all that?" she exclaimed.

"My father," Margarethe replied, surprising her.

"I thought you didn't correspond with your father?"

"I don't, but occasionally he sends me things. As far as he is concerned, I am a good daughter of the Reich now I am nursing rather than 'playing at being a nun', and he likes to reward me." She grinned. "At least I can put it to good use."

It was a perfect day for a picnic, sunny and hot. Margarethe insisted Hannah wear one of her dresses, of white sprigged cotton with a nipped-in waist and flounced skirt.

"It's far too girlish for me," Margarethe said, and Hannah let out an uncertain laugh.

"Then it must be for me. I'm twenty-eight."

"And I'm thirty. You can wear white for two more years, at least." Margarethe was wearing a narrow-skirted dress of lavender cotton, its purple hue suited her dark hair and eyes. As she looped the picnic basket over one arm, Hannah felt a surge of excitement. She had not left the grounds of Am Steinhof in weeks, and she longed to now, to leave it all behind, if only for a few hours.

In addition to the dress, Margarethe had lent her a swimming costume, and had insisted she try the lido.

"I want you to have *fun*, Hannah," she'd said, wagging her finger at her, and Hannah had pretended to look meek.

"I'll try," she'd promised.

They met Lash and Hedji by the gates; Hedji looked underfed and raggedy in his reformatory uniform, but Lash had shaved and looked far neater than when Hannah had last seen him, thanks to the money he'd earned from steady work, and his hair was brushed, his clothes clean and respectable. He smiled at Margarethe before he caught Hedji up in a hug.

They took the tram across the city to the Alte Donau lido, on the shores of the Old Danube, an arm of the mighty river that had, in order to prevent flooding, been forced into a regulated canal fifty years ago. With its sunbathing lawns, paddleboats, and bathing jetties, it was the perfect place to while away a hot afternoon.

Yet, Hannah did not miss the '*Juden Betreten Verboten*' sign at the entrance to the lido—Jews, entry forbidden. She glanced at Margarethe and said in a low voice, "Are... are they allowed in here?"

"They're not Jews," Margarethe replied under her breath. "I doubt there's a Jew left in all of Vienna."

"Yes, but—"

"No one will ask," Margarethe cut across her, "and no one will tell."

Hannah supposed Lash looked respectable enough, and no different than any other Austrian. Hedji less so, in his raggedy uniform, but the lido was crowded with all sorts, and everyone seemed intent on minding their own business and enjoying the day. She decided not to let herself worry about it, not today. Today was for enjoyment and pleasure and fun. For friends.

Margarethe picked a secluded spot near the river, sheltered by several trees, and laid out their blanket and picnic. It was easy enough for Hannah to let her cares slide away under the sunshine, especially when she was replete with ham and cheese, bread and jam.

While Margarethe and Lash sat sprawled on the blanket enjoying the sunshine, Hannah took Hedji into the shallow bathing waters of the lido. They stood side by side, the warm water lapping their bare feet. He reached her shoulder, just as Willi had done.

"Isn't it lovely?" she remarked, and he nodded, splashing the water with one bare foot. "Do you swim?" she asked, and then she laughed a little when Hedji gave her a surprisingly haughty look.

"Of course I do."

"I'm not very good," Hannah admitted. She'd only been to the lido in Berlin, by the Wannsee, a handful of times. Her mother had not had time for such things.

"Shall I show you?" Hedji asked, eagerly.

"Yes, please."

She watched as he demonstrated various strokes, cutting through the water with a boy's ease. He was painfully thin, but he was still strong, and the pleasure he took at being in the water gave Hannah her own pleasure, almost painful in its intensity. She could not help but think of Willi. She did not know if he'd enjoyed the water, if he'd been able to swim. Had Georg ever taken him to the Wannsee? She could almost imagine it. He'd have been playful, she was sure of it. He would have splashed her and then chortled in glee, his eyes sparkling as she laughed and wiped the water from her eyes...

"Hannah, are you watching?" Hedji had stopped swimming, standing waist-deep in the water as he looked at her seriously. "Are you sad?" he asked, and Hannah let out an uncertain laugh as she realized her eyes were full of tears.

"Sad and happy," she told him, and he nodded in understanding.

"It's often like that, isn't it?" he asked soberly. He splashed the water gently with one hand. "Come swim with me."

"All right," Hannah answered, a bit recklessly, for she wasn't a particularly strong swimmer, and then she dove into the river, feeling the cool water close over her head, so for a few blissful seconds the whole world fell away and she was alone and clean and so very free—legs kicking out, arms reaching, lungs aching as the sunlight sparkled on the water above her head and she swam on and on, longing to feel like this forever.

Finally, she burst through the surface, droplets of water streaming down her face and bare arms, gasping for breath as she found her footing on the slippery rocks of the riverbed.

Hedji swam up to her, looking both concerned and cross.

"I thought you might have drowned!" he exclaimed and she laughed in abashed apology.

"No, no, it was just so lovely. So quiet and peaceful under the water."

"Let's race!"

"I can't," Hannah protested, laughing again, but Hedji was already off, cutting through the water, heading across the lido, and so, with a groan, Hannah followed, knowing she was much slower.

"I beat you," Hedji crowed when they finally reached the end of the bathing jetty, with Hannah gasping for breath.

"Yes, you did."

"If you're tired, you can float on your back," Hedji offered kindly, and they both flipped over on their backs, faces tilted up to the sunshine as they drifted lazily through the warm water.

There was not a cloud in the achingly blue sky, and as Hannah drifted along, the only sound the occasional burst of laughter or birdsong, she felt almost as if she could fall asleep, a smile on her face, lulled by the gentle waves like a baby in a cradle. If only life could be as simple as this.

And why shouldn't it be? Why should there be wars, and

unjust laws, and cruel people like Jekelius ending lives with the stroke of his pen? She wanted to pretend none of it existed, for a few more hours, and yet already she felt a shadow creep over her mind, if not the sun, and she stood up in the river, shielding her eyes as she glanced back toward the bathing lawn.

Margarethe was bundling up their blanket, she saw, and a scowling man was moving them on. Rage burned through her. Someone must have suspected Lash was Roma.

"Come on, Hedji," she said, and she swam out, back toward the bathing jetty, away from Margarethe and Lash, and what was happening there.

By the time Hannah and Hedji got out of the water, Margarethe and Lash had moved to another place in the lido, away from whoever had been bothering them.

"Just a busybody with nothing better to do," Margarethe replied dismissively to Hannah's silent question as she and Hedji walked up to them. "He had no authority, at least."

"And we pretended we were leaving," Lash interjected with a wry smile. "People so often wish to feel important."

"I'm sorry," Hannah said quietly. She sat, dripping, on the blanket, while Hedji flopped down next to his father.

"I beat Hannah in a race!" Hedji, unaware of what had happened, grinned at Lash.

"How gallant of you," Lash remarked, stroking his son's shaven head with a look on his face that Hannah couldn't bear to see—an ache of love and longing, mingled with both fear and loss. She had heard from Margarethe how his wife had died back in Hungary, after they'd been turned out of their home for being Roma. How hard it must be for him, she thought, to have no choice but to leave his son at that place, just as Georg had.

"It was completely fair," she assured him with a small smile. "Hedji is simply a better swimmer than I am."

"What about boating?" Margarethe asked with a playful gleam in her eyes. "Are you adept with a paddle, Hedji? Shall we see?"

Lash looked both abashed and alarmed. "I don't—"

"My treat," Margarethe stated firmly. "I've always wanted to boat on the Danube."

She left them to pay for the boat, while Lash gave Hannah an embarrassed look. "It is better if I don't make the arrangements," he told her, and she nodded her understanding, knowing he could run into trouble if he attempted such a thing.

"I'm sorry it is this way."

"It has always been this way for our people, sometimes better, sometimes worse, but never fair." He sighed. "I try to live as best as I can, in peace with everyone."

"That is wise," Hannah told him. "But also difficult."

Lash smiled wryly in acknowledgement, and Hannah could understand why Margarethe's cheeks went pink when she spoke of him. Clean-shaven and dressed respectably, he was a handsome man, with hazel eyes like his son, and soft brown hair that fell across his forehead. There was a touching dignity to him, as well as a surprising strength and a rare humor. When he looked at Margarethe, Hannah had noticed, everything about him softened.

Soon enough, they were all clambering into the boat, and then pushing off into the river, far enough away from any other potential busybodies as they drifted downstream.

"Isn't this lovely?" Margarethe murmured as she leaned back in her seat, her elbows braced behind her, one slender leg raised to trail her toes in the water, while Lash paddled. She tilted her face up to the sky, her languorous post as artful as a statue of Venus. "You can almost believe there isn't a war on."

"That's what I was thinking earlier, when we were swimming," Hannah replied.

"One day there won't be a war." Margarethe lowered her

head from her perusal of the cloudless sky to gaze at them each in turn. "What will you do after the war? Hedji?"

"We'll go to the mountains," Hedji answered promptly. "And have a little cottage. And we'll have a garden, and chickens, and maybe a cow, for milk. Or a goat."

"And don't forget a dog," Lash put in with a smile.

"Yes, and Papa will make things," Hedji continued. "Chairs and tables and shelves." He smiled with childish certainty, and Hannah suppressed the pang of fear and grief she felt, that such simple dreams had little chance of coming to pass. *After the war...* would such a time ever come, for Margarethe, for Lash, for Hedji, for her?

"And you, Lash?" Margarethe asked, a playful lilt of challenge in her voice. "Do you share that dream?"

"I think it's a good one." His gaze lingered on hers as her lips curved in a pleased and knowing smile.

"Yes," she agreed, "it is." Hannah, sensing they were sharing something private, had to look away. "But what about a cat?" Margarethe continued. "I have always wanted a cat. Is there room in this cottage for a cat, Hedji?"

"I don't like cats," Hedji informed her solemnly, and Margarethe pulled a disappointed face.

"Oh, dear! A kitten, then?"

"Maybe."

"But kittens," Lash reminded him gently, "grow up into cats, *fiacskam*, remember?"

"Ye-es..." Hedji agreed reluctantly, and Margarethe laughed and clapped her hands.

"So they do, more's the pity! What about you, Hannah? What will you do after the war?"

"Me?" Hannah gazed down at the gently flowing river, the water smooth and opaque as she trailed her fingers through its silky coolness. She could see nothing beneath. "I don't know."

"Not allowed in this game!" Margarethe told her cheerfully. "You must think of something."

"Must I?" Hannah returned with a small laugh. Yes, she supposed, today, with its sunshine and blue skies, was a day for dreams and not worries, hope and not fear. She glanced back at the water, as dark as the lake by Heim Hochland, when she had stood outside and tried to forget about a baby being born with blue eyes and a cleft lip. That felt like a lifetime ago, but it had been less than a year. "Then I suppose..." She hesitated, staring into those dark waters now swirling into eddies from Lash's paddle so she could not see anything—not the sky, not the riverbed. "I suppose I'd like to live quietly somewhere," she said slowly. "And be at peace." As for other, vague notions—of a husband, a home, children... she did not dare speak of those. She could not even think about them.

She glanced up to see Margarethe looking at her thoughtfully, while Lash gave her a smile full of sympathy and understanding.

"That," he said, "sounds like a good dream."

And that was all it was right now, Hannah thought as she trailed her fingers through the water, sending eddies rippling away. A dream. A dream she would hold onto.

The sun was sinking toward the horizon, a golden ball of fire, when they finally, sleepy and sunburned, made it back to Penzing. At the gates of Am Steinhof, Lash embraced his son tightly, murmuring endearments and prayers against his shaven scalp before he finally, with tears in his eyes, released him.

He turned to Margarethe. "I can never thank you enough for today—"

"You don't need to thank me at all."

They stared at each other, and Hannah moved away a little, conscious once again of the intimacy of the moment.

Hedji reached for her hand. "Will we go swimming again?"

She opened her mouth to say she hoped so, and then smiled down at him. "Yes," she promised, "we will."

Margarethe broke away from Lash, and together she, Hannah and Hedji all headed toward the tall, forbidding gates of the hospital. As Hannah approached, the pavilions looming darkly beyond, she was seized by a sudden, overwhelming dread so visceral and complete she let out a little gasp and started to take a step back, longing only to run away, as far and fast as she could.

Margarethe, sensing her mood, reached for her hand. "Remember," she said softly. "We have work to do."

Hannah nodded, the aftershocks of that awful dread, almost like a premonition, still trembling through her. She couldn't bear it, she thought, not any of it. Not the dreary ward, not her tiny room, not the watery soup, and most of all, not the desperate, pleading eyes of all the children she might never be able to save.

"Come on, Hannah," Hedji said, reaching for her other hand, and together, the three of them walked through the gates.

CHAPTER 25

Hannah struggled to enter Jekelius's study at the end of July; each time she went, the door was locked. She tried four times before she finally succeeded, letting out a gasp of surprise when the door swung open. This time, there was no envelope waiting for her in its tray; she had to riffle through the papers on his desk, rattle drawers uselessly, before she realized there was nothing for her to find.

"Perhaps the letter did not come this month," Margarethe said, frowning, when Hannah gave her the news. "Perhaps it's a good thing, Hannah. We will keep our ears and eyes open, and try again next month."

Hannah nodded, feeling dissatisfied. She had but one part to play in their rescue operation each month, and she was desperate to play it. A whole month without saving any children... but perhaps, like Margarethe had intimated, it meant none had been marked for death.

Even so, it was becoming more and more challenging to go about her duties, weighed down with the knowledge she had. The day at the Alte Donau lido had only made things more difficult to bear, for now that she'd tasted such sweetness and freedom, the long, dispiriting days on the ward felt even more endless, the war stretching on and on.

July had been full of the Wehrmacht's victories against the Soviets; they had secured the Baltic states, crossed the Dnieper, and were within a few dozen miles of both Kiev and Leningrad. Despite the staggeringly heavy losses, victory seemed almost certain, at least according to the newspapers.

"Wait until winter," Margarethe had told Hannah, unimpressed by the blazing headlines in the *Wiener Zeitung*. "Hitler, it seems, hasn't heard of Napoleon."

"How can you be so sure?"

"Because I am sure that Germany will lose this war," Margarethe had replied in a clipped, matter-of-fact tone. "Of that I *must* be sure."

In August, Margarethe got hold of an illegally printed copy of a sermon Bishop von Galen had preached in Münster earlier in the month. "Read what he says," she exclaimed to Hannah, defiant and rejoicing. "Finally, someone is bold enough to proclaim the truth! At last people must listen!"

Hannah scanned the printed text, her heart leaping at the bishop's brave words: *This ghastly doctrine tries to justify the murder of blameless men and would seek to give legal sanction to the forcible killing of invalids, cripples, the incurable and the incapacitated... The opinion is that since they can no longer make money, they are obsolete machines, comparable with some old cow that can no longer give milk or some horse that has gone lame... Here we are dealing with human beings, with our neighbors, brothers and sisters, the poor and invalids... unproductive—perhaps! But have they, therefore, lost the right to live? Have you or I the right to exist only because we are "productive"?... My dearly Beloved, I trust that it is not too late. It is time that we realized today what alone can bring us peace. We must openly, and without reserve, show by our actions that we will live our lives by obeying God's commandments. Our motto must be: Death rather than sin. By pious prayer and penance we can bring down upon us all, our city and our beloved German land, His grace and forgiveness.*

Slowly, Hannah lowered the leaflet. "He'll be arrested," she said, her tone one of both awe and foreboding. "Sent to a camp or killed."

"Perhaps, or perhaps Goebbels and his ilk will realize that doing such a thing will only stoke the fires of rebellion. People are outraged, Hannah, now that it has been brought into the light. There have been protests all over Austria and Germany, letters by the basketful to Berlin... Hitler cannot ignore it." Her face shone as she finished softly, "Perhaps this means it will finally end."

"End...?" Hannah stared at her in incredulous hope. "Do you really think so? There won't be any more orders...?" She could hardly dare to dream of such a thing. She realized she had not been able to imagine an end to the killing, the suffering, the fear, the grief. But on a single order from Hitler...

"No, there won't," Margarethe told her with joy, before adding more somberly, "God willing."

A week later, amazingly, it seemed their hopes were confirmed. "Hitler himself has given the order," Margarethe announced, grabbing Hannah's hands and spinning her around in her room. "I heard it from Helga, because, of course, she can't keep a secret! She heard it from Nurse Bertha, who had it from Jekelius himself. All the sanitoriums and hospitals have received it straight from Berlin—there will be no more names given. The program is officially stopped, because of the protests."

"I can't believe it," Hannah whispered. It felt too easy, and yet it had been so *hard*. So long. Could it really be over, in the snap of a finger? It almost felt wrong, somehow, and yet, of course, it was so right. No more children killed. No more names on dreaded lists.

"Nor can I." Margarethe dropped her hands to gaze out the window at the parkland in summery bloom, her exultant expression turning pensive. "No more sneaking into Jekelius's office. No more creeping about in the night." For a second, her face darkened and then she shook her head, as if to discard a memory. "We can finally dream of a future, Hannah, for when after the war is over."

"And who knows when that will be," Hannah couldn't keep from retorting. Imagination only took one so far.

"Still, we can hope." There was a stubborn note in Margarethe's voice, and Hannah smiled, feeling, for the first time, strangely maternal toward her friend.

"And are you hoping for a little cottage in the mountains," she teased gently, "with some chickens and a goat, a dog, and yes, a cat? Or at least a kitten."

Margarethe blushed as she gave a little laugh. "Am I so obvious?"

Hannah's smile deepened. "I'm happy for you, Margarethe."

"I never expected to fall in love." She ducked her head, abashed, blushing. "And with a penniless Roma! But he's a good man, you know."

"Yes," Hannah agreed, "I do. A very good man."

"He must survive the war." Margarethe stared out the window, her expression turning bleak, her voice fierce. "He *must*. You know they have started to round up the Roma along with the Jews? To send them out east."

"Perhaps it is better out east," Hannah offered hesitantly.

Margarethe gave a harsh laugh. "And if you believe that, you believe Nurse Katschenka really is just feeding her little patients raspberry juice, and out of the goodness of her heart, as well."

Hannah could not keep from shuddering. "Do not mention that woman to me." Even now, she could recall her smooth face, those pitiless eyes, as she'd told her about Willi.

Margarethe laughed again, this time the sound one of joy. "I never will again, because I won't have to! She will not prepare a cup of cocoa or juice again, I hope."

"I pray that it is so," Hannah agreed.

Margarethe looked at her in sudden earnestness. "Do you, Hannah?" she asked. "Do you pray?"

"Oh, I..." She let out an embarrassed laugh; the words had come thoughtlessly. "I don't know."

"I hope you do," Margarethe told her. "I *pray* you do. For the war will end for both of us, and I pray I will find my cottage in the mountains, and you... you will find your peace."

"Yes," Hannah replied, but she heard the creeping note of doubt in her voice. When she closed her eyes, even now, she sometimes still thought of that baby boy, his cleft lip. And what of Willi as well as all the others? There would be no future for them, no hope for when the war ended. How could she then find her own peace? Even now, with the good news brought by Bishop von Galen, it felt elusive.

A week passed where peace felt, while still elusive, not quite as far away. Margarethe was more playful than ever, made buoyant in hope; the sun shone; Hannah received a letter from Georg praising the announcement of the end of the killings—couched in vague language, of course—and wishing her well. He'd written to her once or twice a month, to ask after her wellbeing. Two German U-boats had been captured by the British; the Soviets were pushing back in both Kiev and Smolensk. As much as Hannah dreaded the possibility of Germany's defeat, she welcomed it, too. Perhaps the end of the war was nearer than any of them dared hope, no matter Georg's dire predictions.

Then, in the first week of September, she saw an unfamiliar orderly pushing a stretcher toward pavilion fifteen. "No..." she whispered from the window of the hospital ward, her palm pressed against the glass. Before she could even think what she was doing, she ran down the stairs and out of the pavilion, hurrying down the path toward the man.

"*Verzeihung*, but where are you going?" she called. "Where are you taking that patient?"

He stared at her, surprised by her outburst. "He is being transferred to pavilion fifteen."

"But—" She stared at him in confusion. "But why?"

The man simply shrugged. He started pushing again and Hannah took a few steps toward him, so she could see the child lying in the stretcher. It was little Leon from pavilion five, the boy who had liked to bang on the piano. He gazed up at her with dazed eyes, his lids heavy from sedation. The orderly started to push the stretcher once more and Hannah stopped him with one hand.

"There's been a mistake."

"I don't think so, *Schwester*—"

"Trust me on this." She gave him a hard, glittering smile. "This boy is meant for pavilion three. He's burned himself, and he needs to be treated."

For the first time, the orderly looked confused. He was young, Hannah realized, barely more than a boy. "But I was told—"

"By Nurse Scholz, I suppose?" Hannah cut across him, shaking her head, the lies springing to her lips with sudden, surprising ease. "She's hopeless, that one. Always getting confused. She'd rather read the *Wiener Illustrierte* than do her job! You know what I mean?"

The boy smiled faintly and Hannah knew she had guessed right.

"You know she's already been reprimanded twice? Imagine if you took the wrong patient to pavilion *fifteen*?" She rolled her eyes. "Trust me, you'd be in big trouble. You're new here, I know. You don't know the ropes yet, perhaps." She clapped a hand on his shoulder. "Don't worry, I'll help you. I'll take it from here."

"But..."

"Go on, now," Hannah said as she began to push the stretcher toward three. "And thank your lucky stars I caught you before you did something really disastrous!"

She kept pushing, walking with an airy confidence she was far from feeling, and after a few seconds, the orderly muttered,

"*Danke, Schwester.*"

Upstairs, Margarethe paced Hannah's room while Leon lay on her bed, just as Willi once had.

"How can it still be going on!" she exclaimed. "Hitler himself gave the order—"

"Or said he did," Hannah interjected. "But why should we believe him, or anyone? The deaths are still happening."

"But..." Margarethe's voice trailed away, her eyes turning wide and dark.

Hannah knew what she was thinking, that she'd wanted to believe they'd stopped. Of course she had, because she had something to live for now; she had Lash. *I died before I came here.* But not quite, not entirely. Not now.

"What about Leon?" she asked quietly, nodding toward the sleeping boy.

"I'll see Heinrich tonight. We'll arrange something. He should be quiet, up here."

"As long as there's not a piano nearby," Hannah said with a

little laugh. She reached down to stroke the little boy's hair away from his forehead. "He likes his music."

"You were brave, Hannah," Margarethe told her. "And quick-thinking too! That orderly didn't know what to think, I'm sure."

"I'm glad of it." Hannah gazed down at Leon, something fiercer than joy expanding in her heart. *Oskar. Ilse. Freya. Friedrich. Anna. Helga. Franz. Otto.* And now Leon.

"I'll have to go into Jekelius's office again," she told Margarethe the next day, when Leon, thankfully, had been spirited away, through the orchard and to the Franciscan Sisters of Charity.

"I suppose you must." There was a new weariness to Margarethe's voice, a defeated tone that bordered on hopelessness. She looked as if some vital element had drained out of her, had left her wrung out and weary, so unlike her normally vibrant self.

"Yes." The prospect did not frighten her, the way it once might have. Hannah felt only determined.

Margarethe shook her head slowly as she sank onto her bed. "I don't understand it. If the killings don't stop, the protests will start up once more. Hitler wouldn't give an order simply for it to be disregarded. He's too clever for that."

"Perhaps there is another order," Hannah suggested.

"But what?"

She shook her head helplessly. She had no idea.

In late September Hannah found her way into Jekelius' office, only to be thwarted yet again. There was no envelope, no list of names. Frustration roared through her. To risk so much—for nothing! What was happening? Children were still being marked out for the ghastly further treatment, but it didn't seem to be coming from Berlin. Who, then?

The weather became chilly, the leaves turned yellow and brown, and Hannah felt no closer to understanding what was happening—or how she could save more children. In fact, things seemed to be getting even worse, despite the order from Berlin. The neglect, starvation and downright abuse that had been a matter more of indifference was becoming both calculated and systemic. Hannah suffered in horrified silence as an urbane, blank-faced doctor came into pavilion three and injected every patient on the ward with tuberculosis; nine of them died within days.

"It's to research a vaccine," Ida explained, as if that made it better.

She saw children who had at least before been fed and clothed now starved and left out in the cold. Helga wheeled a child out into the courtyard behind the pavilion even though it was raining; the poor girl developed pneumonia and disappeared from the ward the next day.

Both Hannah and Margarethe did what they could to fight the relentless tide of cruelty, but it felt like so little. Whenever she could, she closed windows, tucked in extra blankets, smuggled in extra food. At least, she thought, children weren't being sent to pavilion fifteen, as far as she could tell, but in some ways this slow torture was worse.

"It's all around us now," Margarethe said, biting her knuckles as she paced her room, while Hannah sat on the bed, watching her. They were both pale and gaunt from the stress, filled with a nervous energy, an endless anxiety. "It's impossible to stop or contain. There's no way to help them all! And it will only get worse as Germany loses the war. I should have seen how this would be." She shook her head, the movement savage. "They will begrudge so much as a single moldy potato given to the *Unbrauchbar* instead of the Wehrmacht." She gazed at

Hannah with haunted eyes. "And it won't just be the patients, although they will certainly suffer the worst of it. It will be us, too." For the first time since Hannah had known her, her friend looked afraid.

She wasn't, though, she realized. She wasn't even surprised; she was beginning to think that no evil perpetrated in this place would ever take her by surprise again.

"Then we must try harder," she stated firmly.

In mid-September of 1941, the Royal Air Force airdropped leaflets all over Vienna, as part of their anti-Nazi propaganda. In large, black print, they stated starkly *Unbrauchbare*... The Useless. They named the figure of those killed by the Nazis as two hundred thousand, which shocked Hannah into a horrified silence.

"And here we thought only four or five a month," Margarethe whispered as she scanned the leaflet. "They mention Am Steinhof, and even Jekelius! They call him 'the gentleman with the syringe,' and they say Hitler is 'The Urn Handler.'" She shuddered and thrust the leaflet away from her. "Nothing has changed, has it?"

Hannah scanned the leaflet, realization dawning inside her. "If there's no list from Berlin," she said slowly, "it must be Jekelius himself who is deciding, in secret."

Understanding flashed in Margarethe's eyes as her lips twisted. "How powerful he must feel! He must have been given not an order, but a license—death by any means. The public will never even know." She shook her head, and then the derision dropped away, replaced by stark fear as she let out a gasp, the sound as close to a sob as any Hannah had heard from her. "Hannah," she confessed on a moan, "I don't know what to do." It was the first time she had ever said such a thing to her.

"So it will get worse," Hannah stated slowly. Something was

hardening inside her, a resolve that went right down into her bones, her very soul, solidifying inside her, a heavy, purposeful weight. She felt as if she were at the beginning of something, the start of a journey, or the base of a mountain. She had been so afraid things would get worse, so very afraid of all the unknowns looming ahead of her, yet now did not feel any fear at all. "We knew that would happen, Margarethe, if Germany is to lose the war."

"Yes, but..." Margarethe bit her lip.

Lash, Hannah thought, understanding at once. Lash and Hedji. They meant so much to Margarethe now; her *life* meant more to her, because of them. "We must continue to rescue whom we can," she stated with firm matter-of-factness. "It worked before, when I found the names—"

"But there *are* no names now!"

"There will still be names. Jekelius will write them down, or mark them on a list of his own. Somehow, he will, and I will find it." The certainty of it settled in Hannah's bones. "He would enjoy that, wouldn't he? Reading a list of names and deciding some child's fate with the simple stroke of his pen. It will all be up to him, no orders from Berlin to follow, and he will relish it."

"And you'll look for that list?" Margarethe surmised, sounding anxious. Her eyes were wide and dark in her pale face, and she nibbled her lip.

Hannah smiled at her, putting her hands on her shoulders for comfort. "I'll find that list," she promised.

At the end of October, Hannah managed to get into Jekelius's study, but she could find nothing at all. The top of the desk had been tidied; there were no papers, and neither was there a photograph of the dark-eyed *fraulein*. Hannah had no choice but to creep away, frustrated and yet more determined than ever.

The autumn rain had started, dark, drizzly days that wore down the spirit and permeated the soul. The wards had become cold again, and the children's thin chests rattled with coughs, especially as Helga insisted on keeping the windows open in all weathers. What little sense of camaraderie or cheerfulness there had been among the staff, it was utterly gone; the doctors and all the other nurses went about their business in dour silence, without even the pretense of caring, as the patients entrusted to them wasted away.

And then, in early November, Hannah found her opportunity. Helga let it slip that Jekelius had to go into central Vienna to meet with the Youth Welfare Office; once again, he'd incurred their disapproval with his stringent punishments for the pupils of the reformatory school that was under his control, along with the clinic. With the afternoon off, it was easy enough for Hannah to slip away; she was halfway to the administration pavilion when she heard a shout from behind her.

"Hannah!"

She turned to see Karl striding toward her, a sullen look on his face. "I haven't seen you in a while," he remarked. "Where are you off to, then?"

"Just into Penzing, for some errands." Hannah spoke as repressively as she could, but Karl merely shoved his hands into the pockets of his coat, rocking back on his heels as he gazed at her.

"I liked you, you know," he said after a moment, and she thought he sounded more truculent than regretful. "What happened?"

Hannah could only shake her head.

"It wasn't my fault, about Willi," he told her.

"I know."

"Then why—" He frowned, his expression twisting into something ugly. "What did Margarethe tell you? Because if that bit of—"

"She didn't tell me anything," Hannah cut across him. "But what would she tell me, Karl, if she chose to?"

He shrugged, his gaze sliding away. "It doesn't matter."

"I don't suppose it does," she agreed. Things were different now, and perhaps, if they dared another rescue, they'd be better off without Karl, although they'd certainly needed his help before. "I must go."

"Too good for me now, are you?" Karl called after her, and Hannah did not reply as she hurried away.

She was not holding out much hope as she slipped into the administration pavilion; even if she managed to sneak into Jekelius's study, what were the chances she would find something? And yet Hannah knew she had to try. Even if there was nothing, even if she was caught. She could not live with herself otherwise; she could not bear to work, day in and day out, in such a place as this, if she were not doing something, no matter how small, to help. To save the children she could. *Oskar. Ilse. Freya. Friedrich. Anna. Leon. Helga. Franz. Otto.* And, she hoped, someone else, today.

No one saw her slip into Jekelius's study, and just as before, there were no papers on the desk. Hannah let out a quiet breath of disappointment before she moved around to the other side of the desk to try the drawers—all locked, save for the ones that held only pens and paper. There was no mail in the tray on top of the filing cabinets, and the cabinets themselves were locked. There was nothing, *nothing*...

And then, a sound in the hallway—quick, light footsteps. Hannah froze, her feet rooted to the floor, as she heard the footsteps come closer, and then, alarmingly, stop right outside the door. A second passed, an eternity that went all too quickly, and then she stared in mesmerized horror as the knob began to turn. The door had started to open when she finally sprang to action, slipping behind the heavy curtains just as Dr. Jekelius himself stepped into the room.

CHAPTER 26

Hannah knew it was Jekelius from the smell of his aftershave, cloyingly overpowering and expensive. He was humming under his breath, moving around the study, while Hannah shrank against the window, sucking in her own breath, praying he would only be a moment. He was meant to be in the city, meeting with officials! Why had he come back?

She heard the creak of his chair as he sat down and she closed her eyes, offered up a silent prayer. What if he stayed for hours? What on earth would she do then? She could not skulk behind this curtain for very long; she would make a sound, or her legs would cramp. Something would give her away. He was barely more than a meter or two away from her; he would hear her *breathe*.

And if he found her, hiding here behind the curtain? What on earth could be her excuse?

I don't care, Hannah thought with sudden, reckless certainty. *I don't care if he finds me, and I won't give an excuse. I'll tell him I know about his murderous deeds, that I'm working against him. Why not? Why not!*

A bright, blazing courage surged through her, and she

almost stepped forward, if just to see the look of shock on Jekelius's face. *I came into your study, I rescued children you'd deemed worthy only of death, and you never even knew...*

Then Jekelius let out a long, exaggerated sigh. The chair creaked as he sat back against it; Hannah could just glimpse the polished tip of his shoe, his legs stretched out in front of him.

"Why don't you just come out from there, Nurse Stern," he said.

For a single, stunned second, Hannah thought she must have imagined it. He couldn't possibly know she was hiding here, and he sounded so unsurprised about it, as well.

"It must be quite tiring, to stand so still," he remarked. "Are you holding your breath? My dear girl, just come out and be done with it."

Another moment passed while Hannah simply stood there, too shocked even to think, and then, on shaky legs, she stepped out from behind the curtain to see, to her shock, Jekelius smiling at her.

"There," he said. "That wasn't so hard, was it? Do sit down." He gestured to the chair in front of his desk and she lowered herself into it, her mind reeling. "Did you think I didn't know?" he asked, amused. "My dear Nurse Stern, not one thing happens at this hospital without me knowing. Not one single thing."

Hannah simply stared. She would not give Margarethe away, or even Karl, or anything that happened here. He could not know everything. He simply could not.

"You were looking for the list, weren't you?" Jekelius continued. "I suppose you thought you were very clever, opening those envelopes from Berlin?'

Hannah opened her mouth, closed it. He'd *known*?

Finally she forced herself to speak. "You left them there on purpose?" she asked, her voice a croak.

Jekelius shrugged, his gaze sliding away from hers. "The last one, yes. It took me some time to realize what was going on under my nose, I must admit!" He turned back to her, wagged his finger with an awful sort of playfulness. "So you are quite clever, aren't you? When I saw the envelope had been opened..." He leaned forward, clearly enjoying this little denouement. "Well, I had my suspicions. You do not need to be an eminent scientist such as I am to wonder what had happened, especially when Nurse Bertha kindly informed me that you had been looking for me. However, I must confess I didn't think you *quite* so courageous, to sneak in here as you must have done. I suppose you've saved one or two of the children?"

Oskar. Ilse. Freya. Friedrich. Anna. Leon. Helga. Franz. Otto. If he only thought she'd saved one or two, he didn't know as much as he pretended, and she wondered if he'd really suspected at all, before this moment. Dr. Jekelius was the sort of man who liked to think he was smarter than he was.

"Yes," Hannah replied tonelessly, "we managed one or two."

She realized she had nothing left to lose, and it was almost a heady feeling. Finally she could tell this man exactly what she thought of him and it wouldn't matter one whit, because surely her death warrant, or at least the one for her arrest, was as good as signed.

"To risk your life for such creatures," Jekelius remarked musingly. "How strange. How foolish of you."

"Foolish?" Hannah repeated neutrally, allowing it to be a question.

"Yes, foolish!" For a second, the mask dropped, and Jekelius did not look amused or urbane or in control; he only looked annoyed by what he saw as her stubbornness. "Willing to risk everything, and for what? A child or two whose lives are worthless anyway?"

"I don't think their lives are worthless," Hannah stated quietly.

"You realize I could have you arrested? Sent to a camp?" He spoke incredulously, yet also with a smugness that made Hannah realize he enjoyed wielding such power.

"Yes, I do," she replied, her voice thankfully steady.

"You don't even know what the camps are like, you can't imagine," he told her scornfully. "If you did—"

"I'd do the same again," Hannah cut across him. She took a deep breath and continued with determination, "I would do anything I could to stop an evil murderer like you from doing your heinous work. Anything at all."

"Hah!" Her words seemed to have bounced off Jekelius; he was already thinking of something else as he drummed his fingers on his desk. "Well, it hardly matters now, does it?" he remarked. "The die, unfortunately, has already been cast."

"Has it?" she asked, for she sensed now that he wasn't talking about her or even the hospital; perhaps he never had been.

"Indeed." He seemed weary now as well as bored, turning away from her as if she were no consequence, and he had already dismissed her from her mind. "You are fortunate, Nurse Stern," he remarked, "in that I won't denounce you, but don't flatter yourself that it's out of affection or even mercy. It's simply that I cannot be bothered. I have urgent business in Berlin that has nothing to do with you or this hospital."

Fraulein Wolff, Hannah guessed. Had his suit been accepted? Yet he did not look like a man on the cusp of victory, but rather of defeat. But if it had been refused...

"Will you be returning to Am Steinhof?" she asked, and Jekelius let out a huff of humorless laughter.

"God only knows. The die has been cast, Nurse Stern, and yet I must give it one last roll. I go to Berlin to decide my fate—either glory or disaster." He threw his arms wide and Hannah wondered why he was telling her such a thing. Did he have no one else to perform to? He clearly relished the role.

"And what would the disaster be?" she asked and he dropped his arms.

"To die on the godforsaken Eastern Front." He pressed his lips together. "Do you know how many men have died there already? Over a million." He shook his head. "I cannot think of a worse punishment."

"Can't you?" Hannah gave him a hard look. "It seems you are getting a taste of your own medicine, *Herr Doktor*, quite literally."

Jekelius returned her look without expression. "I would rather have a spoonful of Luminal and drift off to sleep than be hacked to death by some barbarian Cossack."

"Pity you don't have a choice, then," Hannah replied, "just as the children under your care didn't have a choice." She could not summon even a shred of pity for him.

"I still stand by everything I said and did," Jekelius stated with stiff dignity. "Those children were suffering. They were not worthy of life."

"You cannot have it both ways, *Herr Doktor*," Hannah retorted. "Either they were fellow human beings who were suffering and you wished to treat them kindly, or you considered them less than human and not deserving of a single breath. Which is it?"

He flicked his fingers at her, as if the question was simply too tedious for a response.

"Is there still a list?" she asked him. "Even though Hitler himself has issued an order to stop the killings?"

"To stop the killings!" Jekelius let out a bellow of genuine laughter. "Do you think that's what he's done? My dear Nurse Stern, after all this time, to still be so naïve."

"What, then?" Hannah demanded. "To kill the children through starvation? To give them tuberculosis, pneumonia—"

Jekelius waved a hand. "Whatever it takes."

"Why not just murder them all in one go?" Hannah burst out. "Shoot them in a... in a field?"

"From the things I am hearing," Jekelius replied mildly, "it is not out of the question."

She shook her head, too angry to feel the despair she knew would come later, swamping her, pulling her under, along with the grief. So much cruelty. So much needless death. "And what about the children who are being sent to pavilion fifteen even now? Do you choose them yourself?"

He inclined his head. "Indeed."

Her stomach cramped. "And how do you choose?"

"Oh, it depends. Sometimes there is a particular case, a child suffering from such a condition that their body—their brain—could be useful for research. Other times..." He shrugged. "Someone has outlived his usefulness, as it seems we all do, one day or another."

He sounded so cavalier, yet Hannah thought she saw something darker in his eyes. No matter his last try for glory, he seemed like a man consigned to a fate similar to those he'd condemned. Had it made him reconsider, or simply feel more defiant?

"And this month?" she asked. "Have you chosen the names?"

With a shrug, he nodded.

"Who?" Hannah demanded, her voice ragged.

He arched an eyebrow, amused. "Do you think you will save them, even now?"

Hannah half-rose from her chair. "*Tell me.*"

Jekelius hesitated, and then he shrugged again. "I can't remember their names."

"You can't..." Her breath came out in a slow rush. "Not even one?" And yet he'd condemned them to death.

He paused, a small, cruel smile flirting with his lips. "Oh

yes, one," he said, his tone deceptively casual. Instinctively, Hannah tensed. "I believe," Jekelius said, "his name is Hedji."

She found Margarethe on the ward, listlessly checking a bandage as Hannah burst into the room, the door clattering closed behind her.

"Hannah—"

"It's Hedji."

Margarethe's face drained of color. "Hedji—"

Hannah shook her head, the words coming too fast, garbled and desperate because there was no *time*. "He knows. Jekelius— he knows! I don't know how long for, not as long as he thinks, but... he knows now." She let out a choked sound while Margarethe stared at her in confusion.

"How can he know?"

"He suspected me of opening the envelopes. He doesn't know everything, but now..." She shook her head as she thought of how resigned Jekelius had looked, when she'd left him in his office. There had been no talk of arrest, of discipline even; he hadn't seemed to care at all. "We were right, Margarethe. He has been choosing the children—and he told me he chose Hedji."

When Hannah had, in a choked voice, asked Jekelius why he had chosen a boy who was healthy, who was wanted by his own father, he had looked surprised, as if he hadn't even considered such things.

"He's as good as a Jew," he'd told her, sounding almost mystified by her horror. "And he's become increasingly difficult to control. It surprises me, Nurse Stern, the kind of children you seem to care about."

"Hedji! What can we do, Hannah?" Margarethe asked. Her voice was high and thin and she was wringing her hands. "What can we do? We must take him from the school—"

"He has already been taken!" Something else Jekelius had told her, in a bored voice. "He's already been moved to pavilion fifteen."

Margarethe's eyes were huge and dark in her bloodless face. "No…"

"We'll have to take him from there," Hannah stated firmly. "We have to try. Perhaps he hasn't been given anything yet—"

"I'll go—" Margarethe turned toward the door.

"Nurse Bauer!" Helga's voice, usually so cheerful, came out like the crack of a whip as she stood in the doorway of the ward. "To your duties."

Margarethe exchanged a wordless glance with Hannah before turning back to the child she'd been checking on. Helga glared at them both beadily for a moment before returning to the staff room, where she was no doubt sipping coffee and reading a magazine rather than tending to her patients.

"If I go now, I'll alert her," Margarethe whispered. "She might stop me, and what then?"

"I'll go," Hannah said quietly. "I'm not on duty until this evening. I'll go. I'll take him from the pavilion and hide him by the orchard, as you have done."

"There's a potting shed—"

"There, then."

Margarethe nodded, her eyes still wide and dark. "I'll get in contact with Heinrich and meet you there after my shift." She reached for Hannah's hand, squeezing her fingers. "Hannah… don't trust Karl."

"I never have," she replied simply, and then she turned and hurried down the stairs.

Hannah had no plan as she marched toward pavilion fifteen, no plan at all except to save Hedji, and yet somehow that seemed enough. It had been enough for Leon, she remembered; she would have to use her wits. When she rapped smartly on the pavilion's door and saw Nurse Katschenka glide down the stairs, it almost felt providential.

"Dr. Jekelius has sent me to tell you there has been a mistake," she stated firmly, and the nurse's dark eyebrows rose in disbelief.

"Again?"

"Indeed, yes. A boy, Hedji, about twelve years old, was brought here from the reformatory school. His case is being questioned at the Youth Welfare Office, after his father complained—you know Dr. Jekelius is under investigation with the office?" The words came so smoothly, easily, that Hannah almost believed the lies herself. "He has already been disciplined, Nurse Katschenka, and he certainly does not wish any more trouble. It will not do the doctor any favors, I assure you, to lose a child whose file is being read as we speak."

The nurse bristled. "I have not heard from the medical director myself—"

"Because he is such a busy man. Do you think he has time to spare for a mere nurse?"

"And yet he speaks to you—"

"My brother is a major in the Abwehr, as you know," Hannah reminded her loftily as she pushed past her and went up the stairs. "Of course he speaks to me." Her heart was thudding, yet she walked with calm purpose toward the ward. "Where is the boy, Hedji?"

Nurse Katschenka pointed to a bed on the end of the ward. "This is most irregular, Nurse—"

Hannah ignored her as she walked quickly to Hedji's bed. He was unconscious, his breathing deep and even. "Has he been given anything?" she demanded. "Have you administered him the Luminal yet?"

"Just a sedative so far," the nurse replied after a second's pause. "When he arrived, he was most unruly." She sounded disapproving, and Hannah had to suppress a wild, pain-filled laugh. Unruly! When he must have known he was meant to die?

She glanced down at Hedji, and then, taking a deep breath, she scooped him up in her arms. He was heavier than she expected, despite being so thin, his elbow digging into her ribs, his legs splayed out, a tall boy for twelve or thirteen. She staggered underneath the weight of him.

"What on earth are you doing, Nurse?" Nurse Katschenka demanded, her eyes narrowing. "You are taking him yourself? This really is *most* irregular. I must speak to Matron Bertha before you—"

But Hannah was already lumbering toward the stairs, Hedji in her aching arms, every step one closer to freedom.

"I will talk to Dr. Jekelius!" Nurse Katschenka exclaimed shrilly, and Hannah let out a huff of laughter as she threw over her shoulder,

"I think you might have to go to Moscow, then."

She'd reached the door, and bracing Hedji against her shoulder, she opened it and then staggered out of pavilion fifteen.

CHAPTER 27

So this was how Margarethe must have been with that first poor child, rushing out into the night with him in her arms, with no thought, no plan but to save him. Hannah had no idea where to go. She did not want to risk taking Hedji to her room, as she had with Willi, in case Jekelius had decided to alert the authorities, after all. She would certainly not put such a thing past him. Perhaps he'd become angry, resentful of her presumption and rudeness. Perhaps he'd already called the Gestapo.

Yet she knew she could not hold Hedji for much longer; already her arms were trembling from the effort. She had to find a hiding place *now*; she struggled even to take more than a few steps. If only there was one of those awful green carts to put Hedji in and pull him, but there was nothing, no one about at all.

Then, in the distance, she saw a familiar figure, surprisingly welcome.

"Karl!" she called, her voice a ragged rasp. "*Karl!*"

He turned, frowning as he took in the sight of her with a child in her arms.

"Hannah," he demanded as he strode toward her. "What the hell...?"

He had no reason to help her, Hannah knew, and Margarethe had warned her not to trust him, yet there *was* no one else and even now part of her wanted to believe in the goodness of Karl's heart, beneath the surly resentment. At least a little goodness, just a little. Enough.

"Please, can you take him? I can't hold him much longer. I need to get him to safety."

"Are you crazy?" His gaze darted around, but fortunately there was still no one else about. "You can't just go into a pavilion and *take* a patient—"

"Actually," Hannah told him, "I can, and I did." She tried to smile, but her lips trembled. "Please, Karl. I will only ask you for this."

He gazed at her for a second, a hard, knowing look, before he gave a brief nod and then took Hedji from her, throwing him over one shoulder like a sack of potatoes.

"Be careful!" Hannah cried.

"He's out for the count, trust me. Where are you putting him?"

She hesitated, not wanting to reveal the shed by the orchard, just in case, remembering Margarethe's warning. "I... I don't know."

Karl let out a sigh as he hoisted Hedji farther up on his shoulder. "There's a disused shed behind the carpentry shop. We can put him there for now."

"Thank you, Karl—"

"You can thank me later," he told her with a hard laugh that made Hannah's stomach roil. She did not want to think about what he might mean.

She followed him toward the far side of the complex, past the kitchen and the theatre, the church on its hill. A few groundsmen passed in the distance, but no one paid them any attention. Hannah could hardly believe it; was an orderly with a body slung over his shoulder not a sight to behold, in this godforsaken place? They probably thought Hedji was dead, and there wasn't a cart to be found. It was awful, *awful*, and yet providential, too. The system was working for them, at least in this.

The shed was a rough building with a floor of hard-packed dirt and a smell of old straw. Karl slung Hedji, still unconscious, down on a pile of old sacks before turning to Hannah.

"Thank you, Karl—" she said again, only for him to give that same hard laugh as before.

"Oh, you'll thank me."

Hannah stared at him in confusion as his hands went to his belt buckle.

"How do you think the so-very-pure Margarethe thanks me?" he continued, the words a taunt. "For a nun, she can get down on her knees pretty damned quick, let me tell you."

Hannah opened her mouth, closed it. *"Margarethe..."*

"Yes, Margarethe. She wasn't too good for me, in the end."

Bile rose in Hannah's throat and she forced it down. She should have guessed, she realized, or at least suspected, and yet even so, she could hardly believe it now. Poor Margarethe, reduced to buying Karl's silence in such a terrible way.

"Not so prim for a nun after all, eh?" He reached out and wrapped one large hand around Hannah's neck, roughly pulling her toward him. "And you're not too good for me, either, Hannah Stern. I was patient with you, I *tried*, and it still wasn't enough, was it? Well, I'll just have to make do with this, I guess, won't I?"

He let out another laugh as he pulled her toward him and Hannah struggled not to retch. This was Berlin all over again—the slow-motion surrealness of it, her dazed confusion, the horror. Without even realizing what she was doing, she lurched back and kicked Karl as hard as she could between the legs.

He let out a startled moan as he clutched himself. "You *bitch*—"

"How dare you?" Hannah choked. "How dare you use Margarethe—use me—like this? You're..." Tears of both rage and grief smarted her eyes. She'd so wanted to believe in his goodness. "You're despicable."

"*I* am?" Karl snarled. "I risked my life—"

"For no more than a cheap tumble!"

"So what? It's more than most men would do, you know. A lot more."

"Am I supposed to be impressed?" she demanded, her voice shaking. "You're pathetic."

His face twisted in an ugly grimace. "You'll pay for this—"

With a growl, she planted her hands on his shoulders and pushed him as hard as she could. He fell backwards, smacking his head on the wall before sliding to the floor. Hannah stared at him in numb horror; he was unconscious, or at least dazed, although she doubted he would be for very long.

Scrambling across his supine body, she hefted Hedji into her arms and headed out once more. The shadows were lengthening under the trees, the parkland shrouded in shadow, as Hannah staggered along the paths, across the complex toward the orchard at the back of the pavilions, where Margarethe had said she would meet her. Hannah needed to find the potting shed she had mentioned...

The trees of the orchard looked twisted and misshapen under the setting sun, their crooked branches black against the darkening sky. Then Hannah spied the little shed, barely more than a lean-to, and a gust of relief escaped her. *Finally.*

She took one staggering step and then another, so close to safety—and then her foot hooked underneath a knobbly tree root, and before she could stop herself, she was pitching forward, stifling her instinctive scream as she twisted her body so her shoulder took the brunt of the fall, and Hedji was protected from the worst.

The ground seemed to come up to meet her, as hard as concrete as the impact of the landing jarred through her and left her both winded and dazed. She glanced at Hedji, and saw his eyelids flutter.

Somehow, everything in her aching with pain, she managed to get to her knees. She tried to stand, but the ankle of the foot that had been trapped by the root was throbbing and she let out a cry when she tried to put weight on it.

Biting her lip hard enough to taste blood, Hannah forced herself to stand. There was no way she could carry Hedji now, but she could drag him at least, even though every step was a blazing agony, and several times she had to stop, afraid she might faint from the searing pain of her swollen ankle.

"Come on, Hedji," she whispered, although she knew he could not hear her. "Come on..."

Step by painstaking step, Hannah made it into the shed, pulling Hedji behind her, and then she collapsed in the doorway, her ankle throbbing, her eyelids fluttering closed.

By the time Hannah came to, it was dark, and Hedji was awake. He'd managed to get himself into a sitting position, propped against an old barrel. As Hannah blinked him into focus, he smiled wryly at her, his eyes glinting in the dark.

"I don't know which of us is worse off."

She tried to laugh, but it ended in a groan. The sweetish smell of rotting apples clung to her nostrils, and when she looked down at her ankle, she saw it was swollen to almost three times its size. Something was either broken or sprained. She would not be able to walk.

She dragged herself up as best as she could, so she was sitting next to Hedji, her head lolling back against the barrel.

"Where are we?" Hedji asked.

"By the orchard."

"Yes, I recognize the smell of apples. They used to set us to work here, picking." Hedji let out a slow breath. "They were going to kill me, weren't they?"

Wordlessly, Hannah nodded.

"You saved me," he said wonderingly.

"I tried."

Clumsily, he reached for her hand. "*Danke*, Hannah."

Her throat tight, Hannah could only nod. Thoughts were flooding through her, filling her with both fear and remorse. Jekelius. Karl. Margarethe... How had she borne the indignity of it? Yet she'd never said a word. Margarethe had tried to warn her, yes, but she'd kept her silence. Had she worried Hannah would think badly of her? Had she been ashamed by what she'd done? Or had she worried that Hannah wouldn't believe her? *Oh, Margarethe...*

Hannah closed her eyes, shifting her position on the cold, hard ground. The air was damp and chilly, and it would likely go below freezing once the sun had set. How long would they have to wait here? Would Margarethe be able to get away? Hannah didn't know if she'd been able to contact Heinrich, if there was anywhere for Hedji to *go*.

And what about her? How could she possibly get anywhere? Yet she couldn't go back to the hospital now. She'd defied Jekelius, she'd kidnapped a patient from a ward. She would certainly be disciplined, likely arrested, and that was at the very least. Perhaps Jekelius had already alerted the authorities. Or Karl had, in his anger... At any moment, she half-expected to hear the bark of dogs, the stomp of boots, the demanding cry of the Gestapo. *Halt!*

But the only sound was the wind whispering through the apple trees, a lonely murmur.

"What will happen?" Hedji asked. He sounded curious

rather than scared, with the trust of a child, despite everything he'd endured. "How will we get out of here?"

"Margarethe will come," Hannah told him, trying to sound more confident than she felt. "And your father. They will take you to safety."

"And you?" Hedji asked seriously.

Hannah hesitated and then replied with the same confidence, "And me."

She gazed out at the orchard, the trees now lost in darkness, the moon a sliver of silver above, sending out a narrow swathe of lambent light. In the stillness, Hedji's stomach growled, and they both laughed.

"You must be hungry," Hannah said.

Hedji shrugged. "I'm always hungry."

"Did they treat you very badly, in that school?"

He was silent for a long moment. "It was the worst thing I've ever known."

Hannah closed her eyes. "You won't ever have to go back," she promised. Indeed, he couldn't.

"I'd rather die," Hedji replied, and she knew he meant it. She could not bear to think of what he had endured, and, needing no words, she reached over and held his hand.

"You'll be safe now," she told him softly. "You and your papa will find your cottage in the mountains. There will be chickens and cows—"

"A goat, I think," Hedji interrupted, and Hannah smiled.

"A goat," she agreed. "And what about a cat for Margarethe?"

Hedji was silent for a moment, considering. "I suppose," he said, "that would be all right."

She could picture it all—the three of them, so happy in their home. She wanted it so much to be true, a promise rather than a wish. It would be true, she vowed. She would make it so.

They were silent again, listening to the rustling of the dry, autumn leaves, the cold, clear stillness of the night. Would Margarethe come? What if she'd been delayed? Arrested? Jekelius might have done anything...

And yet Hannah was not afraid. She realized she had a settled certainty inside her, a faith that defied logic or reason. Margarethe would come. Hedji would be safe. She didn't know how or why, and yet she was sure of those two things.

And you, Hannah, will you find your peace?

She could almost hear Margarethe ask the question; she saw the seriousness in her eyes, heard the playfulness in her tone. Would she?

She gazed out at the orchard bathed in moonlight, the trees' twisted arms raised to heaven. She had the same rush of emotion, of both loss and joy, that she'd felt when Margarethe had played the Mendelssohn. So much beauty in the world, even here. *So much beauty.*

Would she find her peace? Was it even something that could be found, like a lost shoe, a misplaced key?

Hannah put her arm around Hedji and drew him closer to her; he nestled in. Perhaps she already had found it, here, now.

Another hour crept past as the moon rose in the sky and the night grew colder. Hedji burrowed into Hannah, shivering, while she stretched her swollen ankle out in front of her and fell into a half-doze, a montage of memories drifting through her mind. Willi smiling at her in the car, his finger to his lips. Margarethe kissing her forehead. Swimming with Hedji, diving under the water as the world fell away, and she was clean and free. Holding Willi's hands as his last breath had ebbed into the silence. He was free, too.

And this moment here, now, with Hedji, alive and well, against her, his heart beating with the joyful certainty of life. And another boy, so very small, who had stared up at her with unblinking blue eyes and seemed to be saying now, with sorrowful compassion and endless understanding, *I forgive you.*

"Hannah!"

She opened her eyes, blinking groggily to see Margarethe crouching in front of her. "You're here..."

"I came as soon as I could." Margarethe turned to Hedji. "Your papa is waiting for you, *schatzi*, just on the other side of that wall, with a nice man who has a great big motorcar."

"Heinrich?" Hannah asked, and Margarethe nodded.

"I went to him right after my shift, before coming here."

"Thank you." It was going to be all right, just as she'd thought. Just as she'd known.

"We must go," Margarethe said, reaching for Hedji.

"I'll have to stay here," Hannah told her. "My ankle..."

"What happened?" Margarethe cried, noticing her swollen ankle for the first time.

"I tripped on a tree root. It's either broken or sprained. I can't walk."

"Oh, Hannah." Margarethe bit her lip, her eyes anxious. "It's all right, I'll help you back after we get Hedji away. I told Helga you were ill, anyway, since you didn't turn up for your shift. No one should suspect."

Her shift! She'd actually forgotten about it. Did it even matter now? Jekelius knew, and Nurse Katschenka, and Karl. There could be no going back, not for her.

Hannah turned to Hedji. "Go safely," she said, resting her hand against his cheek. "And Godspeed."

Hedji nodded, looking serious. "I'll see you again, won't I, Hannah?"

"Oh, I should think so. I want to meet your dog and your goat, and of course your kitten."

Margarethe let out a soft, choked sound and Hannah smiled.

"They're there, Hedji, waiting for you."

He pressed her hand against his cheek for a brief second before he began to scramble up to his feet, just as they heard the sudden, fearful clamor of dogs barking in the distance. Hannah and Margarethe turned to stare at each other, silent and wide-eyed.

"It can't be," Margarethe whispered.

"Jekelius must have called the Gestapo."

"No, he left for Berlin this very evening! I heard it from Helga."

Of course, his urgent business there. "Then Karl," Hannah said heavily.

"*Karl*—"

"He helped to carry Hedji. And then I made him angry—"

"Oh, Hannah." Margarethe's eyes filled with tears, her face with understanding. "I'm so sorry."

"No, I am the one who is sorry." Hannah gripped her hand. "You never should have had to—"

"It doesn't matter." Margarethe swiped angrily at her eyes. "He's nothing to me, less than nothing. He's a fly to be swatted away—"

The dogs barked again, and Hannah gave Margarethe a little push. "You must go. They can't catch you here, Margarethe—"

"And they can't catch *you*. We'll all go together."

"I can't—"

"I'll help you, Hannah." Already, Margarethe was hoisting Hannah's arm around her shoulders, while Hedji helped her lurch to her feet. "As if I'd leave you here! The very idea." Her old humor sparkled in her eyes, even now. "Come on. Hurry, now. Chop, chop! We don't want to be late, not for this!"

Somehow the three of them made it to the wall, stumbling in the moonlit darkness, Hannah half-staggering, half-dragged between Margarethe and Hedji. In the distance, they could still hear the dogs, coming ever closer.

"Here, by this tree." Gasping for breath, Margarethe rested her hands on her knees. A tree was growing against the wall, with a low branch shaped almost like a seat, perfect for a foothold, and another branch above it, spreading out over the wall. From above it, Lash peeked over, his expression urgent and anxious.

"Papa!" Hedji whispered joyfully.

"My Hedji..." Lash reached down to grasp his son's arms.

"Quickly, now." Margarethe hoisted Hedji onto the first branch as Lash began to haul him up.

In the distance, Hannah saw the sweep of flashlights, their beam brighter than the moon, fingers of light coming ever closer. A dog barked excitedly, followed by another.

Margarethe glanced back at her, her face pale and pinched, her eyes wide and dark. "Hurry, Hedji," she whispered, and then he was over the wall, his pale legs dangling down for a second before he disappeared to safety. Margarethe turned to Hannah. "You, next."

Hannah almost laughed at such a notion. The sweeping arcs of light were coming closer, the dogs' barking a noisy, determined chorus. She was not afraid. "No," she said firmly. "You first, Margarethe, with Lash and Hedji."

"Hannah—"

"I mean it. It must be that way."

Margarethe hesitated, and then she reached over and hugged Hannah tightly. Hannah returned the hug, closing her eyes as she absorbed her friend's vitality and warmth one last time before she made herself thrust her away.

"*Go.*"

They were closer now, burly, shadowy figures through the skeletal trees. Dogs were barking, running toward them, eyes glowing yellow in the darkness, mouths slavering.

"Hannah..."

"Go, or it will all be for nothing."

"But—"

"I'll be fine," Hannah assured her.

"No, I'm not leaving you here—"

"Go." Hannah forced herself, despite the pain in her ankle, to step away from the tree so Margarethe could not reach for her. "Don't sacrifice yourself for me, not when you have so much to live for," she said. "Go now, and Godspeed."

Margarethe's eyes sparkled with tears, and she looked torn, still hesitating despite the dogs, the searching beams of the flashlights. "I can't leave you..."

"You must. Remember, it is not only for this life I have hope." She smiled through her tears as Margarethe gave her one last burning, grateful glance, and then scrambled up the wall, her hands clinging to the edge, legs dangling down.

"*Halt!*"

Hannah saw the gleam of moonlight on metal, felt rather than heard the cock of the pistol. Margarethe clinging to the wall, frozen in fear, her face pale and shocked, her legs still dangling down, a perfect target. It required no thought, not even a split second's hesitation, for Hannah to throw herself in front of Margarethe, shielding her with her body. She heard the crack of the gunshot that split the still night air, absorbed the pain of the hit as Margarethe gazed at her in both horror and gratitude.

"*Hannah...*"

With one last, wavering smile of farewell, Hannah pushed Margarethe over the edge of the wall, so she tumbled down into Lash's arms and safety. She heard the snarling dogs, the thunder of boots, but it all felt far away as she remained there for a second, as if she were floating, weightless, suspended in air. The pain was coming toward her on a red tide, flooding through her body, and then the world was falling away, the water was closing over her head and she wasn't floating anymore, but swimming, swimming alone and free and finally at peace, toward the arms already open to receive her.

EPILOGUE

VIENNA, AUGUST 1946

"Guilty!"

The word rings out, triumphant, as a murmur runs through the weary crowd. Her hand tightens on the boy's as the truth of it reverberates through her. *Guilty... guilty... guilty.*

She hears, as if from a distance, the verdicts. Illing will be executed. Katschenka, that murderous, merciless nurse, will be given eight years in prison. Dr. Türk, ten. Strangely, after waiting so long, the news does not affect her the way she thought it would. She expected to feel satisfaction, but it is only sorrow that sweeps through her now, sorrow and grief. They know now that seven hundred and eighty-nine children lost their lives through deliberate killing at Am Spiegelgrund, thousands more from starvation, neglect, and abuse.

"Margarethe?"

She turns to give Lash a weary smile. Hedji slips his hand out of hers to hug his father. It has been a long, hard war for all of them—nearly five years since Hannah threw herself in front of Margarethe; the bullet would have hit her square in the chest if Hannah hadn't taken it instead. On the other side of the wall, Lash had put his arms around her and Hedji, and Heinrich

Maier had driven them to safety. Her mind had been both buzzing and numb; she'd *left* Hannah. Already she'd known she was dead; she'd felt it, and yet still the terrible treachery of her actions, tormented her.

When they'd reached the church in Wahring, and Lash and Hedji were both safe, Heinrich had turned to her.

"Margarethe, you must go back."

She had goggled at him, shocked to her core. "Go *back*?"

"Yes, because you will not have been missed yet. Go back and show up for your morning shift, wondering where Hannah is. It is the only way."

She had almost laughed at the awful absurdity of it. "Heinrich, I *can't*. They will know what I've done. They will be looking for me. Jekelius, Karl Muller—"

"Jekelius was arrested by the Gestapo when he arrived in Berlin this very evening," Heinrich had informed her calmly. "I learned it from a trusted source. He is not your concern, and you are certainly not his. As for Karl Muller... he is but one man, and a mere orderly at that. He won't want to implicate himself. You must brazen it out, Margarethe. The Gestapo didn't know it was you, they barely saw you for a second. It will be risky, yes, but you can ride it out."

She'd closed her eyes, sickened by the thought. To return to Am Steinhof without Hannah, to pretend nothing was wrong, to continue to work and serve in that wretched, wretched place... "I can't."

"You can save more children," Heinrich had said, and now his voice was gentle. "Isn't that what you want? Otherwise, where will you go? If you don't show up for your shift, they will be suspicious. They will arrest you for that, never mind what happened here tonight."

She had felt the truth of his words even as she shook her head.

"You could try to make it to Switzerland," Heinrich had

allowed, "but it is six hundred kilometers, and even then, you could be sent back." He'd paused. "I can only help you so much."

"What about Lash? And Hedji?"

"I will do my best, but you know the Roma are being sent east, along with the Jews. Perhaps we can get them to Switzerland, but not if the Gestapo are looking for you, as well. You would endanger them with your presence."

She'd let the truth of it soak into her, along with a flicker of hope. Lash and Hedji would be safe, and she could save more children. If Hannah had been brave enough to sacrifice herself, then she could, as well, in this way. Slowly, she'd nodded. "Yes, all right. I'll go back."

And so she had walked once more through those gates, even though it had felt like the hardest thing she'd ever done —harder even than risking her life to save children. She'd shown up for work that next morning with no more than a quizzical smile, and when she'd heard that Hannah had been shot dead, suspected of kidnapping a patient, she'd acted surprised and grieved, of course, but not disapproving, no, never that, because acting outraged would certainly be a step too far.

She'd kept working all through the war, even though the conditions continued to deteriorate, to an unbearable level. She'd saved as many children as she could, however she could— sneaking them food, hiding them in cupboards when doctors passed by, even emptying out precious bottles of Luminal when she'd managed to steal the key to the medicine cupboard. She hadn't involved Karl; he'd left Am Steinhof in 1944, when they'd been desperate for more recruits, to serve as an orderly on the Eastern Front.

She'd done as much as she could, as often as she could, and yet it had still felt like so little. She'd always wanted to do more, had longed for the day when she wouldn't have to do anything at all, because these children would be safe. Free. And now, at last, they would be

Heinrich had been executed in 1945, just before the end of the war; Hannah's half-brother Georg a few months before that, implicated in an assassination attempt on Hitler.

By the time the Soviets had marched into Vienna, Margarethe had been half-starved, a ghost of herself, stumbling through her days, waiting for the end, however it came. Lash and Hedji had never made it to Switzerland; they had been sent to a ghetto in Lodz back in 1942, rounded up with all the other Romas and the last of the Jews. Margarethe had spent the first six months after the war searching for them, weeping with relief and joy when she'd finally received word of them, in a camp for displaced persons outside Munich.

And now, finally, a year after the end of the war, the three of them have, if not true peace, then at least some sort of resolution. Illing, that medical director who came after Jekelius and had been even worse than him in his murderous experiments, his willingness to torture and kill, will pay for his heinous crimes at last.

"It's over," Lash says softly, and Margarethe nods, her body sagging with the knowledge of it. Yes, it is finally, *finally* over. She can put the past behind her, or try to, although she knows she will always live with both the horror of what she has seen and endured and the grief of losing Hannah; those will never leave her.

Hannah... Even now, Margarethe feels a clutch of sorrow, a searing pain of loss. Dear Hannah, the best friend she'd ever had, who had sacrificed her life so Margarethe could live. *Do you believe in heaven?* Surely Hannah did now. She is there, Margarethe is sure of it, smiling, at peace at last, the true angel of Vienna.

"We should go," Lash tells her softly. "There's nothing more for us here." Their train to Salzburg leaves that evening, and from there they will travel to Zell am See, a small town in the mountains, where they feel sure a little cottage waits for them, with room for a cow and chickens and a dog and a cat.

It is there, Margarethe knows it. They just have to find it.

Slipping her hand into Lash's and her other into Hedji's, Margarethe turns from the courthouse, from the past, and heads for the station—and home.

A LETTER FROM KATE

Dear reader,

I want to say a huge thank you for choosing to read *The Angel of Vienna*. If you found it thought-provoking and powerful, and would like to keep up to date with all my latest releases, just sign up at the following link. Your email address will never be shared and you can unsubscribe at any time.

www.bookouture.com/kate-hewitt

The Angel of Vienna was an incredibly challenging book to write, as the subject matter was so terrible and tragic, and yet I felt it was such an important story to share, and one that is not often told, even within the realm of historical fiction set during the Second World War.

In all my stories I look to highlight the often-unsung heroism of ordinary people, and the extraordinary risk—and cost—they faced in helping and saving others. Many of the books I used for research were written in German, but I can recommend the book *Asperger's Children*, as well as *Nurses and Midwives in Nazi Germany: The Euthanasia Programs* if you would like to know more about the subject.

I hope you loved *The Angel of Vienna* and if you did, I would be very grateful if you could write a review. I'd love to hear what you think, and it makes such a difference helping new readers to discover one of my books for the first time.

I love hearing from my readers—you can get in touch on my Facebook page, through Twitter, Goodreads or my website.

Thanks again for reading!

Kate

www.kate-hewitt.com

 facebook.com/KateHewittAuthor

twitter.com/author_kate

AUTHOR'S NOTE

In 1939, at the start of the war, Hitler gave an order for all disabled and mentally ill adults in sanitoriums or hospitals to be systematically removed and murdered, gassed in killing centers such as Hartheim Castle. A year later, the order was extended to disabled children; this secret program of supposed 'mercy' killing was known as Aktion T4, based on the address in Berlin where the orders originated from. When, after Bishop von Galen's sermon in August 1941, the outcry against it became too great, Hitler ended the program, but, in reality, simply changed the order to allow doctors themselves to decide which patients to kill, in what was known as "wild euthanasia", which lasted until the end of the war.

The heroic events of this novel are, alas, fiction; there is no known organized rescue attempt of children at the Am Spiegelgrund Clinic in Vienna. There are, however, courageous accounts of individuals: children from the reformatory school who managed to escape in the manner described, climbing a tree in the orchard (but were later caught and returned), as well as nurses who hid children in closets or cupboards when a doctor came to a ward with his recommendation for "further treatment", or warned parents to continue visiting their children in order to keep them safe.

The characters of Hannah and Margarethe are inspired by real people—Hannah by Anna Wödl, the nurse whose own son was killed at Am Spiegelgrund in 1941 and who campaigned against the euthanasia program, and Sister Anna Bertha Königsegg, a nun in the Sisters of Charity, who protested against the Nazis' policies on the euthanasia of the disabled and was arrested.

Other characters in the novel were in fact real people—Dr. Erwin Jekelius, the first medical director of Am Spiegelgrund, who did have an ill-fated romance with Paula Wolff, and was arrested upon arrival in Berlin and sent to the Eastern Front in November 1941. He died in a Soviet camp in 1951. Nurse Katschenka was also a real person; her character is based on the testimony she gave at the Am Steinhof trials after the war.

Klara Bertha and Marianne Türk were the head matron and a doctor at the clinic respectively. Georg Strasser is fictional, but is inspired by Hans von Dohnyani, the brother-in-law of Dietrich Bonhoeffer, who worked in the Abwehr and was involved in the 20 July 1944 assassination attempt on Hitler. He was executed in April 1945.

Overall, seven hundred and eighty-nine children were murdered at Am Spiegelgrund alone, and thousands died from neglect or starvation. In Greater Germany, the Nazi euthanasia program claimed the lives of over two hundred and fifty thousand adults and children.

ACKNOWLEDGEMENTS

When I started researching the subject matter for *The Angel of Vienna*, I was at a bit of a loss, as there seemed to be very little written about it in the English language. I therefore must thank profusely Professor Peter Schwarz of the University of Vienna, whose focus of research is the Am Spiegelgrund clinic. He provided me with countless articles, case studies from the clinic, photographs of original documents (including the notorious kill list from Berlin) and a very helpful map of the Am Steinhof complex. I had been hoping to travel to Vienna myself to meet him, but Covid measures prevented such a journey. However, I still hope to thank him in person one day!

Many thanks also to my fabulous Bookouture team—my editor Isobel, who was generously willing for me to write about something so challenging (and gave me wonderful feedback on how to make the story more powerful), and all the terrific editorial and marketing support team—Kim, Sarah, Jess, Alex, Mel and Ciara in publicity and marketing; Richard in foreign rights; Alex with proofreading; Natalie and Lauren in promotions; as well as Peta, Saidah, Sarah and Alba, who help with audio and administration. Thank you also to Jade and Tom for helping my manuscript to be as polished as possible.

Thanks also to my writing buddy Emma Robinson, who listened to me brainstorm about the story during a writing weekend away, and gave me great advice about how to balance the light and dark. Also thanks to my husband Cliff, who always listens to me thrash out plot points and then explain to him why his well-intended suggestions won't work. You are a very patient and gracious man! Thanks to my daughter Caroline, for reading the first hundred pages and giving me her feedback, and also to the rest of my children—Ellen, Teddy, Anna and Charlotte. Teddy, I promise in the next book I will name a character after you. Love you all!

Made in the USA
Monee, IL
17 March 2024